JUN 10 — Oct. 10 = 9

The Nobodies Album

ALSO BY CAROLYN PARKHURST

The Dogs of Babel
Lost and Found

The Nobodies Album

A NOVEL

CAROLYN PARKHURST

DOUBLEDAY

NEW YORK LONDON TORONTO

SYDNEY AUCKLAND

DOUBLEDAY

All rights reserved. Published in the United States by Doubleday, a division of Random House, Inc., New York, and in Canada by Random House of Canada Limited, Toronto.

www.doubleday.com

DOUBLEDAY and the DD colophon are registered trademarks of Random House, Inc.

LIBRARY OF CONGRESS CATALOGING-IN-PUBLICATION DATA
Parkhurst, Carolyn
The nobodies album: a novel/by Carolyn Parkhurst.—1st ed.
p. cm.
1. Women novelists—Fiction. 2. Mothers and sons—Fiction.
3. Psychological fiction. I. Title.
PS3616.A754N63 2010
813'.6—dc22
2009041886

ISBN 978-0-385-52769-9

PRINTED IN THE UNITED STATES OF AMERICA

1 3 5 7 9 10 8 6 4 2

First Edition

To my father,

who taught me how to tell a story

Chapter One

/||\

There are some stories no one wants to hear. Some stories, once told, won't let you go so easily. I'm not talking about the tedious, the pointless, the disgusting: the bugs in your bag of flour; your hour on the phone with the insurance people; the unexplained blood in your urine. I'm talking about narratives of tragedy and pathos so painful, so compelling, that they seem to catch inside you on a tiny hook you didn't even know you'd hung. You wish for a way to pull the story back out; you grow resentful of the very breath that pushed those words into the air. Stories like this have become a specialty of mine.

It wasn't always that way. I used to think my goal should be to write the kind of story everyone wanted to hear, but I soon learned what a fool's errand that was. I found out there are better ways to get you. "I wish I hadn't read it," a woman wrote to me after she finished my last novel. She sounded bewildered, and wistful for the time before she'd heard what I had to say. But isn't that the point—to write something that will last after the book has been put back on the shelf? This is the way I like it. Read my story, walk through those woods, and when you get to the other side, you may not even realize that you're carrying something out that you didn't have when you went in. A little tick of an idea, clinging to your scalp or hidden in a fold of skin. Somewhere out of sight. By the time you discover it, it's already begun to prey on you; perhaps it's merely gouged your flesh, or perhaps it's already begun to nibble away at your central nervous system. It's a small thing, whatever it is, and whether your life will be better for it or worse, I cannot say. But something's different, something has changed.

And it's all because of me.

. . .

The plane rises. We achieve liftoff, and in that mysterious, hanging moment I say a prayer—as I always do—to help keep us aloft. In my more idealistic days, I used to add a phrase of benediction for all the other people on the airplane, which eventually stretched into a wish for every soul who found himself away from home that day. My goodwill knew no bounds—or maybe I thought that the generosity of such a wish would gain me extra points and thereby ensure my own safety. But I stopped doing that a long time ago. Because, if you think about it, when has there ever been a day when all the world's travelers have been returned safely to their homes, to sleep untroubled in their beds? That's not the way it works. Better to keep your focus on yourself and leave the others to sort themselves out. Better to say a prayer for your own well-being and hope that today, at least, you'll be one of the lucky ones.

It's a short flight: Boston to New York, less than an hour in the air. As soon as the flight attendants can walk the aisles without listing too much, they'll be flinging pretzels at our heads in a mad effort to get everything served and cleaned up before we're back on the ground, returned to the world of adulthood, where we're free to get our own snacks.

I have on my tray table, displayed rather importantly, as if it were a prop in a play no one else realizes is being performed, the manuscript of my latest book, *The Nobodies Album*. This is part of my ritual: there's my name, emblazoned on the first page, and if my seatmate or a wandering crew member should happen to glance over and see it—and if, furthermore, that name should happen to have any meaning for them—well, then they're free to begin a conversation with me. So far, it's never happened.

The other rite I will observe today concerns what I will do with this manuscript once I arrive in New York. This neat stack of white and black, so clean and tidy—you'd never know from looking at it what a living thing it is. Its heft is satisfying—I'll admit that to hold its weight in my hands gives me a childish feeling of *Look what I did!*—but the visuals are disappointing. Look at it and you'll see nothing more than a pile of paper; there's no indication of the blood that circulates through the text, the gristle that holds these pages together. This is why, when it comes time to surrender a new book to my publisher, I make it a rule to do it in person; I want to be sure no one forgets the humanity of this exchange. No e-mail, no overnighting, no couriers; I will carry my book into those offices, and I will deliver it to my editor, person to person, hand to hand. I've been doing it since I finished my second novel, and I have no intention of stopping now. It makes for a pleasant day. I will have a fuss made over me; I will be taken to lunch. And when I leave, I will keep my eyes turned forward so I won't see the raised eyebrows and the looks exchanged, the casual toss that will land my manuscript in the exact place a mailroom clerk would have dropped it had I saved myself all this trouble. My idiosyncrasies are my right, and as long as everyone does me the courtesy of not mocking them to my face, we'll all get along fine.

Not that any of these people has ever been anything less than lovely to me. I suppose I'm a little more attuned to these kinds of thoughts today, because I know that there have been a few . . . questions about the book I'm turning in. This book is different from anything I've done in the past; in fact, I'm going to puff myself up a little bit and say that it's different from anything *anyone* has done in the past, though there isn't a writer alive who hasn't thought about it. *The Nobodies Album* isn't a novel, though every word of it is fiction. Do you see me talking around it now, building up the suspense? Can you hear the excitement creeping into my voice? Because what I've done here is nothing short of revolutionary, and I want to make sure the impact is clear. What I've done in this book is to revisit the seven novels I've published in the last twenty years and rewrite the ending of each one. *The Nobodies Album* is a collection of every last chapter I have ever written—or at least every one that made it into a book available for public consumption; even I drew the line at rewriting the ending of the unpublished novel that's been sitting in a box in my basement since 1992. But it contains all of the others, each one tweaked and reshaped into something completely new. Can you imagine what happens when you rewrite the ending of a book? It changes everything. Meaning shifts; certainties are called into question. Write seven new last chapters and all at once you have seven different books.

It won't be a thick volume; it's barely a hundred pages. More a companion piece than anything else, intended not to take the place of the original endings but to set alongside them as a bookend. From my perspective, it's an opportunity to take a tour of old haunts. See how they look now that the world and I have moved on to another vantage point.

It's possible, though, that not everyone sees the beauty of this idea as clearly as I do. When I first mentioned my plans to my agent and my editor, they were not entirely enthusiastic. "People love your books the way they are," they both told me in their own separate, ass-kissing ways. "Readers might get angry at you for messing with these novels they care about so deeply." Oh, they were so concerned, so solicitous of me and my legions of fans . . . It was almost enough to make me reconsider.

But of course it's all bullshit. It's true that people come to feel proprietary about certain books, and once the author has done his part, they want him to back away politely; otherwise, he's an embarrassing reminder that these stories didn't spring to life fully formed. I suppose that if Shakespeare were to reappear and say, "I was wrong about Romeo and Juliet—they didn't die tragically, they lived long enough to get married and lose their teeth and make each other miserable," there might be hell to pay. But I'm not Shakespeare, and nobody involved with publishing this book is afraid readers are going to care too much. They're afraid they're not going to care at all.

. . .

I've planned to arrive early—I don't love New York, but I respect it, restless beast that it is, and it seems rude to me to pass through it too quickly. So from the airport I take a cab to the Forty-second Street library; I like to poke around the collection of early-twentieth-century photographs and stereographic cards. A crucial scene in my seventh novel, in fact, was inspired by a 1902 postcard I came across here several years ago, though I can't get too nostalgic about it, since the new version in *The Nobodies Album* wipes that scene clear away.

My favorite picture today is from the same era. Entitled "Morning Ride, Atlantic City, NJ," it depicts several couples (and one standard poodle) being pushed down the boardwalk in a fleet of odd three-wheeled wicker carriages. The women are all wearing extravagant hats; the dog, wind in its fur, looks happier than anyone else. I doubt I'll ever use it for anything. I don't expect to do any period writing in the near future, and the idea of the sheer research that would be necessary to write a single paragraph about this image—are they riding in surreys? landaus? rickshaws?—exhausts me. But I spend an hour making disjointed notes anyway, because you never know where ideas are going to come from, and as my eighth-grade Latin teacher used to say, "Muscles train the mind."

I'm a little uncertain, actually, about what role writing will play in my life from this point forward. Working on this last book has allowed me to see certain uncomfortable truths about the whole process. I've always known that the best part of writing occurs before you've picked up a pen. When a story exists only in your mind, its potential is infinite; it's only when you start pinning words to paper that it becomes less than perfect. You have to make your choices, set your limits. Start whittling away at the cosmos, and don't stop until you've narrowed it down to a single, ordinary speck of dirt. And in the end, what you've made is not nearly as glorious as what you've thrown away.

The final product never made me happy for very long. A year out, and I was already seeing the flaws, feeling the loss of those closed-off possibilities. But I always figured that once a book was published, my part in it was done. Finished; time to move on. But *The Nobodies Album* shines a light behind that scrim. It turns out there's no statute of limitations on changing your mind. You don't ever have to be done. And if you're never done, then what's the point of beginning? I drop my notes in the trash on the way out of the building.

It was my son, Milo, who came up with the phrase "the Nobodies Album." He'd just turned four. He'd developed an interest in music and often engaged in games to stretch our extensive but finite record collection into something that could match the breadth of his imagination. The Nobodies Album was, simply enough, an album containing songs that do not exist. *Have you ever heard the Beatles' version of "I've Been Working on the Railroad"?* he'd ask me, walking around our living room in a wide circle. No, I'd say—I didn't realize they ever sang that. *Well, they did.* His face would be serious, but his voice would swell wide with the excitement of creating something new. *It's on the Nobodies Album.* Oh, of course, I'd say, I love that album, and I could see my words travel through his body. He was so happy I was playing along he'd almost vibrate, until it seemed like he might just crack open with joy.

Milo is now twenty-seven and the lead singer of a band whose songs most certainly exist, even if they're not always entirely to my taste. We haven't spoken in almost four years. My use of this childhood phrase of his is one part appropriation—the writer's narcissistic view that everything I come across is mine, mine, mine—and one part transparent stab at reconciliation. If I were being honest, I would add a subtitle: *See, honey? See what Mommy remembers?*

I walk down the steps, past the lions, to Fifth Avenue. It's a dim day, early in November, and the sky is entirely without color. The air tastes cold and burnt. The sidewalks are crowded, and I join the moving swell.

Milo's band is called Pareidolia, and they've had a fair bit of success, though whether they're here to stay or are simply the taste of the moment remains to be seen. I can never be certain when I open a magazine that I won't come across his face somewhere inside. Not that it's unwelcome when it happens—of course, it's most of the reason I buy those kinds of magazines—but it's jarring, and it leaves me feeling hollow and unsettled for the rest of the day. Still, it's allowed me to keep up with him, after a fashion. I know that he's bought a house in San Francisco, and that he's been dating a pointy-faced little mouse named

Bettina something. I've seen them dancing together at a club he owns a piece of; I've seen them walking on the beach, throwing sticks for dogs whose names I may never know.

I turn left onto Forty-second Street. It's almost time for my meeting, and I should get a cab soon, but I'm feeling suddenly apprehensive, and I'd like a few more minutes on my own before stepping into my public skin. A few minutes in the visual chaos of Times Square, where I am nobody to no one and this book I'm carrying holds no more significance than a pile of handbills. Perhaps less, because who can really say what's worth more in the cool of the day, a parcel of story fragments or the promise of remarkable prices on electronic goods?

It's extraordinary, this assault of color and light, this riot of information, though the people moving through it seem barely to notice. I try to absorb it all—the neon, the colossal ads, the day's news moving past on the side of a building. I dabble in a bit of time travel: if I were a woman from the eighteenth century (or the seventeenth or the fifth) and I found myself suddenly in the middle of this tumultuous place, how would I respond to a landscape so terrible and bright? For a moment I'm able to fill myself with wonder and fear, but I can't maintain it for long. My twenty-first-century eyes are jaded, and in the end, this is nothing I haven't seen before.

Several of my novels have had their origins in game playing of this sort. My last book before this one, a spectacular failure entitled *My Only Sunshine*, came into being when I had occasion to hold a cousin's new baby and I began to wonder what might be going on inside his soft, slightly conical little head. A distancing measure, perhaps, if I'm honest—a way to step back from the indisputable solidity of the child in my arms, the head no bigger than a grapefruit, the compact body wrapped tight.

Still, it's an interesting question. It's the most basic of human mysteries—how do we think when we have no language, when we know nothing more than how to swallow, how to suck?—and yet every person on the earth has the answer stashed away in some jellied gray furrow of brain. Not such an original thought (quite a banal one, really), but on that day it seemed as if I had discovered something new. What if? I thought, which is the way books are always born. What if I wrote a novel from the point of view of a newborn baby? Start in the womb and carry it through the first six months or so. Finish before she can sit without toppling, before she can lift a cup or blow a kiss. What will she make of the family she's been born into? What will the reader understand that the protagonist herself cannot?

Not much, according to critics and consumers alike. Except for one reviewer, who said a few nice things about the way my books succeed at capturing "the texture of life," most readers had a fairly tepid response. I'm sure that people will see a link between the failure of that book and my decision to write *The Nobodies Album*, and it's true that *My Only Sunshine* was the first book I thought about revising post-publication. But I'm not that easy to sway. If writers ran to change their books every time they got a few bad reviews, then libraries would be very confusing places.

I hail a cab, suddenly anxious to get this process started, to get this manuscript out of my hands and release it into the wild. I open the door and get inside, tell the driver the intersection I'd like to go to. As he's pulling away, I happen to turn and look out the window, and the news crawl catches my eye. The tail end of a headline pulls at me, but I can't be sure I've read it right, and then it's gone around the side of the building.

"Wait," I say. My voice is strange. "I need to get out."

The driver makes a noise of disgust and pulls over to the curb. Even though he's only driven me thirty feet, I take a couple of dollars from my bag and drop them through the slot in the Plexiglas partition. I notice with some surprise that my hands are shaking.

I get out and stand on the sidewalk, watching the news stories slide by. People push around me; I'm touched on every side. There's a headline about the salaries of professional basketball players and one about wildfires in the Pacific Northwest. And then the one I've been waiting for comes around again, and the world changes in a series of cheery yellow lights: "Pareidolia singer Milo Frost arrested for the murder of girlfriend Bettina Moffett."

In the moments that follow, as I stand mute in the middle of the humming crowd, the thing I'm most aware of is my own response to this news. I don't scream or faint or fall to my knees; I don't burst into tears, or lean on a wall for support, or worry that I'm going to be sick. I feel utterly, pervasively blank. I'm consumed with trying to understand what I'm supposed to do. If I were writing this in a book, I wonder, how would my character react? But this isn't fiction; apparently, if my senses are to be believed, this is life.

For a blink of a moment, I think about getting another cab and continuing on my way to my meeting. But of course I don't. I find my phone in my purse and call my editor; I tell her that something's come up and I won't be able to make it to lunch. I don't say what's wrong, and I can't tell whether she already knows or not. As for the manuscript, I tell her I'll drop it in the mail.

And then I'm free and lost. I force myself to begin walking again, though I have no idea where I'm going. Sometime soon I'm going to feel this blow, and I'd rather not be standing on this radiant bruise of a street corner when that happens. I count out the things I'm going to need: solitude, a television news channel, access to a computer where I can read the rest of this story. Someplace soft to lay my body when the spasms finally hit.

I see a hotel down the block, and it gives me something to work toward. Don't crack apart here in the city's guts; it's not going to be much longer. Keep it together for the length of time it takes to talk to a desk clerk, ride an elevator, walk an anonymous hall. Swipe the card and feel the door click open. That's all you have to do.

This is happening; this is not fiction. And the thing about life? It doesn't have texture at all. Go ahead, feel the space around you. Do it now. See? It's nothing but air.

From the Jacket Copy for

MY ONLY SUNSHINE

By Octavia Frost

(Farraday Books, 2009)

/||\

How does the world look to its newest inhabitants? In this astonishing and daring new novel, Octavia Frost takes us to a place we've all visited, though we can't quite recollect its landscape: infancy. Starting from the one experience we all share—birth itself—and moving into the tragic particulars of one baby born into one family, Frost sheds new light on how we become who we are.

The night of the day she rolls over for the first time, she is wide awake at her two a.m. feeding, her eyes open in the dark, her legs continually flexing and unflexing, as if her muscles simply cannot contain this jubilant new information. She nurses without focus, stopping to find her mother's face, the crack of light that makes its way through the blinds, the long mountain of her father lying next to them in the bed. Then the nipple is covered up, and she finds herself being carried back to her crib. "Sleepy girl," she hears, and "sleepy time." The click of the door, the narrowing light, and she is alone.

But the sleep isn't there. She can't keep her body from moving. She rolls onto her stomach and finds she can't get back. Up on her arms, head high, stuck like a turtle, she hollers until her mother comes back and flips her. They do this again and again.

Finally she's too tired, and she can't make herself wind down to the place where she wants to be. Back arching, legs kicking, body flopping back and forth until, as if she were a fish losing breath on the pier, her movements grow less frequent and less spirited. The upper half of her body seems ready for rest before the lower half. She collapses forward onto the sheet, eyes falling halfway shut, mouth working the pacifier, but her backside is up in the air, and her knees bend, bouncing her up and down. She can't keep still, and she roars with anger. Nothing is right, it can't be right; her mother lifts her and swings her back and forth, makes the swishing sound that she hears sometimes in her dreams, but now it doesn't help, nothing is ever going to help. She goes rigid, she resists, she yells. And then her mother leans forward, touches their foreheads together, and in the sudden close room their faces make, she's able to let her eyelids drop. Another moment, and she's away.

. . .

Light and noise, the morning sun and the cracking thunder of her parents' voices. The frogs hanging over her bed are there again, back from the shadows, and the air rises and falls with sound: this is how she knows the night is over. But something isn't right. Her skin is warm, her chin slick and wet. Her mouth hurts; her gums are beating like a heart. In one place there's something new, a rough edge poking up, and she doesn't like the way it scrapes against her tongue. A muffled slam from the other side of the wall, a bellow and a shriek, then the sound of something clattering to the floor. She begins to cry. After a moment, the other noises stop. This is how it always happens. She doesn't know who will come to get her this time—milk smell or spice, soft skin or rough—but she knows that for the length of time it takes for someone to walk to her room, pick her up loosely, and cradle her close, her crying will be the only sound there is.

. . .

She's undressed to her diaper, sitting on her mother's lap in a cold, bright room. Her mother is talking to a woman wearing a white jacket. There's a small bear stuck to a necklace of long tubes on the woman's chest.

It sounds like she's meeting all the milestones. What's your home situation like? Is she in day care?

Her attention moves from the bear to the panel of lights up on the ceiling. Her cheek is against her mother's chest, and she feels her mother's voice before she hears it. *No, she's home with me.*

Any pets in the home?

No.

Any smokers?

No.

Good. Are there any guns in the house?

She's still watching the light above her, but suddenly everything grows tight and quick: her mother's arms around her, the soft pulsing beneath her cheek, the rhythm of the noise against her ear. She squirms, and the grip loosens a little, but her mother's body doesn't slow.

14

No, her mother says.

Laughter from the woman with the little bear: *I hate asking that one, but you never know.*

Sure, her mother says. *Right.*

Well, once she starts crawling you'll need to think about baby-proofing the house. The nurse will give you a handout. The woman leans toward her, waves the little bear in her direction. *Let's take a look.*

Unhappy things now: a cold weight against her chest, her belly, her back; light in her eyes; something sharp in her ear. She twists away, but her mother holds her in place.

Everything looks good. She's scheduled for four immunizations today. I'll tell the nurse to come on in.

The door opens and closes. Her mother's hands are shaking against her belly. A knock on the door, and a new woman comes in, carrying a shiny tray.

Hi, sweetie, the woman says, holding out a fat finger for her to grab. *Boy, are you going to be mad at me.*

. . .

Bundled into her car seat, she's transported backward to the store. Her mother threads her legs through the openings in the metal cart, and she rides high through the aisles. She loves it here: the brightness, the activity, the tall walls of color. Leaning forward, she opens her mouth against the bar and presses the hurting place against the cold metal. *No*, her mother says, pushing her body back up. *Yucky*. But now that this cool comfort has been revealed to her, it's impossible to resist. She must put her mouth to this new star of a thing, must press her sore flesh to its chilly mass and feel it warm against her tongue. Eventually her mother gives up trying to distract her, and she sucks and gnaws until there's something new to fill her mind. When they reach the aisle with the balloons, her face floats upward as if it were suspended by a string.

. . .

At dinnertime she's placed in a new chair, one that's as tall as the table. Her father is sitting next to her, and she's never seen him this way before, so close and at her eye level. He's eating something with his hands, a triangle of color; the smell of it makes her want to put it in her mouth. She reaches out, but it's too far away to grab.

There's a white tray in front of her, and she bangs on the plastic surface with one loose fist. A piece of stiff fabric is placed around her neck from behind—she fidgets and tugs at it but can't get free—and then her mother picks up a small white bowl and a spoon edged in pink rubber.

Cereal, she says, dipping the spoon into the bowl and scooping up a small mound of white mud.

The spoon comes toward her, pushes her lips apart, and her mouth is filled with terrible lumps. She gags and propels the substance back out with her tongue. Her parents laugh. *Get the camera*, says her mother.

I know what you want, her father says to her, holding the wonderful triangle toward her. It's almost close enough for her to touch.

Michael, no, says her mother, still laughing. She's moving toward her with another spoonful of white. *You can't give her pizza. It'll make her sick.*

The triangle comes closer. Her mother's mouth still curves upward, her eyes cast down toward the spoon. *She'll be fine*, her father says, and then the food is at her mouth. She opens wide to receive it. The tip of the triangle lands on her tongue, but she can't taste anything but heat. She jerks her head back and shrieks, outraged and brokenhearted.

Michael! her mother yells, pushing him away from her. *You burned her. I told you she couldn't have that*. Her mother reaches into a glass of clear liquid, holds a cold block to her tongue. The feeling is magnificent. *She's only six months old.*

When her father speaks, his voice is very quiet. *Well, thanks for educating me*, he says. *Thanks for filling me in on that little detail. I certainly can't be trusted to know how old my own baby is.*

Her mother stops moving. *I didn't mean that. I just meant . . . it burned her tongue.*

Her father drops the pretty slice of food to the table so hard it makes a slapping sound. *Which was an accident. But I know nothing like that ever happens to you. You're the fucking baby expert.*

No, her mother says. *Michael.*

Watch out, folks. The goddamn baby queen is here. Whatever you do, don't try to have fun. Whatever you do, don't try to be a father.

Her mother unbuckles the high-chair straps, her hands clumsy. *I'm not going to sit here and listen to this.*

Motion and noise, and everything is on the floor—the lumps and the bowl, the bright triangle and the pink spoon. She begins to cry again.

Put her to bed, her father says.

It's not time yet.

Put. Her. To bed.

And she's whisked away through the rooms and up the stairs, her mouth spilling water as the beautiful smell gets fainter and fainter.

. . .

It's not morning, but her mother is taking her from her crib and wrapping her in a blanket, putting a hand over her mouth as she begins to fuss. They're moving fast, down the stairs and out into the cold. When the car door opens, she can see in the sudden light that her mother's face is bumpy and wet, with patches of darkness that aren't usually there.

She sleeps and wakes, sleeps and wakes. When she's lifted from the car again, the sky has a new color. Her mother carries her to the door of a small red house, but before they get there, the door opens and a woman with black and white hair comes out.

You made good time, she says. This new woman reaches out and scoops her right out of her mother's arms. *Do you remember Grandma Kay?* she asks in a voice like singing. But this woman doesn't smell right or feel right, and she yells until her mother takes her back.

She's been a little clingy lately.

Already, at this age? Well, you know, they pick up a lot from their environment. Grandma Kay holds out a finger, moves it in slow circles until she reaches out for it. *This isn't just about you anymore.*

Mom, stop it, okay? I'm here, aren't I?

Inside the house, a man wearing a gray shirt kisses her, a warm whisper on top of her head.

Is this for real this time? he asks. *You know he's going to show up here.*

This house is different. This house has brown wings that spin on the ceiling and a soft rug that covers the whole floor. When her mother sets her down, she lays her cheek on the carpet and tests the hairy strands with her tongue. She watches the wings go around and feels the wind they make. She rolls over once, and then again. She rolls until she reaches the wall and can't go any farther.

She sleeps in this house—not in her crib, but in a soft box with mesh walls—for two naps and one night before she sees her father again. When he comes, she hears his voice first. She's on the soft rug, chewing on the ear of a rubber giraffe, when the buzzing noise comes from the front door. The grown-ups move all at the same time.

Shit, says her mother.

Should I call the police? asks Grandma Kay.

Her mother picks her up and runs with her into the other room, puts her down in her sleeping box, and leaves her there. She yells and yells, but no one comes, and when she stops to take a breath, she can hear that her father's voice is one of the noises in the swell of sound coming from the living room.

She cries out for him. After a few minutes there are footsteps in the hallway, and there he is in the doorway, tall and smiling down. She kicks her legs with happiness at the sight of him. *Hi, Teddy Bear*, he says, and the sound of his voice fills her like warm milk. *Come see Daddy.*

She reaches out to him with both arms.

. . .

At home, in her swing, she floats back and forth as smoothly as a shadow moving across a wall. It's the time of day when food smells come from the kitchen and the trees outside the windows disappear, the time of day when she usually can't get happy, but the motion of the swing and the rubber comfort of the pacifier are making her feel calm and a little dazed.

Her mother walks into the room and kneels in front of the swing. She speaks with a voice that sounds rougher than it usually does—*I'm so sorry, baby, I love you so much*—and she stares at her mother's face, so big and so beloved. She smiles underneath her pacifier as her eyes begin to close.

Seventy-one years from now, on the last morning of her life, she will wake from a dream that she has been sitting on a porch swing while a woman she does not recognize stands in front of her, moving closer, then farther away. She's a young woman, but somehow she knows the woman is old, too, and she speaks to her in a language she does not understand. She will wake with a depth of peace she rarely feels in her daytime life. The feeling will last as she gets up and dresses, careful not to wake her husband, and puts on makeup, careful to cover both the new bruises and the old ones. It will last through her morning work (she has to be careful that she doesn't leave streak marks when she wipes down the glass table), through the usual flitting thoughts about her father and her children (she has two sons, though it's been a long time since she talked to either of them), all the way until her husband goes out to take his walk and she sits down to drink a cup of coffee, as if it were any other day.

But on this evening in her swing, the evening that will someday be longer ago than she thinks she can remember, she knows nothing of death, or makeup, or even coffee. She dozes and rocks until a new sound wakes her. It's short and sudden and loud—louder than a voice yelling on the other side of a wall, louder than a pile of blocks falling to the floor. All at once the room is filled with a smell that burns her nose. Startled and furious, she begins to cry, her body pushing the sound louder and louder until her father walks through the front door and sees her there.

Her father looks around the room and lets out a wordless howl, loud and fierce. His face is red, and he looks at her in a way that makes her scared. He takes her out of the swing roughly—*Goddamn it, stop crying*—and walks to the table where they keep the phone.

As they walk through the room, she takes in what she sees: toys in a basket, an empty glass on the coffee table, her mother sleeping softly on the floor. She reaches out toward where she lies. She'd like to put her fingers in the dark bath around her.

Her father's forearm is too tight on her chest, and she struggles, and he lets go of her and drops her to the floor. For a moment, in the shock of it, her mouth won't make a sound, and she stares, frozen, as he picks up the phone. Then the air rushes in and she begins to cry, knowing that if she yells loud enough, her mother will come to get her.

At home, in her swing, she floats back and forth as smoothly as a shadow moving across a wall. It's the time of day when food smells come from the kitchen and the trees outside the windows disappear, the time of day when she usually can't get happy, but the motion of the swing and the rubber comfort of the pacifier are making her feel calm and a little dazed. She hears the front door open, and after a minute her father comes into the room. He stands in front of her and speaks to her gently—*Hello there, Teddy Bear*—and she stares at his face, so big and so beloved. She smiles underneath her pacifier as her eyes begin to close.

Seventy-one years from now, on the last morning of her life, she will wake up from a dream that she has been sitting on a porch swing while a man she does not recognize stands in front of her, moving closer, then farther away. He's a young man, but somehow she knows he is old, too, and he speaks to her in a language she does not understand. She will wake with a depth of peace she rarely feels in her daytime life. The feeling will last as she gets up and dresses, thinking of the day ahead of her (she has a job in a casino, making change behind a grubby pane of acrylic glass), through a phone call from one of her children (she has two sons, each of them now older than she ever imagined being herself), all the way until her midmorning break, when she sits down to drink a cup of coffee, as if it were any other day.

But on this evening in her swing, the evening that will someday be longer ago than she thinks she can remember, she knows nothing of death, or casinos, or even coffee. She dozes and rocks until a new sound wakes her. It's short and sudden and loud—louder than a voice yelling on the other side of a wall, louder than a pile of blocks falling to the floor. All at once the room is filled with a smell that burns her nose. Startled and furious, she begins to cry, her body pushing the sound louder and louder until her mother comes and picks her up.

As they walk through the room, she takes in what she sees: toys in a basket, an empty glass on the coffee table, her father sleeping softly on the floor. She reaches out toward where he lies. She'd like to put her fingers in the dark bath around him.

Her mother carries her upstairs, lays her on the padded table, changes her diaper, and wiggles her out of her clothes. She dresses her in soft pajamas, then plops her down in her crib. *Just a minute, baby girl*, she says. Her voice sounds rougher than it usually does.

Her mother walks away and makes some crashing sounds in the next room. When she returns, she's carrying a big blue bag.

We're going for a ride, she says. *Let's get you fed, and then we're going for a long, long ride.*

Her mother plucks her from the crib and sits down with her in the chair, lifting her shirt to nurse. Her face is brought close to the nipple, but everything is shaky and wrong. The arms around her are too tight. Even the smell is different. She pulls back, afraid. Her mother breathes deeply, says *It's okay, it's okay, it's okay*. Wetness on the top of her head. The two of them rock together until finally her mother's limbs begin to still. *It's okay*, she breathes, and it's like a lullaby. As she begins to suck, her body relaxes. Soon she'll be asleep again. She flexes her legs, pushes a foot against the spokes of the rocking chair, the pale moon of the breast all she sees, the milk as warm as her mother's body.

Devastate me
Punch holes till the light shines through
Desecrate me
I'll lie under water for you

From "Devastate Me" by Pareidolia
Lyrics by Milo Frost, music by Joe Khan
As quoted in the New York Times, *Wednesday,*
November 10

Chapter Two

When at last this day is finally over, after I've made it through a wretched afternoon spent in faceless hotel splendor and a plane ride during which I became airsick for the first time since I was a child, a taxi lets me out in front of my house in Newton, and I discover I've been found. My yard is scoured with artificial light, and fifteen or twenty people with cameras and microphones and other technological paraphernalia are standing, waiting for me, in the drizzle. As I open the door of the taxi, they move toward me in a single clot.

For a moment I hesitate, and I'm surrounded, pushed back against the door of the cab. Immediately, there's yelling: "Ms. Frost!" "Octavia!" "Have you spoken to Milo?" "Did he do it?" "Was Milo violent as a child?" "Does he have a history of drug abuse?" And other questions I can't make out.

I glance back at the cabdriver, who has begun to honk. I think about getting back in and fleeing, but that's ridiculous. I stand up straighter and draw a long breath. "I have no comment," I say to the bouquet of microphones in front of my mouth. I feel like I'm reading from a movie script, but what else is there to say? I repeat it over and over as I push through the crowd and work my key into the lock. They yell after me as I slip inside, but they can't come in with me. It ends at the threshold.

I close the door and stand for a minute in the dark hall. I moved into this house with my husband, Mitch, when Milo was three and Rosemary was an infant. It was new then; we're the only family who've ever lived here. As I reach for the light, I realize I'm expecting the house to be different than it was when I left. Something dramatic, some visible sign of disintegration or decay. I imagine my belongings sunk in a foot of water, my walls covered with a creeping mold. But of course everything's the same as it was when I walked out the door thirteen hours ago. Mess of mail on the hall table. Pictures hanging on the walls: the four of us, and then the two of us.

I take off my shoes, use the bathroom, get a box of crackers from the kitchen. I pause for a minute to lean against the counter, without bothering to turn on the light. It's a big room, warm with sun in the mornings, cool and empty now. Framed finger paintings over the breakfast table, artwork created by children who no longer exist. A shadow box displaying two baby hats, one tied with blue ribbon, one with pink. Provided by the hospital and slipped on their heads moments after they were born. One thing that can be said about me as a mother: I've always enjoyed the artifacts.

I walk around the first floor, drawing curtains and blinds, keeping myself away from the edges of windows, though it appears that most of the reporters are packing up to go. Dining room, office, living room, cozy and familiar, more cluttered than they ought to be, considering that only one person lives in them. I don't know whether it's nostalgia or laziness, but I've never once thought about leaving this house. After Milo left for college, I waited for it to hit me: the wish for walls never touched by crayons, for floors unscratched by scooters that weren't supposed to be ridden indoors in the first place. A willingness to trade pencil marks on a doorjamb for space that's indisputably my own. But it never did, and tonight I'm glad. I can't imagine how I would absorb this news in a place where my children never lived.

In the living room, I sit down on the couch—relatively new, bought to please no one but myself—and pull my laptop from its case. I'm not going to check my e-mail, but I open it up long enough to send one note, attach one document. Type in the first letters of my editor's address, let the computer fill in the rest. *Dear Lisa, Sorry to cancel lunch, but I'm sure you've heard what's happened by now. Just wanted to get this to you before it slips my mind. I look forward to hearing your thoughts. Best, O.* Press Send before I can formulate any questions about whether this is a reasonable way for me to be spending my time on this particular night.

My voice mail tells me I have thirty-three new messages, and I run through them slowly, listening for the one voice I'd like to hear. It's mostly journalists, a couple of prank calls, a message from a police officer in San Francisco, notifying me of the arrest. There's one from my mother, who sounds upset; I'll have to call her tomorrow. A scattering of messages from friends and acquaintances: some offer kind wishes; others clearly just want the pulpy details. When I've finally waded through it all, I lean toward the coffee table and pick up the remote.

I have a habit of recording newscasts so I can watch them at my leisure, and never before have technology and personal need seemed so perfectly in sync. I turn on my TV, push two buttons, and there's Milo, walking with police officers, his hands clamped behind his back. I've already seen this footage, in my hotel room and in the airport lounge, but now I take time to really study it. He's wearing a red T-shirt and black jeans. I can't get a good look at his face; he's keeping his eyes down, the way they all do in these situations, unless they're Manson-level crazy. He looks skinnier than he was the last time I saw him, and his hair—dark like mine, though mine now requires artificial means to keep it that color—falls to his chin. A lock of it slips over his face as he's led forward. Somewhere, in an envelope, I have a few strands of that hair, saved from his first haircut. It was lighter then, and finer. If I wanted to, if I was willing to spend some time with the boxes in the basement, all my cardboard archives, I could find that envelope and run my fingers through that hair. I could marvel at how silky it once was.

After I've watched the news story all the way through a couple of times, I pause the recording so that Milo's image is fixed on the screen. I look at the picture, my son in handcuffs, and use it to test myself. How does it make me feel? I don't cry; I did that in the hotel and on the plane ride home, and for the moment I've run dry. I feel instead the way I felt for a stretch of months eighteen years ago, when Milo was a nine-year-old boy, forever sticking out at odd angles from pajamas that had grown too small, and I was a widow who had never published a word. A great welling fear, and something that might be called despair. A feeling of intangible loss; a certainty that nothing is ever going to be okay again.

When Milo was little, before I'd suffered any *real* losses, I would look at him sometimes and imagine that I'd just heard the news of his death. That was a test, too. The horror I felt, the surge in my guts and the stinging at my eyes, the need to reach out and touch the solidity and wholeness of his body, would satisfy me. Yes, I would think. That's how a mother is supposed to feel. Before Milo was born, I'd imagined the love a mother feels for her child to be a solid thing, completely unshakable. I thought it would be like a coat—rather cozy, something that can be added to the self without changing the flesh underneath. I didn't understand yet the way that love can scoop you out; I didn't know that each time a new channel of care and attachment forms, it carves something else away.

I think sometimes of the Etch A Sketch Milo had as a child. When he was nine or ten years old, he took it apart to see how it worked. I was surprised by what he discovered; it turned out I had the whole thing backward in my mind. I had imagined that by turning the dials to move the stylus, the user was drawing metallic dust to the other side of the glass. I'd thought it was this dust that made up the lines. In fact it's the opposite: the inside surface of the screen is coated with aluminum powder from the moment you shake it, and when you turn the knobs, you draw the particles away. The lines you draw represent an absence of the dust, not its presence. It's possible, with enough time and care, to draw a design dense enough to clear the screen completely. Scribble over a big enough area and you can see right through the glass to the machine's dark innards.

My love for Milo—and for whatever reasons, it was not quite the same with his sister—has always been fierce, but it has not been unchanging. Sometimes the lines of it are drawn so clearly, are so complex and overlapping, that they seem to cover every inch of me, laying open everything that lies below. But when something happens to shake the ground between us, the surface of that emotion can turn—for just a moment—blank and opaque. Looking at it, you'd never know there had been a picture there at all.

. . .

Morning. Today begins, as yesterday did, with me sitting on a plane. This time, however, my fondest wish is *not* to be recognized. I'm going to San Francisco. Of course I am. I have little idea of what I'll do once I get there, but sitting at home is not an option.

I made phone calls on the way to the airport—the head of the English department where I teach, canceling my upcoming classes; my mother in Fort Lauderdale, who needed reassurance, though I had nothing reassuring to say. I haven't yet made any attempt to contact Milo; I don't have a current number for him, and as far as I can tell, he's still in police custody.

I've got three newspapers on my tray table, and each of them has a front-page story about my son. In this strange age of technology and information, in which news is practically injected straight into our veins, replaced with a fresh drip each quarter hour, nothing is ever final. I'm sure that by the time I disembark, the story will have already changed. But at this particular moment, the world knows only this: Bettina Moffett, age twenty-six, was found in the home she and Milo shared at eight-thirty in the morning on November 9. She was lying in bed; her skull had been crushed with a ten-pound exercise weight. She was discovered by their housekeeper, Joyce Tung. (Odd to think of my son as a man who employs a housekeeper. It's not something I ever would have expected of him.) When Ms. Tung arrived, she used her key to let herself in, as she always did; the door was, as usual, locked from the inside. What was not usual was the view she came upon when she walked into the house: Milo asleep on a couch, his face and hands smeared with dried blood. Ms. Tung left the room quietly, without waking him, and continued upstairs with a feeling of unease. Shortly thereafter, she found Bettina's body and called the police. Milo woke sometime later, dazed and apparently hungover, to find an assortment of officers surrounding the couch, looking down at him impassively. (Please note that the expressions on the cops' faces are not explicitly discussed anywhere; that detail is my own contribution to the Milo Frost mythology currently under construction.)

The three articles contain largely the same information. Each one lists the same key points about Milo's background—*He is, along with guitarist Joe Khan, a member of the band Pareidolia, whose most recent album,* December Graffiti, *has produced four top-ten hits, including "Devastate Me" and "Your Brain on Drugs"*—and each paper has found some high school classmate of Milo's who's willing to say he was occasionally sullen as a teenager. Each story ends with a quote from Bettina's mother, Kathy Moffett, guaranteed to bring tears to the reader's eyes. There are several to choose from; she's been busy in the last twenty-four hours. It's like she's been practicing for this moment. *Bettina was born on Christmas Eve, and I always said she was my angel here on Earth,* one paper reports. And another: *I always knew she was too good for this world.* And perhaps my favorite: *The last words she ever said to me were "I love you, Mom."*

This isn't the first time that Bettina's mother has entered my consciousness. Though it's easy for me to make fun of her overblown phrasing, I believe that she is telling the truth about having a close relationship with her daughter. I've seen her in photo after photo, hovering and trailing, always at the edges of the scene; her presence in Milo and Bettina's life together has been impossible to miss. Milo, Bettina, and Kathy carrying Starbucks cups. Milo, Bettina, and Kathy arriving at the airport. She and I look nothing alike—she's tall, blond, firm, where I'm smaller, darker, softer—but she's become a kind of doppelgänger for me. Living a life that could be mine, if I could only figure out how to swap our positions. This is where a mother might go; in today's performance, the role will be played by Kathy Moffett.

Milo has said (through a statement by his lawyer) that he's not guilty. He says that he was sleeping on the couch because he and Bettina had argued over dinner—indeed, witnesses place them in a nearby restaurant, speaking in intense, hushed tones around nine-thirty—but that they had gone their separate ways afterward and he hadn't come home until almost two a.m., at which time Bettina was (he says) upstairs, sleeping peacefully. He passed out on the couch and remembers nothing more until the police arrived. But a man who was out walking his dog around eleven p.m. says that he saw a car resembling Milo's in the driveway, and two different neighbors have reported hearing shouting from the house and a crashing noise less than a half hour later. The police have found traces of her blood on his skin and on the upholstery he slept on. They've found—and here I have to stop and take a breath before I read any further—they've found bloody footprints on the stairs that match the tread of his shoes.

I look at the picture that all the papers are running, a shot taken a couple of months ago at an awards show. He's wearing a bizarre velvet tuxedo, bottle green; it looks like it came from a thrift store, but it's more likely that he paid some designer a ridiculous sum of money for it. His hair looks tangled and dirty—though again, I'm sure he went to a great deal of trouble to get it that way—and his jaw is stubbly. Bettina's wearing a short beaded dress, meant to evoke the flapper era, and ripped black tights; her blond hair is done up in elaborate pin curls, and her makeup is heavy. She's got both arms around Milo and is leaning her head against his arm, with a wild happy smile on her face. Milo isn't smiling. He's gazing down at Bettina with an intensity that would frighten the mother of any daughter. It may be an accident of timing, the expression lasting for only that split second when the photographer moved his finger. But he's looking at her as if he couldn't stop if he wanted to, as if the sheer act of watching her is the only thing that can sustain him. As if he's afraid that if he looks away, even for a second, one of them might cease to exist.

Bettina didn't deserve this—that's another statement her mother made at her little press party. I've always been wary of that idea—that any of us deserve anything, that we're owed a particular outcome for our lives—but this is one of those black-and-white cases that wipes away the gray areas pretty neatly. Bettina Moffett did not deserve to have her cranium shattered, her blood spilled on her sheets. And Kathy

Moffett—I will say this as someone who knows how it feels to lose a daughter—does not deserve what she's been given, either.

I fold up the papers and stuff them under the seat in front of me. I also have a book I picked up at the airport, a novel written by a woman named Sara Ferdinand, who's an old friend of mine from college. A onetime rival, really. She's done very well; she's won a lot of awards, but I've never really understood the appeal of her work. She writes stories like spindly wooden dolls with no clothes on them, stories that are often admired but, as far as I can tell, seldom loved. Her prose is like an empty room: bare, not a speck of dust, each sentence reduced down to its very essence. Emotion leached out with all the other debris. This book is called *The Dying Brain*, and there was a huge display of them at the airport newsstand. It's just been released as a film, and the paperback has been given a makeover, celebrities on the cover as if you might actually find them inside. I don't know why I chose today of all days to buy a book written by a colleague I have decidedly mixed feelings about, but it doesn't surprise me that I don't even want to read the first page. And so I'm here, in a metal box in the sky, trapped with my own thoughts.

One more thing about the newspaper articles: they include me as well. Each story has managed to squeeze in something like the following: *Frost is the son of best-selling author Octavia Frost, whose novel* Tropospheric Scatter *contains a scene in which a musician kills his wife.* (They do not mention that the scene in question—which has little bearing on the larger plot—is about an eighty-nine-year-old flautist who backs over his wife with his car.)

It's not the first time since we've been apart that Milo and I have been discussed in the same flutter of newsprint. Articles about Pareidolia mention me only rarely; I imagine that the group's target audience would be frightened by the very mention of books (not to mention mothers) and would skitter off to find a band with a less literary pedigree. But publicists and journalists working on my behalf never fail to bring up who my son is. And despite the troubles we've had, I always enjoy sharing print space with Milo. I imagine him, alerted to these articles by some digital clipping service, forced to read my name and gaze upon my image, however much he'd prefer not to. This is how we've kept up with each other in these past few years. I don't think I'm the only one who's been looking.

. . .

After half a day of travel, I arrive in a place where it's still morning and bright as spring. Once I'm installed in my hotel room, tired and dazed, I turn on CNN to see what news may have broken during the few hours I was moving through the air. I find out immediately—it's printed on the screen, I don't even have to wait for the words to be spoken aloud—that Milo has been released on bail. It's a relief, though perhaps it shouldn't be. It changes nothing about the larger situation, but I'm glad to know that, for the moment anyway, he's not being raped or threatened with a shank or whatever goes on in a prison inhabited by real criminals and not Hollywood actors, which is my only point of reference. The fact that he's been released also implies a judgment about the severity of his crime: the police may still think my son is a murderer, but if they're willing to let him walk the streets, then they must not think he's the very worst kind of murderer. It's a matter of degree that would have been too subtle for me to grasp twenty-four hours ago. Strange how reassuring I find it now.

Milo's lawyer is on the screen, talking to the news anchor. His name is Samuel Zalakis, which I copy down onto the hotel-letterhead notepad next to the phone. I don't know if Milo picked this man himself, but he seems like a good choice. He's in his mid-fifties, sleek and well groomed, charismatic but not unctuous. He could perhaps be called fatherly, but only if your father had a taste for thousand-dollar ties and appeared comfortable speaking in front of fifty million people.

"At this point," the anchorwoman asks, leaning forward, "it does not look likely that prosecutors will seek the death penalty, is that correct?"

A snake moves through my belly. Living in Massachusetts, where no one's been executed since—when? the forties?—I hadn't even thought of that.

"That's right. The charge is first-degree murder without special circumstances, which in the state of California is punishable by twenty-five years to life."

"And if, during the course of the investigation, the district attorney were to determine that there were special circumstances, such as lying in wait or mayhem, which we've seen before in high-profile murder cases . . . ?"

"We don't expect that to happen, but yes, it is possible that additional charges could be filed, which might affect the sentencing."

I lie down across the bed, resting my cheek against the rough silk of the bedspread. My heart beats; I breathe in, I breathe out. I don't know how I'm supposed to do this.

The show goes to commercial; I stretch for the remote and turn off the TV. I'm certain there will be more coverage, but I don't want to see it right now. After a few moments, I force myself to sit up. I didn't come all the way across the country to lie on a bed. I reach for my cell phone and call directory assistance to request the number of Zalakis's firm.

"Zalakis, Sampson, and Dugger," says the receptionist who answers.

"Hello," I say. "I'm trying to reach Mr. Zalakis. I'm Milo Frost's mother."

I'm hoping for a shocked pause, perhaps even an expression of disbelief, but she's a pro. "I'm sorry," she says, "Mr. Zalakis isn't available right now." Of course not; I just saw him live on CNN. Did I think she was going to give me his private cell? "If you'd like to give me your name and number, I can take a message."

I give her the information and hang up. I've got one more vague idea. In my purse I find the old address book I pulled from my desk this morning, and I look up the home number for Rana and Salima Khan, the parents of Milo's bandmate Joe. I've known Joe for a long time. He and Milo go way back—junior high, at least. I can remember the two of them holed up in Milo's bedroom, listening to music so loud the house shook. On more than one occasion, I went in to turn the music down and caught them with contraband they shouldn't have had: a girly magazine, firecrackers, a joint. I remember the startled panic on their faces at my appearance, the rush to hide whatever they didn't want me to see. This is how I imagine Milo reacting yesterday morning when the police stormed into his house.

Salima answers. The conversation is awkward—we haven't spoken in probably ten years, and this isn't the best week for getting in touch with old friends—but when I hang up, I have Joe's number written on my hotel pad.

Joe spent quite a bit of time with us when he and Milo were teenagers. I was happy to have him there; with just me and Milo in the house, it was helpful to have someone else around to act as a buffer from time to time. He was a nice kid, smart and funny, more even-keeled than Milo ever was. I think he'll be willing to talk to me, though I don't know how much my absence from Milo's life over the past four years will have influenced his ideas about me.

He answers on the second ring. "Hello?" he says, like it's a question. Now that everyone knows who's on the phone before the first words are spoken, a call from an unfamiliar number is cause for suspicion.

"Hi, Joe," I say. I'm nervous suddenly. "It's Octavia Frost."

"Mrs. Frost," he says. I tried for a while, I remember, to get him to call me by my first name, but it never took. "I was wondering if I'd hear from you."

"You were?"

"Well, yeah, of course. I figured, with all this going on, you might be trying to get in touch with Milo."

"Have you seen him?" I say. "Since he . . . was released?"

"No, not yet, but I talked to him. He sounds, you know, okay."

"Where is he staying? Not back in the house?"

"No, the police are still there. He's going to stay with Roland Nysmith for a few days."

This takes me by surprise. Roland Nysmith, the venerable rock god from the seventies band The Misters, has long been a hero of Milo's. I had read that they'd become friends, but I had no idea they were close enough for Milo to call in a favor like this. It's a brilliant move, actually, probably the work of some PR damage-control guru. Roland Nysmith's one of the few celebrities who's managed the curious transformation from tight-trousered rebel to elder statesman without stumbling into the murk of self-parody, and his support lends an air of respectability to the whole sordid mess.

"I see," I say. "Can you give me the number there, or maybe even take me to see him?"

"Oh, you're here? In San Francisco?"

"I flew in this morning."

"That's funny. When I talked to Milo a little while ago, I asked if he'd talked to you, and he said no. I said, 'I bet she'll want to see you,' and he said he thought you'd probably want to watch everything unfold from a distance. He said he thought you'd just want to know how the story ends."

I don't say anything. It's just a bratty throwaway comment, typical Milo, but it hurts me.

"Oh, God," says Joe. "I can't believe I said that. I'm sorry, I haven't gotten any sleep in, like, thirty hours."

"That's okay," I said. "Well, I'm here and I would like to see my son. Do you have his phone number?"

"Well, here's the thing. He told me that if you did get in touch with me, I shouldn't tell you anything."

"Oh," I say. I'm not surprised, but I still feel a buried thrum of grief.

"But now that you're actually here," Joe continues, "maybe he'll feel differently. Let me give him a call, and I'll get back to you in a few minutes, okay?"

I thank him and we hang up. The last time I saw Milo, he was getting ready to board a plane. He'd been home for Christmas, and I saw him off at the airport. Pareidolia's debut album had just come out, and the first single was getting a lot of airplay. I was in a professional honeymoon mood myself, having written the last pages of my novel *Carpathia* the day before he'd arrived. We'd had a lovely visit; there had been a sense of things about to happen. I wish now that I'd gone into the airport with him—he'd had some time to kill, which turned out to be a crucial factor in everything that followed—but I had some errands to run, so I dropped him at the curb. We hugged good-bye, and I kissed him on the cheek. Neither of us knew, not yet, that by the time Milo stepped off that plane, our relationship would have changed irrevocably.

The phone rings. "Hi, Joe," I say.

"I'm sorry, Mrs. Frost. He said no."

All at once I feel nothing but angry. *The little shit*, I think, then immediately feel guilty, as if I'd said it to his face. I suppose I have to admire his backbone. Why turn this into a melodrama? The tearful mother pressing her hand to the jailhouse glass, the wayward son ashamed to meet her eyes . . . no. Not us. I'll leave, I'll fly back tonight. The next time I come, it will be because he asked me to.

"Mrs. Frost?" says Joe. "Are you okay?"

"Fine," I say, my voice tight.

"Where are you staying?" he asks.

I tell him.

"Do you want to meet for coffee or something? I could be there in a half hour."

. . .

There was a girl I knew, growing up, named Lisette Freyn. She was a quiet, bending willow of a girl; she smiled a lot, but she never seemed to have any friends. She left home at fifteen, and the story was that she'd run away to become a groupie, following rock bands on the road. To me, naive and still comfortable in the straitjacket of home life, it was like hearing she'd run away to become a peacock. To be part of a crowd every night, losing your edges in a thudding gush of music; to lick the sweat from the faces of men whose albums you'd bought with your birthday money . . . I couldn't imagine anyone I knew living such a life.

A few years later, in the mid-seventies, when Bramble Wine came out with their song "Lisette Spins," we all knew (or thought we knew) that it was about her. A girl with "burning eyes and a firefly smile," a girl "young enough to spin across the room, old enough to land here on the bed." A girl who "whispers her mama's name when she thinks

I can't hear." The song comes on every so often on the oldies station, and for a long time, before the Internet made ignorance quaint and unnecessary, I would think about her and try to imagine what had become of her.

She died of an overdose. Or she married a chiropractor.

She hates the song, she calls herself Lisa now, her kids don't even know.

It's a story she tells at parties. Or she never talks about it but she makes sure the hostess points her out to every guest.

She's moved on; she doesn't even recognize that young girl anymore.

Or maybe it's like this: maybe she's spent every moment of her life listening for the rising arc of those opening notes, waiting for the words to remind her of who she's supposed to be.

Of course, the romance of letting an old friend fade out of your life is a luxury of the past, and I'm far too curious a person to have let this one rest. I looked her up a few years ago, and we've been in touch sporadically. We're closer as online "friends" than we ever were as friends in the flesh, and her Facebook updates have turned her from a mythical icon to an ordinary woman living her life. She lives in San Francisco, and if this were a trip for business or pleasure, I'd certainly take the time to get in touch with her, to see if she wanted to get together.

But now, as I sit in the café where Joe has agreed to meet me, I'm thinking about Lisette the wandering girl and not Lisette the fifty-two-year-old divorced real estate agent. The people around me don't look much different from people buying coffee in any other American city, but I've absorbed enough of the California mythology to imagine that each of them is in the grip of some sharp-flavored ambition, aching to be known and remembered. I'll bet any one of them would be thrilled to have a song written about them. I know I would.

As I wait for Joe to arrive, I tune in to a conversation at a table on my right. Two guys with laptops, one typing away, the other sitting back reading something. From time to time one of them will talk on the phone to someone else. It's a different model of companionship than I'm used to, but they seem content.

The one who's been reading looks up. "Hey, here's a good one. What's the name of Pareidolia's follow-up to *December Graffiti*?"

His friend looks up from his screen, smiling already. "What?"

"*Dismember Your Sweetie.*"

His friend shrugs, makes a noncommittal gesture with his hand. "Eh," he says. "I've heard better."

Much is being made already about the dark nature of the lyrics Milo has written. Everyone's scrutinizing his songs, looking for violence, misogyny, anything that can be sharpened and used to poke with. The results are iffy at best, but when people see a puzzle, they will find pieces that fit. In one song, "Saskatchewan," Milo sings, "Be a whore for me / You know how, you've done it before." Not my favorite lyric, but not terribly out of the ordinary when placed in the context of modern pop music. And the irony of it is, "Saskatchewan" is a love song. The narrator (who may or may not be Milo, let's not forget) is telling his girlfriend that he doesn't care how many men she's been with before, as long as she stays true to him. It's as close to gallantry as this type of music gets. Another song, "Plutonium Kiss," contains the following couplet: "She had poison between her lips and poison between her thighs / We played Russian roulette to find out who should die." This one makes me laugh. I'll bet even Milo can't keep a straight face when he sings those lines. It's ludicrous; it's posturing for effect; it's a ninth grader showing off for his friends.

But the song people are really excited about is "Diesel Lights," which describes a lovers' quarrel at a highway rest stop. As the song builds and the tension rises between the couple in the story, the speaker tells his girlfriend:

> *I grabbed you hard*
> *There was no one else around*
> *I'll tell you now*
> *I could have beat you to the ground.*

In light of what's happened . . . well. But I don't think it's particularly revelatory. I know from personal experience that this kind of treasure hunt is not useful. When Pareidolia's second album came out, I spent hours with the lyric sheet, looking for anything that might mean something to me. Some hidden wish for immortalization à la Lisette Freyn. And sometimes—a verse about long-standing anger, a line about betrayal—I thought I might have found it. But I was never sure.

Anyway. Young men don't write songs about their mothers; you'd worry about them if they did. Milo is not some folksinger, composing sentimental ballads about his childhood home, and he's not a country singer belting out odes to his mama. He's going for rock star; he's going for hard, pointed, edged like a sword. And how much can you tell about a person from what he writes anyway? He has a lot to juggle, I imagine—he's working with rhyme and meter, making the story fit the music—and he's trying to manufacture a particular image. You can't assume he's telling the truth about anything.

. . .

The door opens, and there he is, Joe Khan, all grown up. He's wearing a baseball cap and sunglasses—the half-disguise of the semicelebrity—and he's affected a careful scruffiness that seems miles away from the true slovenly disregard of his adolescence. It's a strange sensation to see him here. We haven't been in a room together for five years or more, but I can't say that I haven't seen him in that time. I'd seen enough recent pictures to know what to expect—I knew his hair would be shorter than the last time we met, and that his face would look slightly more angular—but I had forgotten about texture and curve and depth, all of the corporeal minutiae that can't be conveyed on film. Looking at him in the flesh—in 3-D, as it were—makes me realize that I've come to picture Milo in that same flat way.

Joe takes off his sunglasses, and I see his eyes, wide and brown as a seal's, just exactly like they always were. I feel lifted, somehow, just standing in his presence. To see him after all this time, this man whose boyhood was so entwined with Milo's, who ate noisily at our table and broke the sugar bowl from my mother's wedding china, who once couldn't look at me for a month after reading a novel of mine that included a few racy scenes—it's like letting out a breath I didn't know I'd been holding. There's a surrogate pleasure in it, a chance to extend some maternal warmth by proxy.

"Joe," I say. I give him a hug. "You look good."

"Thanks," he says. "You too. You really do."

"Thank you," I say. I look okay, I suppose, for a middle-aged woman lost in catastrophe. My hair is shorter now, too, but it's softer and wavier; I used to blow-dry it straight in a way that looks severe to me now in pictures. And though I'm a little travel-rumpled, I took care to dress up today, in the apparently foolish hope that I might be seeing Milo. Perhaps Joe had imagined I'd look worse than this. I've been using the same author photo for ten years, so he may not have known what to expect.

He gestures toward the counter. "Let me just grab a coffee."

I watch as he goes up, orders, pays. No one seems to take any notice of him, though his picture's been in the paper nearly as much as Milo's.

"So I should tell you," he says as he sits down at the table. He pulls the plastic lid off his cup, blows ripples across the surface of the coffee. I can see he has a small tattoo on his forearm, just above his wrist; it looks abstract, some kind of runic design, but it's partly covered by his sleeve. "My lawyer has advised me not to talk about the case."

I nod. "Sure," I say. "That's fine." I expected as much, though it does leave us with some awkward holes in the conversation. "So," I try. "How are your parents doing? I talked to your mom briefly, but we didn't really have time to catch up."

"They're good," he says. "My dad's retiring next year."

"Good for him," I say.

"Are you still in the same place?" he asks. I nod.

"I always liked that house," he says, and I have a sudden flash of an image, Milo and Joe sitting on the carpet in front of the TV, video game controllers clutched so tightly their knuckles were pale. In the very room where I sat last night and watched my son move across the screen in handcuffs.

I sigh, and Joe sips his coffee. The conversation is stagnating, but

I'm not sure what I can ask him. *How's the band going?* is clearly not the right question. We sit in silence for a few moments, drinking our coffee studiously.

"Without asking about the case," I say, "can I ask about Milo?"

"I guess so," says Joe. "What do you want to know?"

I think about it. How does this happen? That's one thing I want to know. How is it possible that we find ourselves in this situation? And, did he kill Bettina? And, will I ever lay eyes on him again without a screen of television glass between us?

"Well, whatever you want to tell me, I guess. How was he before all this happened? Just anything. It's been a long time since I've seen him."

"Before this," Joe says. He sounds almost wistful, as if he's forgotten such a time existed. "He was okay, I guess. He was ... I don't know. He's, you know ... Milo."

I look down at the paper cup in my hands, the cardboard sleeve around its middle. I feel suddenly that I might cry. Of course. He's just Milo.

"What was Bettina like?" I ask. What I really mean is, what was Milo like when he was with her, but that seems to veer too closely to danger territory.

He doesn't say anything for a minute. "Honestly, I was never crazy about her," he says. "God, that sounds awful after all this."

I shrug. "You don't have to start liking someone just because they're dead. What didn't you like about her?"

"She was just annoying. She was kind of childish, always throwing tantrums when she didn't get her way. And she was very possessive of Milo. Not that he minded—he was way too into her, and I could never really figure out why."

He stops talking. I think he thinks he's gone too far. I don't want him to be uncomfortable, but I'd give any amount of money to know his definition of "way too into her."

"So how's the writing going?" he asks. He wants to talk about something else.

"Okay," I say. I feel like I'm sitting in a cloud of anxiety as it is, and

I don't want to think about *The Nobodies Album* waiting in my editor's in-box. I wonder instead if the publishing company will be sending me a sympathy fruit basket or something. I wonder if I'll be staying here long enough for it to molder on the porch before I get home. "Fine."

"I read one of your books a couple of summers ago," he says, livening a little. "The one . . . the ghost story, if you can call it that. The one about the guy who had been on the *Titanic* when he was a kid."

"Carpathia," I say.

"Right. It was really good."

"Thanks," I say. "I'm glad you liked it."

"It was crazy, though—just having it in my house was all cloak-and-dagger. I had to hide it every time Milo came over, to make sure he didn't see it." He laughs, as if it's cute that my son can't even stand to lay eyes on something I've written.

I drink the last of my coffee and set the cup on the table. Casting about for a new topic, I ask if he has a girlfriend. He does, which I already knew—a woman named Chloe, who has a young daughter from a previous relationship. She designs jewelry and sells it online. And we're back to silence.

I'm about to ask if his parents' cockatoo is still alive, but at the same moment Joe says, "I have something for you."

He picks up his messenger bag from where he's dropped it under the table. When he opens it, I can see the edge of a laptop, a coiled cord, some papers, two CDs. And a square white gift box, which he pulls out and hands to me.

"You're kidding," I say. "Really?"

"Yup," he says. He smiles for the first time since he sat down. "Just a little something."

I open the box and find a porcelain sugar bowl painted with yellow roses. My mother's pattern.

"Oh, Joe," I say. A thread of warmth snakes through me. I'm truly touched. "This is lovely. I can't believe you did this."

"Yeah, well," he says, looking embarrassed. "I always felt bad about breaking it. I actually thought right away that I wanted to get you a new one. I saved a little piece of the one that broke—I put it in my pocket while we were cleaning it up, so I'd have something with the pattern on it. But I never did anything about it. And then, after the band started making money, I was buying presents like crazy—it was a little insane, actually, like I bought my mom a car, and I got my dad this signed baseball that cost twenty-five hundred dollars."

I smile and try to look charmed. Milo never sent me anything.

"So anyway, I remembered that I always wanted to replace the sugar bowl, and it became like my life's mission to track one down. Milo was no help—he didn't know the name of the pattern or who made it or anything, but I still had that little broken piece, and eventually I figured out the details. You know they don't make this stuff anymore?"

I nod. "I almost never use my pieces anymore because they're so hard to replace."

"Yeah. I'd pretty much given up. With everything that happened between you and Milo, it would've seemed weird to just send you a sugar bowl out of the blue."

Weird. I guess I would have thought it was. It's very sweet, but it's well beyond what you might expect from a man his age. I think he might have had a bit of a crush on me when he was a teenager.

"So how'd you end up finding it?"

"Chloe finally tracked one down online. She likes those kind of challenges, so she'd do searches from time to time. It actually just arrived this morning."

"Wow," I say, rather inelegantly. I nestle the bowl in its tissue paper. "Well, thank you. I really love it. It's a great gift."

"Well, good. I'm glad." He pulls his phone out of his pocket, checks the time. "I've got to go," he says. "I've got a meeting with our manager at four. We've got to figure out what the rest of the band is going to do until all this is resolved. We've got tour dates to cancel . . . it's a mess." We stand up. "How long are you out here for?"

"Not long. Not much I can do if he won't even talk to me."

"It's still good you came, I think," says Joe. "Even though he won't see you."

I look at him. "Really?" I say.

"Yeah. For what it's worth, I think he's being a prick. He could use having you around right now."

I reach up to hug him again, run a hand through his bristly hair like a mother might do. He's always had beautiful hair, dark and thick. *Wasted on a boy*, my grandmother would have said. "It was great to see you," I say. "Take care of yourself."

"Yeah, you too," he says. I start to gather our trash from the table.

He picks up his bag and his phone and looks toward the door. "Well, have a good flight back. You have my number." I don't want him to go, I want to keep him here, but there's nothing to do about that. He wouldn't tell me anything anyway. "Bye," he calls, without looking back. The bell over the door jingles.

I sit back down, even though I've already thrown away my coffee. I try to go over the conversation I've just had, but everything seems slippery. There's nothing to grasp. I lift the sugar bowl from the box. It's identical to the one Joe broke all those years ago. I remember spooning sugar from that bowl onto my oatmeal when I was a child, and spooning it onto Milo's cornflakes a blink of an eye later. It really does look the same. It's almost like having the old one back.

I lift the lid to check for chips, and as I look down into the smooth white curve of the interior I see something inside, a piece of paper folded into a small, thick wedge. I try to reach in to grab it, but my hand is too big for the delicate opening. I turn the bowl over, dumping the paper onto the table. I unfold it to find three words written in careful block letters. The ink is black, and whoever wrote the words went over them several times with the pen.

Oh, for Christ's sake. What kind of a B movie is this? Three words. "Someone is lying."

who cares if he did it? pareidolia rocks!!!!!!

Comment from a message board on FreeMilo.com,
Thursday, November 11

Chapter Three

/||\

My first impulse after finding the note is to call Joe right away, but I remember that he's on his way to a meeting and won't want to be disturbed. And the absurd spy-novel nature of this transaction makes me wonder if there's some reason he doesn't want to discuss this with me directly. I can't for the life of me think why he would sit with me for half an hour, saying nothing of any import, then pass me this cryptic message in such an oblique way. Did he think someone would be watching us? I look around the café, but no one seems to be paying any attention to me. What made him think I would look inside the bowl right away? I might well have put it in my suitcase, carried it home, and not opened it up until the next time I decided to have a tea party. And above all, why go to all this trouble to convey something so vague? "Someone is lying" isn't exactly "Colonel Mustard in the conservatory with a candlestick." Maybe he's gotten eccentric in his celebrity, and this is just his preferred method of communication. Maybe I should write the word "Who?" on a piece of paper and pass it to him in a coffee creamer.

Carrying the box gingerly back to my hotel, I try to convince myself that the note means nothing. Joe said that he hasn't had the thing for very long; the note was probably already in its hiding place, left over from a game of charades two or three owners ago, when Joe's girlfriend received the sugar bowl from some anonymous eBay seller.

But.

I wonder for a moment if it could be a message smuggled to me from Milo, but I realize immediately that that's pure fantasy. Milo is, for the moment, a free man. If he has something to tell me, there are more direct ways he could do it.

Back in my room, I place Joe's gift on the dresser and lie down once more across the bed. It's late afternoon and I'm exhausted. I don't know what I'm supposed to do now. If this were a mystery novel, the note in the sugar bowl would spur me to take some action. With my child's life in the balance, I would charge forward and begin investigating the case on my own. I would track down waiters and convenience store clerks; I would visit seedy nightclubs and interview the victim's friends. More clues would follow: there would be a bellboy at my hotel who would turn out to have an unusual connection to the crime; a stranger would hold a door open for me, then press a phone number into my hand as I passed through. Everyone would have an easily describable quirk. And the murderer would turn out to be the last person anyone would suspect.

I fall asleep wondering how good a writer I would have to be to bring us to a happy ending.

. . .

There's a story I haven't been able to get out of my head, one you might have heard: A family of three, by all appearances happy and self-contained, falls prey to an intruder. A thief enters their home and ransacks their belongings, leaving the family's most vulnerable member, their beloved child, hungry and bereft. Happily, the mother and father rise up and do what is right: they eject the invader, thereby protecting their child and maintaining the careful balance of their lives. Is there any parent who wouldn't do the same?

During the months after my daughter, Rosemary, was born, Milo asked to hear the story of the Three Bears at least five times a day. Mitch and I were pleased at how well Milo seemed to have adjusted to the presence of the new baby, but we did notice that he clung to small rituals in ways he hadn't before, wanting to keep his baseball cap on even in the bathtub and insisting that his cereal be served in the same bowl every day. (This is only one of a hundred scalpel-edged memories I've been scraping myself with over the past few days; the image of Milo, small and worried in his red cap, never fails to break the skin.) The Three Bears became a part of our daily cadence in those months, as regular as feedings and diaper changes.

Somewhere around the three- or four-hundredth reading, it occurred to me that I had never before noticed the subtext of this story, the ancient familial rites of betrayal and reassurance that get played out within its narrative. *The baby will wear your old clothes*, we tell our children; *she'll sleep in your old bed, and we're proud you're such a big boy that you don't need them anymore.* Fuck that, the story says. Three is enough for any family. And no matter how many times the narration is interrupted by the screeching cry that belies the story's message, no matter how distracted your mother seems as she recites the words from memory while fastening the soft little leech to her breast, the ending is always the same. Baby Bear always wins.

Children, with their feral sweetness: it can break your heart. Once I understood, I made an effort to put the baby down in her crib or on a blanket before sitting down with Milo to read the story, so that he could lean into me, sad little turnip, without finding that my arms were occupied by somebody else. But the truth was—and maybe I already knew it—that this was a balancing act I would never quite get right. In the metaphor of the family romance, when you fall in love with a second child, does it mean you're betraying the first? Sometimes it feels that way. And sometimes, holed up in bed with my new little one—sleeping, nursing, sleeping, while Mitch attended to Milo's more complicated needs and questions and occasional tyrannies—I enjoyed the illicit pleasure of it.

Every moment leads to every other. Volcanoes don't erupt without warning, and now, in this new Pompeii, my task is to sift through the levels of ash and pumice to find artifacts of lives lived before the disaster. Do I believe it's possible that Milo killed Bettina? I don't know; I really don't. I have no idea when it is that I stopped knowing him utterly, which moment marks my first failure of maternal empathy.

And so I examine; and so I dig. And in the ruins of my memory, I find evidence that supports both versions of history.

. . .

I wake up in that state of grief where you can tell you've been mourning even in your sleep. I've been dreaming of Milo as a child, in a series of fragmentary scenarios: Milo hot with fever, Milo digging a hole, Milo lost in a crowd. It's just after four a.m., and I'm pretty sure I'm up for the day.

Apparently room service doesn't begin until six, so I brew weak coffee with the machine provided in my bathroom and sit to drink it in an armchair in the corner. I feel agitated; I can't stand the hush, the middle-of-the-night solitude. I'm too distracted to read, and turning on the television feels like an assault, so I turn to the new-world cure for loneliness: I open up my laptop.

I'd like, I suppose, some comfort or fellowship, but I'm not sure how to find it. I type my troubles into a search engine like it's a diary. I find articles about murderers from every corner of the world and about the million ways their mothers pray for them, but nothing that tells me how I can make this situation more bearable. Finally, steeling myself, I type in "Milo Frost." I just want to see a picture of his face.

An onslaught of horrible links follows—news stories, blog screeds, one site that purports to have video of Bettina's body being taken away in a bag—but one phrase catches my eye: FreeMilo.com. I click.

The site is profoundly distasteful, I can see that right away—it bills itself as "out to protect our boy Milo, whether he killed the bitch or not"—but I'm fascinated by it. I browse the message boards, which cover topics ranging from fairly cogent analyses of the facts that have been made public to speculations about which Pareidolia song would be the best soundtrack for murder. There's an entire thread devoted to the band's name: what it means, which band member chose it, whether it might shed any light on the current situation. Here, at least, I feel I have a little more insight than the average reader. I'm the one who taught him the word.

Pareidolia describes the human tendency to find meaning where there is none. Take the man in the moon, for example: we raise our eyes, and there, in lifeless markings of bedrock and basalt, we find a human face. We're hardwired to look for patterns in the Rorschach of the natural world: a woman's reclining form in the curve of a mountain range, the Virgin Mary in a water stain on a concrete wall. We want the world to be both known and mysterious. We're looking for evidence of God, or maybe just for company.

When Milo was small and afraid of the dark, Mitch told him that he didn't have to worry because the man in the moon was always just outside his room, looking out for him. Milo's bed was under a window, and sometimes I'd catch sight of the two of them looking out, checking to make sure that the pale gatekeeper was still out there, keeping watch. (Note where I am, by the way: not quite in the scene and not quite out. That was me as I often was in those days, hovering in doorways, unsure how to move in and sweep up my child as confidently as Mitch seemed to. Always happy for him to be doing the work, so I could have a moment to myself. "Time to myself," that grail forever sought and lost by mothers of young children—that was what I thought I lacked back then. I was always waiting for Mitch to come home or the babysitter to arrive so I could slip away to spend a clandestine hour inside my own mind. And then, coming upon the two of them in a moment as sweet as that one, I'd stand and observe, my heart in my throat, my arms hanging empty. Sometimes I'd even snap a picture.)

Later, maybe a year after Mitch and Rosemary died, I went into Milo's room to see if he was ready for bed, and I found him looking out the window. "What *is* the man in the moon?" he asked. "I mean, really."

He would have been about ten, I think. Too old for Santa and the Easter Bunny, but still willing to play along with the ruse of the tooth fairy. He'd shown some interest in science and astronomy, so I told him what I could about the surface of the moon, and I explained the idea of pareidolia. He listened and nodded and asked questions. And I never saw him look out his bedroom window at the moon again.

The FreeMilo Web site continues to disgust me, and I continue to read it. What amazes me most is that these people—mostly young men, I assume—think they know my son. They've pieced together a man from song lyrics, videos, fragments of interviews, and they believe it's genuinely Milo. Not that I can be so sure I know him much better, I suppose; I've just built my version of him from a larger sample of material.

I'm almost ready to put an end to this unhealthy gorging when I see a new headline, screaming at me from the top of the list: VIDEO OF THE MURDER HOUSE—BEFORE THE MURDER!!!

The Murder House. Of course, I've never been to Milo's house, and it hadn't yet occurred to me that it would now take on this added significance. I know that houses where murders take place become stops on a gruesome pilgrimage route, and I wonder if there are people there—right now, a matter of blocks from here—camping out alongside the yellow crime-scene tape, taking pictures and toasting the dead. I wonder if the house will be demolished eventually. Sometimes they are, more for real estate reasons than symbolic ones: the property values, the privacy of the neighbors, the decency of letting the dead rest. Still, it has the feel of an ancient rite. Purification by fire. On this site, blood was spilled.

I click on the subject heading. Inside, there's a link, accompanied by the following explanation: "My cousin's a film editor on *Turf Wars*, and he got this amazing footage of a Milo/Bettina episode that was supposed to air next month. They filmed it three weeks ago. It's a rough cut, so it's not as smooth as it would be if it were actually on TV. Check it out!!!!"

Turf Wars, I know, is a TV program that showcases rock stars' homes. In each episode, two different celebrities lead the cameras on tours of their houses; afterward, viewers call in to vote on which house they like better. I've seen this show once or twice, and I've wondered, who are these children, and why are they living by themselves? They don't seem fully formed somehow, even the ones in their forties who are already doing comeback tours. Video game rooms and waterfalls, ceilings painted with stars and clouds. Gold fixtures and shark tanks.

Rooms full of shoes. I didn't know Milo was slated to appear, though in the past I've followed the show's listings carefully in the hope I might get to see where he lived.

I click the link, and my computer's video player pops up. I press Play.

The clip begins with a shot of a white stucco house against a blue sky. It's a Spanish mission–style building with a red tile roof and a wrought-iron gate. It's a beautiful house, but I can't imagine the process by which Milo would have chosen it above any other. I try to imagine Milo house hunting, ticking off his preferences for a real estate agent. It's as foreign an idea as seeing him in a military uniform or a ball gown.

The camera lands on the door, a tall, imposing thing made of dark wood and intricately carved. The door opens a crack and Milo sticks his head out. "Yeah," he says. "I'll take two boxes of Thin Mints."

A prickle of nerve endings at the sight of him. A muted ache in my belly. The camera pulls back and Milo opens the door wider. He's wearing a ratty maroon T-shirt with the word "Fizz" written on it—I'm not sure whether that's the name of a band or some kind of product or simply an ironic statement I don't understand. He's wearing jeans and a dark wool hat, and he's barefoot. You can see how tall he is—lanky. He's looking down into the camera, which must be held by a cameraman of average height. Milo steps backward and gestures us in.

"Welcome to my turf," he says. This, I gather, is the standard greeting for participants on the show. Milo voices it with a kind of smirking affection: *Yes, this is corny, but I'm happy to be a part of it.*

We're in an entryway painted blue-green, bright like the pebbles you find at the bottom of a fish tank. There's a heavy black iron chandelier hanging high enough that Milo doesn't have to duck when he walks underneath it. In the background, off to the left, I see an oversized red couch. I wonder if that's where Milo was sleeping when the police arrived.

"I don't know who we're going to be up against," he says to the camera, "but I can tell you, you're looking at the winner right here. You ain't gonna find too many houses out there that can beat this one." He's clearly playing around, but I'm fascinated by his grammar decisions. I've never once heard Milo say the word "ain't."

We follow Milo into the dining room, which is surprisingly ornate. The walls are papered with flocked cranberry velvet, and there's an old-fashioned light fixture of glass globes hanging from the ceiling. There's a long bench along one wall, upholstered in red velvet, punctuated with a line of small round tables. Across the opposite wall there's a full bar with a zinc counter and tall mahogany stools.

"I wanted to have fun with this place," Milo says. "I was going for a kind of hyperreality, like an amusement park, you know? The way that when you walk through Disneyland, one minute you're in the Old West, and the next minute you're in outer space." This is so completely Milo that I laugh out loud. I remember that when he was a kid, he tried to talk us into decorating his room with wallpaper made from undersea photographs, so that he would feel like he was living in the ocean. I can't remember why we said no.

"So this room was modeled on a picture I found of a nineteenth-century French bistro. I didn't really want some big table taking up the whole room. This leads to smaller, more intimate groups. We've had some nice dinner parties here." He stops walking and addresses the camera with faux solemnity. "I take my duties as a host very seriously," he says. "Later I can show you my four-car garage—I like to make sure my guests don't have to park in the rain."

He turns around and leads us into the kitchen. And there, suddenly, is Bettina, chopping fruit at the counter.

Somehow I'd forgotten she'd be here, though of course I've just read that it's video of both of them. I've been so absorbed in watching Milo, this unfamiliar man, this *homeowner*, that I forgot that this house was more than just his. It was theirs: their love nest; their refuge; the laboratory where they built their particular monster.

Bettina's wearing a white T-shirt and black shorts. Her hair is bleached platinum, styled in a pixie cut, shorter than in most of the pictures they've been running in the paper. Her makeup is light, natural. She looks very young.

"There's my little homemaker," Milo says. "Always busy whipping up a healthy meal, whenever she's not darning my socks or scrubbing the floor."

Bettina looks up and smiles. She kisses him quickly, on the lips. "Kill me now," she says.

I press Pause.

I need a moment. Besides the inadvertent horror of the exchange I've just seen, the unfortunate sound bite that I know will be grabbed up by every morning DJ and gossip column, I'm breathless with the impact of seeing Bettina moving around the kitchen, living her life. Up until now, Bettina has been a creature of my imagination, a cipher to be filled in whatever manner suits me best. At some moments she's innocent, a tragic victim, someone to be pitied; other times, you can't believe what a bitch she can be.

But here she is, slicing mango for a salad, giving my son a kiss.

All right. All right. Play.

Milo's already moving on, leaving Bettina to her fruit. "We don't have any room called the living room," he says, crossing the kitchen to a doorway on the other side. As he talks, there's a burble of sound in the background; it's a cell phone ringing.

"Hang on," says a man's voice, off-camera. "Bettina? Can you turn that off?"

The camera turns back to Bettina at the counter, looking slightly irritated, the phone at her ear. "Yeah, just a second," she says to the man who's just spoken. Then, lower, into the phone, "Mom, I can't talk. The *Turf Wars* people are here. Gotta go." There she is again, my maternal double, making her presence known. Intruding in ways I've only dreamed of.

Bettina rolls her eyes in Milo's direction as she turns off the phone. "Sorry," she says to the room at large, smiling in a way that's both self-deprecating and disarming. "I could've sworn it was off."

"Okay," says the male voice. "Milo, can you go back and walk across the room again?"

He does. "We don't have any room called the living room," he says again. It takes him a minute to get back to the easy, jovial tone he had before. "That's way too vague. We like to live in all our rooms."

He's talking in sound bites; the repetition of the moment makes it more obvious. Nothing he says is genuine or revelatory. I'm not going to find my child here. I'm just another member of the audience.

Milo leads us to a room filled with media equipment: a huge TV mounted on the wall, various shiny black boxes for playing music and movies. Instead of a couch, a wavy mass of overlapping cushions, several layers deep, fills the whole floor. He flops down, stretches his limbs like he's making a snow angel.

"This is the padded cell room," he says. "This is where I come when I start to be a danger to myself and others." He grins widely for the camera.

I close my eyes. Already this video clip has the aura of a holy relic. Meaning has already shifted, lighting up some areas that would have been opaque a week ago. Emphasis added. It's like someone's taken a yellow highlighter to the dialogue.

More rooms, more themes. More explanations from this fictional character made up of pieces of my son. A guitar room with a built-in stage; an office, wallpapered with letters and artwork Milo's admirers have sent. "Pretty soon I'll have to move to a bigger room," he says. "It gets pretty crazy. There's one girl who cuts my horoscope out of the paper and sends it to me every damn day."

Upstairs there's a library—I scan the bookshelves for my books, their spines as familiar to me as the spines of my own children, but I find nothing—and a guest room I've never been invited to sleep in. A bathroom Milo calls "the sea monster room."

He walks us down the hall. "We used to have a beach room," he says. "But the sand got really annoying. Not to mention that we've got the actual ocean right out back. But I'm always changing stuff up. I'm kind of like that crazy lady who was afraid to stop building her house— you know who I mean? Her husband invented a new kind of rifle or something, and she thought that if the house was ever finished, all the ghosts of people who had been killed with those guns would come and get her."

The Winchester Mystery House. I feel a brief electric twinge. I remember Mitch reading about it in a travel guide and telling Milo the story. We even made plans to visit it once, but we never made it there. It's in San Jose, I think, not too far away. I wonder if Milo's ever been.

He turns into the last room. "And finally," he says, "the bedroom."

The camera pans the room. It's a big, airy room, colored in different shades of white. A corner window looks out on the Pacific Ocean; you can actually see the Golden Gate. The bed itself is massive and simple, a block of dark wood. A comfortable-looking chair with an ottoman, a night table with an art deco lamp. And in one corner, almost out of sight, a rack of exercise weights.

"We figured the bedroom didn't need a theme," Milo says. "Bedrooms kind of have their own theme."

The sleep room. The comfort room. The lay-your-body-down room. The sex room, the sweat room, the fuck-me-any-way-you-want room.

"There's just a really nice vibe here. I love waking up to that view."

The sick-in-bed room. The pillow-wet-with-drool room.

"Top-of-the-line mattress. There's, like, a three-year waiting list for these babies. Crazy expensive, but man, is it worth it."

The waking-up-with-a-hangover room. The alarm-clock-ringing room.

"I hate staying in hotels now. They're never as nice as this."

The screaming room. The beating room. The skull-bashed-in room.

Bettina walks in. "You're not telling them all our secrets, are you?" She puts her arms around him.

The breath-turning-shallow room. The falling-heart-rate room. The choking, the gasping, the bleeding-out room.

"Naw, baby," he says. "But if walls could talk, right?"

The viscera room. The crime-scene room. The last-thing-you-see room.

"If walls could talk," says Bettina, "we'd never get any rest."

. . .

Later, after the sun has risen and the city has stopped holding its breath, I get myself dressed and head out for a walk. It's still too early to call

Joe—what time is acceptable? I wonder. Do rock musicians still sleep all day, or have they all turned into savvy businessmen who keep regular hours? And I need to get out of my room. Walking out into the pale morning, I try to imagine the landscape around me as a map of my son's footprints. Milo has lived a life here, in this city of muted colors, this city as misty as a black-and-white photograph. He has walked these vertical streets and slept in these listing, seasick houses. I know nothing about the times he's had here, though I've imagined them often enough: mornings in cluttered kitchens of group houses with shabby furniture and coffee in thrift-store mugs, nights stretched on couches I wouldn't want to lay a finger on. Playing jagged, noisy music on a crowded stage plastered with gaffer's tape; tracing a finger along the outline of a girl's tattoo at some dark, rowdy party. Arguing with landlords. Living on pasta and cereal. And somehow, through luck and work and miracle, becoming the man I saw on my computer screen, the man who lives in a house on the ocean with a gold record on his wall. The man whose tragedies are front-page news.

I could have been a part of that long stretch of life if I'd tried harder. If I'd . . . what? Shown up on the doorstep of his mission-style house with a suitcase? Told him that the man in the moon was real? I don't know where the magic line might have been. That's how it is with children, or at least how it's been with mine: you have chances and chances and chances. And then you have none.

I walk along the streets surrounding Union Square, but I have no real destination. I remember reading that there's a plaque somewhere around here, a plaque that was put up to mark the site where Sam Spade's partner, Miles Archer, was killed. A monument to a fictional event, a murder that never took place. In this present situation, I have no desire to track down such an artifact, but I like the idea that the stories we write can occupy that kind of space on our own physical plane. I've always hoped that my characters will outlive me, though in my darker moments I suspect my books aren't important enough for that. Walking a still-empty block of Mason Street, I wonder how long anyone's characters will last. Sooner or later we will bring this world to its end; that much seems all but certain. My own self dead, the demise of everyone I have loved—we all know to expect that. But the thought of an empty world, all our books waterlogged or turned to dust, with no eyes ever to see them again . . . it fills me with terror. The story to end all stories, and no one will be left to tell it.

As the streets begin to repopulate themselves, I find myself trying to meet people's eyes as they pass by. Just a single smile, a compassionate look, would mean so much to me. But they're all good city dwellers and they keep their eyes to themselves.

Solitude is a much more shaded condition than I used to think; it's not just a matter of being alone or not alone. It would not be wrong to say that I've been alone for eighteen years (if we start counting from the time Mitch died) or nine years (since Milo moved out of our house to go to college) or four years (since the last time we spoke). But it would also not be entirely right. I'm not a hermit, though the isolated nature of my job means that I spend more time by myself than a lot of people do. Still, I teach writing classes; I meet friends for dinner; I get invited to take part in literary events. I visit my mother several times a year, and I'm in touch with a sprawling group of cousins and their children, some of whom are willing to serve as my informants on the rare occasions they hear anything from Milo. In the years since Mitch died, I've dated a few men (either four or five, depending on whether I'm counting the ill-considered night with the author of angel-themed mysteries that I met at a conference in Atlanta), a few of them almost seriously. I receive e-mail from readers, and I have daily opportunities to chat with neighbors and supermarket clerks. There are baristas who know me by name.

But there's no one to watch bad TV with, and no one to run to the drugstore when I'm sick. When something happens that strikes me as funny, it's sometimes weeks before I find anyone who might like to hear the story. And when underpaid interns writing jokes for late-night talk shows build entire monologues around the topic of my son's guilt, there's not a fucking person on Earth who knows exactly what I'm feeling.

. . .

I stop at a coffee shop for a listless breakfast, which I spend trying to avoid reading the headlines in other people's papers, before returning to my hotel, once again at loose ends. Time to myself—I certainly have it now. I check my e-mail. There's a note from my agent, listing seven different magazines and newspapers that would like to interview me about Milo. A month ago I would have been thrilled by the interest.

I page through the other debris that has accumulated in my little corner of digital space. My in-box is filled with messages of support and curiosity, some of them from people I haven't spoken to in years. One of them is from Lisette, offering condolences and asking if I'm coming to town. Just yesterday I was thinking that this wasn't the kind of trip where there would be time for social calls, but her e-mail to me is kind—the surprise smile I was looking for a few moments ago on the street. I write back, briefly. "Yes, I'm here. Don't know if I'm going to be wallowing in free time or busy every minute. If it's the former, maybe we could have lunch . . . ?"

I consider going back to bed. Enough time has passed that I might be able to will myself to sleep. But then my cell phone rings. It's Joe's number; I remember it from yesterday.

"Hello, Joe?" I say.

"Uh, no." It's a woman's voice. "My name is Chloe Treece. I'm Joe's girlfriend."

"Oh," I say. "Okay."

"I'm sorry to bother you, Mrs. Frost, and I'm just noticing how early it is, but Joe mentioned he'd seen you, and I wanted to talk to you."

"All right," I say. I wait. "Does it have to do with Milo?"

"Yes," she says.

"Well, if you have any information that might help his case, please, please talk to his lawyer about it."

There's a pause. "It's complicated," she says. "I'd like to talk to you first." She surprises me by laughing softly. "You have no idea how long I've been wanting to meet you."

This catches me off guard. So . . . what? She knows something about the murder, or she wants me to sign her copy of *The Human Slice?* When I don't answer right away, she goes on. "And if you want, I know where Roland Nysmith lives. I could take you by to see Milo afterward."

My blood speeds up. "He's made it clear he doesn't want to see me."

"Oh, please," she says. "He's just being a douche. Big stubborn guy—does he get that from you?" She doesn't wait for me to answer, which is fine, because I don't know what to say. "Come with me. We'll go over there. Roland will be able to convince him to talk to you."

"All right," I say evenly. "Where and what time?"

"We're in Pacific Heights," she says. She gives me an address. "Can you make it around eleven? Joe will be out then."

"Fine," I say. "See you then."

I hang up. I feel jubilant and terrified. I need to take a shower and figure out what to wear. I turn back to my computer and write a quick reply to my agent: "Please decline these and any future requests. I'm not talking publicly about any of this. Thanks, O." I close my laptop and start getting ready for whatever comes next.

From the Jacket Copy for

CARPATHIA

By Octavia Frost

(Farraday Books, 2007)

/||\

It's 1935, and animator Oscar Clough's life has reached a new low: his fiancée has left him, he's drinking heavily, and the cartoon studio he works for is struggling in the face of competition from Disney and stricter censorship rules resulting from the new Hays Production Code.

As Oscar sinks into depression and uncertainty, unexplained images start appearing in the cartoons he has drawn: a playing card hidden in a garden of flowers; a bell drawn into the pattern of a woman's dress; a ship's oar nestled among the swirls of bark on a tree trunk. As the images accumulate, Oscar wonders whether he's losing his mind, or whether someone is sabotaging his drawings, or even—perhaps—whether there may be supernatural forces at work. With the help of Cecily, a receptionist at the studio and the only person who shares his ability to see the hidden pictures, Oscar is forced to confront an event he's long tried to forget: his trip on the ill-fated *Titanic* at the age of nine.

Excerpt from

CARPATHIA

By Octavia Frost

ORIGINAL ENDING

/|\|\

We sat in the sand as the daylight began to fade. It need hardly be said that I am not one of those souls who take great pleasure in visiting the seaside, but on this day it seemed like the only thing left to do. Somehow I'd thought that if I took Cecily out, if we spent the day together, then we would get to the bottom of this. Cecily was the key, I thought—the only other person to see what I saw, when everyone else said it was just an accident of the way a particular line curved, the way the camera caught the movement of the drawing from cel to cel. But now the day was ending, and I knew nothing more than I had that morning. So I took her to the ocean, and I waited to see what would happen.

I'd picked up a number of stones as we were walking, and now that we'd settled ourselves, Cecily was looking at them. "Do you think this might be a moonstone, Oscar?" she asked, holding up a rough gray rock.

"I don't know," I said. "It looks pretty ordinary to me."

"Well, they are ordinary, until you polish them up. My mother told me that there used to be piles of moonstones on this beach. She and my father came here once, before we kids were born. She said there were mounds of them, four or five feet high, and people would wade through them, looking for good ones."

I tried to picture it—ladies in long dresses, perhaps carrying parasols, holding the arms of men with mustaches and summer suits. All of them taking an afternoon to search the ground for holiday treasure. "So where did they all go?" I asked. "I can't imagine they were all gathered up, if there were that many of them."

She shrugged. "I don't know. Maybe they've been washed away."

It could be. We think the ocean doesn't change, but its borders are never fixed. I thought about the sandy floor littered with bright gems: a payment from the land to the sea, compensation for a debt we couldn't begin to understand.

I returned to the topic we'd been circling all day. "Langer could have my job for this, don't you think? If he were to find out—I mean, if he could see the pictures. He already thinks all the animators are slipping racy messages into the artwork. You know he lives in fear of the Hays people shutting him down."

"Oh, I can't imagine he'd do that," she said.

"The censors would find some reason, I'm sure. These are the men who put a skirt on Flossie the cow."

She smiled. "Well, we couldn't have her udders showing, now could we? Simply scandalous."

We laughed. I felt happy to be on this windy beach with Cecily, happy just then that I wasn't anyone else, not one of the shopkeepers selling postcards and ices or the ragged men fishing for their dinner from the pier. So recently I had been on the verge of becoming a different man: angry, lonely, perhaps even unhinged. It was extraordinary, this effect Cecily had on me. Extraordinary that even in the midst of such turmoil and confusion, I could actually feel lucky.

But I couldn't let the other matter go. In my mind I went over the sequence of events once again. There was the day it all began, when I'd gone to the pictures after running into Ettie and her new boyfriend in the coffee shop, when I'd seen the playing card hidden in the flower bed in the Cappy Penguin cartoon; the day at the studio when the bell appeared right on the production cel, woven into the pattern of Delilah Pufkin's dress; the terrible morning when I'd discovered the ship's oar carved into the bark of the tree where the Singing Sparrows built their nest. Most recently there was my date with Cecily, when we'd both noticed the seagull-shaped cloud in the background of "Farm Funnies." I'd gone through it all a thousand times, and there was nothing new to know about any of it.

I looked out at the sea. There was a young man out there with a wooden board, gliding over the surface of the water. I didn't understand how he didn't get swept under, and it made me very uneasy to watch. How would it feel to stand on the skin of the waves, to ride the galloping ocean as if it were a beast? I felt a lick of panic run through me, and in the tensing of my body, a memory clicked into place.

"I know what it was," I said to Cecily. "That day in the theater, when I saw the card."

"What about it?"

"Well, remember I said I'd been reading the papers before the show started, and there was something that had left me feeling troubled?"

"Yes?"

"I couldn't think what it was, but I knew I'd been feeling worried about something before the cartoon even started. Well, I just remembered—it was a story about the tidal wave, do you remember? The one in Japan, that wiped out all those villages?"

She nodded. "That was awful."

"That's what it was. I had just read that the number of lives lost was much higher than they'd thought, somewhere around fifteen hundred. And you know, fifteen hundred, that's the same number as . . . well, those lost on the *Titanic*." I felt embarrassed, as if by mentioning this unpleasant bit of my past, I was emphasizing a character flaw.

She was looking at me a little doubtfully. "I'm not sure I understand you. That's a coincidence, certainly, but are you saying that reading that article had something to do with the picture of the bell appearing in the cartoon?"

"I don't know," I said. Just a minute ago, it had seemed like a momentous revelation, but now I wasn't sure. It was hard to put into words, and I wasn't sure I wanted to. But to say I'd felt "troubled" was not quite accurate. What I'd felt that evening, as I thought about that sudden rush of water, whole families drowned in their beds, was a sudden, welling terror, almost as if I myself were in danger of being crushed by a wall of water. I nearly left the theater, because I felt I couldn't breathe in that crowded space, the air weighted with popcorn grease and smoke. So when the lights went low and the projector started its rattle, I could barely even watch the cartoon, the figures I myself had drawn and coaxed into motion. Until I saw the playing card, and I remembered the way my brother, Archie, used to call me Ace. And I felt as if I'd just stepped onto solid ground.

"I'm being haunted," I said suddenly. Neither of us had spoken for several minutes. It was going to be dark soon, and cold, and it would be time for us to leave this place and ride the train back to the city, with all of its loneliness and gaiety.

"Haunted?" Cecily repeated. To her credit, if she felt any dismay at my words, her face didn't betray it. Or maybe I just couldn't see it in the shadows.

"Yes. Or maybe, anyway. I think I'm being haunted by my brother, Archie."

If I had heard myself saying these words a mere two months earlier, I would have wondered about my own sanity. But it made a certain amount of sense to me now. Tidal waves, scientists say, are sometimes caused by the eruption of an underwater volcano. An explosion beneath the surface, unsettling everything that lies submerged. Think what's down there, never to be seen by human eyes: treasure ships and the carcasses of sea monsters, the empty bones of sailors and pirates and virgins offered up in savage rites. Our glorious rescue ship, the *Carpathia*, is under there somewhere, torpedoed during the World War and gone to her rest. And, of course, the *Titanic* herself, broken in two and sunk in some forgiving patch of silt. If a single twitch of the earth can raise a wave as big as the greatest buildings men have ever made, then who's to say it can't also wake the dead?

"The playing card," I said. "It was an ace, and that was always his nickname for me. It's almost a little joke for that to be the first one. That was his way of getting my attention."

"And the others?" Cecily asked. I was grateful for how normal her voice sounded, how willing she was to listen to me, no matter how strange my musings became.

"Well, the bell . . . when I first saw it, I immediately thought of the bell on the *Titanic*, the one they rang to alert the passengers that there was danger. And the oar seems clear enough—it's meant to remind me of the lifeboat. I remember even my mother took a turn at rowing. By morning her hands were bloody."

There was a breeze, and Cecily wrapped her arms around herself. I took off my jacket and laid it on her shoulders.

"And the last one?" she asked. "The seagull?"

I didn't answer her question right away. It seemed impossible to talk about the seagull without explaining what had come before, but that wasn't the story I'd meant to tell. Though in a way, she knew it already. Who didn't?

Someday, I thought, I'll tell her everything. Someday there would be time enough for all the small details. My brief memories of the voyage itself, before the disaster—games of tag with Sally and Lovie in the corridor outside the second-class library; the novelty of eating food brought by waiters; the charts my father showed me, which tracked how far we had come and how far we had left to go. My anger at Archie, seventeen and suddenly fancying himself an adult, who wanted nothing to do with me or our sisters but spent his days smoking with the men and talking to a pretty girl from Philadelphia. The argument he and I had on Sunday afternoon when I tripped walking past them on the promenade, dousing them both with lemon squash from a glass I'd been carrying. He knew I'd done it on purpose, but I wouldn't admit it, and we spent Sunday evening glaring at each other without saying a word.

And then it was night, and here begins the part that would have been familiar to any listener. Why tell it at all? I woke to a long scraping noise, which didn't sound like the beginning of any kind of end. My mother pulled us from our beds. We dressed and went to join the strange scene on deck, where the mood was almost festive: children running here and there, barefoot women wearing nightclothes and fur coats. My father handed us into the lifeboat, Archie standing tall beside him, and assured us that all this would be sorted out soon. My parents didn't even kiss each other good-bye, so certain were they that they would be reunited.

It wasn't until we'd been rowing for an hour or more under the cold stars that we began to hear cries from the ship, and I understood that this wasn't some midnight adventure. As I pressed close to my mother, her arms full with my two sleeping sisters, everything seemed to happen at once: explosions and gunshots and the music of an orchestra; the sudden dark as the lights onboard were extinguished. The ship rising vertical in the night—and a terrible crack—and the strange, gentle way she disappeared under water, almost without making a sound.

And still the dark and the cold and my sisters crying softly beside me. Loud wailing from the water. A sailor in our boat slumping over, still. A man in evening clothes floating dead on a cake of ice, so close I could have reached out and touched him.

It's occurred to me in recent years that I don't know exactly how my father and Archie died. Drowning, of course, is the most obvious answer, but it's also possible that they died from cold or from the impact of slapping hard onto the glass of the sea. They might have been crushed under a bed or a piano; or perhaps my father's heart, never strong, took him before the water could. They might be on the ship yet, wherever she has rested, their skeletons held in place by the wreckage that has pinned them, the seaweed that has tied itself around their bones.

But Cecily hadn't asked about any of that. She had asked about the seagull. And if I'd been able to find the words to explain, I think she would have listened. But it was too much to tell, and people don't change that much. I'd been alone in that lifeboat, even surrounded by my mother and my sisters and a crowd of determined survivors, and it was my fate to remain alone now. So I didn't answer her question. We sat quietly for a few more minutes, and when we stood to begin our walk to the train station, I didn't take her hand.

God is generous, but he's not a pushover. You don't get rescued twice. The pictures in my cartoons got more and more obvious, until Langer had no choice but to fire me. Cecily married one of the soundmen from the studio, and most likely went on to have a houseful of children, though I couldn't tell you for sure.

I don't live in Hollywood anymore. I packed up my pencils and went to live someplace where dreams happen only while you sleep. My life is as ordinary as I can make it, at least until I lie down and feel myself drift, setting sail for destinations I haven't chosen. I don't know if it's a premonition I should heed or a message from Archie or simply my own mind tormenting me. But when I close my eyes, I drown every single night.

But Cecily hadn't asked about any of that. She had asked about the seagull, so this is what I told her:

The life belts we wore were white, and the morning after the great ship sank, the sea was dotted with bright, pale specks, like a flock of seabirds lighting on the waves. My father and Archie were almost certainly among them, though I didn't know to look, because at that time we were still searching for their faces among the rescued souls aboard the *Carpathia*. I was left on my own for the better part of that day, my mother being wholly consumed with caring for the little ones and with making a home for the ballooning grief her life now contained.

I stood on the deck and looked out at what remained. I saw a barber pole floating in the water, and a deck chair, and a flight of wooden stairs. I saw the body of a woman clutching in her arms a small dog. And everywhere the mountains of ice like great meringues, making it seem as if we were floating in a very grim fairyland.

Seagulls: that was what the dead looked like to me that day. Seagulls balancing on the water, looking for food.

Cecily took my hand. We sat like that together for some time. When finally we stood to begin our walk back to the train station, she broke the silence.

"I'm still not sure I see it, Oscar," she said. "Certainly the images seem to fit your own experience, but another person might see the same objects and think of something completely different. What kind of message do you think your brother is trying to send you? And why should I see the pictures, too?"

I didn't have an answer for her then; perhaps I still don't. But after that day, the pictures stopped appearing in my drawings—or I should say they stopped for a while. Because there was one more, nearly a year later. It appeared on a production cel I was working on for a Boots Byzantine short, the day before Cecily and I were to be married. I'd been sitting at my drafting table, drawing a spiral staircase in a castle tower, which was proving rather tricky. I got up to clear my mind, have a drink of water, and walk around the office, which I found was almost empty. Cecily wasn't there, having been spirited away by some of the other girls for an impromptu bridal shower, and some of the men had gone to look at a new set of offices Langer was thinking of leasing. When I failed to find anyone to talk to, I returned to my desk, and there it was: the outline of a ship, written into the bricks on the wall. It was not the *Titanic*. I could see that at once. It was a long steamship with a single funnel. It was the *Carpathia*.

Seeing the image, I had none of the terror I'd felt upon confronting the bell and the oar and the seagull. I felt, rather, as if I'd been walking in an unfamiliar city and had chanced to meet an old friend. I understood at last that there was nothing sinister here, nothing hateful or destructive. If there was any meaning here at all, if it wasn't just a grand trick of my imagination, it contained nothing but blessing.

It's rare, I think, for a man's life to be saved twice. But I'm happy to say it can happen. The next day, when I looked at Cecily walking down the aisle on her father's arm, this is what I saw: Warmth after freezing. A ship growing nearer. Lights in the dark.

\\|||/

"I don't talk about my family."

Milo Frost, in an interview with Esquire,
April 2007

Chapter Four

Joe and Chloe live in a big white block of a house planted on the vertiginous corner of one flat street and one lurching one. It's a pretty building, more modern than Milo's, if I can judge from the brief glimpse I got on the video, with unexpected angles and tall arching windows that I imagine must make the most of the city's anemic sunshine.

I walk up a steep flight of steps and ring the bell. The woman who answers is tall and slender, with dark hair pulled into two tufty ponytails. They jut out of her head the way a little girl's would, a toddler who doesn't really have enough hair yet but whose mother can't resist trying anyway.

"Octavia?" she says, smiling and studying my face. I imagine she's looking for traces of Milo.

"Yes," I say. "Are you Chloe?"

"Uh-huh. It's so great to meet you, finally. Come on in."

She's about Milo and Joe's age, or maybe a year or two older. She's wearing brick-colored yoga pants and a black scoop-necked T-shirt. When she turns to lead me down the hall, I see that she has two small earring studs in the back of her neck. It takes me a minute to understand that they must be connected to each other by some sort of post that enters through one pierced hole and emerges from the other.

"Thanks for coming," she says, looking back at me over her shoulder. We're in a narrow hallway that opens into a bright kitchen. The walls and floor are white, and there are brightly colored accents: red table and chairs, an orange throw rug, yellow planters by the windows. It's a big room, and one end of it has been turned into a sitting area, with a moss-colored couch and an overflowing toy box.

"You have a child," I say. I'd read that, somewhere. A little girl, I think, from a previous relationship. How strange to meet someone and already know the facts of her life.

Chloe nods. "Lia," she says. "She's three. Can I get you some coffee or, let's see, we have juice and water. Or a real drink, if you want. I'm sure this has been a terrible week."

"Water would be nice," I say. I sit down on the couch. "Thank you."

Chloe brings me a heavy square glass; it feels expensive. These boys, I think, looking around me and remembering Milo's lush funhouse: they've done well for themselves. I expect Chloe to sit down, too, but she doesn't. She goes back into the hall and calls up the flight of stairs, "Jilly, could you and Lia come down for a minute?"

She receives some sort of answer and comes back to the kitchen. "Jilly's our nanny," she says. I nod and smile. Honestly, I don't really want to meet her daughter. Children aren't easy for me; being around them forces a plunge into the cold water of my own regrets. Little girls spinning in dresses like bells; little boys climbing onto any surface that will hold them. Speckled light penetrating the slats of my shuttered mind. All the things I ever did wrong. It's unwelcome.

"I work from home mostly," Chloe is saying. "I make jewelry, and I used to think I'd be able to do that and watch Lia at the same time, but it just doesn't work." She looks at me appraisingly. "It must have been the same for you, with writing."

"Yes," I say. Pleasant conversation feels creaky to me after all the time I've spent alone lately. "Well, sort of. I didn't really start writing seriously until my kids . . . until Milo was a little older."

Noises from the stairs as the little girl and her nanny come down. The nanny has an accent—Caribbean, maybe?—and I hear her say, "Hold hands now. Go slow."

Lia and Jilly reach the bottom of the stairs, and Lia runs into the kitchen. "Mommy," she yells, throwing her arms around Chloe's knees.

She has dark hair, like Chloe's, but with some curl to it. She's wearing a purple dress and a headband with cat ears. Chloe picks her up and sits with her in a yellow armchair. Jilly, a tall black woman, younger than I would have guessed from her voice, says hello, then walks to the other end of the room and opens a cupboard.

"Hi, sweetie," Chloe says, kissing the child's forehead. "I want you to meet someone. This is Octavia. She's Uncle Milo's mommy."

Lia hides her face in her mother's neck.

I give it a try. "Are you a kitty?" I ask. My voice sounds skeptical, though I don't mean it to.

Lia nods. "I'm a baby kitty," she says, her voice muffled. She pulls back and puts a hand on her mother's face. "This is my mommy kitty."

"I like kitties," I say.

Lia turns her face to me shyly, pushing the side of her head into her mother's chest. Big, searching eyes; an expression like she's waiting for something. She juts out her top lip, then her lower one. She hasn't yet decided if she's going to smile.

Something happens to me. Somehow I'm still here, holding a glass of water, sitting on a sofa, but I feel like I'm falling, and suddenly I understand why I've been asked to come. That pursed mouth; those fathomless eyes. She looks like my own children when they were little. She looks like Milo.

I stare at her for what must be a very long time. I'm unable to speak. My eyes ache, as if my dry old body is unable to find enough liquid to make tears. Lia watches me back, and finally the corners of her mouth turn upward.

"Meow," she says.

. . .

Later, after I've regained the power of speech and Chloe has put enough plates on the table for all of us, I sit and watch my grandchild eat. She uses her fingers, picking up cubes of cooked chicken, spirals of plain pasta, slices of pear. Chloe has found something more adult for us to have, leftover pumpkin risotto, but I love the simplicity of Lia's meal.

I love the care she takes in lifting each piece of food to her mouth, the way her steady ribbon of chatter gives way to silence while she focuses on the task at hand.

It's not until the plates have been cleared and Jilly has carried Lia upstairs that I'm able to talk to Chloe and confirm that I'm not deluding myself. I sit again on the green couch, and Chloe sits across from me in the yellow armchair. She stares at me, and I stare at her.

"Her father?" I say finally.

She nods. "It's Milo." I look for something in her expression: Anger? Rejection? But her face is blank.

"Does he know?" I ask. A stupid question, I suppose. She wouldn't tell me if she hadn't told him. But to think of everything that's been here all this time—this room, this child, this potential for joy—and to know he chose not to tell me . . . it's very painful.

"He knows. And Joe knows."

Yes. I suppose that would have been my next question.

"I'm sorry I didn't get in touch with you sooner," she says. "Milo was really against it, and I figured I should respect his wishes, at least about his own family. So I promised him I wouldn't track you down all the way across the country. But I said that if I ever found myself face-to-face with you, I wouldn't lie." She smiles. "So. Here we are."

I smile weakly. I don't mention that she called me and invited me to come. It's not like we ran into each other at the supermarket. "So you and Milo . . . dated?" I know I've never seen a picture of them together, and I've been quite vigilant about following any gossip about Milo. How is it possible that none of this has ever been public?

"No, not really," she says. "I was living in Italy, and one of my American friends there was a friend of Milo's, so when Pareidolia came to Rome, a bunch of us went to the concert, and that's how we met. It was just a brief thing. He was already with Bettina."

I nod as if I'm absorbing all this, but I'm not really getting it. It's too much information, and yet not enough. I mean, yes, I understand: they slept together, they conceived a child. That's not the part I mean to dwell on. It's the *story* I want, the narrative of how this child and this configuration of lives came to be: the scenes played out, the words spo-ken, the rooms walked through on the way to other rooms. There are so many gaps in my knowledge of Milo's life, and they're too big to be filled in with the skeletal details of who introduced whom.

And the fact about Bettina. I suppose I'd rather not have known it. It makes me unexpectedly angry at Milo, and my feelings about Milo are complicated enough right now.

"And when you found out you were pregnant . . . ?" I ask.

"Yeah, I got in touch with Milo and told him. I let him know I was perfectly happy to just raise the kid on my own, but that he could be involved to whatever degree he wanted."

"And what was his reaction?" Were "Don't tell my mom" the first words out of his mouth, or did that come later?

"Um, kind of distant. He said he'd help support the baby and all that, but he didn't really want to play a parental role in her life."

I shake my head. My stomach is filled with stones. I keep waiting to hear something good about Milo, some bright strand to add to the tan-gled nest. But it's not here.

Chloe's watching me. "Yeah, I know. Way to step up to the plate, right?" She sounds slightly aggrieved, but then she shrugs. "But, you know, it hasn't been terrible."

I nod. I feel tired, and old. "And when did you and Joe start dating?" I ask finally.

"Well, I moved back here while I was still pregnant—I grew up around here, my parents are on the peninsula." I don't really know what that refers to, but I nod. "Milo came to see the baby a few times when she was little, and one time he brought Joe with him. We started seeing each other when Lia was four or five months old, and we moved in together when she was maybe one and a half. As far as she's concerned, he's Daddy."

"And so 'Uncle Milo' was born," I say.

"Yup. It's just kind of the way it's worked out."

So casual. I like Chloe, but her attitude about all this is a bit cavalier for me. And the moment this half-negative thought enters my mind,

I'm aware, in a cold rush, of the power this woman holds. She's the mother of my granddaughter. And I'm nothing more than Uncle Milo's mommy.

"I'm glad you came," Chloe says, smiling at me. "I'd like Lia to know someday that she has a famous grandma."

"Oh," I say, embarrassed. "Well, I don't know about that. Less famous than her father, certainly. Either of her fathers."

Chloe stands up, rolls her head to stretch the muscles in her neck. "Tricky situation," she says. "Wrong kind of famous, after this week." She picks up my water glass from the table and carries it to the sink, then turns back to me. "You want to go visit your son?"

Warmth and fear, hope and panic. "Okay," I say.

I get up from the couch and gather my jacket and purse. Something occurs to me. "I understand you're the one I have to thank for the sugar bowl," I say.

"Oh, yeah," she says, brightening. "Joe told me the story once, and it became kind of a thing for me, you know? Like, how is it possible in this day and age that I can't locate a simple piece of china? I was psyched when I finally found it. And now it's served another purpose, too—it's kind of led to this." She draws a line in the air between the two of us. "You know, us getting together."

I'm not sure I follow her logic, but I don't want to get off topic. "Did you happen to look inside it?" I ask. "When it came in the mail? When I opened it up, there was a note inside that said, 'Someone is lying.'"

She bursts out laughing. "Are you kidding?"

"No. So you don't know anything about it?"

"Well, no, but I doubt it's anything. I got the box, literally, like four days ago, and I only looked inside long enough to make sure it was in one piece. Who knows why anything else would be in there? But I doubt it had anything to do with you."

"Oh," I say. I feel strangely let down. "Okay."

"But you know," she says, "it's funny. That's something Bettina used to say. Like, if the guys stayed out all night and tried to give us a lame excuse or something. She'd say it in this funny way, like she was imitating someone. It was kind of a private joke, I think, between her and Milo."

"Huh," I say. I have no idea whether or not that's relevant. I follow Chloe back down the hall. She takes a sweater from a hook by the door. "Ready?" she asks.

I shake my head. "Probably not," I say.

"It'll be fine," she says. She opens up the door, and we step outside.

. . .

The last time I saw Milo, as I think I've mentioned, he was getting ready to board a plane. That's the way I tell the story in my mind, incidentally; those are the words I always use. I've often wondered if writers are the only ones who feel compelled to narrate their lives as they live them, to stand in the shower and wonder whether there's a less predictable word than "lather." I used to think it made me a good writer— look at me, honing my craft as I stand here to pour a cup of coffee, drafting and revising my descriptions of the mug, the smell, the sound of the hot splatter! Now I just find it tiresome, though it doesn't seem to be something I can stop. An end to narration: that's what I imagine death will be like.

In any case, this sentence is as good as it's ever going to be: the last time I saw Milo, he was getting ready to board a plane. It was the week between Christmas and New Year's, and we'd had a good time together. That's the unhappy irony; if we'd had the kind of visit we usually had, tense and angry and haunted by old ghosts, then the next link in the chain of events might never have been forged. But Milo was in a good mood and, presumably, feeling rather generous about the foibles of his old mother; at least, that's the conclusion I drew from the terse note he sent the following week. Like thousands of travelers every day, he stopped at the airport newsstand to buy a book. And for the first time in his life, he decided to pick up one of mine.

I've wished sometimes that the book Milo bought at the airport that day had been *The Human Slice*. Published just five months after the events of 9/11, *The Human Slice* was not my most critically acclaimed book, but it was my biggest seller. The popular theory is that readers were in exactly the right place to appreciate a novel about characters whose minds are magically wiped clean of trauma and sadness. Maybe this is true, and maybe it's not; the reasons people buy books are personal and arbitrary, and trying to analyze it does nothing but clutter a writer's mind. The fact remains that, for whatever reason, in 2002 people bought this book in droves. If four years later Milo had picked up that book, my gentle fable of forgetting and perhaps even forgiving, then he might have come away with a different understanding of my intentions.

But when he took his seat in first class that day and read for the five hours he had between taking his last breath of Boston's air and taking his first of San Francisco's, the book he was holding was not *The Human Slice*. It was *Tropospheric Scatter*, a messy, sprawling splotch of a book that had been nominated for two important prizes. And as he read, he wasn't thinking about terrorism or firefighters' widows or national tragedy. He was turning the well-worn pages of his own great loss, and mine. He was thinking about the day we lost Mitch and Rosemary.

\\\|//

- Milo Frost ACCUSED KILLER Autograph on Back of Envelope, $25.00
- "219 Sea Cliff" Replica of ACTUAL number sign from Murder House, Pareidolia, Milo, $7.99
- ORIGINAL copy New York Times, 11/10/10, MILO FROST front page, $9.00

Items listed on MurderAuction.com,
November 11, 2010

Chapter Five

⁄⁄⁄⁄⁄

I follow Chloe to her car, which turns out to be a Checker, like the old taxicabs, but painted red. As I get in, I peek into the cavernous backseat and see a child's car seat with a leopard-spotted cover perched on the red vinyl. I feel an unexpected pulse of tenderness at the sight.

"Nice car," I say.

"Oh, thanks. I always liked the way these looked. Joe gave it to me. That's kind of his thing, giving people cars." She laughs at the way that sounds. "It's kind of a pain, though. It's hard to find a mechanic who can track down the right replacement parts and things like that."

She turns the key, and a blast of music fills the car—nothing I recognize.

"Sorry," says Chloe, turning the radio off. It's a new stereo system, clearly not something that came with the original car. "I was listening to that earlier. Can you believe I still listen to Pareidolia by myself in the car? I'm such a groupie, even after all this time."

"But that wasn't Pareidolia," I say. I'm certain I'm right, but it sounds like I'm asking a question.

"Yes, it was," she says. "It's 'Traitor in the Backseat.' You never heard it before?"

"No," I say. I feel a little stunned. "It's not on any of their albums."

"Yes, it is," she says. "It's on *December Graffiti*." She looks over her shoulder, pulls out of her parking space.

I'm more agitated than I should be by this, and I feel like snapping at her that it's not on my copy of the album, or any other that I've ever seen (and I've seen a lot of them, because, crazy lady that I am, sometimes I visit the P section of a music store just to pick one up and turn it over in my hands), but I stop myself.

"Oh, you know what?" she says after a minute. "You're right, it's not on the American version. It was a bonus track on the European release. It's one of those hidden tracks—you know what I'm talking about? It's not listed in the credits, it just starts playing after the last song is over."

I absorb this. Given the number and scope of the surprises I've had this week, this one shouldn't even register. But it does. I thought I'd done such careful research. I thought I knew every song Milo had ever recorded.

"Why did they do that?" I ask. "Why didn't they include it on the American album?"

"I'm not sure," she says. She stops for a red light. "I don't follow that stuff. Probably their label didn't think it was commercial enough or something. It's kind of a funny song for them. It's about little kids, you know, like brothers and sisters on a car trip? It's about how they create this little world apart from the adults, until one of them tattles and brings in the parents. Then that person's the traitor in the backseat."

She sounds so casual, as if this is something that may or may not be of interest to me.

"Can I hear it?" I ask. My voice sounds tighter than I'd like. I take a breath.

"Sure," she says. She turns the stereo on again, presses the back arrow on the CD panel.

The song begins, and I see what she means about its being a departure for the band. It's softer, more melodic than most of their other work, and it has the same sort of rhythm as a waltz. It's the kind of song you enter like a corridor; from the very first notes, I'm inside the music, traveling toward an uncertain destination.

Milo begins to sing, his voice vibrating in my chest.

Dad drives, like always
Mom asks, "Did you pee?"

Look over the guardrail
down to the bright sea
We might stop for ice cream or some other treat
if no one turns traitor in the backseat

Yesterday Disney,
Tomorrow San Fran
Remember the guy with
the bright orange tan?
My side's a mess, but you keep your side neat
It's a whole separate world here in the backseat

We laugh and we fight and
we ask every minute
when we'll get to the house
with the mystery in it
Up front they use phrases like "power elite"
And for now there's no traitor in the backseat

I stare at my hands in my lap. I'm hardly breathing.

You call me a retard
I call you a gnome
With both of us here
we're not far from home
We play license plate games till I see you cheat
It's my turn to be traitor in the backseat

There's an instrumental bridge here; the music swells and then drops away for one final quiet verse:

Now there's darkness and firmament, water and foam
With only me here, I'm a long way from home
And I'm wishing you were here to notice me cheat
It's your turn to be traitor in the backseat.

Chloe switches off the CD. My throat aches. I focus on the registration sticker in the corner of the windshield, reading the backward letters to keep myself from crying.

I'd like it if Chloe wouldn't talk right away; I need a minute. But she asks, "So what do you think? It's a good song, isn't it?"

"Yes," I say. "It is."

"Milo's good at capturing those kinds of little moments," she says. "I totally remember what that was like, going on road trips with my family."

I look at her. Does she not understand my own connection to the song, the emotional undertow I'm fighting? Perhaps not. She's very young still, and I don't know how much she knows about Milo's family history. He's made it a rule not to discuss it publicly.

But I'm wrong. "How old was Milo when he lost his dad and sister?" she asks.

"Nine," I say quietly.

"Poor kid," she says. And already she's understood something I was not entirely willing to see when we were in the midst of it: that Milo's loss was at least as profound as my own. For all the energy I've spent in my writing life considering the taxonomy of human pain, for all the times I've told students that the key to creating a sympathetic and three-dimensional character is compassion, I turned out to be spectacularly unsympathetic when it actually mattered. My grief was proprietary. I wanted it all to myself.

"I can't even imagine," says Chloe. "I mean, I sort of can—I know what it's like to lose someone you really love. But now that I'm a mom . . ." She trails off. "You know, I guarantee you, that's something that people are going to try to use against him, now that all this is going on."

"What do you mean?" I ask.

"Oh, you know, that he suffered this huge loss when he was little. Like that might've warped him or something. I'm sure people are looking for ammunition to explain why he might've killed her. I remember reading once that some huge percentage of serial killers had traumatic experiences going to their grandparents' funerals when they were at a formative age and seeing the bodies in the caskets."

I stare at her. "Lots of children lose family members and don't grow up to be murderers."

She laughs, which startles me. "Oh, God, I know. I wasn't saying that *I* thought that. Just that, you know, people are ruthless about this kind of thing."

I sigh. "I'd like to talk about something else, if you don't mind."

"Oh, sure. Sorry." She gives me a rueful smile. "I wasn't thinking."

"That's all right." I wait for her to change the subject.

"So what was Milo like when he was little?" she asks. "I've heard some stories about his teenage years from Joe, but I've always wondered what he was like as a little boy."

I try to think how to answer. As a little boy, Milo was many things, and he was not the same child at eight that he was at eleven. If it were possible for me to sum him up with a few adjectives, our relationship might be simpler. I settle for generics. "He was a great kid. Funny. We never knew what was going to come out of his mouth." It's all true, but it doesn't begin to tell the whole story.

She grins. "Sounds like not much has changed. Any embarrassing anecdotes I can torture him with? Pants wetting or thumb sucking or whatever?"

Her voice is completely jovial—no edge that I can discern—but the question makes me uncomfortable. I don't understand yet what we're supposed to be to each other. She's not a daughter-in-law by anyone's definition, but we're bound together by a child I didn't even know existed until a few hours ago. And I still don't know exactly how she and Milo get along. Do they act like friends or exes or something completely different?

"Well, since I'm hoping to stay on Milo's good side, I think I'll keep those to myself for the moment."

"Wise woman."

I need to put an end to this conversation. I can't think about it now, not when I'm so close to seeing Milo. "Where does Roland Nysmith live?" I say.

"Near the Presidio. His house is amazing, you'll see."

"And what's he like?"

"Hmm," she says. "Not what you'd expect."

I'm not sure what I'd expect. Roland Nysmith has lived a very public life, and I know as much about him as anybody does. I was in high school and college in the mid-seventies, when his band, The Misters, first started making headlines. The Misters were a progressive rock band from England—someplace south of London, I think. In 1977 they released a concept album called *Underneath*, which told the story of a futuristic world in which human beings have built domed cities under the sea. It was trippy music, ponderous, self-indulgent, very seventies: music to get high to. Everyone in my dorm had a copy. The following year a full-length concert film was released, documenting several weeks of The Misters' tour of Japan. I remember seeing it at a midnight showing on campus—that was the kind of movie it was—and falling asleep partway through. Later, after the emergence of VCRs, I heard that the movie had gathered a cult following and that there was a drinking game in which viewers had to take a shot every time Roland Nysmith used the word "consciousness." But by then I was older, married, and a mother, and my interests lay elsewhere.

Roland Nysmith now, in his fifties, is not someone I know much about. But he's the kind of artist whose name evokes respect, if only because of the longevity associated with it. In more than thirty years, he's never stopped making music that people like.

"It sounds like he's been very supportive of Milo," I say. During that last Christmas together, I remember Milo telling me that Roland Nysmith had taken an interest in Pareidolia; later I read that he had helped produce the band's second and third albums. But that kind of involvement doesn't automatically translate into housing an accused murderer. What I'm getting at here is, *Roland must believe Milo's innocent, right? Do you think so, too?* But I can't ask those questions straight out.

"Yeah," says Chloe. "He's a loyal guy. He also just likes Milo. He's been kind of a father figure to him since early on."

I think of Mitch—down-to-earth, wry man that he was—and wonder how he would feel to think that his role has been filled by a person who once appeared onstage in a bodysuit covered with fish scales. I suspect, actually, that he'd be amused, and I spend a moment trying to imagine what joke he might make, but I'm not as funny as he was. In any case, Mitch isn't here, and for quite some time I haven't been here either. I suppose I'm glad Milo has had someone to look up to.

"Were you . . ." I hesitate. "Were you and Bettina friends?"

Chloe shrugs. "We didn't really know each other that well, in spite of Milo and Joe spending so much time together. She wasn't . . . This sounds awful, but she wasn't the type of woman who has many other women friends, you know what I mean? You kind of got the feeling she'd spill all of your secrets when she was drunk and hit on your boyfriend when you were out of town."

I make a noncommittal noise. Something else occurs to me. "Did she know about Lia?" I ask.

"No," Chloe answers in a tart tone that suggests she doesn't like this piece of the story. "She did not."

"Really?" I ask.

"I never wanted it to be some big secret," Chloe says, "but the fact is, Milo did cheat on Bettina to be with me. She was a fairly possessive person, and I guess Milo didn't think she'd react well to the news."

I absorb this quietly. I've only just come into this drama, and I don't feel it's my place to comment on it.

"The weather's changed," I say. When we left Chloe and Joe's, the sky was gray and overcast, and now there's sun lighting the street and reflecting on the bay.

She shakes her head. "It's not that the weather's changed, it's just that we've driven across it. This neighborhood is always sunny. Microclimates. We're almost there, by the way."

We've come into a neighborhood of astonishingly big houses, and I know which one is Roland's as soon as Chloe turns the corner. The street is clogged with parked cars, and at least a dozen men with cameras stand in the road, talking and smoking, all of them careful to keep one eye on a white stone mansion rising above them. It's a beautiful house—I suppose a real estate agent would refer to it as neoclassical or some such thing—and it towers over its neighbors, owing to a combination of hilltop placement and a street-level garage that makes it look as if the house doesn't really begin until the second floor.

"Crap," says Chloe. "We'll go around back."

As she slows the car to turn it around, the photographers swarm to peer in the windows. I don't know whether they recognize me or Chloe, or if they're just covering their bases, but there's a frenzy of picture snapping and video recording until Chloe leans on her horn and revs her accelerator and they scatter.

"Leeches," she says. She drives around the corner and approaches a wrought-iron gate with an intercom. She opens her window and presses a button. "It's Chloe," she says, and after a minute the gate swings inward.

She parks in a paved courtyard, and we get out of the car. She leads me up a winding brick staircase and rings the doorbell.

"He must be here," Chloe says. "Those guys"—she gestures down toward the street—"would know if he'd gone out."

The door opens, and Roland Nysmith stands before me. His face is angular, the structure of it more pronounced than it was when he was younger, and his hair is cut down to gray stubble, but I recognize him immediately as the man I've seen in magazines and on album covers since I was seventeen. I never hung a poster of him on my wall, but I knew plenty of girls who did, and even under these circumstances, I'm aware of a faint charge of astonishment running through me in a flimsy twitter. I actually feel some measure of awe at finding myself in this man's presence. Are there people who feel this way around Milo?

"Chloe," he says, leaning in to give her a kiss on the cheek. I'm surprised to find that even his speaking voice is familiar to me. "And who is this?"

"This is Octavia Frost," she says. "Milo's mother." And to me, "Roland Nysmith," as if I may not know.

Roland smiles and holds out his hand, giving me a curious and frankly appraising look. "A pleasure," he says. "So you're the famous writer."

I actually blush as I shake his hand. The phrase is embarrassing and untrue, especially coming from a man who has lived in the bone-white light of true fame for all of his adult life, but I don't think he means it to be sarcastic.

"Nice to meet you," I say. I pause. He's still looking at me in that strange way, as if he's trying to soak me up. "And, belatedly, thank you for all of the kindness you have shown my son."

He puts up his hands in a gesture of modesty. "Not at all," he says. "Don't be silly." He steps backward for us to pass. "Come on in, both of you, won't you?"

We walk into an entryway with yellow walls and a black-and-white marble floor. I look to my right, down a hallway that leads into a dark-paneled room with a grand piano, then straight ahead into a sitting room with a boldly patterned rug and several orange couches. I'm hoping to catch sight of Milo before he knows I'm here, but he's nowhere to be seen. The scope of it all amazes me. This is a city where you certainly pay for space.

"If you don't mind," Roland says, "I'm expecting a phone call, but I hope you'll make yourself at home. I'll just be a trice."

It finally occurs to me that we're dropping in unannounced. "Of course," I say to Roland. "I'm so sorry to bother you. But can you tell me . . . is Milo here?" My voice rises, betraying my nervousness.

Roland smiles at me. "Yes, of course, Mum," he says, and I'm not sure I like that. I'm not *his* mother. "Milo and Joe both. They're up in the library." He turns to Chloe. "You know the way, don't you, darling?" He turns away from us and walks toward the room with the piano.

"Yup," says Chloe. "Don't tell them we're here, okay?"

"Not a word," says Roland, over his shoulder. I watch as he walks through the paneled room and disappears through a door at the other end.

Chloe gives me a smile. "Here we go," she says.

I follow her up the stairs and down a wide hallway. There's deep carpet that muffles our footsteps, though I don't know if this is a good thing or not—do I really want to take him by surprise? As we walk toward an open doorway at the end of the hall, I hear voices. First Joe talking in a quiet monotone, and then Milo's voice rising with emotion. I can't hear what he's saying, but he sounds like he's crying.

My heart is beating like crazy. Chloe stops and stands to the side. She points to the room ahead of us and nods. She's sending me in alone.

I walk the last few yards slowly. I'm frightened in a way that strikes me as ridiculous.

I step into the room and stop. Joe is slumped in a red armchair, leaning his head on his hand. He looks miserable. And there's Milo, my beloved, my boy, pacing the floor and sobbing. His hand is on top of his head, pulling his long hair away from his face. His face is red, and he has a jagged line of scrapes and bruises on his forehead and one cheek. He looks like he hasn't had a bath in days.

He sees me and freezes. I'm prepared for anything except what actually happens.

"Mommy," he says.

He walks over to where I'm standing and crumples against me. I put my arms around him cautiously, then pull him closer when he doesn't move away. He rests his head heavily on my shoulder, and I turn to whisper into his hair, the way I did when he was a child. "Milo," I say. "It's all right. It's going to be all right."

He pushes his face into my shoulder. I can't hear what he's saying. "It's all right, baby," I say again.

He pulls back and looks at me wretchedly. "I did it, Mom," he says. "I killed her. I think I killed her."

From the Jacket Copy for

THE HUMAN SLICE

By Octavia Frost

(Farraday Books, 2002)

/|||\

T he day we all began to lose our memories was
a Tuesday." So begins Octavia Frost's startling and
poignant new novel, *The Human Slice*. When Hope Russo
begins to forget her most painful memories, her family wonders if it's a psychological defense mechanism; after all, she's
still reeling from the recent death of her young son, Jonah. But
it soon becomes apparent that Hope is not alone. People all
over the world are suffering similar memory losses, a phenomenon soon dubbed WSA (Widespread Selective Amnesia):
happy memories stay in place, but unhappy ones simply disappear. Only a small minority, including Hope's mother-in-law,
Linda, seem to be immune from this epidemic.

Narrated in turn by each member of the Russo family—
grandmother Linda, mother Hope, father Rich, fifteen-year-old
Macy, and twelve-year-old Kyra—*The Human Slice* combines
fable, science fiction, and family drama to create an all-too-
realistic tale of tragedy and that malleable substance called
human nature.

Excerpt from

THE HUMAN SLICE

By Octavia Frost

ORIGINAL ENDING

/ʼ¡\\

LINDA

It's been a year now since Hope walked into the living room and asked if anyone had seen Jonah. A year of being the only one in the family who knows anything about Jonah's death. It's starting to become a little bit lonely for me in this house.

We have a name for this thing now, at least; an international group of doctors have gotten together and settled on a few terms. The winning name for this act of forgetting, of losing oneself in layers, is Widespread Selective Amnesia (WSA). People are calling themselves "Ammies."

As for the Heavies, we've been renamed NAs: the Non-Afflicted. (The joke, of course, is that we're more afflicted than anybody.) We're not as small a group as it seemed at the beginning; doctors estimate that NAs make up 3 to 5 percent of the population. But we're enough of a minority that the switch in terminology doesn't seem particularly urgent to the general public. Most people still call us Heavies, though I'm still not sure whether it's because of the weight they imagine we must feel all the time or the damper we seem to put on any lighthearted conversation.

RICH

Honestly, I've never been happier. I'm more productive at work than I've ever been, and when I leave at the end of the day, I can't wait to walk into my house and see my family. Hope and I are getting along the way we were when we were first married, at least first thing in the morning, when she's had a good night's sleep and a chance to forget whatever my mother was putting into her head the night before. We're even starting to talk about having another baby.

The four of us—me, Hope, and the girls—are all doing great, but my mother is running around like some kind of reverse Cassandra, insisting we try to regain some hold on the things that used to torment us. Uh . . . thanks, but no thanks, you know?

MACY

Today at school, Ryan comes up to me and tells me he thinks we should get back together. And I want to say yes—I'm standing here looking at him, and all I want to do is reach out and put my hands on him. But I keep thinking, "How can I do this when I don't even know why we broke up the first time? What did we do to each other that was so bad neither one of us can remember it?"

KYRA

School has gotten crazy. Kids are bailing on tests, saying, "Oh, sorry, I tried to read about the Holocaust, but it made me too sad, it wouldn't stay in my head." And this one kid beat someone up and got sent to the principal's office. His defense was, "What does it matter? He's not going to remember it anyway." Even teachers are forgetting stuff. Mrs. Kantner, my English teacher, told us she had to reread *Romeo and Juliet*, even though she'd been teaching it for sixteen years. She said she didn't know what kind of past experience she'd had with *Romeo and Juliet*, but it must have been pretty bad.

And as for the Heavies, people either ignore them or pick on them. Most of us, at least as far as I can tell, just aren't admitting it. Even my mom still hasn't figured out about me. Even my grandma.

HOPE

There's a laundry tip I know, a little piece of household alchemy passed down to me from my mother: if you ever need to get blood out of a piece of clothing, hold the item over the sink and douse the stain with hydrogen peroxide. It's like magic. The liquid fizzes and bubbles. The fabric turns hot, as some unseen chemical battle takes place within its threads. And then the blood is gone—all of it, every trace. Sometimes the item feels a little stiff after it dries—peroxide is harsh and can wear down material over time—but the stain is gone. The liquid runs clear, and the fabric is clean and wet as spring.

I keep trying to tell myself that it's a relief that I don't remember anything about Jonah's death. But part of me doesn't want that spot to be gone.

Rich is fine with a few gaps in his memory, but I don't like this hungover, what-did-I-do-last-night feeling. Doesn't this make us vulnerable, this inability to remember our pain? A world of clean, bright-eyed innocents—that wasn't the way things were meant to be. A world of babies with no adults to warn them that fire is hot.

I think: a woman whose husband has beaten her twice a month for the last thirty years will no longer know that when he starts talking in that particular tone of voice and examining his fingernails with the most casual air in the world, it's time to go lock herself in the bedroom and dial the first two numbers of 911. According to a new study, laboratory rats are no longer able to learn that pressing a certain lever will give them a shock. I imagine them jolting themselves over and over again, looking for rewards and finding only pain, until their fur is singed and their paws have lost all feeling.

MACY

One of the things I still haven't gotten used to is the way that not everyone forgets the same things. It can be useful—like when I was thinking about getting back together with Ryan, I asked my friend Lauren if she could remember what happened the first time around, and she told me this whole story about him cheating on me with some girl when his family was on vacation. It didn't sound familiar—it was like she was talking about someone else—but it was bad enough that I decided this reunion wasn't going to happen.

But it can also make you feel kind of lonely and almost scared. Like, why do you know these things about me that I don't know? And why didn't that hurt you so much that you forgot it, too?

RICH

So tonight Macy comes home with a tattoo on the nape of her neck. I'm not particularly happy about it, but I'm trying not to make it into a big thing. The thing I don't entirely get is the picture she chose: it's a figurehead, like from an old ship.

You know, those busts of women jutting out from the bow? Well, this is a head-on view of one of those. A wide-eyed woman with flowing hair and a pale face, pointing one finger out to sea. The artwork's pretty good, actually. But when I ask her why she picked that particular image, she doesn't seem quite sure how to explain it.

"I don't know," she says. "I just think those things are kind of creepy and interesting. They give me the chills, you know? And also I like the idea that there's someone looking behind me, keeping an eye out on the things I can't see."

"Watching your back," I say.

As is so often the case these days, I have this feeling that Macy and I are just on the verge of some connection, but our hands can't quite reach.

"I like it," I say. "I think it's cool."

Macy rolls her eyes. "God, Dad," she says. And she walks out of the room, her second set of eyes watching me as she leaves.

KYRA

The tattoo comes close to being the thing that pushes me over the edge. I'm really tempted to tell Macy I'm a Heavy. I mean, for God's sake. She doesn't have any idea why she's picked that thing. But I'm managing to stay low-key.

"Yeah, I've seen those before. We saw some at the museum, right?"

"Which museum?" she says. Oh, come on.

"The Museum of Science and Industry. We . . ." My voice starts to crack, but I save it by clearing my throat. "We saw them when we went there with Mom a while ago, remember?"

"Not really," she says. "Funny that you remember it and I don't. Maybe I had a fight with Ryan right beforehand or something."

"Yeah," I say. "That's probably it."

"Well, we should go there," she says. "I'd like to see them again—it's kind of my new thing. Maybe this weekend. We can get someone to drive us."

What can I say? She knows I don't have anything else going on. "Yeah," I say. "We should go."

LINDA

For a while this spring, Hope joined a support group for people who were troubled by the effects of WSA. But it was frustrating, she said, because while they could talk around their vague feelings of loss and identity confusion, they could never really get to the heart of any of it. You could say, for example, "I'm upset that I can't remember my mother's death," but it was hard to maintain much fire when you in fact could not remember your mother's death.

They tried different strategies. For a while they were doing weekly exercises in which they'd go home and ask friends and families, and sometimes mere acquaintances, to help them fill in the gaps. How did my husband become paralyzed? What happened that Christmas when I was nine? Have I ever hit my children? They'd write down the stories and bring them in to read aloud. But it was as if they were reading a newspaper article or a piece of overblown fiction: somebody else's tragedy.

Hope eventually stopped going to the group—as I think most of them did. But that little homework assignment ended up helping her. The trick is finding someone who knows your history but hasn't been personally affected by the same things as you. Or—and this is where Hope is lucky, if you can call it that— you can ask an NA.

HOPE

Usually, before bed Linda reads for a while at the kitchen table and has a glass of wine. Lately I've started joining her; we both have books, but from time to time we put them down and talk a little. One night, finally, I asked her to tell me about Jonah. That was how I phrased it, but she understood that I meant *Tell me about Jonah's death.*

The ironic thing is, the absence of that one enormous memory has made room for a whole flock of smaller happy ones to come skittering back. I think that before WSA, I had deprived myself of my good memories of Jonah. They were too painful in light of what happened later. But once that boulder had been lifted out, a million little bits of gravel spilled in to fill the hole: the unexpected pleasure of having a baby who was all mine (or so it always feels when they're tiny) again after so many years; the way he loved strained carrots so much that they turned his nose orange; watching him toddle after the girls in the yard, shrieking and holding out a handful of grass.

I knew that hearing the story of his death would probably take those memories away again, at least until the WSA did its work once more. It was a strange trade to be making, but I wanted to hear the story.

LINDA

"It was a Wednesday in August," I tell her. "The girls' summer camp had already finished, and they were kind of at loose ends. So you had told them you'd take the day off and drive them into Chicago to go to the science museum."

RICHARD

I come in one night, right in the middle of this morbid tête-à-tête, and once I figure out what they're talking about, I'm disgusted. Why does my mother insist on forcing these things on us? Why can't she let us move on?

MACY

I know my mom and Grammy have these nightly meetings, and from the way my dad grumbles, I gather they're talking about Jonah. Honestly, I don't really get it. I mean, I remember Jonah, too; he was a cutie. But I'm happy to remember him as he was, a cheery little guy, always getting into everything. Why bring up all the dark stuff if you're lucky enough to have forgotten it?

LINDA

We speak about it every night, and every morning she's forgotten again. But it's important to both of us. I think of Penelope, weaving and unweaving. I think of Scheherazade, warding off her own death by telling stories.

"There'd been a lot of back-and-forth," I tell her, "about whether you were going to take Jonah to the museum with you or Rich would drop him off at day care as usual. You thought he might like the big heart and maybe the whispering gallery, too, but you also knew he wasn't going to sit in his stroller quietly while the three of you took in the exhibits."

By this point, Hope always has a wary look on her face, but she never wants me to stop.

"So finally you decided to send him to day care, but I hadn't heard that part. And when Kyra came up and said, 'Mom said, can you put Jonah in the car?' I thought it meant you'd decided to take him with you.

"I put his coat on him and carried him outside. He'd been fussy all morning, and I thought, 'Good. He'll probably take a nap on the way.'"

And always I speak this part clear and loud, always, always: "I was the one who buckled him in. I gave him his pacifier and rubbed his head for a minute. He was asleep before I shut the door."

"I don't understand," Hope says every single night. "How could I not have noticed he was there? Or the girls? And if Rich was supposed to take him to day care...?"

And I go through the chain of error. "Well, I was on my way to the dentist's, so I didn't even go back inside after I'd put him in the car. I knew you were all getting ready to go and you'd be out in a minute. When Rich got in his car and saw the baby wasn't there, he figured you'd decided to take him with you after all. So he called day care and told them Jonah wasn't coming, which is why they never called you when he didn't arrive."

"But," she always says. I know. "But" was the game we all played for months afterward.

"It was the week after Macy's sleepover, and Rich had moved Jonah's car seat to the back row so that all the girls could fit when you went to the pizza place. And he was still facing backward, remember, because even though he was almost eighteen months, he was still such a little guy. He slept all the way there. From what everyone said afterward, he didn't make a peep. That's all, honey. I'm sorry. That's all there is to it."

KYRA

As it turns out, Grammy's going to be the one to take me and Macy on this WSA-fueled field trip back to the museum. Which makes things a little more difficult, because she knows, you know? She understands what that place means. But whatever. I've been faking for a year. I can handle a stupid museum trip.

LINDA

I'm actually glad to be going with them. I wasn't there the day it happened—the dentist appointment, remember—so my memories of that day have little to do with the locale. They're precious to me, those memories of horror and grief, locked up safe in the same place I keep all my treasures of birth and laughter and falling in love. This is what people don't seem to understand anymore: that we need to know all of our extremes in order to know ourselves. I'm happy that I still know I made fun of a girl in grade school because her family was poor and she spoke with a lisp. Happy that I remember the pain of both a broken arm and a failed marriage. Happy even to remember the exact wording of Hope's phone message, the one I picked up in the parking lot of the dentist's office, my face still numb with Novocain.

KYRA

So Saturday comes, and we head off to go to this place I thought I never wanted to see again. At least Grammy parks on a different level, thank God. That purple paint is burned into my mind forever.

MACY

We go right to the ship exhibit first, so I can look at the figureheads. It gives me a cool, creepy déjà-vu feeling that I can't quite put my finger on. I stay there awhile, just looking. There are two of them, a woman and a man. And the woman one looks just like my tattoo. I must have subconsciously remembered the design when I sketched it out for the tattoo guy. I wonder if the gift shop has a postcard or something.

KYRA

She's just standing there, staring at these statues like an idiot and saying how they're all scary and mystical, and I just want to scream at her: *This is where you were, you moron. This is where you heard the news.* And now she thinks she's some kind of art history student, because her malfunctioning brain has forgotten every detail of the day except this one.

HOPE

"Once you were inside the museum," Linda always told me as we sat at the kitchen table with our wine, "you all went to look at the Fairy Castle for a while."

I knew about that, at least. "The girls always loved that."

"And then you went and looked at the coal exhibit with the elevator and the hard hats, because Macy was supposed to write her family history for English class in the fall, and you'd told her your grandfather was a coal miner. And then you split up, because Kyra wanted to go see the body slices, and Macy thought they were gross. So you went with Kyra, and Macy stayed downstairs to look at the exhibits on the first floor."

MACY

There's this horrible thing at the top of the blue stairs that people call "the human slice." It's so creepy: it's the real bodies of two real dead people from, like, the 1930s or something, and they've been cut into slices and preserved in plastic. There's a man and a woman, and they cut one up vertically and the other one horizontally. And you can just walk through and look at all these slices of dead bodies, and see all the cross-sections of veins and organs and teeth and whatnot, and admire the wonders of the human body.

And then you can just go home and kill yourself because you're such a freak. I mean, seriously, what the fuck?

KYRA

I just think it's interesting. I mean, yeah, it's kind of disgusting, but it's kind of amazing, too. I always used to like walking through that part; I was never afraid of them until afterward. But going to the museum today, I was pretty sure I wouldn't go up there. Because that's where Mom and I were standing when the message came on the loudspeaker.

HOPE

"Hyperthermia" is the word; I learn it every day. Even on a moderately warm day, the temperature in a car can get up past a hundred in no time. And this was the middle of summer.

The only thing that ever gets me to sleep is knowing I won't remember a thing about it in the morning.

LINDA

I tell the girls I'm going to the bathroom, and I go to see the body slices myself. I don't want to take Kyra with me, in case there's some scrap of a memory that the WSA has missed. That was the thing she had nightmares about, afterward. Not the loss of her brother, baked to death in his car seat, but the sliced-up people under glass. She was afraid someone was going to do the same thing to her.

I walk through the display, and honestly, it doesn't have much of an effect on me. It's like looking at bodies in a textbook. Strata of muscle and bone. Bloodless. Clean. Whatever made these cadavers human was lost a long time ago.

KYRA

Macy's still mesmerized by the stupid ship lady, so I tell her I'm going to go buy a bottle of water. And then I go stand for a while, looking up at the blue stairs.

Even as I'm walking up, I'm telling myself I could still turn around. I almost don't expect I'll get all the way to the top. But I do.

It's just . . . I don't know. As horrible as that memory is, it still means something to me, you know? I want to visit this spot the same way people visit graves. I want to be there again, even if it means I'm going to feel horrible afterward.

Right before I turn the last bend in the stairs, I suddenly wonder if I'm going to be the only one up there. And whether I want that or not. Whether it's better to be alone with the slices of dead people that I've been dreaming about for a year and a half or to be in a crowd of people making jokes about how disgusting it is.

And then there's my grandmother, standing right there where I need her to be. And I can't help it. I just start crying.

LINDA

I know right away, as soon as I see her face. My God. My poor baby. How has she managed to keep this a secret all this time?

KYRA

I can't believe it, after so long trying to fit in, but I actually feel better now that someone knows. I'm still not ready to tell anyone else, but she says she'll keep it a secret until I'm ready for it not to be one. We've started having our own daily talks, happier ones, I think, than the ones she was having with Mom. She tells me that she thinks it's important for people like us to be around. After a while, I may even start to believe her.

LINDA

And so it seems that the world is just as wide as it's ever been, even if my granddaughter and I are the only ones who can see it. I've forgiven my son for being happy to spend the rest of his life squinting, and I've begun to shorten my evening storytelling sessions with Hope.

On the first truly sultry night of the season, we cook hot dogs and hamburgers on the grill and eat dinner in the yard. Macy has spent all afternoon making potato salad, and in a burst of festivity, she's piled it into a cut-glass bowl that belonged to my mother. As she walks out to the picnic table, her foot catches on an uneven stone in the patio, and she trips. The bowl shatters. Potatoes and mayonnaise, shards of glass and pieces of hard-boiled egg spill across the grass.

I'm closest, and I stand to help her up. "Are you all right, Macy?" I ask.

She looks like she might cry. "Grandma," she says. "I'm so sorry. Your bowl . . ."

Poor little bug. So soft and unprotected. As far as she knows, a broken dish is the worst thing the world has to offer.

"It's okay, sweetie," I say. "Forgive and forget." And then we're all laughing.

Excerpt from

THE HUMAN SLICE

By Octavia Frost

REVISED ENDING

/////

KYRA

The morning after the cookout, I walk into the kitchen. Grammy's sitting at the table, reading the paper.

"Monday's Memorial Day," I say, opening a cupboard to get a glass. "Will you take me to put some flowers on Jonah's grave?"

She looks up, smiling. Her voice is pleasant and curious. "Who's Jonah?" she asks.

"It was strange: I brought them their entrées, and they were laughing and holding hands, and by the time I came back to take away the plates, Bettina was crying and Milo was sitting back, looking . . . I guess I'd say annoyed."

—*Sean Bowers, waiter at Zana, as quoted on People.com, November 11, 2010*

Chapter Six

/|||\

I hold on to Milo. He's taller than I am—has been for a long time, but it's still a surprise—and he's bent over, crying onto my shoulder. His smell is so familiar to me, and the plain, pure presence of him, his undeniable solidity, sets off a spit of recognition in my skin's own memory. I'm left with a feeling of quiet elation that stands quite apart from the horror of the statement he's just made.

Ever since the news of the murder broke, I've been thinking about how I would react if I were faced with some incontrovertible proof that Milo is guilty. I expected I might feel frightened, protective, sad. Some dusty maternal hope that I might still be able to make it all go away.

Now that the moment is here, it's not what I expected at all. That's the fundamental flaw in the illusion that writers like to maintain, the idea that we can craft anything approaching truth. No matter how richly we imagine, no matter how vividly we set the scene, we never come close to the unambiguous realness of the moment itself. Here's how I feel, faced with my child's confession that he has committed murder: I don't believe it's true. Not for a single minute.

Chloe comes into the room from the hallway, and she and I speak at the same time.

"What did you just say?" she asks.

"What do you mean, 'I think'?" I say.

"He doesn't know," says Joe from the armchair where he's sitting. "He doesn't remember."

Milo pulls away from me and wipes his wet face with his sleeve, like a child.

"What do you mean, you don't remember?" I ask. "What don't you remember?"

"A whole period of time from that night. A couple hours or more."

"Were you on drugs?" I say. What a cliché of a mother I can be, given the right opportunity.

"No, but I had a lot to drink."

Roland appears in the doorway. "I see you found your way," he says jovially. He takes in the mood of the room. "What's happened?" he asks.

"Sam Zalakis called," says Joe. And to me, "Milo's lawyer."

"He got some of the police reports," says Milo. He shakes his head.

"Tell me what he said," says Roland.

The room seems suddenly very full, and I have an impulse to stop Milo before he says anything more. I don't know the first thing about any of these people. Milo obviously trusts them, but that doesn't mean I have to.

"Milo," I say. "Can we just spend a couple of minutes together?"

"Oh, right," says Roland. "Of course."

Joe stands up. "We'll be downstairs," he says. I watch the three of them leave; as they go, I overhear Chloe whisper to Joe, "Do you think he really did it?"

I sit down in a vast armchair, the mate of the one where Joe was sitting. Milo sits down in the other one. He looks at me, confused, and for the first time slightly wary. "What are you two doing here, anyway? How did you meet Chloe?"

"She called me," I said. "I guess Joe told her he'd seen me."

He laughs humorlessly. "Right," he says. "Face-to-face. I guess she told you?"

I nod. I have a grandchild, I think, astonished once again. Next time, maybe I'll be able to hold her in my lap.

"Figures," he says. "She's been looking for an opportunity for years. I guess it wouldn't occur to her that this might not be the best week. She can be a little . . . single-minded. She's been trying to get Lia into this preschool, and Joe said she's called the director every day for a month."

"I met Lia, Milo. She's beautiful."

"She looks like Rosemary," he says.

"She looks like you."

There's a pause. As important as this is, it's not what we need to talk about. There will, I hope, be time for that later. I can't stop looking at him. Four years, my God. There he is.

I pull my mind back to the issue at hand. "You can't really think you killed her," I say.

He looks at me evenly. "Why not? I think I'm capable of it."

I shake my head. "You loved her," I say, though of course I know nothing that I haven't read in a gossip magazine. "Right?"

"I loved her," he says. "And she was leaving me."

This is news. I've read that Milo and Bettina were seen arguing in a restaurant earlier in the evening, but I haven't heard anything about a breakup. I don't know if this is information the police don't have or just information they haven't released to the public.

"What happened?" I ask. "What's the part of the night you do remember?"

"We went out to dinner," he says. He looks annoyed with me, vaguely sullen, like he resents me for not knowing the story already. There's my Milo, I think, then do the mental equivalent of biting my tongue.

"And I told her I thought we should get married."

I stare at him. "You proposed?" I say.

"No, I didn't *propose*," he says, sounding exasperated. "I didn't get down on my knees in the middle of the restaurant or have them hide a diamond ring in her salad or whatever. I said that it seemed like we were headed in that direction, and I loved her, and we should just go ahead and get married."

Really swept her off her feet, I think. But what do I know? Maybe girls want different things these days. Maybe this one did, anyway.

"And what did she say?" I ask.

Milo looks down at his lap, and for a quick private moment I see his face soften. "She said yes," he says. "For, like, ten minutes we talked about what kind of wedding we'd have and where we'd have it, like should we go to Bali or someplace and just make it really small and intimate, or should we do it here in town and have a big blowout . . ."

I'm touched by the poignance of these half plans; I imagine flowers, tears in my eyes, an aisle on a beach or in a city cathedral. But then I remember: I wouldn't have been invited.

"So what happened?" I say. "When did you start arguing?"

"Oh, God," he says. "We were having champagne, and she called her mother, and I called Joe . . ." He shakes his head. "God, she was just so happy. And then she said, 'Are you gonna get me pregnant on our honeymoon?' and I just thought, I have to tell her about Lia."

I feel suddenly irritated. *Of course* there was no way for that to end well. What kind of denial, what shortsightedness, made him think that lying to Bettina for more than three years was a good way to handle things? "I have to say, Milo, I don't really understand that whole arrangement—"

He puts up a hand. "Stop it, okay?" he says. "Jesus Christ. Just . . . stop it."

I back off. Take a breath. "Okay," I say finally. "So you told her. And she didn't take it well."

"No," he says, his voice like a rock. "She didn't take it well."

I look at this man sitting before me with bloodshot eyes and a two-day growth of beard, and I think about a younger, more awkward Milo, fourteen years old and just beginning to date his first girlfriend. Her name was Melody, and she was a slippery, insecure little thing. In those years, young girls were windows for me, or crystal balls: Can I glimpse Rosemary in this one, or this one, or this one? What struggles would we be having now, she and I, and what shared pleasures? And when Milo first brought Melody to our house, I thought, If this were my daughter, I'd be worried.

This was 1997; Rosemary, if she'd lived, would have been eleven. Girls then (and probably now, though I'm not looking in the same way) were such a strange mixture of sheltered and worldly. Melody was brassy, trying hard: she had scarlet hair and a pierced eyebrow, but her face was the face of a baby. She could be opaque in that way that torments teenage boys—*What does she want?* I remember Milo saying. *Why can't it just be fun?*—and she could turn sharp and vindictive in an instant if she felt she'd been wronged. I could see almost immediately that she was just beginning the process of growing up to be a damaged young woman.

Which is not to say that she was solely responsible for the unhappiness they nurtured between them. Melody was in and out of our lives for the better part of a year, and by the end of it, the relationship had become a study in miniature of many of the bad marriages I've seen from the outside. They made each other miserable. Milo was baffled and resentful to discover that romance could have rules, and Melody was hurt and angry that he didn't already know what they were. They had gotten close very fast, and there was an almost immediate blurring that unnerved me and, I think, them. They were so bewildered, both of them, by the intensity of this thing they'd created, and neither one had any idea how to unbraid themselves back into separate strands.

Melody was too thin, and she smoked; I could smell it on her jacket, thrown across the arm of the couch. I remember at the time starting to wonder, what is my responsibility to these girls, the ones my son brings home? Was it my job to call Melody's mother and tell her to intervene? I decided it was not, just as I decided, almost without thinking about it, that it was not my place to lead Milo step by step through his first romance. He needs to learn, I thought. He'd want me to stay out of it. But I see now that I was wrong. I never left my children's shoes untied until I was confident they could perform the maneuvers with their own hands; what made me think that Milo's education in adult relationships was any less my responsibility?

I think of Bettina, sitting in that restaurant on the last night of her life, newly engaged and heartbroken. If I'd been present in Milo's life in any meaningful way, would I have done anything to prevent that moment? I imagine an alternate reality in which I make different decisions and these four years of estrangement never happen. In this version of things, I move to the West Coast and come to know Bettina. I go to their house for dinner; Bettina and I go shopping together when Milo is out of town. I stay back, not interfering but offering gentle advice when it seems appropriate. They invite me along when they have an extra ticket to something; my picture appears at the edges of magazine photos, half cut off because I'm not the important one. Perhaps I become friends with Kathy Moffett, that master of pithy and heart-tugging newspaper quotes. We would have been uneasy allies, not sure whether we were destined to be grandmothers to the same babies or strained acquaintances armed with intimate, unflattering details about the other's child. (I'm sure that this current scenario, our faces on the same page of the newspaper, our eventual seats on opposite sides of a courtroom, would not have occurred to either of us.) But working together, like mothers whispering lines to their children onstage in a school play, we might have helped them navigate this course more smoothly.

Milo is sitting in his chair, worrying a small hole on the hem of his T-shirt. "Okay," I say. "What happened next?"

Milo closes his eyes for a moment, pushes his hair away from his face. "She left," he says. "She told me not to come home, she'd get a taxi. She was going to pack, and she'd be gone in the morning."

"What did you do?"

"I went to a liquor store and bought a bottle of scotch, and I sat in my car and drank it."

"In your car?" I say. I'm appalled, and I'm afraid it's clear in my voice.

Milo raises one hand idly, palm up: a spare version of a shrug. "I can't go to bars anymore," he says. "I get recognized."

Which would have provided an alibi. See? I'm thinking. He couldn't have done it. He would've been smarter about it, if he'd known he'd need to account for his whereabouts. But that raises questions about premeditation and crimes of passion and people snapping in the heat of the moment. And that's where I stop pursuing it. "What time was this?" I ask.

"I don't know," says Milo. "Ten, maybe. Ten-thirty?"

"And do they know . . . have they determined a time of death?"

"Yeah. That was one of the things in the coroner's report. Between midnight and two a.m."

"Okay." I drum my fingers on my thigh, made newly anxious by the existence of this timetable. "How long did you stay in your car?"

"No idea. I listened to some music and drank about half the bottle of scotch, or maybe a little more. I tried to call Bettina about a million times, but she wouldn't answer."

"So is that the last thing you remember, sitting in your car and drinking?" I'm waiting for the moment of relief, the detail that disproves everything.

"It *was* the last thing I remembered," he says. "When the cops were questioning me, everything was really patchy in my mind, and most of the night was a blur. I had a clear picture of sitting in the car, drinking, and then nothing else until I was back home, trying to get my keys in the door. I guess I was making a lot of noise, because someone came outside and yelled that I should quiet down because it was two a.m."

"And you remember more now?"

"Yeah, a little. Things have been coming back to me slowly, just bits and pieces. This morning, I was reading the news, and it said that someone saw me at the house around eleven, and I was just wracking my brain. It didn't sound familiar at all. Then I took out my phone to see what time it was, and I had this flash from that night. This memory of looking at my phone and feeling really pissed off that Bettina wasn't answering my calls and thinking that I should just go over there and talk to her." He shakes his head. "I don't know whether to trust these things, you know? Like my brain could just be inventing memories that match the other parts of the story."

I nod. I don't know much about posttraumatic stress disorder or alcoholic blackouts, but I did do some research on amnesia when I was writing *The Human Slice*. I wasn't interested so much in the physiology of it as in its metaphorical possibilities, the way that its exaggerated lines can bring our more ordinary memory losses into sharper focus. Amnesia as we usually think of it, as we see it played out in books and movies—the man who wakes up in a strange city with nothing in his pockets and no idea of his own name—is rare. But we're forgetting all the time; we forget more than we remember. It's necessary for our sanity, for our self-preservation, to reduce the noise in our brains. But the haphazard nature of our recall, the idiosyncrasies of which details linger and which ones vanish, has always struck me as sad.

My own powers of memory are robust, strong, and sinewy from constant work, and I can remember the prickle of loneliness, the jolt of something akin to betrayal that I felt whenever I would realize that Mitch had forgotten something I still remembered. It was never anything much—a joke one of us had made, the details of an evening out, a waitress or cabdriver who'd made a vivid impression—but to me, it felt like a chipping away, an erosion of our shared experience. A rehearsal, in retrospect, for the time when my memories would be the only ones left.

Back to the matter at hand: memory loss brought about by physical or psychological trauma. It's a real phenomenon—whatever happened that night, it was distressing for Milo, and it's not a surprise that his brain is concealing some details from him, like a mother skipping over the scary parts in a storybook. Memory is not an exact science, for all its attendant terminology of amygdala and hippocampus, and whether or not Milo will regain access to those moments remains to be seen. But for now, his body is doing what it needs to do to protect him. The repression of painful memories is also called "motivated forgetting." Whatever Milo saw that night, whatever he did, whatever he felt, it was something he had a reason to forget.

"Okay," I say. "Do you actually remember being at the house and going inside, or do you just remember deciding to go there?"

"Yeah," he says. "Well, no. I remember trying to go in, but while I was looking for my keys, Kathy opened the door and told me to leave." He glances up at me absently. "Kathy's Bettina's mom."

"Why was she there?" I ask.

"I guess Bettina must've called her. They were really close—she was over all the time. She was always the first one Bettina went to when she was upset."

"Okay, so . . . ?"

"So I tried to go in, and she wouldn't let me. She was really pissed off, and she said she wasn't letting me anywhere near her daughter. And I freaked out and started yelling that it was my house and I had every right to be there, blah blah blah. I said that Bettina was an adult, and that she should tell me herself if she didn't want to talk to me, instead of sending her mommy to do it."

"Did you see Bettina at all?"

"No, but she shouted down from upstairs. She told me to go away until I'd calmed down."

"And did you leave?"

"Eventually. First I yelled some more, and then I picked up a planter we had by the door and smashed it on the stairs. God, I was so mad." He shakes his head wearily. There's almost no emotion in his voice. "Then Kathy came out again and said she was going to call the cops if I didn't leave. I remember yelling that she couldn't keep me away, that it was my house and I'd be back. But I had enough presence of mind that I didn't want to get arrested, so I got back in the car."

"And where did you go?"

"Well, first I just drove a few blocks, to get away from the house, and then I pulled over. I remember suddenly feeling really scared, like maybe it finally occurred to me that this was real and that Bettina might really leave me. I couldn't stand it; I felt like I couldn't breathe. So I called Joe and asked him if he could come meet me, because I was really freaked out and didn't want to be alone. But he couldn't leave because Lia was asleep, and he was the only one home. He said I could go over there, but I didn't want to."

"And then?"

"I took a couple Xanax, and I just started driving. After that, it's pretty patchy."

I press my lips together in an almost literal gesture of biting my tongue as I work to keep myself from saying anything about mixing drugs and alcohol or driving under the influence. Or, for that matter, about lying or infidelity or the throwing of ceramic pots in anger. "What *do* you remember?"

"Well, at some point I got out of the car, because I remember being outside someplace. It was cold and dark and windy—I didn't have a jacket—and I remember falling down at one point." He touches one of the scrapes on his face. "Some of the blood they found on me was mine. I hit my head on a big slab of rock—that part I remember pretty clearly. There was a design carved into it, almost like a tombstone or something, so the surface was kind of jagged? It hurt like hell. I'm surprised the pattern didn't end up, like, embossed on my face."

"Do you think you were at a cemetery?"

He shakes his head. "I don't think I've ever even seen a cemetery around here. I wouldn't know where to find one."

"Okay. Do you remember anything else?"

"Well, I didn't until I talked to Sam this afternoon, right before you got here. I mean, when I said I was innocent, I believed it, or mostly I did. I mean . . . fuck." He makes a searching gesture with his arms. "I could never do something like that, right? But there was a little part of me that wasn't sure. I knew I had been there, and I knew I was upset. The next morning, when the cops told me Bettina was dead, it was like it wasn't a surprise. I already knew what they were going to say."

"Well, that doesn't mean much. You wake up and find yourself surrounded by cops, you know they're not there to give you good news."

"Yeah, I guess. Maybe. The thing I kept hanging on to was that I was absolutely sure I hadn't been in the bedroom. I came home, I knew Bettina didn't want to see me, I passed out on the couch. End of story. And then when they started turning up evidence that I *had* been in the bedroom—the footprints on the stairs and all that—I started to question things."

I tap my fingers on the arm of my chair. "But what happened *today*, Milo? What did Sam say? You said something about a report?"

"Yeah. He was telling me there were some new wrinkles we were going to have to deal with, new evidence we didn't know about. And there were two things that kind of freaked me out. One was that they checked my cell phone records, and I called the house at twelve-thirty. Or I got through at twelve-thirty—I'd been calling for hours."

"So you talked to Bettina?"

He shakes his head. "I have no idea. I don't remember it at all. But the records show I was on the phone for seven minutes."

"What was the other thing?"

"They found something on the table by the bed. A little plastic bubble with a toy inside, like you get out of a vending machine? It had my fingerprints on it. They called Kathy in to ask her some more questions, and she told them that it wasn't there when she left at midnight, because the first thing they packed up was all of Bettina's stuff from on top of the dresser and bedside table."

I think about this. "Okay, so you bought her something from a vending machine. You'd had a fight, you wanted to make up with her. I don't see why that upsets you."

He's quiet for a minute. "It wasn't just the fact of it," he says. "It was that suddenly I could see how it looked, just for a second. I could remember walking up the stairs in the dark, holding this thing in my hand. I knew what was inside the container before Sam even told me."

"What was it?"

"Oh, like some fake jewelry. A necklace and a ring with big pink plastic gemstones. I don't know if I can explain why it freaked me out so much, it was just . . . suddenly there was evidence of this whole part of the night that I don't remember. And I just thought, My God. I could have done this."

I sit with him and look at this picture he's creating for us. I know what it's like to construct a scene so vividly that you're practically there. I also know what it's like to remember something painful you've previously blocked from your mind.

"Have you ever blacked out like that before?" I ask.

"No."

"And have you ever . . ." I don't know how to ask this. "When you and Bettina fought in the past, did it ever get violent?"

He doesn't answer right away. "Not really," he says. "But the way I felt when I imagined her leaving . . . it was pretty intense."

His face is hard, set. He really believes he might have done this.

Okay. Follow it through: I imagine Milo going up the stairs of his house. I've seen the staircase in the *Turf Wars* video: curved wrought-iron railing, wooden steps, risers decorated with a mosaic of colorful ceramic tiles. It's the middle of the night—are there any lights on? He's unsteady; he holds on to the banister as he goes. He reaches the top, walks down the hall, opens the door of the bedroom. He finds Bettina sleeping in their bed. And then what? He climbs in beside her? He picks up the exercise weight and kills her while she sleeps? Or she wakes up, and they argue, and he beats her while she begs him to stop? No. Just . . . no.

"What else did Sam say?" I ask.

"Oh, I don't know. Stuff about . . . blood spatter and . . . the angle of impact . . . Of course, my fingerprints are all over the place, but you know, it was *my house*, so that doesn't necessarily prove anything."

"Right," I say. I feel tired and heartsick. What happens after this? I'm wondering. He may go to prison, whether he's guilty or not. He may spend the rest of his life in a cell. I have a sudden impulse to take him away somewhere, to break the law, get him out of the country, hide him away where they won't find him. And like every wild plot twist that seems full of possibility until I see how implausible it is, the idea shines for an instant and then fades away.

The room fills suddenly with the chorus of a Pareidolia song, "Under the Muddy," and I realize it's the sound of Milo's phone ringing. He takes it out of his pocket and answers it, keeping the conversation to monosyllables, then hangs up.

"It's Joe," he says. "They're all downstairs. They don't want to interrupt if we're not finished, but . . ." He trails off.

"Okay," I say. I don't feel as if our conversation is finished, but I don't know what else to say. I wonder how long it will be before this happens again, me and Milo sitting in a room, talking by ourselves. Am I back in his life for good now? Do I use my return ticket to Boston (four days away and counting), or do I stay in San Francisco until this thing is settled?

We walk out of the room together and follow the curving hallway.

We go down the stairs, and Milo leads the way into the kitchen, where Chloe, Roland, and Joe are sitting.

"Oh, hey," Chloe says to me. "I've got to get home and relieve the sitter, and I wondered if you want a ride back to your hotel."

I wait a fraction of a moment to see if there are any other offers— Roland asking me to stay and have dinner with them, Milo saying he can drive me back later—but none are forthcoming. "Yes," I say. "Thank you."

Roland retrieves our jackets from a closet in the hallway behind the kitchen and helps us into them. "Lovely to meet you," he says to me. "I hope we'll be seeing you again soon."

"So do I," I say. I walk over to Milo and give him an awkward hug. "Please call me," I say. "Let me know what I can do to help."

"Okay," he says, in a tone that tells me nothing.

I follow Chloe to the front door. "Joe just got a call from Bettina's mother," she says to me in a low voice. "The funeral is tomorrow, and she wanted to make sure we know that she doesn't want any of us there."

"That's ridiculous," I say, though I don't really know if it is.

"Ready for the circus?" Chloe says, her hand on the door handle. I look at her blankly. "The photographers, I mean," she says.

She opens the door, and before I step out, I look back down the hall to the kitchen. Through the frame of the doorway I can see Roland and Joe, but Milo is out of my view.

For a period of several years in my late twenties and early thirties, every wish I made on a birthday candle came true. The wishes were things I had some measure of control over, mostly—babies being born, a house that we loved—though certain details (a *healthy* baby, a house we could *afford*) were out of my hands, and I liked the idea that I had wished them into being. After a while, though, coming up with the right wish became something of a burden. I didn't want the lucky streak to end, but I knew it couldn't last forever, and each year I'd think, Is this going to be the one that doesn't come true? It was magical thinking and I knew it, but it had become a solemn little tradition for me, and I didn't want to give it up willingly by wishing to win the lottery or live on the moon or something else outside the parameters of wish alchemy.

On my thirty-fourth birthday, when Rosemary was six and Milo was almost nine, we had dinner at home, and when Mitch brought out the cake he'd bought at the bakery, I suddenly realized that I hadn't given any thought to what I would wish for. The candles were burning, the children's fingers were inching toward the frosting, and I had to come up with something. What did I want most? I'd been working on a novel called *Hamelin* for years and years at that point, and it still wasn't coming together. In my more honest moments, I knew that it probably never would. But that was the dream, that was what I'd have told you I wanted if you'd asked me when I was twelve: a husband, children, books with my name on them sitting in the window of a bookstore. Mitch and the kids finished singing; I drew in my breath and blew. In the space of an inhalation I imagined *Hamelin* finished, sold, published. And I wished for something I knew I wasn't going to get.

Milo, as I've said, was almost nine that year, and we'd been having a hard time of it, he and I. From very early on, there was something about my personality that clashed with his, and we'd just recently come into an unpleasant pattern of pushing and pushing back; sometimes it seemed like we spent all our time not getting along. That night we ate our cake, Milo and I squabbled over bedtime, and I went downstairs, exhausted by the conflict, to watch a movie with Mitch. Then, just before midnight, as I was turning out the lights to go to bed, I started to panic. Knowing my time was almost up, I went into the dark kitchen and cut myself a slice of leftover cake. I stuck a candle in the hardened crust of the icing, lit the wick, and blew. I wished for what I should have wished for earlier—peace for me and my child, patience and generosity on my part, overflowing love. I took a bite of the cake—the cut edge was already growing stale—and I went to bed, hoping I'd done the right thing.

That year, neither of my wishes came true.

Chapter Seven

〵〴〳〲〱

A few minutes later we're back in Chloe's Checker, Lia's empty car seat a benevolent presence behind us, like a sleeping pet.

"So what do you think of Roland?" Chloe asks.

I shake my head briefly; all my thoughts are on Milo. "He seems nice," I say. "I didn't really get a chance to talk to him."

"Oh my God," she says. "You should date him!" I turn to stare at her. She throws me a happy, teasing smile. "You totally should."

"I'll keep that in mind," I say. I honestly can't tell if she's a little bit strange, or if I'm just no longer used to being around young people. "Finding a boyfriend isn't really at the top of my list right now."

"Right," she says, sobering a little. She comes to a stop sign, waits for a woman to cross. "So listen," she continues. "I just want to let you know that I'm not going to say anything to anyone. About what Milo said when we first got there."

My skin prickles. I suppose I had assumed that that should go without saying.

"I mean, I wouldn't lie under oath or anything, if it comes to that. But I'm not going to go running to the police or the press or anyone and say that I heard him confess." Right. *I won't tell your mother about Lia unless we're in the same room. I won't point a finger at Milo unless I'm under oath.*

"Thank you," I say. "I should probably clarify, since you weren't there for the whole conversation, that Milo's actually very confused about what happened. After hearing his side of the story, I think it's unlikely that he had anything to do with it."

She nods and stays quiet for a moment while she looks over her shoulder and changes lanes. "I keep going back and forth about whether it would surprise me or not. You know, to find out he did it. It was definitely a . . . passionate relationship. A lot of ups and downs."

Her tone changes. "Oh, I know what I wanted to ask you—is there anything I should know about your family history? Like, for Lia's medical records or whatever?"

Not a question I was expecting. "Um, let me think. Not really. My mother's still alive. My dad died of lung cancer, but he was a lifelong smoker, so. Mitch's parents both lived fairly long lives. He had a heart attack in his sixties, and she died during surgery a few years later." I think some more. "One of my aunts was diabetic. Is that the kind of thing you mean?"

"Yeah, just the basics. They ask for all this information on the pediatric forms when your kid is born, and Milo didn't seem to have many of the answers." She smiles. "He wasn't much help with the family tree in the baby book, either."

I shake my head. "No, he wouldn't be. If you remind me after I get back home, I can e-mail you some of that information."

She pulls to a stop in front of my hotel. "That would be really great," she says, turning to smile at me almost shyly. "There are times I've felt kind of alone in this, you know?"

I nod. "I can imagine."

"When I first told my parents I was pregnant, my mom said something that really bothered me. She was telling me that it was going to be hard to be a single parent and that having a kid would make it harder to get involved with anyone down the line, and she said, 'You only get one chance to make a family.' But I don't think that's true at all. Do you?"

I think of the familial groups I've been a part of in my adult life—chaotic family of four, shell-shocked family of two, heartsick family of one—and I realize how much I've staked on my hope that those numbers will change again. "No," I say. "I don't. And it looks like you and Joe have proven your mother wrong."

She smiles, though her expression is still wistful. "Yeah," she says. "You're nice to say that."

I let a moment pass, feeling slightly awkward. "Well. Thank you for the ride."

She looks up, her face snapping into more pleasant lines. "No problem at all," she says. "It's been really great meeting you. I hope we'll be seeing more of each other."

"Thanks," I say. "Me too. Have a good night."

. . .

Later, after going upstairs and studying the room service menu with more absorption than it really requires, I have a sandwich in my room and think of almost nothing at all. I feel as if my brain has shut down from the intensity of the day, the way an infant will sometimes fall asleep when you run a loud vacuum. Tomorrow, I think, but I don't get much further. Eventually I get undressed and slip into bed, though it's still early evening. It's a long while before I finally sleep.

A year or two ago, during one of my Milo-intelligence-gathering missions, I came across a Web site that featured the backstage riders of various musical artists, the document that lists a band's technical and hospitality requirements for before, during, and after a concert. There was one for Pareidolia, and I read it eagerly.

It was like discovering a cave painting. Here, in washed-out color, was a trace of a rich and unknown culture, an artifact that might provide exegesis of an entire way of life—but only if you knew how to interpret it the right way. Sifting through pages of notes about guitar stands and speaker cables, the amount of space needed to park a string of buses forty-eight feet long apiece, I felt as if I were close to discovering the secret of my son's daily life. There were requirements for clean bath towels and Chopin vodka, a stated preference for lighting in shades of mauve and violet. Requests for ginger beer and vegan snacks, a kind of tea designed to soothe a sore throat. Here, a hunter following a stag; there, a tracing of a human hand.

He's in here somewhere, I thought. These are the details of how he spends his days, he and the band of dozens he must travel with;

somewhere in here are the foods he craves, the comfort he seeks. But in this roughly rendered form, rinsed of context and nuance, how was I to know what any of it meant? Black hand towels for use onstage. Full-length mirrors and "clean ice." But nothing to tell me if my son was happy or how often he thought of me. Nothing to say that it's only because of me, the family I created and raised, nurtured and destroyed, that any of this exists at all.

. . .

I wake up in the morning feeling determined and frightened, thinking about everything I have learned and everything I may yet lose. This new hope, this frail peace . . . it's all very precarious. And as for my role here—in this disastrous situation, in the life of my only surviving child—it's no clearer than it was yesterday.

I go down to the hotel restaurant for breakfast and, steeling myself, open up my laptop to read the news. Milo's case is lower on the page today, but still prominent. Some of the details from the coroner's report have been made public, and I can see that journalists are working hard to piece together a narrative from the list of bald facts. I take a small notebook out of my purse—my obligatory writer's "You never know when inspiration will strike!" notebook, which is filled mostly with grocery lists and calculations of how much of a tip to leave—and start to make a list. I need to keep track of what they think they have on him.

Some of it is not news. Cause of death: blunt-force trauma to the head and subsequent bleeding in the brain. Weapon: a ten-pound exercise weight that had been in the bedroom already. But some of it is new, and so terribly specific. Number of blows Bettina suffered: three. Places where investigators found traces of her blood: the soles of Milo's shoes, the palm of one hand, the pillows on the couch where he slept. Such clear directionality. There's practically a map drawn from the scene of the crime to the snoring body the police found on the sofa the next morning.

I sigh, take a sip of my coffee. Focus. At the time of Bettina's death, her blood alcohol level was 0.03; she'd had something to drink, but she was barely even tipsy. Standard toxicology screens were negative for whatever substances they routinely test for. Blood was taken from Milo, too, and urine; here, in bold letters on my screen, discussion of my son's urine. His blood alcohol at the time of his arrest was not high, but several hours had passed since the time of the murder, so police say that the result is not particularly significant. In addition, it's been revealed that Xanax was present in his bloodstream, and every journalist who's taken the time to spend five minutes on Wikipedia is pleased to report that in rare cases alprazolam can cause aggression, rage, and agitation. Combining it with alcohol, of course, may intensify these effects.

I close my computer and put down my pen. I'm not sure what I think I can do to help here; I'm not a detective or a lawyer. Like everyone else, I've read a few mystery novels and seen a few crime shows and I think that qualifies me to form an opinion. There was blood on the ceiling of the bedroom, the paper said, cast off from the surface of the dumbbell as it moved upward from Bettina's skull to come down again after the initial blow. Blood on the ceiling. I don't know a fucking thing.

I signal for the waitress. A few tables away from me, there's a little girl sitting with her parents. I judge her to be younger than Lia, but not much, and I watch her with interest while I pretend to look at the screen of my cell phone. She's sitting in a booster seat, and the table in front of her is littered with torn-up napkins and crusts of toast; she has jam on her shirt and on her cheek. Apparently done with her meal, she displays extreme concentration as she scribbles on her hand with a green marker. Her mother and father are sitting silently, gazing at nothing in particular. They look tired.

I remember that one of the other requests on that Pareidolia rider I saw was "one room to be designated as a Family Room." It was to be stocked with, among other things, "one play yard (Pack 'n Play or similar) with two clean sheets" and "six jars of organic baby food, assorted vegetables and fruits."

At the time I knew that Joe was dating a woman who had a child, and I had some idea that this might be the baby in question. I remember wondering rather snippily what kind of mother feeds her child organic baby food while dragging it all over the country and subjecting it to the decibel levels of nightly rock concerts.

Now I wonder something else: what kind of father knows his

daughter, sees her often, even travels with her, but doesn't acknowledge that she's his? I picture the little family unit of Joe and Chloe and baby Lia, sitting cozily in a made-over room in the belly of a stadium, eating an evening meal together before Daddy goes to do his job onstage. And where's Milo? Someplace else, filling a glass with Chopin vodka and clean ice.

. . .

After breakfast I go back to my room and try to call Chloe, but I get her voice mail. Joe's not answering either, and somehow I left yesterday without getting Milo's number, or Roland's. I'm practically back where I started.

The morning passes slowly, and I spend it in a languorous panic, pacing my hotel room, refreshing news sites, calling people who don't answer their phones. It's all a spectacular waste of time, but what else am I supposed to do? I use hotel stationery to make timelines and lists of motives, as if I'm plotting a novel. On my computer, I shift between ten different tabs, all open to Google, skimming results for "gravestones, San Francisco," and "posttraumatic memory loss." Hoping that I just need to find the right search terms. Looking up "vending machine jewelry" and "locked room mystery" and "mother of the accused."

Finally, at a time that feels like late afternoon but is only eleven a.m., I spot a news item that gives me focus. Something tangible for me to investigate, some action that is at least actually related to the matter at hand. I plug in the iron provided by the hotel and carefully press the wrinkles out of a dark brown skirt and cream-colored blouse, an outfit I packed because I thought it would fit any number of occasions where I might need to look respectable. On my way out of the hotel, I stop in the gift shop to buy sunglasses—my picture really is everywhere these days—and a small, soft item in a white paper bag that I stick into my purse for some unspecified later time. A present I hope I'll have the opportunity to give while I'm in town. A half hour later I step off a city bus, disproportionately proud of myself for navigating an unfamiliar transportation system, and begin to walk down Arguello Boulevard. It's sunny and warm; whether this is typical for November, I have no idea. I walk down a wide sidewalk, past a long stretch of houses and apartment buildings. The garages here all seem to be built on the bottom floor, with the rest of the house above them, and I wonder briefly if it has something to do with earthquakes.

I cross a wide street and go past a gas station and an animal hospital with a rainbow painted on the side. At first my steps are quick and agitated, my body humming with nervous energy, but eventually my pace and my breathing begin to slow. I remember that whenever Mitch and I had a fight, my first impulse was always to get out—out of the house, out of the car, wherever we were—and start walking. Sometimes I had a half plan, ridiculous when I thought of it later (I could go to a hotel, I could get on a bus), but most of the time I just wanted to be elsewhere, as if I might be able to leave my fury and hurt feelings behind me. And often by the time I'd charged around the block and arrived back at the house I'd stormed out of just a few moments before, I had.

I come to the corner of Arguello and Anza and turn left. There are species of trees here that I've never seen on the East Coast, some of them knobby and stunted, others blooming in big green globes, almost like topiary. I'm going deeper into what seems to be an entirely residential neighborhood, and I like the solitude. For a few more minutes I can be outside my life, not the mother of an accused murderer, not a writer wasting time on a project no one seems to understand. Just a lady with sunglasses, walking through a landscape designed by Dr. Seuss.

Up ahead there's a corner where I've seen several cars turn in the last few minutes, and I strain to see the street sign. Yes, it's the right one. I turn into a tiny cul-de-sac, maybe four houses on each side, which dead-ends at a strange little building with a domed roof and a crowd of people outside. The building is round, ornate, neoclassical—not quite a church, not quite a museum—and it's an odd sight in the middle of this ordinary neighborhood.

I walk closer, and the crowd outside comes into sharper focus. It's a collection of news crews, photographers, and curious onlookers, similar to the one gathered outside Roland's house yesterday.

Then two things happen simultaneously: I see the sign on the gate that says COLUMBARIUM OF SAN FRANCISCO, and a man comes out of the building carrying two cases of soda.

He sets them down before the wriggling mass. "Mrs. Moffett asked me to bring these out," he says. "She said she'll be happy to talk to you afterward."

And that's when I know I've come to the right place. I've found Bettina's funeral.

From the Jacket Copy for

TROPOSPHERIC SCATTER

By Octavia Frost

(Farraday Books, 1999)

〃〢⧹

In 1964, engineer Howard Liles moves his wife, Marie, and ten-year-old son, Tom, to the far edge of the earth: Kotzebue, Alaska, thirty-three miles above the Arctic Circle, where Howard has a job working on the military's White Alice Communications System. Shortly after they arrive, in the midst of adjusting to their desolate new home, Marie makes a startling discovery while doing some charity work for her church: she finds a six-year-old girl, raised in terrible neglect and squalor and now orphaned. The family takes this nearly feral child into their home and raises her, learning from her as much as she learns from them.

From its captivating beginning to its tragic and shattering climax, *Tropospheric Scatter* is a novel you won't soon forget.

/||\\

They were exactly the wrong two to die. Nights, after the accident—that was the thought Howard kept returning to. Any other combination, even for him and Marie to lose both children, or for Tom and Beecy to have been orphaned, would have been better than this gutted fish of a family that flopped grotesquely, slowly suffocating on the pier. It was a horrible thing to think, and worse probably because Tom was his child by birth when Beecy hadn't been, but Howard found some grim comfort in the stark defiance of it. So many of the facts of his life now involved confinement—the close quarters of the cabin, the brutal wind that kept everyone indoors, the days without sunlight, the bed that seemed somehow smaller without Marie in it. He'd be damned if he couldn't roam where he wanted in the terrain of his own mind.

The two of them barely spoke in the days and weeks after it happened, though perhaps it had less to do with their feelings about each other than with the way they both seemed to have settled out of human society like debris sinking to the bottom of a water glass. Howard worked and came home and spent his evenings smoking at the table, and Tom lay curled on his bed for hours at a time, sometimes from the moment he came home from school until it was time to turn around and go there again. Howard kept his distance and left food out, as he might for an injured animal. He knew Tom was hurting, and that it was his job to help in whatever way he could, but he didn't even trust himself to open his mouth, knowing the things that might come out. Howard could examine the events of that terrible day objectively, call it an accident to anyone who asked, but when he looked at Tom, slumped at the table with his schoolbooks, he would repeat to himself "Your fault your fault your fault" until the words became non-sense and the rhythm began to soothe him.

The bottomlessness of his anger surprised him. Tom was his son, and he loved him; that wasn't in question. But it seemed, all of a sudden, irrelevant. He could picture Tom as a baby, Tom as a toddler, Tom on his first day of school, and listen for that automatic note of tenderness, but it was far-off now, muffled. It was as if there were static in his chest, white noise keeping him from picking up signals that should have been clear. Had it always been there, that crackle of interference? He no longer had any idea.

. . .

Three days after the bodies had been recovered, when the men went to dig the graves, Howard went with them. It was much the same as it had been when he joined in after Wally Forman died—clearing the snow, building a fire to soften the earth. The thermos of coffee passed from hand to hand, the quiet talk of fishing, the backache that told you you were doing something worthwhile.

Howard was glad, just then, to be here in Alaska, glad he could do some-thing so tangible for his two lost girls. When his turn came, he climbed into the hole, and with each shovel of frozen dirt, he thought, This is for you, and this is for you, and this is for you.

The funeral was well attended, despite the snow that drifted up to the church's bell tower, and the same newspaper reporter who had come to Kotze-bue after they'd found Beecy showed up now to put an ending to the story. Within a few weeks, Peller's Trading Post was selling copies of the *Anchorage Daily News* with a handwritten note posted on the wall above the pile: "Beecy's story inside." Howard, in the store to buy powdered milk and bear lard, walked right by without even a sideways glance, but someone (with what kind of inten-tions, Howard wasn't sure) left a copy in his locker at work. And that night, after Tom was in bed, Howard sat at the table with a glass of whiskey and opened to the right page.

"The Short, Strange Life of Beecy Liles" was the title. As if she were a charac-ter in a film. Howard tapped his fingers and took a drink.

"The child that newspapers dubbed 'the Kotzebue Closet Girl' was chris-tened Elizabeth Ann Liles by her adoptive parents, who intended to call her Betsy.

But the name that will be engraved on her tombstone is the one that she gave herself when, after nearly two years of patience and intense work on the part of her new parents, she attempted to say her name for the first time. On that day, transplanted to a loving home, with the ordeals of her early life long behind her, she looked into Marie Liles's face and said, 'Beecy.'"

Howard's eyes stung, though the word that came into his mind was "manipulative." It was the same as it had been before, the first time that the shape of their family had caught the newspapers' attention: hours plucked from his life at random and placed within a framework they hadn't seemed to have at the time. It was still his life, recognizable and even capable of provoking emotion, but it was missing some kind of essential texture.

He skimmed the next part, a repeat of all the same details that had been published before. People were in love with this story; why, Howard didn't quite know.

"Everyone in this small town knew Beecy's father, Malcolm Barnett; as the owner of one of Kotzebue's two general stores, he was familiar to everyone. But no one seemed to know much about him. He was a quiet man, and a bit of a recluse. Townspeople would sometimes make bets with each other about how many words they'd be able to get him to speak during a visit to his store. Rumor goes, the record was eight. People knew that he'd married an Eskimo girl some years before, and that she'd died soon after. What they didn't know, what nobody knew, was that she'd died giving birth to their only child, a daughter. When Mr. Barnett died in 1965, with no apparent heirs or family nearby, several ladies from St. George's in the Arctic Episcopal Church volunteered to clean out his cabin. They were shocked by what they found. The squat two-room building contained a level of filth few of those good women had ever seen. And it contained something else, as Marie Liles found out when she opened the door of a closet in Mr. Barnett's bedroom: a six-year-old girl, naked and shivering, lying on a pile of rags on the floor."

Howard flicked the paper with his forefinger in a childish, vaguely hostile gesture. He hated seeing this hashed out yet again. It gave him the feeling that even if Beecy had lived to be a hundred, she still would've been known as the Closet Girl of Kotzebue. And of course he never liked the way they insisted on referring to that crazy bastard as Beecy's father. Howard's ideas of heaven were vague, but he did believe that one day he would be reunited with the people he'd loved. He wondered if Marie and Beecy were still together in that place or state of being or whatever it might be, or if Beecy had been returned to her natural mother and father. It was a gray area, certainly not something that any priest he'd ever listened to had addressed in a sermon, but it killed him to think of Beecy's soul being given over to the safekeeping of the two people who had abandoned her, one through death and one through cruelty and neglect.

He read on, because it was there and because it was about his child, but when he came to the paragraph about the accident, he felt the need to physically avert his eyes. The idiocy of the impulse annoyed him. He knew what had happened, didn't he? There was nothing new in those words, no reason he should feel like he couldn't catch his breath. So he pushed himself to look down for seconds at a time, absorbing a phrase or two at each go.

"An ice bridge had formed across the surface of the river, and Tom urged his sister to climb out onto the sparkling surface ..."

Take a break. Look up at the wooden slats of the ceiling, pick a knothole to focus on, gulp the air.

"... terrible crack ... Tom ran for help ..." Press a tender place where he'd accidentally hammered his thumbnail a couple weeks before.

"Marie Liles, doing the washing, heard her son's shouts ... rushed together toward the riverbank ... jumped in after her daughter."

Close your eyes. Breathe in, breathe out.

"Helpless and horrified ... frozen ... trapped under the lip of the ice."

Even though two people had died that day, the article barely mentioned Marie at all. It was a reversal of the way most people seemed to want to talk about it, Howard thought, at least when they were addressing him directly. He'd noticed that his friends and neighbors and coworkers seemed to expect him to divide his grief in two. And if they saw fit to offer their comfort, they expected that in return Howard would tuck one half of it away out of sight.

Losing Marie was a panic and a weight. It was a hole so deep that he wasn't sure he'd ever climb out of it. But at least it was something everyone seemed to understand. Pete Johansen took him aside one day at work and told Howard that after Gloria died, he went a full year without eating a hot meal. And Marty Willoughby over at the Kalakaket Creek site, whom Howard had never met but had spoken to over the radio often enough, told him that he still had dreams about a girlfriend who'd died when they were in high school. Even people who'd barely known Marie felt comfortable grabbing Howard's arm and telling him she'd been a saint. That was the word he heard over and over again, and he appreciated the kindness of it, though he didn't think of Marie as having the sort of bland goodness, the pale porcelain virtue, he'd always imagined when he heard that word.

But almost no one knew what to say about Beecy. There were a couple of men Howard knew who'd lost children (and one of them a cripple), but none of those guys seemed to draw any line between their own experiences and the airless, choking feeling Howard got whenever he pictured Beecy's face. And maybe it was better they didn't say anything; the ones who did couldn't have gotten it more wrong if they'd tried. After the funeral, when the men moved from the church over to the Royal, Sheet Jennings clapped Howard on the back and said, "It's better this way. There was no way she was going to grow up to be somebody's wife. You and Marie would've been taking care of her till the day you died." And not too much later, on his way back from the toilet, he overheard Don Mizulski, drunk and shushed quickly but not soon enough, say, "I used to look at that girl and think, they better not let her out after she starts bleeding, or they're gonna end up with a whole litter just like her."

It was hard for Howard to put into words what he had seen in Beecy that made her so dear to him. She was his daughter, certainly, almost from the first moment she entered their home, but she was also his most precious responsibility. He understood her, and she was a child he knew not everybody would understand. She wasn't wild—that was the thing he kept coming back to. Every single article that had been written about her had used that word or a variation of it: feral, savage, like an animal. But putting her face in a plate of food because she didn't know any other way to eat, soiling herself because no one had taught her any different—that didn't make her an animal. It was the very fact of her humanity that caught in Howard's chest. She was a child, a hurt, frightened little girl. And Howard's only job was to show her that people in this world had the capacity to be kind.

It was Howard's hands she'd been holding the first time she crossed the floor on two legs, Howard's lap she was sitting on the first time she looked at the fire and said "Fa." Of course, Tom had done those same things, back in his own infancy, back in Minnesota, and Howard had been as proud as any father. But when you buy a car new off the lot, it's no surprise that it runs when you turn the key. The unexpected thing, the miraculous thing, is when a car that's been shattered in a crash, that's been left in the rain to rust for years at a time, can be coaxed to growl to a start and slowly begin rolling down the street.

. . .

Time passed, and Howard waited for the thaw. Walking the mud road to the base, slapping at mosquitoes, he looked at the landscape around him and tried to find some wonder in it. He remembered their first summer here, how thrilled they'd all been by the wildflowers and the racks of drying fish, the spectacle of a whale slaughter, the surprise of a bear cub eating blueberries from a bush. And later summers: Tom jumping from oil drums and Beecy laughing at husky puppies rolling in the dirt, Marie sitting outside the cabin after dinner, her hands empty for once, no basket of mending, no work to keep them busy. Now the world was melting again, and Howard wondered if the only thing he'd remember from this summer would be the shameful relief he felt whenever he arrived home to find his son wasn't there.

Tom had found a girlfriend, which Howard couldn't begrudge him, and he spent most of his time over at her house, where things were, presumably, less bleak. Tom's life was going to keep going, even if Howard's didn't—a few more years and he'd be off to college or the army, a job in a less frozen locale, and eventually there would be marriage and children and days full to bursting. Howard knew that certainly a time would come when he would be sorry for the way he was behaving now, when he'd wish for the kind of connection with his son that he was all but murdering. The hell of it was, knowing it didn't change a thing.

In early June, the sun rose and didn't set. Through the nightless weeks that preceded Tom's fifteenth birthday, Howard tried to imagine a way he might make things different. He suggested to Tom that they might want to take a trip—they could go camping, or even fly into Anchorage—but Tom wanted to stay in town and go to the July Fourth fair, just as they'd always done, though Howard was sure they were both thinking that there could be no more "just as they'd always done," not really, not ever.

He had meant to go down to Peller's to see about ordering Tom a camera, but the time got away from him, and so he ended up buying him a set of binoculars from the shelf above the counter. They were nice ones, and they'd be good for hunting or for hiking and climbing. A million uses a boy might have for binoculars here—wasn't that exactly the reason they'd packed up their house and moved to this end of the earth in the first place?

When Howard woke on the morning of the Fourth, early as he always did in the summer here, in spite of the thick blankets Marie always hung on the windows, he lay in bed and smoked for a while before getting up. *His birth day*, he thought, testing himself, remembering the smoky waiting room and the tiny weight in his hands, Marie's happiness and indeed his own. He remembered the sudden shyness he felt, walking into his wife's hospital room with a bouquet of irises, and he remembered his mother spontaneously singing "Yankee Doodle Dandy" when he called to tell her the news. He remembered looking at the clock and savoring the phrase "three hours old" as he held a bottle to the baby's lips and watched him drink for only the second time in his life. Howard focused on these things, pushing out everything else, and he was rewarded with a small piercing feeling, but it was distant and bewildering, like hearing a few lines of a language you'd studied in high school.

He let Tom sleep late, then woke him with pancakes like Marie used to do. The line between nostalgia and playacting hadn't quite solidified in Howard's mind yet, but he guessed this would be something Tom would miss if he didn't do it. They ate together, and Howard presented the binoculars, which Tom seemed pleased with, and then they set off for town.

They walked toward the water and Front Street, where the crowds had gathered. In the distance was the otherworldly silhouette of the White Alice site: the Martian-city radar domes and the billboard antennas that looked for all the world like the drive-in movie screens that had thrown patterns of light on the twining bodies of Howard and Marie in the days before they were married. He wondered who was working today at the site. Strange to think that as he and his son walked in silence, there were words flying through the air above their heads: messages and signals, invisible, bouncing off the lowest level of sky. People throwing their voices hundreds of miles, a modern miracle dressed down with secular words like "communication" and "defense."

"You gonna join the blubber-eating contest this year?" Howard asked Tom. Trying. "They say it tastes like coconut."

Tom looked at his father with half a smile. "I will if you do the blanket toss."

Howard smiled, too, or something like it. It had been a joke last year, how Howard was the only one who wouldn't take a turn being thrown up and down on the circle of sealskin. Well, that was something, he thought, a way of stepping out of the trap of "the way things used to be."

"You got it," he said.

They could hear the sound of drumming now, and Howard saw a banner strung up outside the Royal: "Happy Independence Day! 10 Years of State-hood: 1959–1969!" A makeshift stage had been set up down by the water, and the beautiful-baby contest was in full swing. Later there would be more competitions—sled dogs pulling weighted carts, men kicking fur balls hung above their heads, children drawing lengths of string into their mouths without using their hands. Already young women were lining up in parkas and fur boots to compete for the title of Miss Arctic Circle. It was a warm day, maybe seventy-five degrees. There were men grilling caribou sausages and Eskimo children holding miniature flags. Who would ever have thought that America would grow to encompass all this?

Soon after they arrived, Tom found some friends from school, and Howard stepped aside. He wandered around, talked to neighbors and coworkers he ran into. When the muktuk-eating contest began, he watched Tom up onstage with the others, gulping down black-and-white cubes of blubber and whale skin. And when the blanket toss got under way, he approached his son and tapped him on the shoulder like a boy asking a girl to dance.

They joined the group standing around the edges of the leathery blanket, everybody holding a piece and working together to move it up and down, pro-pelling one person after another up into the air. There was a cheery feeling in the crowd, and Howard tried to breathe with the same rhythm, to enjoy the sur-prised cry of each new person who climbed up onto the blanket and felt them-selves, for a few moments, freed from the ties of gravity.

When it was Tom's turn, Howard jerked the blanket with the others, and he saw his son bounce up into the blue. He felt his body loosen, just the tiniest bit, and he laughed out loud at Tom's shout when his feet hit the sealskin and he soared up again. Howard kept his eyes on Tom's face as he flew and fell, coming in and out of focus. With each ascent, he became a blur Howard wouldn't have known in a crowd, and with each drop, he settled back into the young man, nearly grown, who roused such a complicated range of feelings in his father's chest. Howard remembered that when Tom was a baby, he hadn't known how to answer the question "Who does he look like?" because there seemed to be such changeability to his newborn features. Howard could watch his son sleep and see one moment his own father and the next Marie's mother, and so on through a dozen different expressions, until he understood finally what it meant to call a child "my flesh and blood."

When Tom came off the blanket, he looked at his father with an open, questioning smile, and Howard smiled back and nodded. He worked his way onto the blanket and stood up in the very center. For a moment he was still, looking around at the circle of people he knew, friends and neighbors and coworkers who might or might not know him. And then they moved as one, and he was in the air.

It was not like jumping; it was not in his control in the same way that jumping would have been. He had no agency in this transaction. He simply rose and plunged, lifted by the hands of the community below. He was with them, then apart, with them, then apart. At his highest, he could see shacks of wood and sod, the ragged edge of the land and the dark water beyond. Radio towers and the White Alice antennas, and his son below him, his son.

He wanted to go higher, until he reached night, until he pierced the skin of the bright, endless day. He wanted to go until he hit the edge of the troposphere, wherever that invisible boundary might be, where men's words flew back and forth, propelled by his own work. His voice was going without him, sounds flying out of his body without any volition. He yelled until even he wasn't sure whether he was making angry noises or joyful ones. He rose and fell, free and weightless, a creature of earth and air. For a few moments he existed in a place between, nobody on any side of him, no one to hear him but the sky.

Excerpt from

TROPOSPHERIC SCATTER

By Octavia Frost

REVISED ENDING

/||\\

Hi Lisa,

Still working on this one. I'll get it to you ASAP.

Best, O

Chapter Eight

I stand for a minute at the edge of the crowd outside the Columbarium and study the scene. Of course, I knew that this would be a high-profile event, and that there would most likely be some media presence—the very reason I went to the trouble of buying new sunglasses and putting them on four blocks away. But now that I'm here and I see what a spectacle it is, it seems less likely that I'm going to be able to slip in undetected.

I feel I must clarify that I wasn't worried someone might identify me from the covers of my books. Few writers enjoy that kind of fame, and I'm not deluded enough to think I'm among their ranks. I don't get recognized, not when I sit on a plane with a manuscript on my tray table, title page up, not when I stand in a bookstore and purchase one of my own novels with a credit card bearing my name. Normally—or in the normality of the life I lived until Tuesday—it wouldn't even have occurred to me to worry that someone might know who I was. But my picture has been broadcast so widely these past few days, always in pointed association with the murder of the very woman whose funeral I'm trying to crash, that I didn't think I could count on not being noticed.

It turns out, however, that you can't just walk into a celebrity funeral—which is what I suppose this has become—and casually join the rows of mourners, sunglasses or not. There's security; I hadn't counted on that. A man in an expensive suit is standing at the door with a clipboard, checking people against a guest list. And I don't imagine my name is on it.

I stand back and try to figure out my next move. I feel foolish; I'm not even sure what I thought I could accomplish by coming here. I had some vague idea—not from any true insight into criminal behavior, but from a novel or movie, some other writer's assertions about sociopaths and the way they act—that sometimes a murderer will feel compelled to join in the activity that follows his crime. Watch the faces in the crowd scene when the body is discovered; keep an eye on the guests who come to pay their respects. If I have any talent at all in social situations, it's my ability to fade into the background and observe, and I suppose I thought that if I put myself in the right room, I might be able to zero in on a suspicious figure filling a plate at the hors d'oeuvres table, telegraphing his guilt to me and only me.

I watch the comings and goings for a little while. Guests arrive—no one famous, or at least no one I recognize—put on somber faces, and walk gracefully up the steps, pretending they don't know they're being photographed. Every so often someone comes outside to have a cigarette or to make a phone call. The windows of the building are all stained glass; no way to see inside.

I watch one of the smokers, a tall, slender woman who I think must be around my age, though she might, from a great distance, be mistaken for someone younger. She looks familiar, but I can't place her—is she an actress? She has dark hair, short and artful, and she's wearing a black skirt with a sleeveless, beaded top: funeral meets cocktail party. She looks good, though. It's not something I could pull off.

She lifts her head and sees me watching her. I look away, embarrassed, and pretend to search for something in my purse. I consider approaching her and asking for a cigarette, but I've never been a smoker, and I don't think I could make it believable.

When I close my bag and glance up again, I see she's still watching me. She finishes her cigarette and drops it on the asphalt; then she begins to weave through the crowd in my direction.

I smile pleasantly, noncommittal enough that it won't be too awkward if it turns out she's going to see someone else. She walks closer, peers at my face.

"Octavia?" she says.

So much for my brilliant disguise. "Yes?" I say mildly. I'm nervous, ready to turn and retreat if she starts yelling that the murderer's mother is here. But instead she puts her arms out and pulls me into a hug. I'm slightly uncomfortable—I still haven't placed her—but I'm touched by the gesture, so unexpected, here of all places. It occurs to me that I've been hugged more this week than I have in a year or more.

"I didn't expect to see you here," she says after she lets go. "Though of course I've been thinking about you. I got your e-mail that you were in town."

The pictures lock into their proper slots. "Lisette," I say. "Lisette Freyn."

"Bingo," she says, taking out another cigarette.

. . .

There's an analogy I came up with once for an interviewer who asked me how much of my material was autobiographical. I said that the life experience of a fiction writer is like butter in cookie dough: it's a crucial part of flavor and texture—you certainly couldn't leave it out—but if you've done it right, it can't be discerned as a separate element. There shouldn't be a place that anyone can point to and say, *There—she's talking about her miscarriage*, or *Look—he wrote that because his wife had an affair*.

So Lisette Freyn—the living, breathing girl who dropped out of school to follow a rock band from city to city, the embodiment of all of our mothers' worst nightmares, rediscovered years later as a casual online friend—has never found her way into my books. Just as it's true (do I even need to say it?) that none of the fictional husbands I've written are Mitch, not exactly, and none of the children—loved and mourned and resented and worried over—are Rosemary or Milo. And none of the protagonists are me, except in the sense that of course they all are.

But the teenage girl in *The Human Slice* owes some of her fragile self-assurance to Lisette (or at least to my fragmented memories of her), and if Lisette were to peer into the surface of my books, looking for her own reflection, she'd find a handful of minor characters who share one or more of her traits: a gesture, a verbal pattern, a little piece of life experience. The story of Lisette Freyn has become part of my own inner mythology, a drop in the reservoir of history, memory, and invention that I dip into when my pen begins to run dry, until I almost forgot there was a real person at the center of it. But here she is, standing in front of me.

"What are you doing here?" I ask abruptly. "I mean, *here* . . ." I gesture toward the rounded building, the crowd of watchers. "Did you know . . . do you know the family?"

She nods, blows smoke through her lips. "Her mother's an old friend of mine, from way back. Bettina was a beautiful girl." She shakes her head. "It's a terrible, terrible thing."

"I agree," I say firmly. "It's awful."

"I've never met Milo," Lisette says, looking at me intently. "But I'm just about the only person in Kathy's life who's sticking up for him at this point. I keep telling her, there's more to this story, and we can't just make assumptions when we don't have all the facts."

I nod. "Thank you," I say.

She crushes out her cigarette. "Well, I should get back in there. The service will be starting soon." She looks at me curiously. "What are *you* doing here?" She points toward the Columbarium, as I did a minute ago. "I mean, *here*."

I pause. "I don't know," I say. "I knew that it was happening today, and I just wanted to come. I don't know why, I thought . . ." I trail off. Honestly, I don't know what I thought. "I didn't realize I wouldn't be able to go inside, though."

"Oh, you want to go in?" she asks. "I can get you in." She smiles conspiratorially. She seems excited, as if we're kids who are about to get away with something.

"Really?" I say. "Are you sure?"

"Sure. But keep your glasses on, and try to stay away from Kathy. She'd probably freak out if she saw you. And she can be a little . . . dramatic."

That almost stops me. This isn't a game; there's a woman in there who has lost her child. I think of the memorial service we had for Mitch and Rosemary: a double funeral, rarer even than a double wedding. It was wrenching but also, strangely, the best day of the ghastly year that followed their deaths. It was a day when I was not expected to be strong for my son or to put the tragedy behind me and move forward to whatever might come next. There was no embarrassment in crying, no awkwardness in talking about the two of them as much as I wanted to. And I wasn't alone, left by myself with a child I could hardly look at.

Paradoxically, that's the thing—the memory of Milo, nine years old and so lost, my shame over being the kind of mother I was in those years—that makes me follow Lisette as she turns and starts walking through the crowd. I follow her up the marble steps, right up to the man with the clipboard.

"Hi again," she says to him with a wide smile, holding up her pack of cigarettes. "I'll probably be in and out a million more times. It's an addiction." And then, casually, as an afterthought, she puts her hand out toward me, as though she's going to introduce us. "She's with me, by the way," she says. "She's a dear friend." And then she takes my arm and sweeps us inside before he can even answer.

. . .

The building is beautiful inside, everything marble and mosaic and gold leaf. There's a central rotunda, three stories high and topped with a stained glass dome, surrounded by a circular path that edges the circumference of the building. I keep my head down as I walk through groups of funeral-goers, talking quietly to each other and pausing to examine the compartments lining every wall: little brass doors up to the ceiling.

"So," I say softly to Lisette as we walk around the bending pathway. "A columbarium is a place where people store ashes?" I'm trying to remember my Latin. The root derives, I believe, from the word for "dove," and I imagine each of those alcoves on the wall as a home for a bird, cooing and rustling and laying eggs, instead of a place that holds piles of ashes, the barest remains of human lives.

"Right," she says. "There are no cemeteries in San Francisco—did you know that?"

"I did," I say. "I was just reading about it this morning." And I was, in my search for gravestones-that-aren't-gravestones, trying to figure out where Milo might have gone on the night of the murder. But it's also one of those things I might have filed away once in my mind: a corner of society so desperate for space that the dead are unearthed to make room for the living. A city that holds no ghosts; a metropolis reserved for the breathing. Present company excepted. "What happens to people who don't want to be cremated?"

"They get buried in Colma, a little ways south of here. It's all cemeteries there, cemeteries and car dealerships."

"How far away is that?"

She shrugs. "Maybe twenty, twenty-five minutes down 101." Unlikely, I think, that Milo would have driven that far in the condition he was in. I make a mental note to add this information to my hotel-letterhead timeline.

We walk slowly, looking at the vaults and niches on the walls. There are plaques with names and dates, as in any repository for the dead, but there are also glass-fronted cabinets where people have arranged mementos that remind them of their loved ones. I see a toy car, a picture of a man with a dog, a full bottle of brandy. Handwritten letters, silk flower leis, a thermos from a Batman lunch box.

"It's a beautiful building," I say.

"Yeah," says Lisette. "Actually, this is where I vote. They put the machines right there." She gestures toward the central rotunda, currently filled with folding chairs and a couple of tables set up with food and drinks. And then, vaguely, she continues: "Harvey Milk is in here somewhere." Certain things are coming back to me about Lisette. I remember that she speaks in non sequiturs and then acts surprised that you haven't been inside her mind to follow the same path.

"Not a huge turnout," I say, looking around.

Lisette shakes her head. "The capacity's pretty small. I don't think you're allowed to have more than fifty or sixty people. And Kathy wanted to keep it exclusive. She's been negotiating selling the photo rights to a couple of different magazines. I think *Us Weekly* is ahead in the bidding." I stare at her, and she shrugs. "It's for charity," she says. "She just didn't want it to be a total circus."

Lisette excuses herself to say hello to somebody. I've been deliberately keeping my back to the center of the room; I haven't spotted Kathy Moffett yet, and I want to keep a low profile. But when Lisette walks away, I turn and scan the room. Even though the crowd that's gathered here isn't large, it's decidedly glamorous. One thing that always strikes me as false in funeral scenes in films and TV shows is that everyone's always dressed entirely in black: no dark blue suits, no splashes of color, no print blouses because that's what you had in your closet and you didn't have time to go out and buy something new. But that's the way it is here. These people might have been outfitted by a costume designer.

There's a stack of programs on a low table nearby, and I pick one up. The paper is thick and heavy. On the front there's a picture of Bettina, standing in the sun, smiling, and the words "A Celebration of the Life of Bettina Amber Moffett, December 24, 1984–November 9, 2010."

Lisette returns and puts her hand lightly on my arm. "People are starting to sit down."

We walk toward the rows of folding chairs, and finally I catch a glimpse of Kathy Moffett, standing in the center of a tight knot of people. I feel somewhat relieved when I see how occupied she is. She'll always be in a group today. I should have no trouble staying out of her way.

Lisette and I take seats in a row toward the back. I open my program and pretend to read it while I look at Kathy. She's a tall, slim woman with blond hair down to her shoulders. She has the kind of face—strangely thin nose, overly round cheeks—that I associate with plastic surgery. And I was wrong, not everyone here has followed the dress code so scrupulously. Bettina's mother is dressed entirely in white.

There's a harp set up on one side of the rotunda, and a woman sits down on a low stool and begins to play. It takes me a minute to recognize the song; it's "Someday We'll Be Together," by the Supremes.

When the song ends, a man in a suit steps up to the podium at the front of the bank of chairs. He's younger than I am—in his forties, maybe—and he has red hair and very pale skin. He clears his throat and waits while everyone settles down.

"Good afternoon," he says. "My name is Tom McGinn, and I'm a pastor at St. Jerome's. On behalf of her mother, Kathy, I welcome all of you to this gathering in remembrance of Bettina Moffett. I've had some time over the past few days to talk to some of the people who loved Bettina, and I hope I'll be able to do justice to the memory of her short but charmed life.

"Bettina was born here in San Francisco on Christmas Eve, 1984, to a nineteen-year-old girl named Kathy Moffett. I didn't know Kathy then, but it sounds like she was a remarkable young woman. She told me that even though she was young and unmarried, she made a promise to her daughter the night she was born: *My darling girl*, she said, *I will do everything in my power to take care of you and to give you a good life.*

"Bettina was a beautiful child, bright and happy and lovable. She showed early talent in dance and in art, she always did well in school, and she was a joy to everyone who knew her."

I let my eyes drift to a table set up next to the podium, scattered with framed photos of Bettina. Some of them are too small to see from here, but there are several I can make out. There she is, a baby in a high chair with frosting on her face, and then she's eight or nine, wearing a green bathing suit and sticking her tongue out at the camera. There's one of a toddler Bettina, two or three years old, sitting on her mother's lap; they're both wearing black leather jackets, and Bettina's wispy blond hair has been gelled into points. (Halloween? I wonder. Or just a glimpse of a younger, hipper kind of parenting than I'm used to?) I look at the girl in the pictures and try to figure out what I feel about her.

"By the time Bettina was a teenager," the man is saying, "she had grown into a beauty, and she did some modeling work, though Kathy was careful to make sure that it didn't interfere with her having a normal teenage life. Bettina and her mother had an extraordinarily close bond—many people said that they were more like sisters than mother and daughter."

On one end of the picture table there's a vessel of hand-blown glass in swirls of red and purple and blue and gold. It looks like a vase, or an oversized perfume bottle, and I realize with a bit of a jolt that it's the urn. This girl, this woman, whose life is being summarized so neatly for us, the one my son lived with and loved and believes he might have killed—she's there, in that bottle. That's all that's left. I look at the round stopper stuck in the urn's fluted mouth, and I imagine that it's holding in something more vital than dust and rough fragments of bone. Some spirit, some misty essence that might fly out if I were to step up there and simply remove the lid. I look at the girl in the green bathing suit, and I think about genies and wishes.

"Bettina went on to college, and she graduated with flying colors. She was a smart young woman, and her options were limitless. Family members speculated that she might go on to law school or medical school. But like so many before her—her own mother among them—she fell in love with the music scene, and she never looked back."

It's all so pat, as if she sat at her desk looking at brochures for "cardiologist" and "rock star's girlfriend," making lists of the pros and cons. I wonder what kind of absurd simplifications will be made someday to my own life story. And then I wonder, idly, whether I'm famous enough for the *New York Times* to have a prewritten obituary on file.

"And so," Pastor Tom McGinn is concluding, "we can all take comfort in the fact that though Bettina's life was cut tragically short, it was indeed a life well lived. And now Bettina's mother, Kathy, is going to say a few words."

As Kathy rises from the first row and walks toward the podium, I look down at the program on my lap so that a hank of hair falls over my face.

"Thank you all for coming," she says. "This has been, obviously, an extremely difficult time for me, and I'm so grateful for everyone's kindness and support."

There's a pause. "Bettina was my life," she says abruptly. "I always tried, above all things, to teach her that she was precious, that she had value in this world. I believed that self-worth would be enough to ensure that she would stand up for herself, that she would never let anybody hurt her. And to learn that this beautiful, vibrant woman, my baby girl, was a victim of domestic violence, and had been for possibly years before her death, has been utterly heartbreaking to me."

A note of anger begins to hum in my chest. I glance up at Kathy, still angling my face down. She looks fervent, purposeful: a crusader. I see for the first time that she has a button pinned to her white silk lapel, a badge with a picture of Bettina's face.

"Every year," she says, "two to four million women are assaulted by a domestic partner. Studies show that fully half of all women who are murdered are murdered by a husband or boyfriend."

I lean close to Lisette's ear. "She certainly has her statistics down."

I've forgotten for a moment that they're friends, but Lisette doesn't seem offended. "She does a lot of charity work," she whispers back. "She has this cat that only has one eye."

"The last time I saw my darling girl," says Kathy, "was about an hour before she died. The last night of her life was a turbulent one. She called me early in the evening, more excited than I've ever heard her. She was with the man who would later kill her, whose name I will not speak aloud, for fear of polluting my daughter's final resting place. But she was with that man, a man I had welcomed into my home, a man I did not yet know was capable of violence or brutality, and he had just proposed to her. She called me to say they had decided to get married."

There's a little bit of a rustle among the guests. This is not a detail that the police have made public. No one's rude enough to whisper, but everyone sits up a little straighter.

"Less than an hour later," Kathy says, "she called me back, in tears. She had caught this man, whom she had trusted and loved, in a lie. A lie of such huge magnitude that she could no longer imagine spending her life with him. I wish I had told her then to get away from him and stay away. I wish I had told her to come to my house—" Her voice breaks.

There's a pause, a single muffled sob. Kathy clears her throat. "But I still didn't understand what this man was capable of, and Bettina wanted a clean break. She asked me to come over and help her pack her things."

I clasp my hands together in my lap, tightly, and watch as the knuckles turn pink. I'm furious, but I don't know if I have any right to be. If this were my daughter, instead of my son . . . I don't know.

"And so I went over, and I did my motherly thing. I supported her and hugged her and let her talk and cry. When she'd calmed down, she told me she was going to go to sleep and finish packing in the morning.

I felt uneasy about her spending another night there, though I couldn't have said why. But I knew that my daughter was a grown woman and that it was not my role to tell her what to do. So instead I gave her a hug and told her she could call me anytime. It was the last moment I ever spent with her. I remember reaching over to brush the hair away from her face, just like I did when she was little. *Good night, my love*, I said. *Things will look better in the morning.* And she smiled and said, *I love you, Mom.* And then I walked down the stairs and out of that house, which is something I'll never be able to forgive myself for."

She hasn't mentioned Milo coming home drunk. She hasn't mentioned him yelling as she stood in the doorway or smashing the planter on the concrete.

"I have been to hell this week," she says. "And that's nothing compared to the pain and terror Bettina must have felt in those last moments. Her death was vicious, and it was senseless. But I've decided that maybe I can use this tragedy to make sure that some other mother and some other daughter don't have to go through this kind of hurt. I have a legal battle ahead of me—seeing this man behind bars for the rest of his life is my first priority—but when that's done, I'm starting a foundation that will help young women get out of abusive environments before it's too late. And I'm going to call it Bettina's House."

I'm afraid people are going to applaud, and they do. I want to get out of here, and I want to do it without being noticed. I don't see any choice but to wait until she's finished talking.

"If you'd like to contribute to this worthy cause, there's a box by the door. You can also pick up a flyer with information about the Web site I've started, and please, everyone, take a button. We owe this to Bettina."

More clapping, and finally Kathy says, "And now, please stay and have something to eat. After a short break, we're going to reconvene, and I hope some of you will get up and share your memories of Bettina."

She steps away from the podium, and we're released.

I lean over to whisper to Lisette, "I'm going to make my exit before anyone spots me."

We hug briefly, and I keep an eye on Kathy over Lisette's shoulder.

She seems to have started a one-person receiving line, so I should have a few minutes to get out without being seen.

I leave the rotunda and make my way around the outer circle toward the door. There's a sudden roar of sound from the crowd outside, and I step into an alcove and pretend to study a memorial niche that contains a china teacup and a photo of a Labrador retriever. If there's something going on, I don't want to be in the middle of it.

I hear the man with the checklist addressing someone outside the door. "I'm sorry, sir," he says, "but I can't let you in. I've received very clear instructions."

A male voice answers, though I can't make out the words.

"Well, like I said, my instructions were clear, and if I need to call security, I will."

Another reply I can't hear.

"Thank you for understanding," Checklist says, his voice a little lower. "If it were up to me, I'd let you in. I'm a huge fan."

I wait another moment and then leave my nook and head for the door, as casual as any invited guest. I smile at Checklist as I go.

When I step outside, I see that there's still a bit of a commotion, with people taking pictures and yelling questions. Everyone's attention is directed at an expensive black car stopped just outside the gate. I see a dark suit, the back of a man's head as he opens the rear door. And then, just before he disappears inside, he looks up and glances over the assembled crowd. His profile is unmistakable. It's Roland Nysmith.

"Roland!" I shout, but there are thirty people shouting the same thing, and he doesn't hear me. The door closes, the car begins to move, and I take off after it like it's 1964 and I'm a teenage girl hoping to touch the hallowed flesh of a Beatle.

The car speeds up, and of course I'm no match for it. The driver turns the corner, and they're gone. I'm breathing hard, and I nearly twist my ankle while I'm lurching to a stop. As I walk away from the Columbarium, I look back just once to confirm what I imagine I'll see behind me: a crowd of people staring at the spectacle I've become, a middle-aged woman running after a rock star's car.

\\\|//

"What I did on my summer vacation is I killed my sister and my dad."

Excerpt from an essay by Milo Frost,
September 1992

Chapter Nine

Mitch and I met when we were in college and married shortly after graduation. At the time he died, we'd been together fourteen years. Our marriage was . . . well, it was many things. Is there truly anyone who can say *My marriage was* _____ or *My husband was* _____ and think they've said anything at all? Complexity, that's what it's all about. The simplest thing that can be said about any person, any relationship, is that it's not simple at all. (You should see me when I get called for jury duty and the judge asks me if there's any reason I might not be able to approach a case impartially. It sounds like a riddle to me; I genuinely don't know what to say. Have I ever been impartial, about anything? Is impartiality even possible within the confines of human nature? Usually after a few moments of this I'm free to go.)

So Mitch and I were . . . happy, yes, but happiness isn't what people think it is. There is no synonym for "happiness" that could possibly describe the entirety of a life shared by two people. Bliss? Joy? Ecstasy? Not outside of romance novels and the expectations of twelve-year-old girls. Contentment comes closest, but it errs on the other side. Say your marriage was content, and it sounds like you're damning it with faint praise.

So this is how I'll describe it: our marriage was affectionate and tiresome, passionate and dull. After so many years together, the quality of love changes. It's not that it fades or weakens, but it doesn't follow the same clear path it did at the beginning. There's a certain clogging of the arteries; each resentment, each disappointment leaves its trace, and those narrow passages become built up with detritus, making it harder for blood to pass through. The heart, whose job is not to love or to warm or to break but simply to move that vital fluid from place to place, becomes strained with new effort. It grows bigger, not because its capacity has changed, but because that's what happens to a muscle when you make it work too hard.

And so you focus on the minutiae of each day and lose sight of the larger picture, and slowly the miraculous becomes commonplace. You board an airplane without thinking that it should be impossible for such a machine to take flight; you live with another person, forging good days more often than bad, and never stop to think how unlikely it is that the two of you should be so lucky. A change of perspective is all it takes to shake loose your assumptions: a cloud seen from above instead of below; a husband gone, when you thought you had time to spare.

To say I've been lonely since Mitch has been gone isn't quite right. I live inside my head, and I've always been my own best company. But to be fully known? To be wholly and tenderly understood? That's something I haven't had in eighteen years.

. . .

I limp away from the Columbarium—my heels aren't terribly high, but they weren't intended for running—and make as dignified an exit as possible after my apparent descent into adolescent frenzy. You could say I'm feeling battered, or you could say I'm feeling sorry for myself; either way, the seemingly endless series of hits thrown in my direction this week is catching up with me, and for a moment I think I might actually cry. But I summon . . . not strength, exactly, but emptiness, neutrality, and I concentrate on moving one foot in front of the other until I've put some distance between myself and the roomful of well-dressed people who are so easily convinced that my son is a brutal man.

I'm at a loss as to what to do next. I've felt this way on book tours, when I'm in an unfamiliar city for a day or sometimes less: it's an opportunity of uncertain nature. There's free time to fill, but not enough to see very much, and anyway, I'm not here for pleasure. My only home base is a hotel, and to retire indoors, to lie down and watch a pay-per-view movie in the middle of the afternoon, much as I may want to, feels like the kind of pathos I might write into a book if I wanted to paint a character as particularly unadventurous. But what am I supposed to do, go to Fisherman's Wharf?

I take my phone out of my bag and check my messages; there are none. And then I do something that requires a surprising degree of determination: I turn it off.

Immediately I feel better, the kind of relief a bleeding animal might feel upon finding someplace hidden to lie down. I walk aimlessly until my feet begin to hurt, and as I go, I think about nothing except the question *Where do I want to be?* The answer, as it turns out, is that I want to be nowhere at all.

I stop on a corner and find a cab—more difficult here than in any large city I've been to—and I ask the driver to take me to a movie theater. A big one, I say. One with a lot of screens. Mitch and I did this a few times in the years before we had kids: go to a theater and see the next show that's starting, no matter what it is. Mostly we saw films that were forgettable (and one or two that we both truly hated), and at the time it was just a way to occupy an afternoon, to combat the kind of lazy, affable boredom that we took for granted until our first child was born and then never had again for the rest of our marriage.

But in the years that I've been alone, especially since Milo's been out of the house, it's become something different for me. It's a way to let chance into my life, relinquish control and see what the universe has to show me. New Agey of me, I know, and a bit grand, especially when so often the universe has nothing more to offer than a romantic comedy about a bland couple who meet when his mutt impregnates her purebred. But I believe coincidence can reveal connections that might not have emerged otherwise, and I think this is as good a means of divination as any. Study the flight of birds in the sky on any given day; stand a book on its spine and let it fall open to whatever page it may. Or enter a dark room with no expectations and see what images come to life.

The driver drops me in front of an ornate building on Van Ness Avenue. I walk through an enormous arched portal of bronze and glass set in the middle of four terra-cotta columns, into a cavernous lobby. Fourteen screens—that's what I like to see. I walk up to the ticket counter—it's a little after four in the afternoon, and there's no line—careful to keep my eyes away from the electronic schedule above my head.

I'm about to ask the young man behind the glass for a ticket to the next movie starting, and I'm ready for the look he's sure to give me, skeptical and world-weary in the way only a twenty-year-old can be. But then I stop. As it turns out, I don't want to leave it up to the universe.

"Hi," I say. "Can you tell me if *The Dying Brain* is playing?"

I'm absurdly tempted to elaborate further: *The Dying Brain*, based on the novel by Sara Ferdinand, my old writer friend from college. Sara Ferdinand, winner of the prestigious Jeanne Kern Prize for Fiction. My partner in a thirty-year-old rivalry that perhaps only I am aware of.

The boy behind the counter looks pointedly at the timetable on the wall, which indicates that the movie is occupying not one but two of the theater's screens. Well, good for Sara Ferdinand.

"Next show?" he asks, and I nod. He pushes a button on the panel in front of him, and a ticket pops up cheerily through the slot.

I pass my money under the glass and take the ticket. "How long until it begins?" I ask.

More exaggerated looks, this time at the written information on the ticket and the clock behind him. "Fifteen minutes," he says. "Theater nine."

"Thank you," I say, smiling sweetly. "You've been a big help."

I walk across the lobby, and now that I'm no longer keeping secrets from myself, I stop to look at the posters. The one for *The Dying Brain* has the same picture as the cover of the paperback I bought at the airport the other day: two women in profile (both well-known Hollywood actresses in their thirties, in the midst of that dizzy flip where beauty and substance switch positions of importance), facing away from each other, against a background of undulating lines that I suspect are supposed to be brain waves, though they could just as easily be points on a graph charting, say, the rise and fall of paper sales in the mid-Atlantic region.

I fight the impulse to turn on my phone and check my messages quickly before the show starts, try one more time to reach Joe or Chloe. No one in the world knows how to reach me—a vertiginous place to stand in this day and age. But isn't that why I'm here?

I buy myself a box of Junior Mints and ride up a series of escalators, find a seat in the nearly empty theater. I sit back to wait and think for a few moments about Sara Ferdinand.

Sara and I met in a creative writing class our sophomore year of college. We both already considered ourselves Writers-with-a-capital-W in a way that makes me cringe now, but it was also clear early on that we were the two most talented students in the class. We weren't as good as we thought we were, of course, nor as good as we'd later get, but it would be disingenuous for me to pretend there wasn't something there, some spark, some flow of blood that separated our work from our classmates' graceless sex scenes and moony dissections of unrequited love in a philosophy seminar.

And so we were drawn together. But always, at the back of my mind—and hers, I can only assume—the question remained: which of us had a stronger hold on this gleaming, ineffable thing? Which of us could stretch it further? More than thirty years later, I still don't know the answer.

As I've mentioned, I haven't read *The Dying Brain*—I stopped buying Sarah's books five or six novels ago, though I'm quite thorough about reading her reviews—so I don't know much about the plot, but I do know that it has something to do with academia; a woman who's a professor, I think. Sara has taught, off and on, for most of her career, and her novels often take place on a college campus.

One of the best parts of having friends who are fiction writers is that you get to mine their work for psychological bombshells: unspoken yearnings, unflattering preoccupations, neuroses blooming from a bit of history you've seen firsthand. Yes, I know: butter in cookie dough, I said it myself. But that's not to say that there isn't a fair bit of tangling between life and fiction. We are the people we are. We each have one mind to tap, one life to learn from. We're fairy-tale emperors, all of us: we're naked, but we have you convinced we're dressed in the richest silks.

Not too long ago I met a woman at a party who, I gathered, was familiar with my work. I was careful not to ask her opinion—I've learned the hard way that that's not always something you want to hear—but as our conversation progressed, she began to speak more frankly. "Your books are beautiful," she said. "But so many children die."

Well . . . yes. I may spend more time on trees than forest, but I'm not so obtuse that I hadn't noticed that pattern. But in spite of the simplicity and obviousness of the observation, I found myself completely at a loss. I'm afraid I wasn't very polite, though it wasn't that her comment had angered me. I felt ashamed, somehow, that I'd inserted so transparent an obsession into the books I'd written, and there was no way to get it back out. She was watching me, waiting; she genuinely thought she'd asked something I could easily answer. I smiled unconvincingly and made some kind of nonreply. And then I walked away, naked in a roomful of people.

The lights go down, and the previews begin. I've often imagined what it would be like to sit in a movie theater and watch a trailer for a film based on one of my books; for some reason, that's almost more exciting to me than seeing the actual film. *Coming this fall, based on the novel by Octavia Frost* . . . which one would it be? *Carpathia* has been optioned and is supposedly "making the rounds" in Hollywood, though that doesn't appear to mean anything. I suspect the general feeling is that there have been too many movies about the *Titanic* already. For a while it looked like *The Human Slice* might go forward, but it seems to have stalled somewhere along the line, and maybe it's for the best. Do I really want to see my delicate and complex novel, a story I lived inside for almost three years, reduced to *A wife who wishes she could remember; a husband who's glad to forget* . . . ?

A reminder to turn off our cell phones (which I ignore, with a rather irrational feeling of smugness), several film company logos, and then the credits start to roll. On the screen . . . yes, it's a woman walking across a college campus. Way to be fresh, Sara; way to try something new.

I'm suddenly jumpy, and I realize it's because I'm waiting for Sara's name to go past. The screenwriter gets billed first, I notice. And then, on the screen for a full three seconds, there it is: SARA FERDINAND, big, big, big. I suck the chocolate skin from a Junior Mint.

The film takes a while to get going, but the basic story is this: Our heroine, a woman named Frances, is a neuroscientist. She teaches graduate seminars and does research that involves studying the pain receptors of mice. She's recently divorced and about to take a sabbatical, during which she intends to write a book about phantom pain—the sensations that, for example, an amputee feels in the limb that has been removed. So nothing heavy-handed there.

While Frances is away, the university will be hosting a visiting professor. (Also a female neuroscientist—what are the odds?) This other woman, Cleo, is British; she's a single mother with a young son named Felix. Her research, however, is a bit more controversial than Frances's, and also less obviously useful: she's studying what happens to the brain during a near-death experience. For better or for worse, Cleo is portrayed from the very beginning as being more of a free spirit than Frances; in one early sequence, we see Frances preparing a meal of brown rice and vegetables, intercut with shots of Cleo allowing her son to eat waffles and ice cream for dinner because they've both "had a rough day." The two women correspond, and they decide that it makes sense for them to swap houses for the duration of the semester.

Incidentally, Cleo's research is where the film gets its title. Certain phenomena that occur during near-death experiences are inexplicably universal: people across many different time periods, regardless of culture or religious belief, have reported seeing tunnels, bright lights, a feeling of floating and looking down on one's body from above, and so on. Those who believe in such things take this commonality as evidence of a life hereafter; scientists and skeptics, on the other hand, have suggested that these effects are merely hallucinations caused by neurons misfiring as the brain shuts itself down at the moment of death. Logical Frances subscribes to the dying brain theory; flighty Cleo would like to prove it wrong.

So, all right. Sara's got her metaphors all set up and neatly packaged: science and faith, the tangibility of pain and the uncertainty of heaven. The symbolism's a bit precious for my taste, but I suppose I'm with her so far. Writing the story forward in my own mind, I'm expecting that moving into each other's houses will change the women more than they expect. Settling into the neat lines of Frances's life, Cleo will learn to be a more responsible mother; Frances, living in Cleo's crowded, whimsical cottage, will loosen her restraints and have an impetuous and slightly self-destructive affair with Cleo's brooding ex-boyfriend. In the process, Frances's research will benefit from a more creative approach, and Cleo will discover that the dying brain theory and life after death are not mutually exclusive after all. If that's the way it goes, then as a viewer, I'll leave the theater fairly satisfied; as a long-time friend-slash-rival of Sara's, I'll be positively giddy at the predictability of it all.

But that's not the way it goes. About an hour in, the story takes a turn I don't like. Frances, wandering through her borrowed house one rainy day, comes upon some of Cleo's journals. After an unnecessary and rather drawn-out "will she or won't she?" scene in which Frances stares at the pile of books as she drinks an entire bottle of wine, she finally opens one up and begins to read. And she learns something disturbing about Cleo. She learns that Cleo has given some thought to the possibility of "inducing" a near-death experience in her son.

It may already be clear that my feelings toward Sara are rather prickly. Our friendship has gone through its share of ups and downs over the years. Once when we were still students, I told her about a humiliating experience I'd had in high school gym class, and she listened with an expression of casual interest; her next short story contained the episode, almost verbatim, and I watched in shocked silence as our professor and fellow students praised her imaginative plotting. Still, we were close for a while; she was at my wedding, and she sent gifts for each of my children when they were born. She published her first book quite a long time before I did—hers came out in 1985, while mine wasn't until nearly a decade later—but we were good writing friends, exchanging manuscripts long-distance and taking each other's comments seriously. I didn't know many other writers, and I valued both her insight and the sense of companionship forged by our shared experiences.

Then Mitch and Rosemary died, and Sara was among the first batch of people that I called. Her reaction was like everyone else's at first—shocked, sad, kind. And then she said something that absolutely stunned me.

"This is going to sound horrible," she said, and for one last moment, I still trusted her enough to think that no honest thing she could say to me now would be horrible. She went on: "But I'm almost jealous in a strange way." I remember her laughing then, awkwardly, a hollow sound. "At least you've found your material," she said. "I'm still waiting for my tragedy."

I can't draw the lines easily here. It's not that she's Frances and I'm Cleo; it's never really that simple. And Sara has never once suggested that I was in any way responsible for what happened that day. But the emergence of this plot twist—a mother actually putting her child in danger because it will further her work—reminds me of that comment all those years ago, and suddenly I know that she was thinking of me when she wrote it. And it makes me sick.

I consider getting up and leaving, but endings matter to me, and I want to see how she's going to wrap this up. There's some convoluted business about the sudden death of Frances's mother, whose last words are about a beautiful, shining light, and it turns out I'm right about Frances's affair with Cleo's ex. But eventually Frances discovers that Felix truly is in danger, and she rushes back home to save him. Cleo is sent to prison for attempted murder, and in a bit of writing requiring a rather substantial suspension of disbelief, Frances is granted custody of Felix. To top it all off, Frances hits pay dirt in her research and discovers a new way to alleviate human suffering, for which she wins a fictitious award that seems to be just one notch down from the Nobel. And I can only assume that this particular university never again supports scholarship involving any aspect of the afterlife.

I stay in my seat all through the credits, until the lights come on and someone comes in to sweep up the popcorn. I'm thinking about a particularly colorful critique I heard once, years ago, when I was teaching a writing seminar. "Jeff's stories," this young woman said, "always make me feel like I've stepped in vomit." (With a mind like that, I don't know why she wasn't a better writer.) I've been waiting a long time to use that phrase myself, and I've finally found the opportunity, even if it's only in my own head.

I leave the theater and make my way down the escalators. Finally I turn my phone back on, and I see that I have a new voice mail. I listen to it expectantly and find that it's from my agent, who on most other days is the person whose messages I'm most interested in hearing.

"Hi, Octavia," she says. "It's Anna. I hope you're doing okay in the middle of all this . . . God, what a horrible situation. I wanted to let you know that I've heard back from Lisa at Farraday about *The Nobodies Album*. Which is pretty remarkable, given how short a time it's been since you sent it to her. Give me a call when you get this. It's not exactly what we were hoping for, but I think it might be good."

Her vagueness makes me uneasy. I don't know if what I'm feeling is typical nervousness—my opinions about my own work are spectacularly unstable, bouncing between swollen overconfidence and debilitating insecurity—or a hint of doubt about the project itself, but I'm apprehensive about hearing Lisa's reaction to the manuscript. When I first told her the idea for *The Nobodies Album*, the question she asked was, *Why?* It seemed like something I should have an answer for, but the reasons that came into my head—*because I can; because as long as I'm alive, nothing has to be set in stone*—seemed paltry, not nearly substantial enough to justify the outlay of risk and money required to publish a book.

I won't pretend that there were no personal factors involved in my decision to revisit my earlier novels. From this remove, it's hard to recapture the desolation of the Octavia who began this project, the woman who was afraid she might die before she ever saw her son again, who would have bet money that she'd never sit on a sofa with a grandchild at her feet. It had been almost three years since I'd spoken to Milo, almost three years since I'd received his brusque note saying that he'd read *Tropospheric Scatter* and would appreciate it if I wouldn't try to get in touch with him.

My thinking about *The Nobodies Album* with regard to Milo was not quite as simple as "Writing caused this problem; maybe writing can fix it," but it was along those lines. Rock stars are good at making themselves inaccessible to the general public, and that was the group I had become a part of. Letters and e-mails were ignored; packages were returned undelivered; phone calls dead-ended in high-pitched tones and automated voices that told me the number was no longer in service. I was running out of ways to reach him, and *The Nobodies Album* felt like a loophole, a back door: the plot twist where the guy delivering the balloon bouquet serves you with legal papers. I'd made a name for myself, and I might as well use it to my advantage. I couldn't make him read it, but if I did it right, there was no way he could prevent it from entering his consciousness.

I didn't realize then how important the timing would be—that the very day I intended to place the book in someone else's hands would be the day it became too late. The situation I find myself in now, this gnarl of doubt and accusation and lives irrevocably changed: *this* is what I was trying to prevent.

But redeeming myself to my son was not by any means my only concern. I can't emphasize this strongly enough. My work matters to me, and I hope that it matters to my readers; I may be self-absorbed, but I would never presume that a public gesture of apology was any basis for a work of literature. The day I began writing *The Nobodies Album* was a day of artistic epiphany for me. It was a day of wonderment and humility and assumptions tumbling to the ground.

I suppose you could say I'd been thinking about endings. I'd had a biopsy; my doctor had found a mass in my breast, and I was waiting for him to call with the results. It was a morning like a blank page, and I couldn't really do anything but wait and see what kind of words were going to fill it.

My Only Sunshine had been published a few weeks earlier, and lines from some of the reviews were still floating around in my head. I've mentioned, I believe, that critics were not exactly rising to their feet as one to cheer my achievement, and one writer had suggested (not particularly kindly) that the problem with the book was that it covered the wrong period in the protagonist's life. He said that the only time the novel captured his interest—and this is where I can almost garner some sympathy for the downtrodden reviewer: can you imagine hating a book so much and not being allowed to simply put it down?—was the second-to-last page, when we flash forward to the hours before this unnamed woman's death. This character lives seventy-one years, he wrote, seventy-one years amid the aftermath of her mother's committing suicide, leaving her to be raised by an abusive father, and this is the part of the story the author has chosen to show us? Teething and diaper changes?

It wasn't that I necessarily agreed with him. But from the vantage point of the tightrope I found myself walking that day, I suddenly wished, very much, that I had given that baby girl a chance at a better life than the one she ended up living. It hit me with a force as strong and sudden as grief: I had created this character, made her out of nothing and set her down in the world, and then carefully and systematically sucked away every bead of hope. And I felt I had made a terrible mistake.

Which is not to say that I thought everything should be happy and sunshiny. Her life was her life; unless I started from scratch and wrote something completely new, there were a lot of circumstances that neither she nor I could change. But I wanted to remove some of the bleakness I had written for her so blithely. I wanted to give her a chance.

I went into my office and pulled a copy of the book from one of the boxes I'd received from the publisher. Just as an exercise, just to lessen my own guilt, I wanted to see if there was any way I might have done things differently. I've always said that the ending of a novel should feel inevitable. You, the reader, shouldn't be able to see what's coming, but you should put the book down feeling satisfied that there's no other way it could have gone.

And yet, as I paged through the story I'd settled on, I could see the traces of the hundred different stories I'd rejected. *Here* I'd made a choice, and *here*, and *here*. It was all butterfly wings and tornadoes: even a slight deviation in any one of those places would be enough to set the whole book on course for a different outcome.

I hadn't felt so invigorated by an idea in a long time. It seemed to me powerful, and revolutionary, and . . . inevitable. The questioning of the artistic process; the redemption of character and author in a single blow. By the time the phone rang—and I picked up to hear the voice of the doctor's receptionist instead of the doctor himself, which told me everything I needed to know—I was sitting on the floor, surrounded by all the books I'd written, looking for ways to change the course of history.

I look at the time to see if it's too late to call Anna. It's after nine p.m. on the East Coast, nine on a Friday night. I have her cell phone number, but I've never used it, and it doesn't really feel appropriate to do so now. She usually answers e-mail over the weekend, so I'll just have to hope I can get in touch with her that way.

I walk out of the theater. I see that it's gotten dark, and I feel a sense of loss: another day in my life spent without Milo. A week ago such a thing wouldn't have been extraordinary at all, but now it feels like a fresh wound. I wonder if he's punishing me, making me sweat before he reaches out. Or has he decided to cut me off completely once again?

I'm trying to decide whether to go back to my hotel or get some-thing to eat at the diner I see across the street when my phone actually rings. I look at the number; it's Chloe.

"Hello," I say, sounding regrettably eager.

"Octavia," she says. "It's Chloe. I was just wondering—did you get Milo's text?"

It takes me a minute. "No," I say. "I don't even know how to read text messages on my phone."

Chloe laughs. "See, that's what I told him. You're lucky I'm around. I mean, not that you're not totally-I'm-sure tech-savvy, but texting is kind of a generational thing."

"Right," I say. "So . . . what did it say? Is everything okay?"

"Oh, everything's fine. Well, you know, not fine, but not worse than yesterday. I think he just said that you should come over to Roland's for dinner if you want to. We're just ordering some takeout."

"Thank you," I say. "Yes, I'll come. Can you tell me the address again?"

She does, and I repeat it. "Lia will be glad you're coming," she says. "She was just talking about you."

"Really?" I say.

"Mm-hmm. She asked me what Uncle Milo's mommy's favorite color is."

I look around me: rust-colored taillights, red and green neon, black-denim sky. And I think of Lia as she looked when I met her, violet dress, auburn eyes. "Purple," I say. "Tell her it's purple."

"She'll like that," Chloe says. "That's her favorite, too."

We hang up, and as I start to look for a cab, I'm thinking about time-lapse video and the way that it can reveal the aging of a flower from bloom to wilt or turn a dotted procession of headlights into an unbroken white line. Imperceptible movements made visible; the sum of our progress revealed. I think of the furrow my footsteps have made upon the earth, my life's passage written as a single continuous crease, and I wonder what obeisance I can make, what prayer I can offer, to keep that line moving in this direction, on and on, until my time is through.

From the Jacket Copy for

SANGUINE

By Octavia Frost

(Farraday Books, 1997)

〃〃〵

Matilda, a young widow in sixteenth-century England, supports herself and her son, Hugo, through her work as an "empiric" lay healer. Her skill at bloodletting and delivering babies has made her an indispensable member of her community. But now, as more and more female healers and midwives are charged with witchcraft, Matilda reluctantly puts away her lancet and her herbs. Until Hugo falls ill.

A novel about redemption, maternal responsibility, and that vital substance that flows through our veins, *Sanguine* is a poignant and gripping achievement.

On the tenth day of June in the year of our Lord 1572, I was taken to the Court of Assizes held at Chelmsford for the County of Essex, before Sir Edward Saunders, Lord Chief Baron of His Majesty's Court of Exchequer. When I was called to the Bar, I proclaimed to all assembled that I wished to plead not guilty, whereupon the jury heard the details of the Crown's evidence, as shown in my examination before the Justice of the Peace in the Quarter Session in my own town of Maldon.

The jury—fine men all, I'm sure—heard how Sarah Baker had come into my house carrying a basket of eggs and found me kneeling beside Hugo's bed, my hands splashed with blood. (No matter that he had been cold and melancholic a half hour before, and that bleeding him was the only way to release the evil black bile. No matter that any physician or barber would have done the same.) They heard that I had been present at the birth of Sarah Pilly's baby, and that the girl had been born blue and still, and again that I had been with Beatrice Spynk at the birth of her son, which child is now a drooling idiot who spends his days tied to a pew in the church in the hope that the divine words of the Mass will soothe his mad soul. They heard how Margery Carter examined me and found me to have a Devil's mark in the shape of a crescent moon between the blades of my shoulders. (This I have never seen, but I know it is there because my husband would sometimes put a finger on it and say that it must be good luck to have a wife who carried the moon on her back.)

There seemed to be no end to it all. I keep a frog; I have used love magic to provoke a depraved infatuation in the chaplain Thomas Corker; my son was once heard to say that "Mama can see me even when she's not looking," and subsequently I was discovered to have two freckles that appeared as eyes on the back of my neck.

When at last the alleged evidence of my wrongdoing had been presented, the jurors retired with a list of the prisoners whose fate they were to judge. There were sixteen of us, and the jury took only an hour to return with their decrees. I watched as a vicar was ordered to be pilloried for slander and a peddler was sentenced to hang for stealing birds' eggs. And then the judge read my name, and one of the jurors—a bony man who I suspect suffers from a harmful excess of phlegm—pronounced me guilty. The judge had me brought forward so that he could look at my face as he told me my lot: death by hanging, for the crime of witchcraft. I shall be executed tomorrow week.

. . .

In the gaol, as I starve and freeze, I have much time to reflect upon my various crimes and to ready myself for my reckoning. I am kept with the other women who are awaiting punishment. We sleep on the floor with the rats and mice, and when the food is brought in, we fall upon it like wild beasts. None of us is above using our fingernails or yanking at someone's hair to try to get a larger share for ourselves. When villagers pay the turnkey tuppence to come and jeer at us, we take it in turns to stick an arm through the metal grate in the hopes that one of them will pass us a bit of hard bread or an apple gone soft and brown. How many times have I given a penny at church for the Souls in the Hole, thinking it would provide them with something more than this?

Because I am known as a witch, I am given a bit of space. There is one other here who is to be hanged for witchcraft, but as her crime was merely attempting to learn the span of the Queen's life through divination, she is not as feared as I. I am the one who killed harmless babes and sickened my neighbors' pigs. I am the one who took a lancet to my child's arm and drained his blood into a basin for Heaven only knows what evil purpose.

My child lives, I tell them. My child lives because of my ministrations, and if I had my herbs and my purgatives, my cautery irons and my urine flask, I could ease all of your ulcers and your hemorrhoids and your apoplexies. But the group of them—thieves and poisoners and heretics—do not want to hear.

When it is dark, though, and the imminence of our souls' departure weighs heavy on us all, sometimes one or another of them will come to ask my help. Mary Gadge, who murdered her husband barely a month ago, wants me to bewitch the turnkey so that he will fall in love with her and help her to escape. Agatha Nanton, a scold who will soon have her tongue cut out, wishes me to teach her to fly. And Susanna Tabart, a habitual beggar, wants me to wring her neck before the hangman has a chance to.

Aside from that, the only time anyone speaks to me is when the Reverend John Wolton comes to offer comfort and spiritual advice. I'm happy to sit with him and listen to his words about repentance and redemption, but I don't tell him that my soul is not the thing I worry about. I have made my confessions, though not all of them are the ones he would like to hear, and I trust that my soul will live on, as God wishes. I mourn for my body, splendid companion that it has been, which two days hence will cease its life forever. I mourn for my broken neck and my stilled pulse, for the blood that will no longer flow through my limbs, for the skin that will waste into dust. The vital apparatus of bone and muscle, nerve and humor, is God's greatest work. And though I am ready for death, I am sorry to leave it behind.

. . .

Thoughts of Hugo are, of course, the last in my head before I rest and the first to rouse me when the sun has begun to creep. In my most pitiable moments, I have wept to think that I have orphaned him so wretchedly. Though my sister will keep him and feed him, though his cousins will find room on their pallet that he may lie down and sleep, he will always now be a boy alone. But I cannot dream a way that it might have been different, and if it pleases our Lord that I die so my son may live, I can have no argument. I cannot believe God will punish me, for I have done no more than He asked. This is what mothers are meant to do, the most important job we're given: we keep our children alive.

. . .

The morning of my death, the guards come to get me soon after breakfast. They put me into shackles and take me outside to lead me to the village green. Though they handle me roughly and though I know where we are going, it is a relief to be out of the dark, stinking gaol.

"Not much time left," one of the guards says to me. "Best be thinking about your crimes and asking God for forgiveness."

I think of the fevers I have eased and the babies brought safe to this world. If I have committed crimes, they were not crimes in my heart.

My first sight of the gallows sets my blood racing, but I gather my courage and stand tall. A crowd has gathered to watch and, I suppose, to cheer for my demise. But I do not know any of them. For good or ill, my kinfolk and neighbors are far from here. If I am to be jeered and spit upon in my last moments, I suppose I would rather it were done by strangers.

As I climb the steps, I'm thinking of Hugo, his stubborn chin, his hair like a haystack. My boy. I will never see him again. But he lives. My child lives.

The crowd is noisy, but I'm high above them. All the times I have stood in such a throng, standing on my toes so I might see some scoundrel brought low, I never knew how distant we seemed to the poor soul climbing to his judgment. Their shouts and gibes are no more to me than the buzzing of flies. I am apart from them already. I walk on feet that will never again touch the dirt.

The headsman places the rope around my neck. The day is bright, so bright. And I find myself, in a frightened moment, whispering "God forgive me," though I do not know what guilt I might be confessing.

I breathe in, steady myself on the platform. A cracking noise, an instant of movement. And I feel myself go.

Excerpt from

SANGUINE

By Octavia Frost

REVISED ENDING

/||\\

The crowd is noisy, but I'm high above them. All the times I have stood in such a throng, standing on my toes so I might see some scoundrel brought low, I never knew how distant we seemed to the poor soul climbing to his judgment. Their shouts and gibes are no more to me than the buzzing of flies. I am apart from them already. I walk on feet that will never again touch the dirt.

The headsman places the rope around my neck. The day is bright, so bright. And I find myself, in a frightened moment, whispering "God forgive me," though I do not know what guilt I might be confessing.

I breathe in, steady myself on the platform. A cracking noise, an instant of movement. And for a curious moment I find myself back in our little house in Maldon, kneeling by Hugo's bed. I've been bleeding him for what must be a very long time, and I fear the treatment has stopped working. But still I keep at it. I move feverishly; this is my child, and I will get the poisons out of him. I hold my bowl aloft and gently squeeze his flesh until Sarah Baker walks through the door and sees the poor pale babe, lying lifeless on his little cot. She drops the eggs she's carrying and lets out a woeful cry. "Matilda," she says, her voice full of fear. "What have you done?"

A cracking noise, an instant of movement. As I feel myself go, sliding out of the sieve of my body, I have a terrible moment of pain and of knowing. I am overcome by my grief and my shock and my guilt, and I fear that God has abandoned me, or that I have abandoned Him.

But it only lasts a moment. For there he is, my Hugo, a figure of light at the edge of the crowd. Waiting for me. He holds out his hand, and I go forward to meet him.

Chapter Ten

/|||\

The cab pulls up in front of Roland's house, and I pay the driver. I step out into the shallow bath of artificial light produced by the photographic equipment of those hardy souls who are still camped out here, hoping to get a shot of something valuable.

"Good evening," I say to the assembled group as they document my walk toward the gate, my pressing of the intercom button. I get a few replies, and some shouted questions—*How's Milo doing? Has he said anything to you about the night of the murder?*—but I sense a new listlessness in the effort. I haven't turned out to be very important after all.

A voice I don't recognize—a woman, possibly a housekeeper?—speaks to me through the intercom, and I identify myself and am granted admittance. As I pass through the gates, I'm thinking about *The Wizard of Oz*, the scene where they enter the Emerald City. I should choose my spectacles now, decide how I want to color whatever lies inside.

I walk up the steps and ring the bell. After a moment I hear some unexpected scrambling—quick footsteps, a raised voice—and the door opens, but just barely, no more than an inch or two. Then a man's voice ("Let me get that"), and it swings open the rest of the way to reveal Joe, with Lia in his arms. He steps back, both to let me step in and, I think, to remove Lia from the doorway, from the sight line of the group gathered below.

"Hi there," I say to Lia as Joe closes the door and sets her down.

"You're here," she says in her clear little voice, the ends of the words not quite closing into *r*'s. She looks me over and puts her hands on her hips. "I thought I told you to wear purple," she says.

I look down at my dark skirt and blouse, my drab funeral clothes, smiling at the mimicked sternness in her tone. "Sorry," I say. "Maybe next time. You're not wearing purple either." She's wearing a loose red dress in some kind of jersey material.

"No," she says. "I'm wearing my twirly-whirly dress." And she spins to show me how the skirt billows.

"I have something for you," I say. I open my purse and pull out the white bag containing the item I bought this morning at the hotel gift shop. It's not much, but it was the only child-friendly thing I could find without resorting to candy. I hand her the bag, and she peers inside, then pulls out a small stuffed bear wearing a T-shirt that says "San Francisco."

"Oh," she says happily, "it's my new teddy bear." She rubs its soft nose across her cheek. "I've been waiting for this all day."

I burst into laughter and look at Joe, who smiles and shakes his head with that look of resigned affection that parents have: *I don't know where she gets this stuff.* "And what do you say, Lia?" he asks. But she's already running back toward the kitchen. "Thank you," she calls, without turning.

"How are you, Mrs. Frost?" Joe asks, ushering me in.

"Okay," I say. "Do you think you might be able to start calling me Octavia?"

"I doubt it," he says.

I follow him into the kitchen, and there they all are, sitting around the table: Milo, Chloe, and Roland. Lia has climbed into Chloe's lap, and Chloe holds on to her with one hand while she leans over to pour wine into Milo's glass. They're eating Indian food, fragrant and colorful, and there's an extra plate and utensils on the counter, next to a line of Styrofoam containers.

Still a miracle to walk into a room and see Milo there. He looks tired and unhappy, and I have an impulse to go over and kiss his tangled hair, but I'm not sure if that would be okay. Chloe and Roland smile and greet me, Roland standing and gesturing for me to help myself to some food. Milo smiles, too, and adds his voice to theirs, but he's still looking down at his plate, and I don't know whether that means anything or not. I have a seasick feeling, unsteady, like a dream. Here, in front of me, everything I wanted without daring to say so: my son sitting at the dinner table, waiting for me; a roomful of people who might yet become friends; a radiant child my heart can lay claim to. But the picture's a little off-center, like a filmstrip with a cog out of gear. I don't know how much of it I can trust.

I walk to the counter where the food is. The kitchen is a huge room, beautiful and well appointed but slightly bland. I suspect it was designed to appeal not to Roland in particular but to a generalized profile of the type of person rich enough to buy the house. I pick up a plate, spoon rice, chickpeas, chicken in a coral-colored sauce. Then I carry it to the table and sit down in an empty chair between Milo and Roland.

I touch my hand briefly to Milo's shoulder. "How are you?" I say.

He shrugs, finally turning to look at me. I look at his dark eyes, his long lashes. Strangers used to stop me—at the park, in the supermarket—to comment on how beautiful his eyes were. "Okay," he says. "I didn't even leave the house today."

"That's not good. You should try to get outside." Such a motherly thing to say. I feel like I'm reading from a script.

"It's not worth it," he says. He raises a hand and moves it through the air from left to right to indicate, I gather, reading something. "'Less than a week after the murder of his girlfriend,'" he says, "'Milo Frost was seen buying a pack of Life Savers.'"

Joe smiles grimly. "'Early reports indicate they were Wint-O-Green.'"

Milo continues, "'A source close to the suspected murderer reports that he plans to eat them in a dark room, to see if they really do create sparks when you crunch them.'"

They're laughing now, and Milo's finally looking a little more relaxed. They've always had this, this easy back-and-forth quality to their friendship, and I hadn't even realized I'd been missing it. As I look at them, I'm thinking about the way the house used to come to life when the two of them walked in the door, the sound of them dropping backpacks and ransacking cupboards for a snack, debating different interpretations of sentences girls had uttered in their presence during the course of the day, and I feel a sort of homesickness that doesn't have anything to do with place.

"I need to pee," Lia says, wriggling off Chloe's lap and whirling toward the kitchen door.

"You know where it is," Chloe calls after her. "Call me if you need help."

"So maybe you can see," Milo says, turning back to me, "that I'm going a little stir-crazy."

"Nice to have some company," Roland says, "instead of just me and Milo rattling round the house by ourselves."

Chloe exhales a brief laugh. "The fan fiction practically writes itself," she says.

"Oh, Christ," says Roland.

Joe looks amused. " 'I've heard stories about prison,' Roland said, striding across the room and putting a hand on the younger man's shoulder . . ."

They all laugh, and Milo looks at me as if he's trying to decide whether to translate, like I'm an elderly grandmother in a babushka who speaks a little English but misses most of the subtler notes of conversation. I save him the trouble, look down at my plate, and take a bite of spinach.

I know what they're talking about, in any case. There's not much about Milo online that I haven't seen, and it was a matter of some interest to me to learn that there were people who spent their time turning my son into a fictional character. I don't read many of the stories—they're mostly about sex (most often with Joe, which I wondered about until I learned it's a common quirk of the genre), and like any mother, I protect myself from images I don't want in my head. But with some careful screening—the authors assign them ratings, like movies—I've been able to find a few of the less racy ones, and I'm rather embarrassed to say I've bookmarked them all. I'm fascinated by the glimpses they afford, glimpses as hypothetical as my own, though it's nice that someone else has done the work of imagining it for me. Milo walking into a recording studio. Milo bored on a tour bus. Milo having lunch at a restaurant with friends.

These writers are girls, mostly, and young women, and they want to strip Milo down in every possible way. They imagine a scene and write it a hundred different ways. They can't stop trying to think how it might happen. For all their graphic bravado, they're no more than a roomful of girls pressing Barbie dolls together for the thrill of doing something dirty. I suppose we wanted our daughters to be freer about sex, women of my generation. Now this is what they do instead of scratching "Mrs. Milo Frost" into their school desks.

I understand something about the obsession that motivates these girls, the longing to bridge the distance: Look, here he is, right in front of you. Get as close as you want. I've spent some time lurking in the chat rooms, watching the process by which these fans create their own versions of Milo. They start from the barest of materials—song lyrics, quotes from interviews—and build him up out of nothing. His elasticity as a subject is apparently limitless. Sometimes people request scenarios: Milo as a werewolf, Milo in an alternate universe in which men can become pregnant. It's a commissioning of art, a new Renaissance— payment in enthusiastic comments, marked with winks—and in fanciful moments, I imagine what these writers would make of my requests. Milo goes back to college and graduates this time. Milo calls his mother on her birthday. Milo in an alternate universe where he passes over *Tropospheric Scatter* and picks up *The Human Slice* instead.

"I'll tell you," Roland is saying to Milo, "I miss the days when girls wanted to fuck me instead of wanting me to fuck you." He laughs, and then his eyes settle on me. "Oh, well, strange days," he says, buttoning the conversation closed, remembering that this isn't the way you talk around people's mothers, even if they are several years younger than you are.

Lia comes running back into the kitchen. I wonder if she ever walks.

"Can you eat a little bit more?" Chloe asks her, lifting her onto her lap. She gestures toward Lia's plate, which contains only a scoop of white rice and a samosa with a single bite taken out of it.

Lia pushes it away. "Not hungry," she says, sounding slightly irritable. Then, brightly, "Can I have a snack?"

Chloe stands up, setting Lia on her feet. "Roland, do you mind if I look around for something she'll eat?"

"Oh, sure," says Roland. "Let me think what I've got. Would you like some grapes, darling? Or some toast and jam?"

"No," says Lia. "I want a snack from the freezer."

The two of them head toward the refrigerator at the end of the room, negotiating between fruit and ice cream.

"Octavia Frost," Roland says, turning to me. "I have to confess I haven't read any of your books."

I smile graciously. This is never a surprise. "Oh, no need . . ." I say and trail off. I look sideways at Milo, who's looking down at the table, his face impassive. Joe's looking at him, too, trying to gauge his reaction. I wish the subject hadn't come up at all.

"But I'd like to read them," Roland says, oblivious to the tension, if there is any, if I'm not making it up. "Which one should I start with?"

I'm never sure how to answer this question. I don't particularly subscribe to the idea that writing books is analogous to having children—for one thing, your work on a book *ends* when you see it in print, though that's clearly something I've begun to question—but there's a sort of *Sophie's Choice* aspect at play here that I don't like. *Are you asking me which ones are good,* I want to say, *and which ones aren't worth your time?*

Here, at least, my choices are narrowed somewhat. Clearly I'm not going to mention *Tropospheric Scatter* in front of Milo. I think about what the question means: *Which story will I enjoy spending time in?* or *Which slice of yourself do you want to show me first?* And I say what I never say: "*Crybaby Bridge.*"

Crybaby Bridge is my first published novel. I wrote it the year after

Mitch and Rosemary died, and I finished it in seven weeks. I'd heard stories before then about writers who had been so captured by an idea that they put aside the manuscripts they'd been working on for years, unable to rest until they put these new stories to paper. I'd never quite understood it; my own work had never felt quite that urgent. It was sort of a joke to me: *I'm jealous. Where's* my *six-week book?*

I can say now that it's not an experience I'd like to repeat. It was a horrible time, sharp and raw. I just said that writing a book is not like having a child, but here the analogy seems apt: sometimes a quick birth just means the flesh will tear rather than stretch.

Crybaby Bridge is a dark book, and a bit polarizing; readers either love it or hate it. But when I think about which novel I'm most proud of, which one is *me* to the greatest degree, that's the one I always come back to.

"All right," says Roland. "*Crybaby Bridge* it is."

I resist my impulse to fill the air with talk—*Oh, I hope you like it,* and all that. He'll either like it or he won't. And it shouldn't matter to me either way.

"Are you working on anything new?" Joe asks me.

I hesitate, looking at Milo. In a way, this is what I've been waiting for: a chance to explain . . . well, to explain what, I'm not sure. That I'm changing my novels—my legacy, if I can be grand enough to call it that—and that in some convoluted way, I'm doing it for him? That I've written myself into my books, and I have some kind of overly literal idea that by changing the books, I can write a new ending for myself? I don't know. But whatever it is I want to say to him, it's personal. "Not at the moment," I say lightly.

Chloe and Lia come back to the table with a banana and a dish of chocolate ice cream. Chloe peels the banana and hands it to Lia. "Four bites," she says. Lia takes four bites quickly, one after the other, then chews and swallows the mouthful with some difficulty. Chloe nods and hands her a spoon.

I've finished eating, and I pick up my plate and carry it to the sink.

"Oh, you don't have to do that," Roland says. He stands and gathers a few other things from the table, places them on the counter next to where I'm standing. "You can just leave that in the sink," he says. "There's someone coming in the morning."

"I'll just rinse them," I say, turning on the water. Roland stands and watches me for a moment, then he smiles slightly. He turns and makes another trip to the table, carries back some wineglasses.

"Tell me," I say to him in a low voice. "How's Milo doing really?"

He shrugs. "Today was a hard day," he says. He leans closer and drops his voice. "Bettina's funeral," he says.

I look at him briefly before turning my eyes back to the plates I'm stacking. "Did any of you go?" I ask.

He shakes his head. "No. Kathy didn't want us there."

I can't decide whether to take that as a lie or not. It's certainly true that he didn't go to the funeral, in the sense that he didn't make it past the door.

"Did you know Bettina well?" I ask.

"Oh, yeah, I'd known her for years. I was the one who introduced her to Milo, did you know that?"

I shake my head.

"New Year's Eve party, two thousand ..." He stops to think. "Two thousand six, it was, or two thousand six turning into two thousand seven. Right in this house."

I think about the dates. Christmas 2006 was the last time I'd seen Milo before yesterday. New Year's Eve would have been just a few days after I hugged him good-bye at the airport, a few days after he went inside to buy the book that would set all the dominoes toppling.

Roland hands me a glass, and I glance at him, curious suddenly about what his life is like. "When's the last time you washed dishes?" I ask.

He laughs softly. "Nineteen seventy-four?"

We're quiet for a moment, and then Roland leans in closer. When I look at him, his face is solemn.

"Listen," he says. "I don't know what Milo was going on about yesterday, but I don't believe for a minute that he killed Bettina." He shakes his head. "Not a chance."

I'm surprised how much of a relief it is to hear someone else say it. "Thank you," I say. "Really."

A flash of motion catches my eye, and I turn to see Lia running toward us across the kitchen, her mouth outlined in sticky swipes of chocolate. She's taken her shoes off, and she's wearing tights, and just as I turn, her feet slide on the smooth floor and she falls on her bottom. I see her face, frozen for several seconds in surprise and silent misery until she draws enough breath to cry out, and then her wailing fills the room like a siren.

I'm the closest, so I bend and pick her up with my wet hands—she's so light! I've held cats that weigh more than this—though it occurs to me too late that she doesn't really know me and this might make things worse. She struggles for a moment, legs stiff, back arched, and then she collapses into me, pushing her face into my neck as she screams. I rub her back, make gentle shushing sounds, loving the compact weight of her in my arms and thinking about other crying children I've held: Milo, forever wiggling out of my grasp; Rosemary, holding on for dear life. I rock Lia gently and make quiet noises into her hair until Chloe reaches us and takes her from me.

I see Milo watching me with an expression I can't read, and I turn back to the sink, self-conscious.

"Sorry," Chloe says to me. "She's been a little fragile lately. She can tell something's going on with the grown-ups."

Joe comes over, puts a soothing hand on Lia's back. He speaks quietly to Chloe. "It's not just that she can tell. It's that you *told* her."

"Enough," Chloe says, her voice low and sharp. "There was no reason to lie. It's a part of life."

Chloe turns away from Joe and walks in circles, slow and swaying, until Lia's cries get softer. "We should get going, anyway," she says. She still sounds annoyed. "It's past her bedtime. Octavia, do you need a ride?"

"Oh," I say. I dry my hands on a dish towel. "No, don't go to the trouble. I can get a cab from here, can't I?"

Milo speaks from the table, where he's still sitting. "I can drive you, Mom."

I draw in my breath, my happiness at this small gesture all out of proportion, and duck my head to hide the smile spreading across my face. "Thank you, sweetie," I say. "But are you sure? Don't forget..." I think for a second. "'Milo Frost seen sitting in car outside local hotel.'"

He shrugs. "Can't hide in here forever. And there are fewer of them at this hour."

Joe has gathered up Chloe's purse, Lia's shoes, and the new teddy bear. "Well, have a good night," he says. "We'll see you soon."

"See you," I say.

"Say good-bye," Chloe says, but Lia is sleepy and still hurt, and she doesn't want to talk. I touch her hair, dark and tangled, like Milo's.

"Good night, little girl," I say. They leave, and I feel suddenly shy, alone with Roland and Milo.

"Would you like another glass of wine before you go?" Roland asks me.

"Sure," I say. "That would be nice." I walk back to the table and sit down next to Milo.

"Where are you staying?" Roland asks as he pours.

I tell him.

He sets the glass down in front of me. "You know," he says, "you're welcome to just come stay here. We've got plenty of room."

I take a sip of wine and look at Milo. He's nodding, but he looks a little stunned. "That would be fine," he says in a neutral voice.

I laugh at his politeness and clear lack of enthusiasm. "Well, thanks for the offer. I'll definitely consider it." I'm glad to be where I am, and I don't want to push it.

"Roland, could you tell me where your bathroom is?" I ask.

"Of course," he says. "Go back through the front hall, first door on your left."

I walk out of the kitchen and back through the entryway. On my way, I stop to look at a collection of framed photos on a long table by the wall. In most people's houses you won't find many familiar faces in this kind of display, but here there are quite a few that I recognize. Roland, young and golden, goofing around with his bandmates from The Misters. A publicity still from the film of *Underneath*. One of Roland with Lia on his lap. Several of Roland with other celebrities and public figures: Bob Dylan, Mick Jagger, Bill Clinton. A young Charles and Diana.

There's a picture of Milo and Bettina that I pick up to examine more closely: they're on a jetty paved with cobblestones, water all around. They're sitting on a curved lip of marble right at the edge, their legs dangling over the water. Wherever they are, it has the look of an ancient ruin, or almost: giant plates of rock stacked into tall irregular piles. There are pipes sticking out here and there—I can't guess what their function might be. This may be the first time I've seen a picture of the two of them where they're not dressed up for some public event, the first one I've seen that might have been snapped not by a tabloid photographer but by a fellow tourist they've handed their camera to. They're holding hands; they look ordinary and serene. Happy.

There aren't many faces here that I can't immediately identify. An old wedding photo from the 1940s or '50s: Roland's parents, perhaps? One of Roland standing in a playground, pushing a child in a swing. It's a little girl, blond, maybe five or six years old. I stare at her face; she's so familiar to me, and I can't think why. Then I place her. It's a child I've seen in other photos, just earlier today. It's Bettina as a little girl.

Chapter Eleven

/|||\

When I get back to the kitchen, I make an excuse about the time change catching up with me, and I ask Milo to take me back to my hotel. Roland repeats his offer to let me stay at the house, and he kisses my cheek before we leave.

Milo leads me down a flight of steps to a cavernous garage and unlocks an expensive-looking silver sports car.

"Nice car," I say.

"It's Roland's. The police haven't released mine back to me yet."

"Oh," I say. Blood—they're checking it for blood. "Right."

Milo opens the garage door and pulls out into the street. There's a flurry of lights and camera flashes, but we're past them quickly.

"Can they get pictures at night, through the tinted windows?" I ask. "Or will they just get reflections from the glass?"

Milo laughs humorlessly. "I don't know," he says. "We'll find out tomorrow."

It's not that late, only a little after nine, but I'm exhausted. I yawn, and try to gather some energy.

"So today was the funeral," I say.

I watch his face in the intermittent brightness of the streetlights. He looks defeated.

"I should've been there," he says. "But even if Kathy hadn't . . ." He searches for a word. ". . . *banned* me from going, it wouldn't have been possible."

I think about those mourners in their impeccable clothes, their fervor as they listened to Kathy's words. I imagine how they would have reacted if Milo had walked through the door.

"I was there," I say abruptly.

We come to a stoplight, and he turns to look at me. "What do you mean?" he asks.

"I mean, I went to the funeral."

"Why?" His voice is almost suspicious.

I hesitate. "Because you couldn't, I guess. Because I wanted to know more about Bettina." *Because I don't believe you murdered her*, I don't say, *and I thought that being able to piece together stories made me some kind of detective. Because I'm your mother, and I wanted to know if they were saying unkind things about you.*

"Well, you didn't get inside, did you? I'm sure they weren't just letting anybody in."

"I ran into an old friend, who was a guest. She got me in."

He glances at me, baffled, as if he can't even figure out what question to ask first.

"Only you, Mom," he says. He rubs his eyes like he has a headache.

I'm not sure what he means by that, and I choose not to interpret it.

He shakes his head, still looking bewildered. "Did Kathy recognize you? Your picture's been everywhere lately."

"No. I managed to keep a low profile."

"Well, that's good. I hope no one else did either."

"I don't think anyone did," I say. My voice is a little rough. I'm feeling chastened, though I don't think I did anything wrong.

"Okay." He gives up trying to figure out the details. "How was it?"

"It was nice," I say guardedly. "There were a lot of pictures of Bettina. She was certainly a beautiful girl."

He nods. The light outside the car catches the stubble on his chin and upper lip. I hope his lawyer will tell him to shave before any court appearances. I wonder if he should cut his hair, too; it's almost to his shoulders, though maybe no one cares about that anymore.

"Her mother spoke," I say. I'm sure he's going to hear about this soon enough anyway. "She's starting a charity, or a foundation or something, in Bettina's name. It's for victims of domestic violence."

I watch his face. He looks shocked; then, after a minute, angry.

"Is that what she's saying? That I was abusive to Bettina?"

"Yes," I say quietly.

"But . . . does she . . . is she just talking about the murder, or does she mean, like, the whole time we were together?"

It's an odd distinction, or maybe it's not. Is it worse to commit one crime of passion than it is to terrorize a person you love over a period of years? There's no way to answer.

"Both," I say.

"Goddamn it," he says. He pulls the car to an empty space by the curb, puts on the brake. He shakes his head slowly, raises his hands in a gesture of frustration. "This is so typical of her."

"What do you mean?" I ask.

"I don't know, to . . ." He makes a furious, strangled noise in his throat, like a growl. "To find a way to make this even worse, you know? To make it be about even more than it already is."

I watch him, wait for him to continue.

"It's like . . . okay, this is going to sound strange, but do you remember one Christmas when I was little, we had the news on, and there was a story about a house that had burned down and the whole family had died?"

I shake my head. "No."

"Well, the news people just kept saying, 'And on Christmas, too,' like it would have been any better if it had happened any other day of the year."

"Okay," I say. I'm not sure where he's going with this.

"Kathy's just . . . It's always all about her, you know? If her house burned down, she'd want it to be on Christmas."

I'm quiet for a moment. "They were close, weren't they? Bettina and Kathy." My voice is wistful. Daughters are different from sons, but I wonder what that meant to him, to see such an intimate bond between a parent and a grown child.

But he rolls his eyes. "Too close. Kathy and I got along okay, but it was like she was competing with me to be the most important person in Bettina's life."

There's a flash outside Milo's window, and I realize someone's taking our picture.

"Fuck," he says. He sighs and turns the car on, pulls back onto the road, swerving around the photographer.

I wait until we've gotten a few blocks away. "Did anything ever happen between you and Bettina that Kathy might have misinterpreted?"

"I don't know. I don't think so." He looks at me suddenly. "I never hurt her, okay? I don't know if you think that I might have, but I didn't."

"Okay," I say. "I know." I pause. "But you still think you might've been the one . . . ?"

He sighs. "I don't know, Mom, okay? I just don't fucking know."

We're getting close to the hotel, and I don't want to leave him this upset. "I believe that you never hurt her," I say. "I can tell that you really loved her."

He's quiet for a minute. "I really, really did," he says, his voice still hard. "And it fucking sucks that I don't get to . . . to *grieve* for her, like any other person who loved her."

"Yeah," I say. "That does fucking suck."

He laughs, as I was hoping he would, and the tension dissipates a little. I reach out and squeeze his arm. "I really wish I had had a chance to meet her," I say. "And I hope that someday when things aren't so crazy, you'll tell me more about her."

He pulls up in front of the hotel and stops the car. "Yeah," he says. "I actually think you would have liked each other." And it's more of a compliment than I could have hoped for.

"Okay," I say. "Wait—before I go, I wanted to ask you something. Roland mentioned that he's the one who introduced you and Bettina. How did *he* know her?"

"Oh, God, that's a whole complicated story. Can I tell you tomorrow? I just want to get back home."

"Sure," I say. "So I'll see you tomorrow?"

"Sure," he says. "And you know, if you want to stay at Roland's, it's fine with me."

I lean over and kiss his cheek. "Thanks," I say. "We'll see."

I get out of the car and watch him pull away. As far as I can tell, he's not being followed by anyone looking for a news story. I walk into the hotel and take the elevator up to my room.

. . .

Later, as I'm getting ready for bed, it occurs to me that I still haven't seen Milo's text message. I pull out my phone and spend a few minutes figuring it out. Finally I find the right screen and see that there are actually two messages waiting for me.

I look at Milo's first. It says, "hey mom, dinner at rolands if u want 2 come." I smile. So casual, as if we talk this way all the time.

The second one, I see when I open it, is from Lisette. "Hi O, good to see you, tho sorry such bad circs. Let me know how long your in town. Maybe we can get 2gether."

I send her a message back—I think successfully, though I'm not certain—in which I say, more or less, that I'd like that, and maybe we can talk tomorrow. I write out every single word, without abbreviations.

I open my laptop and send an e-mail to Anna saying that I'm sorry I missed her call, and that if she has a chance to call me over the weekend, I'm anxious to hear whatever news she has for me.

I notice that I still have FreeMilo.com open in a window, lurking in the background. Giving in to my baser impulses, I click Refresh. I want to see if they're saying anything new.

And they are. I catch my breath. Across the screen, in big letters: "Milo's mother speaks!" And just underneath, italicized and flashing: "Read our exclusive interview with Octavia Frost!"

I click on the link. A new page opens, and there I am; they've used my most recent author photo, easy enough to find a copy of. I begin to read.

Q: *Well, first of all, Ms. Frost, thank you for taking the time to speak to us.*

A: Oh, I'm happy to do it. Anything to get the truth out about my son.

Q: *I suppose that answers my first question: do you think he's guilty?*

A: Of course not. I'm his mother. But even if I weren't . . . I know Milo, and I don't think he'd be capable of such a thing.

Q: *What was Milo like as a child?*

A: Very sweet, very likable. But he did have sort of a dark side. He had a temper.

Q: *Was he ever violent?*

A: No, not at all. Well, I mean, just in the usual kid ways.

Q: *Such as?*

A: Oh, you know. He might have hit his little sister a few times, but what brother hasn't? There was nothing we were ever concerned about.

Q: *What do you think of Pareidolia's music?*

A: (Laughs) Well, it's not all my cup of tea, of course. But I'm proud of him. He's always had a beautiful singing voice.

Q: *Ever been to one of their concerts?*

A: (Long pause) No. Actually, I haven't.

Q: *Why is that?*

A: Milo and I haven't been on the best terms in recent years.

Q: *No?*

A: No. We've just grown apart, I guess. It happens when children grow up.

Q: *Did you ever meet Bettina Moffett?*

A: No. But from what I know of her, I don't think I would have liked her.

Q: *Why do you say that?*

A: Oh, I don't know. Just a hunch. You know mothers never think their sons' girlfriends are good enough for them.

Q: *Was Milo a rebellious teenager?*

A: Oh, yes! I can laugh about it now, but at the time it didn't seem very funny. He ran wild. He was out all night more times than I can count. I was always calling the police, afraid he was going to show up in the morgue. I never knew what he was up to. I was widowed, you know, so there wasn't a father figure around to instill discipline.

Q: *Did your writing career have any impact on your relationship with him?*

A: Well, I suppose so. I was always off on book tours and whatnot, so I wasn't home as much as I could have been.

Q: *Are any of your characters based on Milo?*

A: I think I'd better plead the fifth on that one!

Q: *Tell me a little about Milo's childhood.*

A: Oh, it wasn't so different from anyone else's. We were a typical middle-class family.

Q: *Two-point-five kids and a dog?*

A: Well, two-point-zero kids. And we had a number of pets over the years, but we weren't lucky with animals—they all seemed to meet unfortunate ends.

Q: *And I don't want to pry, but . . . you experienced a family tragedy in 1992.*

A: Yes. My husband and daughter died. Milo was . . . let me see, nine at the time. It changed him, it really did. I don't think he was ever the same afterward. It was awful for me, too, of course, but I was able to bounce back eventually. I'm not sure Milo ever has. If you listen to his lyrics, he does seem to have an odd fascination with death.

Q: *Well, thank you very much for your time. We'll all be hoping for a good outcome for Milo.*

A: Thank you. (Pause) He's a complicated person, but I'm sure . . . I mean, as sure as I can be . . . No. He didn't do it. He couldn't have.

Q: *Of course.*

A: And I have a favor to ask you: do you mind including a link to my most recent book?

By the time I finish reading I'm seething, and I'm also feeling the first loose ripples of panic. This is not me—I didn't say a single one of those things—but it's out there with my name on it, ready to be plucked and quoted and fastened tightly to the public idea of who I am. And if Milo should see it . . . well, he would know it's a fake, wouldn't he? The facts aren't right: I hardly ever went on book tours, and when I did, it was never for more than three or four days at a time. And we had one lone pet the whole time he was growing up, a dog who lived to the ripe old age of fifteen. Oh, and for God's sake—I hope he'd know this much—I would never have to stop and think to remember how old he was when Mitch and Rosemary died.

I don't know if this is a joke dreamed up by the FreeMilo people— I scan the interview again for some note of satire, but I'm not seeing it—or if there's really someone out there saying she's me and granting interviews in my name. Whatever the case, I can't imagine what the purpose of it all might be. The Octavia who's interviewed here sounds a bit stupid, and certainly fussier than I am, and she makes a few unsavory implications about Milo (*He hit his sister! Perhaps he killed the family pets!*), but she doesn't say anything particularly shocking or revelatory. What unnerves me about it is that it seems to be an attempt— a clumsy and not very creative one—to imagine what it might be like to live inside my head.

I send Anna a second e-mail, this one rather frantic, with a link to the Web site. I'm not really afraid that we won't be able to fix this. Anna will have some ideas, and I'll probably just have to make a statement that I had nothing to do with the interview. What I'm afraid of is the damage already done, the false witness borne and released into the digital distance. We've come to an age where no word can be unwritten, no idea unthought. And in the land of the anonymous, the attributed quote is king.

My fear is that years from now—perhaps after I am dead, my own ending immutable and fixed in marble—a reader will come across a book of mine and decide she wants to learn more about who I was. She will do her research, and among the billions of documents hovering like ghosts, she will find this one.

My fear is that she—this reader I've imagined, who may or may not ever exist—will believe that this is how I felt about my son.

I try to calm down. If I don't distract myself, I'll never fall asleep. Impulsively, I do a search for "Roland Nysmith." Born in 1955 in Birmingham, England, to a railway worker and his wife. Moved to London at the age of seventeen and briefly studied history at King's College, where he met his first wife, Adelaide Fry, to whom he was married from 1974 to 1977. The Misters formed in 1973; their first hit single was "The Girl in the Window," from the album *War Town*, which was released in February 1975 and spent three weeks at number one on the British charts.

It's all so dry and colorless, even the events that I know must have mattered to him: an arrest for possession of cocaine in Germany in 1981; an Oscar for the title song from the 1989 film *Gray Days*; a bitter and very public divorce from his second wife, model Brooke Audley, in 1992. Why do we think that knowing the events of someone's life will give us insight into the person they are? Certainly we react to the things that happen to us; we are not unchanged by them. But there's no formula to it. You may know that a cascade of water can wear away stone, but you can't predict what shape the rock will take at any given moment. I fall asleep thinking of rushing water and jutting stones, root balls and cataracts and swift-moving streams.

. . .

When I wake up, it's to the sound of my phone vibrating against the surface of the table next to my bed. I look at the number. It's Anna. I clear my throat, try to summon a tone of alertness, and answer the call.

"Octavia," she says. "Am I calling too early?"

"No, not at all," I say. I look at the clock; it's eight a.m. In general, I would say that's a little early, but I'll forgive her. "So what's the news?"

"Well, first of all, I did get your e-mail about the interview on the FreeMilo Web site, and I don't think it's something we have to worry about. I'll get in touch with the legal department at Farraday on Monday, and they'll probably issue a cease-and-desist order. If you can go ahead and put a statement on your Web site, making it clear that you had nothing to do with it, we should be in good shape."

"Okay. Great. And you said you'd talked to Lisa about the manuscript . . . ?"

"Yes, I did." Her tone changes from businesslike to something I'd classify as cheerful but nervous. "She told me that they'd like to make an offer on *The Nobodies Album.*"

My response to this news is more mixed than I would have anticipated. Relief and validation—*they like it; I haven't made a fool of myself*—but it's tempered with a slight feeling of dread I'd rather not investigate too closely.

"That's great," I say, after a minute. "You know, I've thought all along that this could be a really interesting, groundbreaking project, but I know it's a little out there."

"Right," says Anna. She doesn't sound as happy as I do.

"So what are they offering?" I ask. I prepare myself for a low number. My last book didn't sell, and this one's inherently risky.

"Well," she says, "what they're offering is actually a two-book deal."

"Okay," I say. "That's a good thing, right?"

"I think it is," she says. "The stipulation is that the second book—and there's some leeway here for you to make this your own—the second book will be a memoir. About you and Milo."

Of course. Of course. I can't believe I didn't see this coming.

Anna presses on: "Now, whatever you decide, I'm behind you a hundred percent. But while you're thinking about it, I want to emphasize that they're very clearly leaving the subject matter up to you. Whatever angle you want to take is fine. So I imagine that potentially you could do this in a way that could be very positive for Milo, and for his public image."

She tells me the amount. It's a lot, more than any advance I've ever been offered.

"I'm going to need to think about it," I say finally. "When do they want an answer?"

"They want to get moving on this fairly quickly, so probably Monday. Do you have any . . . preliminary thoughts about what your answer might be?"

"No," I say, a little sharply. "None at all."

"Okay," she says. "Because the other piece of this is that if you do decide to do a book like this, then maybe we ought to open it up to other publishers. I think there would be a huge amount of interest."

I just need to end this phone call. "Well, clearly there's a lot to think about." My voice sounds hollow. "I'll let you know on Monday, okay?"

"Okay," she says. "If you have any thoughts or questions over the weekend, feel free to give me a call."

"I will," I say. "Bye."

I hang up before I've even heard her respond. I lie back on the bed and cradle a pillow against my chest. And before I know it, I'm crying, sloppy and ugly and loud. I don't think about why, whether it's just this news or the built-up accumulation of the whole goddamned week. I just cry until my throat is sore and my head aches.

When I'm done, I lie in bed for a few more minutes, my mind blissfully blank. And when I get up, without even realizing it, I've made a decision. I pack up my things and go downstairs to check out of the hotel. While I'm waiting for my turn at the desk, I call Milo and tell him I'm coming to stay.

BR: *So would you agree with the idea that writing can be therapeutic?*

OF: Well, certainly writing can be therapeutic, but when you're writing something that you hope will be artistic and that you'd like to share with the world, therapy can't be your main goal. I mean, it may be therapeutic to write "I hate my mother" on a piece of paper, but that doesn't mean anyone's going to want to read it. That said, it's certainly true that the events of a writer's life, including her emotional life, can and do influence her work.

BR: *So are there aspects of your own books that are autobiographical?*

OF: Well, sure, but not always in a way that's obvious to anyone but me. If you look at my books, there's no character who shares my exact biography. There's no character who's supposed to be me, and there are no characters who are based exclusively on anyone I know. I don't do "thinly veiled." But still, my life is in there. It's oblique, but it's in there.

For example, my novel *The Rule of the Chalice* was very much shaped by the fact that I had lost my husband and my daughter a few years earlier. Even though their deaths were not violent, there was a certain moment in my grieving when I started thinking about blood and violence—what it means to save a life, what it means to take a life—in a way I never had before. And the novel grew out of that.

Excerpt from an interview with Octavia Frost in the Barnstable Review, *February 1998*

From the Jacket Copy for

THE RULE OF THE CHALICE

By Octavia Frost

(Farraday Books, 1995)

/|\\

Nikki is a woman facing enormous tragedy: her young son, Caleb, has been abducted and murdered by her former boyfriend, Gordie. In the aftermath, Nikki makes an unusual career change: she takes a job with a cleaning company that specializes in CTS—crime and trauma scene—cleanup.

As Gordie's trial progresses and Nikki becomes accustomed to this new and difficult kind of work, she retreats further and further into her grief. Then she meets Scott, a gay man whose partner has recently been murdered, and his young daughter, Daisy. Through this new friendship, Nikki finds a way to mourn Caleb and still move forward, and to forgive herself for that most bittersweet crime: continuing to live.

’’’\\\\

The day Gordie was sentenced to die, Nikki walked out of the courthouse, past the reporters and the protesters both pro and con, and went to her car feeling nothing. It wasn't until a half hour later, pulling into the parking lot of a supermarket where she'd stopped to buy milk and soda, that she began to cry. She parked crookedly and put her hands over her face. She wept until she was almost screaming, and she didn't know if it was for herself or for Caleb, or even for the woman she had once hoped would be her mother-in-law, who had been unable to keep herself from moaning out loud when the verdict was read. Or maybe it was because something was supposed to have ended today, but nothing was different, except that now someone else was going to die, and she herself had played an undeniable role in the chain of causation. The phrase "blood on my hands" came into her head, but that seemed to be just another excuse for her mind to bring up all the images of literal blood she'd seen in the slides the prosecution had presented: the spatter patterns on the legs of Gordie's pants, the fingerprint on the steering wheel of his car, the footmarks and drag stains that had appeared like a holy vision when the detectives sprayed Luminol on his basement floor. She stayed in her car for a long time, even after she had finished crying. She sat in a kind of hollow stupor, feeling both thankful and sorry to be living in a time when she could be sure that no one would knock on her window to ask if she was okay.

When she got home—she'd decided to skip the groceries, though it meant she'd be drinking her coffee black in the morning—Nikki checked her messages. There was one from her mother, who'd heard the news about Gordie and was "thrilled." "Call me," she said, "and we can celebrate." Her voice was caustic, and while Nikki understood the depth of her anger, and indeed had spent a lot of time herself looking upward from that same pit, she couldn't match it right now. She decided to put off returning the call until tomorrow.

Scott had also called, and also knew what had happened at the courthouse, though his response was more tempered. "Hope you're doing okay," he said. "Call me if you want to talk." He also reminded her that Saturday was moving day, and that if Nikki still wanted to help out, she should come over around nine.

Finally, there was a message from Jeremy, saying that they had a couple of new jobs and that if she felt up to coming into work in the morning, he was going to put her on a meth lab decon project over on the west side. Nikki knew, from an e-mail she'd gotten from Vera, that there was also a team working on a murder scene in Fairlawn Heights, a high-profile case that had been in the news over the past few weeks. Nikki imagined Jeremy trying to decide where to put her, wondering which location would be less traumatic for her during this particular week, and settling for chemicals over blood, physical hazards over emotional ones.

I could quit, she thought, and waited to see how that felt.

Jeremy had given her an out the day he hired her: "Not everyone can handle this," she remembered him saying. "Sometimes people just wake up one day and feel like they can't come into work. I like two weeks' notice, of course, but I understand that you've got to look out for yourself first."

It was nineteen months now since Caleb had died, and over a year since she'd seen the CNN story that had started her thinking about this kind of work. She had gone into it thinking—what? That it was good money, an important service, a way to help people; yes. But also that she owed a debt to these dead, to their terror and their confusion and their peace. Because she, in a convoluted way, had taken a life herself.

Cause and effect again, strings of events forged into chains, so that she could see the places where her own actions affected someone else's. Caleb would not have died:

- if she had never gone to Tara's Christmas party;
- if, at that party, she had not given Gordie her phone number;

- if she had broken up with him sooner or not at all;
- if she had thought to change the list that told Caleb's teachers which adults were allowed to pick him up from school.

He would not have died if she had been on time that day. He would not have died if she'd gone to Gordie's house immediately instead of calling the police. And so on, and so on, and so on.

But here was the thing: sometime in the ten months since she'd started working for CTSO, another link had been added to the chain. Her work was still about Caleb—it would be, always—but it was about something else now, too. It had to do with respect. It had to do with understanding that *here* a heart had beat and then not, *here* a breath had been exhaled and never repeated.

Nikki had been raised Catholic, and she remembered that once during communion, one of the hosts had fallen during the transfer from the priest's fingers to a parishioner's mouth. Though Nikki had already made her first communion, she wouldn't have understood the significance of the moment if it hadn't been for the adults around her. Her mother, standing behind her in line, drew a sharp breath and squeezed her hands tight on Nikki's shoulders. The woman at the front of the line, the intended recipient, cried out softly. And as the priest knelt down to retrieve the wafer, Nikki could see the distress in his tilted face.

The priest picked up the host and put it into his own mouth, then brushed the floor with his hand, perhaps looking for fragments that might have broken off. Then, in an event that seemed to Nikki much more shocking than the actual dropping of the bread, he bent forward and licked the marble where the host had lain.

Nikki looked around her, but no one else seemed as surprised as she was. The priest took a small white cloth from the altar and dropped it on the spot where the wafer had fallen. Then he took a breath and continued with the service, moving on to the next host, the next waiting tongue.

Later Nikki had asked her mother about what had happened, and her mother had told her that when the consecrated host, the body of Christ, falls onto a profane surface, the priest must himself eat any pieces of it he can find. Later, after mass, he must wash the area with water three times, being careful that no crumbs are left behind. And afterward, her mother said, the water used to cleanse the spot cannot be poured into a regular sink but must be emptied into the soil or into a special drain that will return it directly to the earth. If wine were to spill from the chalice, she added, then the linen cloths used to wipe up the liquid—and even any item of clothing that had been splashed or stained—would have to be burned. Nikki had been impressed by the ritual of it, the solemnity accorded to a task that to her seemed like nothing more than a minor chore.

Now, with her strong stomach and her hazmat suit, Nikki had taken on a job that was not so different. She went into rooms where bodies had broken apart, spaces made foul by spilled blood and all the liquids a living body carries. She cleaned and she purified, and in her careful and methodical work, she honored the dead by recognizing their humanity. And she smoothed the path for those, like herself, who had been left behind among the living.

Nikki called Jeremy's voice mail and told him to expect her in the morning.

. . .

Three days later, on Saturday morning, Nikki drove to Scott's house. Daisy opened the door before Nikki had a chance to knock.

"I saw you," Daisy said, hugging Nikki's thighs. "I saw your car."

"You did?" Nikki asked, bending to pick the girl up. This feeling of holding a small body, arms folding around her neck, feet knocking into her legs . . . there was nothing else like it. "Well, now I see you, too."

Scott came into the room and gave her a kiss on the cheek. "How are you?" he asked in a tone that suggested he wanted a real answer.

"Not bad," she said. She thought for a minute, and then said it again. "Really, I'm not bad."

Scott nodded. "Glad to hear it," he said.

The living room was filled with boxes stacked neatly against the walls. There wouldn't be much to do beyond carrying them out to the U-Haul and unloading them across town. The house seemed smaller, in that way that houses do when their contents have been packed away.

Nikki looked at the fresh paint, the new carpeting that she herself had installed, and thought about the room as it had looked the first time she saw it: the dark stain just a few feet in from the door, the veil of red dots on the wall. The house hadn't sold yet, and might not for a while; Scott probably wouldn't get the price he wanted for it. It was always difficult to sell a house where a murder had occurred, and the specifics of this case—the fact that Ty had walked into the house to find a man with a gun on his way out with a laptop and Scott's mother's jewelry—called the safety of the neighborhood into question. But no one could look at this room and say that it looked like a crime had been committed there. She had done good work.

Nikki knew that Gordie's house had been sold some time ago to help cover his legal fees, but she still didn't know if it was CTSO that had done the cleanup work, or another company, or even Gordie's mother, on her hands and knees with latex gloves and a bottle of Clorox. She'd never asked Jeremy, and she probably wouldn't.

She had thought sometimes that maybe she should move, find a new place, like Scott and Daisy were doing. But it wasn't the same; her house had not been the scene of Caleb's murder. She could picture Caleb playing with his Matchbox cars on the kitchen floor without picturing his blood spread in a jagged stain beneath him. The place where he died was not the place where he lived, she thought. For a moment it seemed more profound than it really was.

Two more of Scott's friends had arrived to help. They all worked together, carrying boxes out to the truck, finding small items here and there that Daisy could handle. When the truck was full, Scott locked the back and got ready to make the first trip over to the new house.

"Are we taking Papa with us?" Daisy asked suddenly. Everyone froze.

"It's okay," Scott said in a low voice meant for the other adults. "They don't really get it at this age. It's too abstract."

He picked up Daisy and kissed the top of her head. "We're taking our thoughts and our memories and our pictures of Papa," he said. "Now, what do you think? Do you want to ride in the big truck?"

"Yeah!" Daisy said, bouncing up and down in Scott's arms.

Scott tossed his house keys to Nikki. "Would you lock up?" he asked. She nodded but didn't speak; inexplicably, she felt close to tears. She thought of Caleb, his chipmunk cheeks, the blue of his eyes. Her boy.

All children are lost, eventually. Nikki remembered Caleb on his fourth birthday, crying because he'd never be three again, and three was the only thing he could ever remember being. If he'd lived another ten years, or seventy, that little boy would be just as gone as he was now. It was like a logic problem: given the same eventual outcome, why was it that one ending was so much worse than another?

Scott lifted Daisy and buckled her into the truck. "You want to ride with us or follow us?" he asked Nikki.

"I'll meet you there," she said. She watched Scott and his friends get into their vehicles, start up the engines, and pull away.

When they were gone, she sat down on the grass. As long as she lived—and it might be a very long time—the central fact of her life would be that her little boy had suffered alone, that he had called out for her and she didn't come. And as long as that continued to be true, she would pay her penance. She would stay behind after others had gone on their way. She would lock doors and clean up. She would spend her days alone, apart, ringing the doorbells of the be-reaved and crossing the thresholds of houses where something terrible had happened.

/|||\

Scott tossed his house keys to Nikki. "Would you lock up?" he asked. She nodded but didn't speak; inexplicably, she felt close to tears. She thought of Caleb, his chipmunk cheeks, the blue of his eyes. Her boy. She covered her eyes, let it wash over her for a minute, and then put it aside, back in the compartment it had come from.

She locked the door and walked down the porch steps. Daisy was walking in circles on the grass, singing a quiet song, just for herself. She was here; that was something. This child was here.

Scott lifted Daisy and buckled her into the truck. "You want to ride with us or follow us?" he asked Nikki.

"I'll come with you," she said, surprising herself. She went around to the passenger side and got in. Daisy sat in the middle, between the two of them.

"Look how high we are," she said. Her face was as bright as the day.

Nikki opened her window. The three of them rode along, washed in breeze. Scott turned on the radio and twisted the knob until he found a station. There was an old song playing, something that her own mother might have listened to as a kid. She and Scott both knew the words.

Daisy leaned her head on Nikki's arm. Nikki felt the weight of the child's body, smelled baby shampoo from her hair. There was music and sunlight, wind and the bumpy movement of the truck. They came to a corner and turned, sliding into each other as they went.

Chapter Twelve

/||\

One day a couple of years ago, I parked my car on a narrow street in the middle of Boston. As I beeped the lock and began to walk away, something unusual happened. Ducklings began to fall from the sky.

I saw first one, then another plummet through the air, to land with a muted thud on the sidewalk. They weren't dead, these two, but they were clearly hurt. They had fallen awkwardly, and were struggling to get to their feet. As I knelt to help one of them right himself, a third duckling landed a little way away, and finally I looked up.

I was standing next to a hotel, and up at the level of the first floor there was a slim ledge that ran the length of the building. A full-grown duck stood up there, looking down at her fallen babies. She let out a husky squawk and paced a few steps from right to left, and as she did, another duckling came to the edge and propelled himself over.

A small group had gathered by this point, five or six of us who had thought we were on our way someplace important until the sky started raining birds like a biblical plague. As this fourth baby fell, we each stretched a hand forward to try to catch it. None of us succeeded, but the toppling yellow body bumped against someone's arm, which was enough to deflect him from hitting the sidewalk with full force. This one stood up immediately, apparently unhurt, and fluffed his feathers while he waited for the rest.

What were they doing up there? I don't know. We were nowhere near the water, and as far as I could see there was no nest. But if she didn't lay the eggs up on that concrete shelf and warm them in that space barely as wide as her own body, then I don't know how they got there, since clearly the babies were too young to know how to fly.

Three more times ducklings came over the edge, and three more times we broke their fall—perhaps not quite saving their lives, but at least minimizing their harm. And then the mother flew down—someone was already on the phone to whomever you call in a situation like this—and she rounded up her babies and led them away toward dangers unknown. And the five or six of us who had taken part in this unnerving incident went our separate ways, having shared something that felt as if it must hold some significance, though its exact meaning remained elusive.

This is troubling me now, as I wheel my suitcase out of the hotel and ask the doorman to find me a cab, because I sense that there's some link between my current situation and the scene I witnessed that day, but I can't quite connect the dots. Something about motherhood and danger, protection and risk. Or trusting fate. Or letting go.

It's the kind of image I might try to put in a book but ultimately abandon. It's too capacious; there are too many possible meanings, and it's not sturdy enough to do all that work at once. Perhaps one day I'll find a place to use it without ascribing it any symbolic significance. Let it stand as a picture, a visual non sequitur. Describe it simply, like a haiku: *Pacing mother duck / Babies dropping from the ledge / Bumping outstretched hands.*

Or maybe I'll never use it, and the entire thing exists only in the minds of those who were there that day, to be wiped from the slate of human experience the moment the last of us dies. What would it matter? Why should that feel like such a loss?

. . .

When the taxi drops me at Roland's house, I say good morning to the photographers and ignore their shouted questions as I pull my suitcase over to the security keypad and punch in the code Milo gave me over the phone. Through the gate, up the stairs, ring the bell. Roland himself answers the door.

"Good morning," he says brightly. He's dressed in shorts and a

T-shirt; his feet are bare, which makes me feel oddly embarrassed, like I'm intruding on something intimate. "So glad you decided to take me up on my offer."

"Thank you again, so much," I say, stepping inside.

"Not at all," he says. "Come with me, I'll show you your room."

He takes my suitcase from me, and I make a feeble show of protesting. He leads me across the chessboard floor to the staircase, and I follow him up, feeling exquisitely awkward. It's hard to make small talk with a man whose Wikipedia entry you read twelve hours earlier.

"Where's Milo?" I ask as we climb.

"Went back to sleep. He got up just long enough to tell me you were coming, then crawled back to bed." He turns to smile at me. "I miss that, you know? Sleeping till all hours. Territory of the young."

"Hmm," I say. "I suppose clinical depression is always an option." I was going for witty, but I'm afraid I ended up with merely odd. Well, I never said I was good with words. Not ones spoken out loud, anyway.

But Roland laughs, and the look he gives me is genuinely amused. "Or opium. Doesn't sound like that Kublai Khan bloke had a problem with early waking."

"Literary references," I say wryly. "Nicely done."

"Comes standard with the room."

At the top of the stairs he turns to the left, the same direction as the library where I sat with Milo two days ago, and starts down the hall, pulling my suitcase along so that it follows him like a pet. He stops at the doorway of the first room on the right.

"There you are, then. I'll let you get settled—make yourself at home. Just so you know the lay of the land, Milo's staying across the hall, next to the library, and I'm down at the other end. My housekeeper's downstairs. Her name's Danielle, and she'll be happy to get you something to eat if you're hungry."

"Thanks," I say. "This is all great material if I ever decide to write a novel about a rock star. 'Seems to know a lot about opium . . . hasn't done dishes since 1974 . . .'"

"I'd better be careful what I say to you," he says. He pauses and looks at me steadily, his face serious. "Listen, whatever you do, you must never open the locked door at the bottom of the basement stairs."

I stare at him, my eyes a little too wide, and he laughs. "Kidding," he says. "See you later. Shout if you need anything." He turns and walks briskly down the hall.

I pull my suitcase inside the bedroom and close the door. It's a lovely room, big and airy, decorated in blues and whites, though like the kitchen, it's a bit anonymous. The room faces the back of the house, and looking out the window, I see a terrace below, with a pool and some deck chairs. I wish for a moment that I had a bathing suit with me—that vague, involuntary response to the mere existence of a pool—and then I realize that there's no way I'd go walking around Roland Nysmith's house in a bathing suit.

I sit down on the bed and allow myself a moment of panic at the reality of being here in this near-stranger's home, without any idea of what I'm supposed to do next. I hadn't counted on Milo being asleep, though I'm certainly not going to wake him.

I take a look around the room—open the drawers, peek into the closets—and find nothing interesting or unusual. For lack of anything better to do, I open my suitcase and start to unpack. There hasn't been any talk about how long I'm staying. I have a ticket back to Boston on Monday, two days from now, but I don't know if I'll be using it.

As I'm lining up bottles of makeup and perfume against the mirror in the bathroom, I hear my phone buzz from my purse. I take it out and look at it. It's Lisette.

"Hello," I say.

"Hi, Octavia," she says. "It's Lisette. How are you?"

"Good," I say. "Actually, kind of weird. I'm sitting in a guest room at Roland Nysmith's house." I think that if anyone will understand the surreal tint my day has taken, it's Lisette. She used to have a true reverence for celebrity, and I don't imagine that goes away, no matter how many rock stars you meet.

"Aaaaah!" she says, in a mock scream I find surprisingly gratifying. "Oh, how funny. Were you a total Misters girl?"

"No, not especially. But, you know . . . I liked them well enough, and

I've been hearing their music for thirty years. I never thought I'd have *Roland Nysmith* carrying my suitcase for me."

I laugh at the way I sound, and she joins in. I've always been wary of school reunions, because of their transformative magic, the way they turn you back into the person you used to be. But there's something reassuring about talking to someone who shared your adolescence.

"So we didn't really get a chance to talk yesterday," I say. "How are you? What are you doing these days?"

We spend a few minutes catching up. She likes working in real estate; she's dating a man who used to play for the 49ers. She has an idea for a book that she'd love to discuss with me sometime. We talk about who we're still in touch with from high school. Her list is long, mine practically nonexistent.

"How was the rest of the service?" I ask.

"Oh, it was nice. Sad, but nice. A lot of people had stories to share about Bettina. Kathy's a wreck, of course. But she's glad to have a project to keep her busy."

"A project?"

"Oh, you know. The domestic violence thing. And, of course, seeing your son convicted." She laughs, which I hope is a response to nervousness.

I don't answer. I'm thinking again of the mother duck, how it must have looked from her perspective. Fragile bodies hurtling toward the pavement.

"God, I'm sorry," she says after a brief silence. "That was so not the right thing to say."

"It's okay," I say. "No one knows what the etiquette is for this kind of situation."

I hear the sound of a cigarette lighter, and she pauses as she breathes in the smoke. "Last week I asked my mail carrier if she was pregnant."

I shake my head, slightly baffled. I assume she's giving an example of another time when she said something that turned out to be inappropriate, but I don't ask her why she's telling me this, or whether it was embarrassing, or how much weight her mail carrier has gained. Instead I think about how to redirect the conversation. "You know, speaking of

Roland," I say finally, though it's actually been several minutes since we have, "after I left yesterday, I saw him outside the building, trying to get into the funeral. The security people asked him to leave."

"Oh, well, I'm not surprised," she says. "It's too bad, though, because I think he really did love Bettina."

I think of the photograph sitting on the table downstairs, Roland pushing Bettina on a swing, and I feel . . . not frightened, exactly, but uneasy.

Lisette continues talking. "He was definitely like a father to her," she says. "Even if he turned out not to be her actual father."

I pause. Now I'm completely confused. "What do you mean?"

"Oh, you don't know the story?"

"No. I don't know anything."

"Well, for years Kathy thought that Roland was Bettina's father. And Roland believed it, and he did his part—he gave them money, and he saw Bettina from time to time. And then, when Bettina was maybe eight or nine, they did a paternity test, and it turned out not to be him."

I try to absorb this. "Wow," I say. "So . . ."

There's a knock on my door. "Mom? Are you in there?"

"Hi," I call. "I'll be out in a minute."

"Okay," he says. "I'll be down in the kitchen."

"Is that Milo?" asks Lisette.

"Yeah."

"You've got hot- and cold-running rock stars over there," she says. "I'll let you go." I feel like I need to ask her more questions, but I'm not even sure what they'd be. "Good to talk to you. How long are you in town for?"

"I don't know," I say. "Everything's pretty much up in the air."

"Right. Well . . . call if you need a break."

A break from what, I'm not sure, though I suppose she means a break from my own project of trying to keep my son out of prison. "Okay," I say. "Thanks. Take care."

After we hang up, I go downstairs. I stop to introduce myself to the housekeeper, who's sweeping the entryway, and then I continue to the kitchen, where I find Milo, eating a bowl of cereal and looking at an open laptop.

"Good morning," I say. "Sorry for waking you earlier. I'm glad you were able to get back to sleep."

"That's okay," he says, looking up briefly. He points toward one of the counters. "There's coffee, if you want some."

"Thanks." I open cabinets until I find a mug. I realize I haven't eaten breakfast, so when I open the refrigerator to get milk, I also take a carton of yogurt. It's a brand I've never seen before, German or Austrian, with pictures of cherries on the foil lid.

As I sit down at the table, Milo closes his computer, which I take as a gesture of politeness, though it could also be that he doesn't want me to see what he was looking at.

"So . . . welcome," he says, looking at me as if he's not quite sure what I'm doing here.

I smile at his expression of vague disconcertedness, his tousled morning hair. "Thank you." I peel the top from my yogurt. "How are you? Anything planned for the day?"

"Yeah, my lawyer's coming over to meet with me around eleven."

I nod. A house call from a lawyer on a Saturday morning. My son is an important man. "To go over anything in particular?" I ask.

He shrugs. "I'm not sure." He takes a bite of cereal. "Also, I guess the police are finished with my house, so I need to . . . deal with that in some way."

"Deal with it?"

"You know, have it cleaned, decide whether I'm going to sell it or whatever. I don't really see myself moving back there, whatever happens."

This, at least, is something I can help with. "Why don't you let me take care of that?" I say. "I'll deal with the cleaning, and I can . . . go through Bettina's things, if you'd like. And if you decide to sell, I can handle all those details."

I try to read his look. Grateful, but wary, like he's not sure he should let me do this.

"Let me help," I say. "I'll be glad to have something concrete to work on." A project. Like Kathy Moffett's.

He sighs, then laughs a little. "I feel like I'm fourteen years old. I'm trying to think if there's anything I wouldn't want you to see."

I know he's talking about the standard kinds of items that might shock a mother or cause her to worry—drug paraphernalia or sex toys or something of that ilk. (Or, oddly, that's what I hope he's talking about. I'd hate to think there's an I-hate-Octavia-Frost-themed room that *Turf Wars* didn't visit, full of voodoo dolls and remaindered copies of *Tropospheric Scatter*.) But the statement raises darker images than I think he intended. There are things in that house that I don't want him to see. Things I'm willing to see so he doesn't have to.

"You've got enough to worry about," I say firmly. "I promise not to snoop. Much." And then, because I'm not sure I'm allowed to make that kind of joke yet, I clarify: "I won't open any drawers or closets. I'll follow the no-search-warrant rule—I'm not allowed to look at anything that's not in plain sight."

He smiles at my cautiousness. "Okay, thanks. You can get the keys from Sam Zalakis, when he comes. My lawyer."

"Good," I say. I finish eating my yogurt, then pick up the carton and look around for the trash.

Milo's finished his cereal and is slumped in his chair, looking into the middle distance. He's so subdued, his whole posture so forlorn. Which, of course, is normal under the circumstances, but I hate it.

"Can I get you anything else to eat?" I ask him. It's the universal script of mothers during times of powerlessness: offer food. He shakes his head.

I stand behind him, reach down to put my arms around him. He lets me pull him into a hug, and he rests his head on my shoulder and sighs. I hold him, silent and still.

In a strange way, when Milo was little, I almost liked it when he was sick. Not that I wanted him to feel bad, not that I didn't hope he'd be better soon. But those were the times when my relationship to him was clearest, and least complicated. There's some truth, I think, to the idea that parents clash most with the children who are most like themselves.

Milo and I are impatient and willful, inventive and passionate and mercurial. We are sensitive to slights; we are quick to anger. And no matter how many books I write, no matter how many characters I knot and untangle, I'm not sure I'll ever have a full understanding of either of us.

He pulls back, and I kiss his forehead before I let him go. "I love you," I say. "And whatever happens, I'll help you get through this."

These are familiar words, ritual or cliché, whichever you prefer. But they're like wedding vows or condolences for the grieving: they adopt new meaning each time they're uttered.

. . .

After Milo goes upstairs to shower and dress, I pour myself another cup of coffee and set about looking for a company to clean the house referred to alternately in the news as "the scene of the murder" and "219 Sea Cliff." I'd like to find a phone book, but I don't know where to look; perhaps people don't even use phone books anymore, though I know the phone companies still give them out. Milo's taken his computer with him, which is probably just as well. I wouldn't look through his files, but I know myself well enough to know that the temptation would be heavily present.

I go upstairs to retrieve my laptop. As I come back down, I'm thinking about coincidence and synchronicity, the way it seems significant when you learn something you never knew before—the meaning of the word "ramellose," or the fact that a group of owls is called a parliament—and then, seemingly all at once, you hear it mentioned in conversation, and you spot it in both a nineteenth-century novel and a newspaper article about local weekend getaways. Lisette Freyn and crime-scene cleanup—the world doubling back on itself, like fabric folded to reveal that two separate holes were made with a single rip. It seems like it should mean something, but it almost certainly doesn't. We don't keep track of the times in our lives when things *don't* match up.

There are a number of listings for companies that handle CTS in San Francisco. One of the interesting things about researching a subject for a novel is that the details you forget to learn are often the practical ones. I know what kind of cleaning solutions these businesses use, and how the workers protect themselves from contact with bodily fluids, but I have no idea what kind of prices to expect or whether anyone will be there on a Saturday to answer the phone.

I've been planning to call two or three places, to compare estimates, but the first phone call turns out to be such an ordeal—I don't know the square footage or the kind of surfaces that have been affected; I don't know whether the blood is confined to a single room—that I just go ahead and make an appointment to meet someone at the house on Monday. If the woman I'm speaking to recognizes the address, if she's exchanging high fives with her coworkers about landing the Milo Frost house, she doesn't let me hear it in her tone.

After I hang up, I find my airline reservation, and after a few minutes of investigating how much it would cost to change the return to later in the week, I simply cancel it. I've decided to make things easy for myself, where I can.

Milo comes downstairs a few minutes before eleven, wearing jeans and a T-shirt, his hair falling in thick, wet stripes. As soon as he walks into the kitchen, I can see that his posture is different than it was earlier: his body is looser, less hunched.

"I remembered something while I was in the shower," he says. He sits down and looks at me intently. "About the phone call, the one at twelve-thirty. I remember talking to Bettina."

"You do?"

"Yeah. It's still fuzzy, and I don't remember all the details, but I remember that I'd been calling her all night, the whole time I was driving—God, it's amazing I didn't kill myself." He shakes his head. "Anyway, she wouldn't answer, and she wouldn't answer, and then finally . . . I was outside, it was wherever I was when I hit my head. And I was freezing, and it was dark, and she finally picked up the phone."

"What do you remember about the conversation?"

"Not much. Bits and pieces. But I think we made up. Or not made up, exactly—she was still pissed, and it wasn't like the problems were just going to go away. But I'm absolutely certain that we ended on a kind of 'let's sleep on it before we make any decisions' note."

I nod, not sure how much hope I can afford to spend on this. "So you think she had forgiven you? Or at least given you the idea that she might?"

He shrugs. "Like I said, I don't remember specifically. But I know I was incredibly happy when I put the phone back in my pocket. I know I felt like things might be okay."

"Well, that's something, anyway."

"Yeah." His eyes are intense. "It's not like I can prove it. But *I* know now. *I* know I didn't kill her."

I watch him. He's relieved and . . . something close to grateful. Glad to have something to hold on to. I'm not sure that this proves as much as he thinks it does, or that Sam Zalakis will be able to turn it into an air-tight defense, but I'm happy he feels he can put that worry to rest.

"I never once thought you did," I say.

The doorbell rings, and I follow Milo into the front hall. As he opens the door, I'm wishing I'd asked him whether or not he'd like me to play any role in this meeting. Because I'm his mother and because I'm here, I feel like I should sit in on the discussion, in case he needs advice or help navigating the legal intricacies. But I suspect that's no longer my job. I wasn't there when he bought his house or negotiated his last two recording contracts or proposed marriage impulsively over dinner; I certainly wasn't there when he stood and listened to murder charges being read to him by police officers. I'll follow his lead on this.

Sam Zalakis comes in, looking much as he did when I saw him on CNN. He's dressed more casually, but he's no less well groomed or expensively outfitted. He and Milo shake hands and exchange their greetings, and then Milo introduces me.

"So nice to meet you," he says warmly, taking my hand. "My daughter will be so excited to hear I met you. She's at Stanford, and she wrote a paper about you in one of her classes. Or not *you*, I guess, but your books."

"Thank you," I say, which isn't entirely the right response but is at least in the ballpark. I'm evaluating him the same way I used to appraise Milo's girlfriends when I met them: *Who are you, and how are you going to treat my son?*

"Before I forget," he says to Milo, setting his briefcase down on a chair and withdrawing a manila envelope, "here are your house keys and the garage door opener. The police are completely finished, so you can go back whenever you want."

Milo gestures to me. "You can give them to my mom," he says. "She's taking care of the cleaning and all that."

Sam hands me the envelope. "It's good that you're here to help him," he says. "These are the times when family is most important." We all nod solemnly, as the script seems to require.

"How's the case looking?" I ask. I know it's not a question he can answer easily, but I imagine that reassuring the family is a part of his job. And I'd very much like to be reassured.

He nods, as if I've asked something that can be answered with a yes or a no. "I'm hopeful," he says. "There are some details that aren't adding up, and the police know it, and the prosecutor knows it. We've got a lot of work ahead of us, but this is not an open-and-shut case by any means."

I smile at him, hoping it conveys my gratitude, because I don't quite trust my voice. "Hopeful" is a better word than I could have expected.

Sam turns to Milo. "Where shall we set up? And are you going to join us, Ms. Frost?"

I give Milo a questioning look. "No, that's all right," he says. "I mean, you can if you want to, but I don't think it's necessary." And then to Sam, "We can talk upstairs in the library."

"Okay, then," I say, as they turn and start up the stairs. I stand in the empty entryway for a moment, unsure what I should do next. I haven't seen the whole house yet, and I'm curious to look around, though I don't want to overstep my bounds.

Idly I walk into the sitting room opposite the front hall, a large, bright space with a window that looks out onto the pool. The black-and-white floor continues in here, though most of it is covered with a plush rug in sunny, saturated shades of red, yellow, and orange.

There are bookshelves built into one of the walls, and I gravitate toward them, as I always do. I didn't have a chance the other day to look at the books in the library, but I imagine that some thought—on the part of someone, Roland or the decorator—went into deciding which books would be displayed in this more public space. These are the books you see if you know Roland Nysmith only slightly, if you're invited in only so far. Dozens of big, glossy doorstops filled with photographs; several shelves about the history of rock music; books about Zen Buddhism and the environment and restoring antique cars. All of it punctuated with awards statues and plaques commemorating high numbers of records sold. Here's an actual Grammy; I can't resist reaching out to touch it.

I see four separate books about Roland himself, and I pull out one with the title *Man Under Water*, only to put it back almost immediately. There's something unseemly about flipping through a biography of a man who might walk in at any moment.

There's a doorway back by the window, and I wander through to the next room, which is the dining room. There's a mammoth table and chairs—dark wood, all very clean lines. Everything's so immaculate, and I wonder if Roland actually uses any of these spaces on a regular basis. I'm headed toward the door on the other side of the room, which I can see leads back to the kitchen, when something catches my eye. There, in a glass-fronted china cabinet against the wall, is a collection of dishes with a pattern of yellow roses and vines.

It's the same kind of china my mother had. The same as the sugar bowl.

I feel suddenly afraid, though I'm not sure why. It's not a particularly rare design. I looked it up once a few years ago, thinking I might replace some pieces, and it appears to have been a popular pattern in the late forties and early fifties; it was manufactured in England but also sold widely in the United States. My parents were married in 1952. I don't know when Roland's parents were married, but it stands to reason that it might have been somewhere in the early part of that time period.

I'm leaning in, still looking at the dishes, when I hear Roland's voice behind me. "Hello there," he says.

For reasons that have never been clear to me—poor reflexes?—I tend to have a slightly delayed startle reaction, and it's only as I turn and see him standing in the kitchen doorway that I flinch and make a small, surprised noise.

"I'm sorry," he says, looking concerned and faintly amused. "I didn't mean to scare you."

"That's okay," I say. "It was just so quiet." My heart's beating fast, and I feel as if I've been caught doing something I shouldn't. But they're just dishes.

"I was looking at your china," I say. "This is the same pattern my parents had when I was growing up. I have a whole cupboard full of it at home."

I watch his reaction, but there's nothing unusual about it. "Funny coincidence," he says, smiling. He steps a little closer, looks into the glass. "I don't use any of it very often, but I like having it around. It reminds me of my mum."

I smile, willing myself to calm down. "I don't really use mine either. But it seems wrong to just get rid of it. I doubt Milo's ever going to want it."

He looks at me thoughtfully. "You never know. We all need something that reminds us of our mothers." And that brings up a whole lot of questions I'm not ready to consider.

Roland points at the envelope I'm still carrying. "Is that something you need to mail?" he asks.

I look down at the package, the tiny hole where the point of a key has begun to poke through the paper. "No. These are the keys to Milo's house. I'm taking care of some things for him over there." On an impulse, I say, "Is it far from here? I thought I might go over this afternoon." I hadn't been planning to go until Monday, but I'm suddenly both restless and curious, and it looks like Milo's going to be busy for a few hours.

"Not far at all. I'd be happy to drop you there after lunch, if you like." He stops abruptly and gestures toward the kitchen. "Right, lunch. That was what I came in to tell you—God, my mind is going. Danielle's put a few things out, if you're hungry. Come on in, if you'd like to join me."

"Thank you," I say. "I'll be right there."

He turns and walks back to the kitchen. After he's gone, I look into the china cabinet again, taking a quick inventory. I see piles of dinner plates, teacups, saucers. Two serving bowls, a covered butter dish. A creamer. But no sugar bowl.

Chapter Thirteen

I join Roland in the kitchen. The lunch that Danielle has set out is simple and lovely—salad, cold roasted chicken, fresh rolls, all so pretty and carefully arranged it could be the work of a caterer. I wonder if it's nice to have this all the time, all these artfully prepared meals, or if it starts to feel like a dinner party that never ends.

I feel on edge, as if I've been presented with an opportunity that I know I might accidentally squander. I think of the games Milo and Rosemary used to play, Jenga and Operation and pick-up sticks, games where everything depends on keeping your hand steady. I never understood the appeal: satisfaction and anxiety laced so tightly.

"I think we may have an acquaintance in common," I say finally. "I mean, besides the obvious."

Roland looks up from his plate, blandly interested. "Oh, really? Who?"

"Lisette Freyn." This is a guess. Lisette hasn't said in so many words that she knows Roland, but it certainly sounds like they've spent considerable time in the same circles.

"Lisette," he says, with a grin so pleased and wolfish that I'm suddenly certain they've slept together. "I've known Lisette since she was a young thing. She traveled with us for a while." He's lost for a moment in some haze of rock-and-roll memory before he pulls himself back. "How do you know her?"

"We went to school together. I ran into her the other day."

His expression turns somber. "Right. I'm sure she mentioned that she and Kathy Moffett are friends."

"Yeah. We didn't get a chance to talk very much, but it sounds like they've known each other a long time." I let it be a question, if he chooses to answer.

He takes a bite of his chicken, nods as he swallows. "Kathy's younger, of course, but they overlapped for a bit."

Overlapped. "So Kathy was a . . ." I pause. Is "groupie" a disrespectful term? Is there some empowering new-millennium phrase for women who trail along behind tour buses, giving blow jobs and doing laundry? "She traveled with the band, too," I finish.

"Right," he says.

"So you must have known Bettina her whole life."

I watch as something rolls through his body, some pulse of sorrow or regret. He sighs. "Yes. I'm lucky enough to say that I did."

"I'm sorry." I reach out to put a hand on his arm, hesitating for a second because . . . why? Because he's famous, I suppose; because he's not quite real to me. But of course his arm, when I do touch it, is as solid as my own. "It sounds like you were very close. She must have been almost like a daughter to you." I wait to see if I've gone too far, if I've added one block too many to the precarious stack.

He smiles weakly. "Very much so. I actually spent several years thinking she *was* my daughter. But that's a saga best left for another time."

He balances his fork and knife on the edge of his plate and looks to see if I'm finished eating. "Ready to get going?" he asks.

"Sure," I say. "Just give me a minute to grab my bag."

There are two cars in the garage, the silver one that Milo drove last night and a black sedan of a make I've never heard of, sleek and curved like a jungle cat. Roland unlocks the black car, and we both get in.

We ride past the photographers in silence. "This will be the first time I've seen Milo's house," I say after we've turned the corner. I don't know how much Milo has told him about our history.

Roland fumbles above his head, pulls a pair of sunglasses from a case clipped to the sun visor. "Kids need a chance to break away," he says after a minute. "Show their independence."

"Yes, they do." That's not really it. But it's nice of him to say.

"So can we expect a new album anytime soon?" I ask after a few minutes.

He turns to look at me briefly, amused. "Are you a fan?" he asks.

I feel myself blush. I'm not sure how to answer. "Sure," I say. "Who isn't?"

"Ah," he says, nodding. "A 'who isn't?' fan." He stops at a red light and turns to look at me, smiling like he finds this all very entertaining.

"I'm just not that familiar with your music," I say. There's a tartness in my voice I didn't entirely intend. "Which album should I start with?"

He laughs, throwing his head back. "Fair enough." The light turns green, and he drives on. "To answer your question, I'm not sure when there'll be a new album. I've been talking to my old bandmates about recording a new version of *Underneath*, but I don't know if it'll actually happen." He glances at me uncertainly. "That's an old Misters album from the seventies," he adds.

"I do know that much," I say. I feel suddenly wary, like he knows more about me than I think he does. I haven't mentioned *The Nobodies Album* to anyone since I got to California, and the coincidence makes me uneasy. "What made you think about redoing it?" I ask.

He shrugs. "Oh, I don't know. Getting older, looking back. What would you do differently if you could—that sort of thing."

We reach the top of a steep hill, and I catch my breath as we go over.

"I've thought about doing something similar," I say, still cautious. "With books."

He glances at me. His expression is friendly, interested. "Really? I don't quite see how it would work with books, but that's probably just my own lack of imagination."

I don't answer right away. "I've thought it might be interesting to change the endings," I say. "Find out how things might have worked out differently for the characters."

"Hmm," he says. He slows to let a dog walker cross the street, five animals of different sizes and colors pulling her forward, leashes tangling.

"What does 'hmm' mean?" I ask.

"Oh, I don't know. I don't read as much as I should, but I always thought part of the appeal is that books never change. You know, that I can read *Great Expectations* or whatever, and it's exactly the same story people were reading a hundred years ago. There's some continuity there."

"That's an interesting example," I say, seeing an opportunity. "Dickens actually *did* write two endings for *Great Expectations*. When he finished the novel, he showed the manuscript to Edward Bulwer-Lytton, and Bulwer-Lytton thought the ending was too bleak. Dickens ended up changing it so that it's more ambiguous; if you want to read a happy ending into it, you can."

"He changed it before or after it was published?" Roland asks.

"Before. The first ending was never published in Dickens's lifetime, but now they're both available. Scholars have all kinds of"—here I wave my hand in the air, though I'm not sure if I mean to be dismissive or not—"spirited debates about which one is better."

"Oh, that's lovely," Roland says. "So after he died, people went through his papers and published the stuff he'd decided wasn't good enough. You know what that is, when you write something and show it to your friends and get some feedback and then change it? That's called revision. It's like when you watch a DVD, and they've got all the deleted scenes from the movie. Usually, it's not hard to see why those scenes were deleted in the first place."

I don't say anything. I'm trying to figure out a rebuttal, but I keep getting tangled in the threads. I've never been very good at debating.

Roland shakes his head. "I don't like it. I want answers—does the boy get the girl, did the butler do it, whatever. That's your job—you're telling me a story, I want to hear a *story*. I don't want to get interested and get all the way to the end and find out you're not going to tell me what happens. It's like when someone tells you a joke but they can't remember the punch line."

This conversation is bothering me more than it should. "But there's also a personal side to it," I say. "We're all submerged in our work, you know? I'm in my books, you're in your songs. And if I've changed since I wrote those books, if the way I see my life events is different, and the way I approach relationships is different . . ." I think about how to say this. It's important, but I don't feel like I'm articulating it right. "If I were writing any of those books now, they wouldn't be the same books. I want to change the way I put myself in them."

He shrugs. "You're getting into some kind of *Dr. Who* time-travel thing now. The only way you got here, to the point you're at now, is by writing those books the way you did . . ." He pauses, then shakes his head and smiles ruefully. "I don't know, you've kind of lost me. I guess I'd just say that if you want to do something new, do something *new*. And whoever you are now, whatever ways you've changed, that's going to show up in the new work without your even trying."

I look at him, his face in profile as he drives. Already he's familiar to me in a different way than he was when we met. It's a little bit like fleshing out a character in fiction; you start off knowing the most basic things about them, but it's only by spending time with them, getting inside their heads, that you learn who they really are. "Well, okay," I say. "But how is this any different from what you're talking about doing with *Underneath*?"

He thinks about it, tapping two fingers on the steering wheel, then laughs. He looks surprised. "I was going to say, music is just a different beast, and it's always interesting to hear an old song played in a new way. But you know what? I think you may have just talked me out of it."

My mouth opens several seconds before I actually say anything. If I were trying to describe it in writing, I'd probably use the word "sputter." "And how did I do that? I'm on the pro side of this, remember?"

"Yeah, but you've made me think about it a different way. People have known these songs for thirty-odd years, yeah? And they've sung along in their cars and played them at parties and all that. I think if we redo them, we run the risk of having people say, 'Why mess with a good thing?' Or even 'Look at those pathetic old bastards trying to cash in on their past glories.'" He laughs. "We've got our place in rock history, such as it is, and our biggest job now is not to embarrass ourselves before we die."

Roland turns a corner, and I realize we're on Milo's street. I recognize it from the *Turf Wars* segment, and I feel suddenly anxious. Milo's house stands out prominently among its neighbors, the front yard wrapped in yellow crime-scene tape, broken and fluttering. There's no one outside the house at the moment, no reporters or murder groupies, but the grass and surrounding sidewalk are covered with trash and flattened debris, like a fairground after the carnival moves on. As we get closer, I can see that the driveway contains a makeshift shrine where people have left a strange mixture of artifacts: stuffed animals and bottles of tequila, black lace lingerie and signs that read JUSTICE FOR BETTINA. I guess there's no consensus yet on what Bettina's legacy will be: will she land on the side of rock-and-roll icon or victim on the milk carton?

Roland pulls up next to the curb and stops. "You all right?" he asks, and I realize that I've been sitting here looking at the scene instead of opening the door. "You want me to come in with you?"

I shake my head. "That's okay. Thanks for the ride."

He nods. "I'm going to run some errands, but it won't take me long. Just give a ring when you're ready to go." He asks for my phone— punches his number right in, which wouldn't have occurred to me— then watches as I get out of the car and walk up the front steps, waiting to see that the keys work before he drives away.

There's a chiming sound as I open the front door, a feature of the house's alarm system that lets inhabitants know when someone new comes in, even when the alarm isn't turned on. I remember this being mentioned in one of the news stories I read, though it didn't sound as if investigators found this detail to be particularly relevant or enlightening.

I step inside, and I'm in the turquoise-painted foyer I remember from the video. The air feels heavy, the way it does when you return home after a long trip. The ceramic-tiled floor is dirty, smeared with dark footprints, and I think of all the people who must have been tramping in and out over the past week, the detectives and forensics experts and whoever else is granted access to the site of a violent death.

I feel vaguely unsettled, maybe just from being here or maybe from the conversation with Roland, and as I close the door behind me, I feel scared. Not scared for my safety—nothing that tangible. But afraid of being here, afraid of entering this house, which no longer has the evolving-organism, blank-slate potential of most spaces where people live. It's been frozen at a single moment, its symbolism fixed and monolithic. And I don't want to walk in far enough to become part of the tableau.

I let the feeling pass through me, like a chill, and then I'm ready to move on. I walk through the velvet-red dining room and into the kitchen, my eyes landing on the counter where the ghost of Bettina might as well still stand, slicing mangoes. It's strange having seen these rooms without ever having been inside them; it's like visiting the empty set of a dream.

If I'm here for any reason other than snooping around, it's to find out the extent of the damage in the master bedroom, but I'm going to need a little time to prepare myself for that. I wander through a doorway into a space that I would probably call a den but that I believe Milo referred to as a "media room." At the time of the *Turf Wars* tour, there were layers of pillows strewn artfully over the floor in a gesture that seemed to mean something like "Why sit on a couch when the whole room can be a couch?" But now the cushions have been tossed into a messy heap, revealing dull off-white carpeting underneath. There's a crack in the face of the TV mounted on the wall, and I wonder if it's something that happened during the investigation.

Walking through the house afterward, I'm thinking, *it was impossible to separate the cumulative ruin into different strands: how much had been caused by the murder, how much by the police, how much by the day-to-day effects of a relationship that, depending on who you asked, was either loving and warm or fierce and treacherous.* This isn't unusual for me, this kind of narration; most of the time, I hardly notice I'm doing it. But now, as I draw back to listen to myself, I'm surprised enough that I stop and stand still. I see what I'm doing: I'm crafting the kind of sentences that might appear in a memoir.

"Write what you know" has always seemed unnecessarily limiting to me. I prefer instead, "Know what you write." You want to inhabit a character who's a banshee or a soil scientist or a Mesopotamian slave girl? Fine. Just make sure you get it right. Make it real; make it true; find the details to convince me.

But it's impossible, isn't it, to escape writing what you know? That slave girl may be able to pickle locusts and read omens in animal entrails, but she also knows how it feels to kiss your husband in the dark. When her hair is shorn so that her forehead can be branded, she will cry your twenty-first-century tears. And if she has a child, he will have your son's eyes and his heartbreaking capacity for worry.

I can't avoid it; that's what I'm saying. I can't *not* write about Milo, because he's there, in every story I try to tell. What I *can* do is look at the two of us as clearly as I can. Give myself time to sort, and distance, and disguise. Set my own rules for privacy; decide what to keep to myself.

I walk past a bathroom that wasn't on the video—it's nicely appointed, but if it has any particular theme, it's too subtle for me to identify—and into Milo's practice room. It's spare and fairly empty, with a stage at one end, set up with various pieces of equipment: amplifiers, microphones, a selection of guitars arranged on stands. There are no windows in the room, and the walls are lined with fabric-covered squares that I think must be soundproofing panels. If a writer had been plotting her murder, Bettina probably would have died in here.

There's one other doorway in the room, and it leads to Milo's office. In the *Turf Wars* clip, it had seemed as if the entire room were papered with fan letters, but I see now that it's only the back wall. Amazing to see, all these things that strangers feel compelled to give my son. There are poems and drawings, photos of topless girls who look barely old enough to be in high school. Love notes and hate mail. An e-mail from a father whose teenage son died in a car accident, telling Milo that they'd played Pareidolia songs at the funeral. A child's letter, written in crayon, asking Milo to come to his birthday party.

There have certainly been times when I've wished that being a writer brought more public recognition with it, more chance of fame.

But I think I've always known that it's not something I'd really want. Several years ago, on a trip to Key West, I visited Hemingway's house and was astounded to find—there in the courtyard, where Hemingway swam and drank and did God knows what private things with assorted wives and friends and guests—a machine for making souvenir pennies with the author's face on them. I thought it was funny, the juxtaposition of art and kitsch, the opportunism of a tourist industry willing to slap anyone's face on a coin if they think people will buy it. But it also made it clear that the tourists they were gouging, me included—and yes, I made my penny, which cost me a total of fifty-one cents—weren't any different from tourists visiting, say, Ripley's Believe-It-or-Not. A group of us, following the tour guide, making notes about six-toed cats and imagining that walking through rooms Hemingway walked through will give us insight into anything besides what kind of pillow he liked to sleep on. Imagining that we're studying literature, when we're really just looking for something to do before the bars open in a town where Ernest Hemingway is accorded the same status as Jimmy Buffett.

I walk slowly through the room. There's a single shelf of books, none of them mine, and I spot Milo's high school yearbook in between a rhyming dictionary and the most recent edition of *This Business of Music*. A sofa next to a table holds photographs; again, no sign of me, but there are several of Milo with Rosemary and Mitch. I pick up each of them in turn, though it's not really to look at them. They're all pictures I have at home: Milo holding newborn Rosemary (adults hovering just outside the frame, on alert for sudden toddler movements), Mitch standing in front of a car he'd just bought. What I want is to touch the objects themselves—solid weight, bright colors behind glass—to hold in my hands something that Milo and I own together.

The last thing I stop to look at is a line of frames on the wall, but they don't contain pictures. When I get close enough, I see that they hold sheets of paper full of lyrics written in Milo's tight, crowded scrawl. All songs I know, songs from the albums, but for the first time I can see the process by which he wrote them. I can see words crossed out and verses abandoned. That "Your Brain on Drugs" started life with the title "Cracking the Shell," and that the couple described in "Atomic Mass" originally met at a party instead of a strip club. It's the creative impulse made visible, and it makes me think that there's always something arbitrary about finishing a song or a novel, choosing the point when we can declare it "done."

I sigh and head back toward the staircase in the entryway. I've got to go up there sooner or later; no point avoiding it. I climb up, thinking about Milo, imagining his footsteps that night, but there's no special insight to be gained from retracing his steps.

On my way up, I'm trying to get my bearings, to think which side of the house the bedroom might be on. I know it faces the bay; I remember the view of water from the windows, the sliver of red from the Golden Gate visible when the camera caught the angle right. But when I get to the top, I see that I'll have no problem finding the right room. All I have to do is follow the marks on the floor, the trail of footprints and dirt and dark coins of blood.

I walk toward the room, which is at the end of the hall. On the doorjamb there's a bloody handprint that I know for a fact is Milo's; it's one of the more lurid details that have been made public. It looks to me like he grabbed at the doorway to steady himself on his way out of the room. I think, incongruously, of kindergarten projects I have stashed in the attic somewhere, hands that share these same fingerprints, but smaller, dipped in brown paint and turned into Thanksgiving turkeys.

I step inside the room and let myself look it over slowly, white linens and wood floor, mottled Rorschach of black and dark crimson. It's a lot of blood, though maybe less than I'd been imagining. The largest stain spills from the flat plain of the bed over the side and onto a downy white rug that I imagine was chosen for its kindness to bare feet. She was standing next to the bed, they've said, when the first blow came. The attacker was standing to her left, and the force of the hit knocked her sideways onto the sheets, which is where she was when the weight made contact with her head again. Amazing that they can know all this, that they can look at a broken body and stained sheets and deduce angles of impact and order of events. That they can find answers by charting the spots where the blood fell as the weapon was raised anew. A story written in droplets. Divination by spatter.

I try to shock myself by slipping my brain this piece of information: whoever stood in this bedroom and lifted that weight, whoever brought it down with full knowledge and intent, it's almost certainly someone I've already met. Perhaps—and I have to allow for this possibility— someone I know well.

This is where the montage would go, if this were a movie: Each of the suspects picking up the murder weapon, one by one. Each of the different paths that might have led, inevitably, to this single outcome. This is where I would lay out clues, sort through timelines of personal betrayal and algebraic equations of romantic entanglement, known and possible. Search the ground for places where anger and jealousy might have taken root.

I realize I've been holding my breath. This, what I'm looking at . . . it's not frightening, the way I thought it might be. This is not a horror movie or a Halloween haunted house. It's the nucleus of a human tragedy. A life ended here, and the circumstances under which it happened—however wretched, however monstrous—should not be the focus. This spot marks a boundary, an endpoint, and I feel unexpectedly solemn. I have an impulse to kneel down, to press the palm of my hand against the stain on the rug, and I do it before I can think of the reasons I shouldn't. I let myself feel it, the place where the fibers go from soft to brittle, and I offer my silent eulogy.

I stay there for a few moments, and it's while I'm paused like that on the floor that I hear the double chime, the one that signals the opening of the front door. I stand up, my heart beating faster even as I run through the reasonable possibilities that someone might be entering the house. Did I say I didn't find it scary, being in this room where a murder has taken place? Apparently that was bullshit.

I walk out of the bedroom as quietly as I can and make my way to the top of the stairs. Looking down over the railing, at first I can't see anything beyond the solid flank of the door, the slant of it blocking whoever's on the other side. Then it closes, and I hear it latch. And Kathy Moffett comes into view.

From the Jacket Copy for

CRYBABY BRIDGE

By Octavia Frost

(Farraday Books, 1994)

/|||\

Alannah Ringgold died angry. After discovering that her husband had been having an affair, she drove off in the rain to confront him, only to skid through a guardrail on a bridge and plunge into the water below.

Now, devastated by her separation from her twelve-year-old son and unwilling to leave her child in the care of the man who betrayed her, Alannah finds herself stuck in the earthly realm, unable to move on to whatever might come next. She haunts the new family whose lines have been drawn in her absence, and places her son in the center of a custody battle between the living and the dead.

/||\\

I wonder how long we might have gone on like that—me hovering, watching you through a pane of glass like a nervous mother on the first day of preschool, making my presence known only through the occasional unexplained thump or flicker of the lights. Maybe years, if I hadn't heard that one sentence pass your lips. If I hadn't heard you call her "my stepmother."

It is said that a mother who sees her child in danger can do amazing things. We are ferocious when we need to be: we will beat off the attacker with a baseball bat; we will find the strength to lift the car off the near-broken body. You called her "my stepmother," and the fury that coursed through me gave me power. I knew suddenly that if I wanted to, I could knock this whole house down with my grief and my need. I could lay its inhabitants flat.

It's the middle of fall by now, a few days before Halloween. Last year—my *last* year—I remember you dressed up as Charlie Chaplin; none of your friends even knew who that was. But this year the tide has turned, and the boys you know have decided they're too old for trick-or-treating. Instead they want to scare themselves and each other. Our town is a little too sterile, a little too tidy, for the kind of abandoned houses that kids can convince themselves are haunted. But we do have one site worth visiting on a dark Halloween night, and it's a nice synchronicity that urban legend and personal history have come together so cleanly. You're going to spend the evening at Crybaby Bridge.

According to tales that have haunted this region far longer than my ragged spirit has, I'm not the first person to spend her last seconds in a shaky drop on the other side of that iron railing. The details vary, depending on whom you ask and what lesson they want to teach, but most people agree that the story begins with a mother and a child. Was the woman an unfaithful wife? An unmarried schoolgirl? No one's sure. But she'd done something wrong, that much is clear, and she wanted to clean the slate. She came to this bridge with her newborn baby, and she dropped him over the side. Some say she threw herself after him, and others say she lived to face her punishment. But ever since, if you sit on the bridge when the moon is out, you'll hear something strange. A baby. The sound of a baby crying.

There's a related legend involving a stalled car—supposedly if you drive to the middle of the bridge and turn off the engine, the car will begin to move under its own power, and later you will find tiny handprints in the dust on your rear bumper. But you, of course, are not old enough to drive, and neither are your friends. You'll be taking Option A, the simpler and purer of the experiments. You'll be listening for the baby's cry.

The boys who are your friends now are not the same ones I knew just a few months ago. There's been a bit of a restructuring, the kind of gerrymandering of friendship that happens so often in adolescence. You, by virtue of having suffered a loss they cannot fathom, have become a kind of shaman figure, a role that will reach the pinnacle of its usefulness on the night of October 31. They want to find a ghost, and they figure that if anyone can summon it, it will be you.

I follow you from room to room as you get ready to go out. You're putting together a costume of sorts—that's everyone's cover story, because what parent would approve of this little anthropological expedition? You put on long-john bottoms, then a pair of black pants—the dress pants I bought you for the holidays last year, too short already—which you roll up to the knee. You tuck in a baggy white dress shirt you've taken from your dad's closet and tie a long winter scarf around your waist like a sash. Black sneakers, because the only boots you have are snow boots, and they're blue. You put on the tricornered hat we bought at Colonial Williamsburg, and you're a pirate, or close enough. If I were here, really *here*, I'd find that old stuffed parrot you used to carry around. I'll bet I could pin it to your shoulder. But I'm not here, and you don't really care about the costume anyway.

You're carrying an old canvas tote bag I got free once from a travel agency; ostensibly, it's to hold all your candy. What it really contains is a thermos—your old Ninja Turtles thermos, for Christ's sake; why is there no adult supervision?—

filled with a combination of Coke and a tiny bit of liquor from every bottle you could find. This is another part of the plan, and I'll bet you anything someone shows up with cough syrup.

You go downstairs, into the living room, and there *they* are, so cozy on the couch, watching TV. They exclaim over your costume, your pathetic thrown-together costume that anyone can see is nothing more than an afterthought. I focus my energy, knock a magazine off the coffee table. The bitch has chosen a new tactic for responding to my outbursts: she's ignoring me. She calmly picks the magazine up and places it back on the table, careful to keep her face neutral. She stands and walks over to you, straightens your hat, and then she has the nerve to lean down and kiss you on the goddamned cheek. And your reaction, your shy needy smile, cuts through me like a blade. I wait until she's stepped away from you, until that hideous light fixture she picked out is right above her head. Then I rally my fury, squeeze it into a tight ball, until one of the bulbs shatters, sending tinkling little shards down into her hair. That gets a reaction: she flinches and I have the satisfaction of seeing a flash of fear cross her face. But only for a moment. Then she composes herself and continues giving you a list of instructions about staying safe while you're out.

You say your good-byes. And they let you go. Later they're going to go over this moment again and again, and they'll never be able to decide what they should have done differently. They may not even make it past the pain that's coming their way—their relationship isn't weathered enough to withstand much thrashing—but I'm surprised to find it makes no difference to me either way. It's you I care about. They can go to hell.

You leave the house without putting on a jacket; you're going to be cold, though I don't suppose that's something I need to worry about for much longer. And you walk off to meet your friends at the site of your mother's death.

I may as well tell you, there are no ghosts at Crybaby Bridge, at least none until I arrive. It's possible that something terrible happened here once—many terrible things, perhaps—but there's no spectral baby crying out for his mama, no wailing woman searching for the child she's forsaken. What there are instead, if you need an explanation, are bare branches and wind, the movement of water and the call of the occasional owl. And several generations' worth of overactive imaginations.

But I feel some kinship with this nameless mother, this imaginary murderess whose story exerts such power over children as they edge toward adulthood. All of those nightmare figures, real and legendary, drowning our children in bathtubs and rivers: we are not monsters. We are human. Nothing less, and certainly nothing more. Ordinary women until you appeared, our children, making us into something else. You, floating, a nucleus. You started off inside us; no wonder we think that to protect you we have to consume you.

I circle you as you walk. I wonder how you would feel if you knew I was here, if you knew what job I'm prepared to do tonight. I remember once when you were small and you had just learned what it meant to die. You were frightened, and it was too big for me to explain, and I was trying to find a way to make it seem less dire. "It's not something to be scared of," I said. "The day you die is the day you find out the answer to the biggest mystery of all."

But it turns out I was wrong, because I still don't know what happens to *most* people when they die. They're not here, I know that much. Those of us who stay behind are relatively few. We are the ones they refer to in Asian folklore as "hungry ghosts." Wanting and empty, we roam around, trying to find what we need to fill us. But it's no use. Our mouths are like pinholes, our bellies the size of the moon.

I don't know where the rest of the dead go, and I don't know if I am fated to join them someday. If there is another realm, I don't want to go there, not unless I can take you with me. I am here because I need to be, for your sake. I have to believe that the choices I've made have been the right ones. I have to believe I've always acted with love.

. . .

Time fades in and out in that way it sometimes does for me, and I'm afraid I've missed my chance, but when I stabilize, I see that you're sitting with your friends on the span of the bridge itself. I hadn't realized they'd closed this part of the road to cars, and I wonder if it has something to do with my accident or it's just part of some long-planned project to streamline the flow of traffic.

You've been drinking the vile mixture you composed in the thermos that I used to fill with chocolate milk, and you're getting a little wobbly. So much the better. You're all taking turns telling scary stories; every one of you, apparently, knows someone who knows someone who found a dead body hidden in a hotel mattress or hatched spiders from an innocuous pimple on her cheek. Whenever there's a quiet moment, someone makes an exaggerated crying noise—*waahhh!*—and you all laugh with relief.

The place where my car broke through the railing hasn't been fixed, just covered with plastic webbing and caution tape, and I see you looking at it from time to time. I'm angry, suddenly, at these boys, who brought you here without thinking that it might cause you pain, and the force of the emotion gives me strength.

I move away from you and drift down until I'm just above the surface of the river, right at the spot where I felt my last terror, where my car filled with water and my human travels came to an end. And with the gathered rage of every mother whose child has ever been taken from her, I make two things happen at once: I flare myself visible, my woeful figure manifesting itself momentarily against the sky, and I make a noise that sounds like your name.

It lasts only a few seconds, and if you look down too late, you'll see nothing but tangled grass and black water. But you look exactly when I hoped you would. You don't call my name—you're too aware of the other boys and what they might think—but you stand up like you've been shocked, and you walk unsteadily toward the broken place in the railing.

Your friends behave predictably: they think you're making a joke, and then they get worried and start telling you to come back. You're at the edge now, looking down, a few sheets of plastic all that stands between you and the drop. I can't see your face, just the angle of your head. We are so close to reunion, so close, and I pull together my hope and my fear and I show myself to you one more time.

You make a mournful noise, a wounded noise, and lean farther over the edge. One of the boys is coming up behind you, and he yells out and tries to grab your arm, and you step away from him and stumble. And you fall.

I watch you plummet, watch you struggle in the air, and for a moment I'm afraid. The part of me that remembers being alive, that knows the rhythm of breath drawn in and breath released, wonders if I have done something unforgivable. But I acknowledge the feeling and let it pass. I am your mother, and you belong with me. Some things are not negotiable.

You break the surface and I plunge beside you. I will stay with you, my baby, during your time of distress, and I will be there when you come through on the other side. Finally I'll be able to pull you to me, and we'll float together, and I'll be holding you close at last.

I wish I could do it for you, but I can't, so I just stay near. Soon there's nothing but the glow around you and your choking voice and my joy lighting the water. We sink down together toward the mud and the silt, and it ends and it ends and it ends.

Excerpt from

CRYBABY BRIDGE

By Octavia Frost

REVISED ENDING

/||\

I watch you plummet, watch you struggle in the air, and for a moment I'm afraid. The part of me that remembers being alive, that knows the rhythm of breath drawn in and breath released, wonders if I have done something unforgivable.

As you come closer, I become aware of an absence of sound, the way you do when a refrigerator stops running its motor. I hadn't quite realized it, but all this time I've been hearing something when I'm with you: an insect twitter, a note of low-frequency static. Something easily tuned out. But I search for it now, and I find it, fainter but still there. I listen as hard as I can.

In this moment, I feel what you feel. Terror. Anguish. And a desire to suck air into your lungs, stronger even than my hunger to pull you close. I understand suddenly how it's been for you. You're lost and frightened and bruised, and it's not just because I am gone. And I try to think what I can do to ease your pain.

Right before you reach the water, you think of your father, and I see him as you do: a person, a living person, who adores you and who is blessed to be adored by you in return. My anger runs dry, and my love for you gathers like a storm cloud. That adrenaline, that superhuman mother strength, kicks in. And I catch you.

Somehow I've got you, and you're swimming, and you're crawling onto the dirt of the riverbank. Your friends are running down the hill, and I feel what you feel: Relief. Comfort. Something not far from joy.

The earth releases its hold on me, and the last thing I see before I slip away is you, sitting up, alive. I have saved you; it's what I was always meant to do. And maybe that's the reason I died. Or maybe it's the reason I lived.

Chapter Fourteen

///\\\

I haven't said it yet, but of course I'm wondering if it's possible that Kathy Moffett murdered her own daughter.

Let's acknowledge, right off the bat, that I don't know anything. There are whole lifetimes to contend with here, scaffolded with overlapping stories of love and resentment that I couldn't possibly uncover. Any number of secrets might still come to the surface—love affairs and Mafia ties, gambling debts and paranoid delusions. It's possible that there are many reasons why Roland might kill Bettina, or why Joe might, or Chloe, or for that matter Lisette Freyn.

But if the police have eliminated the wild cards—thwarted burglar, crazy fan—and if human beings are as complicated and as transparent as I've learned to expect them to be, then it comes down to the two people who loved Bettina most: Kathy and Milo.

Both possibilities are unthinkable, and both are easy to imagine. A spurned lover: *If I can't have you, no one can.* A mother, falling into that place where the lines between parent and child blur: *I brought you into this world. You're mine.*

Either way, the last moments of Bettina's life were a desperate revelation for her; either way, her death was a lesson in the limits of love and the elasticity of human betrayal. If your house burns down and your children are killed, does it matter if it happens on Christmas Day or the ninth of November?

. . .

After closing the front door, Kathy Moffett stands for a moment in the entryway, the same way I did half an hour ago, absorbing the weighted stillness, the postmortem hush. She looks like hell, or maybe that's putting it too strongly. Her clothes and makeup are as flawless as they were for the funeral, but her body sags as if she can barely summon the energy to make muscle and bone work together to hold her up.

I watch for only a few seconds before I start down the stairs. I can't pretend I'm not here. I have to be an adult about this.

"Hello," I call. There's no way to avoid startling her, and she flinches as she turns. As she looks up at me, her expression is afraid, almost panicked, and then, as she recognizes me, it turns hard.

"I'm sorry," I say as I reach the bottom step. "I didn't mean to surprise you." I hold out my hand, though the way she's looking at me, I don't expect her to take it. "I'm Octavia Frost. Milo's mother."

"I know who you are. I'm not going to shake your hand." Her tone is odd, almost conversational. "I should spit in your face."

I'm so shocked I almost laugh—who's writing her dialogue?—but I stop myself. And because she's decided we don't have to follow the rules of conversation, and because I sometimes turn impulsive and inappropriate in the face of anger, I smile at her sweetly. "Likewise," I say.

I regret it immediately, because being bitchy isn't going to help anything. Kathy raises her eyebrows and shakes her head slowly, smiling in a way that suggests this is exactly the kind of behavior she'd expect from me, as though I'm the only one being childish here.

I sigh. "Okay. Let's start again. I'm Octavia. I won't try to shake your hand."

Something occurs to her, and she looks around, a little bit wildly. "Is he here with you?"

"No. It's just me." I pause. "Listen, I know this is difficult, but I do want to say that I'm sorry for your loss."

She shakes her head again, but she looks more haggard than angry. "Yeah, let's not even," she says, looking at the floor.

"I came by," I say, and then I stop. Which one of us needs to explain her presence here? And do I really want to say that I came by to see how much work it will be to remove the damage done by the spill of her daughter's blood?

"You have a key," I say eventually. I'm trying to think of what needs to be said, and I settle on the key as a practical issue. If she won't give it to me, I'll have to arrange to have the locks changed.

She stares at me. "Incredible," she says softly. "Yes, I have a key. I've always been welcome here."

I accept the barb, let it hit its fleshy mark.

"I was going to get in touch with you," I say. "To ask you what you'd like me to do with Bettina's things."

The anger that's been starching her face since I came down the stairs seems to leach away, and she puts a hand out to steady herself on the wall. She looks suddenly lost. "Oh, God," she says. She sounds like she can't catch her breath. "I don't know."

I'm a little bewildered by her reaction. I'd assumed that she'd already thought about the need to sort through Bettina's belongings; I thought that was why she'd come in the first place.

She's breathing fast, and I'm afraid she'll hyperventilate. "Okay," I say. "It's going to be okay." I hesitate, then put out my arms, guide her into the dining room, and settle her on the long velvet banquette.

"Just sit," I say. "I'll get you some water."

I go into the kitchen and open cabinets, looking for a glass. Who picked these out, I wonder when I find the right cupboard and pull out a narrow blue tumbler—Milo or Bettina? Who picked out those dish towels and that toaster oven and those heavy, expensive-looking saucepans? Did they go shopping together, like newlyweds setting up house? Or maybe it wasn't either of them. Maybe when you're rich and busy, you just hire someone to furnish your kitchen for you.

I open the refrigerator, looking for bottled water. There isn't any, but the smell of something just beginning to rot gives me another item to add to my list. I take a moment to look over the inventory, the groceries Milo and Bettina expected they'd be eating together. Soy milk, several varieties of mustard, some sort of salad greens in the crisper. Half an avocado, long since brown. It's like the concert rider I read online: raw material that refuses to shape itself into any kind of narrative.

I find ice in the freezer and fill the glass with water from the tap. Kathy's sitting where I left her, slumped and small. I put the glass in front of her and sit down in a heavy wooden chair on the opposite side of the table.

"It was almost a week ago," she says. She puts her hand on the glass of water but doesn't pick it up. She sounds incredulous, though I can't tell if she thinks a week sounds like too long or too short a period of time to describe what she's gone through. "A week ago I was here and she was here."

I nod, though she's not really looking at me; she's looking at nothing, or else at her hand curved around the blue glass.

"She was so cute when she was little," she says. This is the moment when the interaction crosses a threshold for me. This is where, when I'm telling the story later, I'll say that it "started to get weird." But it's not really that she's saying anything so strange; it's that she's shifting my role, without my permission. She's laying out new rules: she's going to talk, and I'm going to listen, and I don't really have a say in the matter. When I've found myself in situations like this before, taken hostage by a conversation on a plane or someplace else where escape is impossible, my response has always been to draw back just far enough to become a spectator. Material, I always think. Keep listening. There might be something good.

"I remember her on her first day of school," she says. "She was wearing this little white dress with flowers embroidered on it that I'd brought back for her from Mexico. Whenever I'd go away someplace, she'd go stay with her dad, and when I came home, she'd always come running up to me and hug me and say, 'Mommy, I missed you the most.'"

I interrupt. "Her dad?" I ask.

"Roland. She always thought of him as her dad." Her voice gets tight. "I still say he was."

And this is sort of what I mean when I say that I'm looking for material: I'm waiting for the moment when the speaker reveals something about herself that she didn't mean to reveal. A quick glimpse beneath the surface, like rolling back a corner of freshly laid sod. It's a small thing that wriggles into view: Kathy doesn't trust the results of the paternity test. Maybe not so strange—we all have our quirks and our unspoken conspiracy theories, and it's certainly true that lab workers are as prone to human error as anyone else. Roland is a rich and influential man who might be able to make things appear to go his way, and Kathy knows better than anyone else where she was and who she was with when her child was conceived.

But. It's enough to tell me that when it suits her purpose, she can be flexible about things that most people take for granted. It's enough to tell me that she considers truth at least a little bit fluid.

"She was always so well behaved," Kathy says, rubbing at the condensation on her glass. "Such a good little girl."

There's a pause. "From what I hear, she grew up into a wonderful woman," I say. Keep her talking. You never know what you'll find.

She looks at me. Her expression is almost challenging. "We were best friends," she says. "We talked on the phone twice a day, at least. She never made a decision without getting my opinion."

I nod. "That's rare."

"It is. Very rare. You wouldn't know. It's not the same with sons."

You wouldn't know about sons, I want to say, but I don't. "I had a daughter. But I never got to know her as an adult."

She looks at me appraisingly. "That's right," she says. "I forgot about that." I wait to see if she's going to add any of the usual things one is supposed to say here—"I'm sorry," or "What a terrible loss"—and I'm interested that she doesn't.

"Still," she says. "You've got one left, even if he is a psychopath. You've got . . ." She looks at me as if she's accusing me of someting. "You've got a *grandchild.*"

I don't say anything. "Which is worse?" Kathy asks, watching me intently. "To lose a child to an accident and still have one left, or to lose a child to violence and be left all alone?"

I stare at her, stunned. I'm not sure, but I think she may actually expect me to answer, and for a moment I have an impulse to modify her equation, add in the variable of lost husbands and ask her how that changes the balance. "It's always a tragedy," I say finally. My voice is a little bit shaky, and I pause before I continue. "There is no better or worse."

She meets my gaze and gives me an odd smile. When she speaks, her tone is singsong, as if she's talking to a small child. "Someone is lying," she says.

The effect the phrase has on me is almost physical, a jolt, like coming to a sudden stop in a car. I picture the slip of paper, the words written with such force that they're practically embossed. I look at her face, but it tells me nothing.

She stands and picks up her water glass, carries it into the kitchen. And then, because I expect it's coming, because it's the inevitable destination of all those airplane monologues across the armrest, I offer her this, my voice as soft as if it were coming from her own mind: "You should write a book."

She pauses, smiles almost tenderly. "I should. I bet it would sell a million copies."

She pours the water into the sink, ice cubes clanking against metal.

"I'm not entirely sure why you're here," I say. It sounds sharp, rude, but I feel a need to regain control of the situation. "I mean, here at the house, today. Are there things that you left here that you wanted to pick up?"

She looks down, sets the glass carefully in the sink. "I don't know," she says slowly. "I guess I just wanted to be here one more time. I didn't know if I'd get another chance." She looks at me. "Actually, I'd like to go upstairs. Before I leave. If that's okay with you."

I look at her face; her expression is blank. "All right. But just so you know, nothing's been . . . cleaned up."

She nods. I follow her to the hallway and up the stairs. I'm torn between thinking I should give her some privacy and wanting to emphasize that she no longer has free rein here. When she goes into the master bedroom, I stop just inside the door. I turn my body away, so that I don't appear to be watching her, though I can still see her reflection in the mirror over the dresser.

She walks slowly through the room, staying at the edge, reaching out to brush a hand along the wall, the shade of a lamp, a book on the bedside table. Memorizing, maybe; creating a sensory impression. I don't know.

She circles around, then walks to the center of the room and stops in front of the largest of the bloodstains. She looks down at it for a moment, starkly curious, then reaches out a foot and brushes at it with the toe of her shoe.

"I know you're watching me," she says, her eyes still on the floor.

"Sorry," I say. I don't stop looking.

She stares at the rug for what feels like a long time, maybe a minute or more. When she looks up, her face is set into lines I can't quite place. Irritation? Distaste?

"I guess I'm done," she says. She walks past me, out of the room, without looking back, stepping on the bloodstain as she goes.

I follow Kathy back down the stairs and lead her to the front door. She stops and looks around, a little bit dazed.

"I can't make it be okay," she says wonderingly. She shakes her head. "I pushed a piece of hair away from her face. That was the last thing I did."

I nod. She mentioned that at the funeral, too. I know how strong that impulse can be, to invoke details, to enumerate the fine points. There's hope that if we examine the sequence of events carefully enough, we might find a loophole.

We stand in the foyer, neither of us moving toward the door. "She was planning to go to bed after you left?" I ask.

She nods. "She was tired. She told me she loved me. I went over and over it with the police."

There's something that hasn't seemed right to me in any of the versions of the story I've heard. Not for a mother who managed to set up a domestic violence foundation before the week was out.

"Why did you leave her here alone?" I ask. "Weren't you worried that Milo would come back?"

She gives me a scathing look, as if I'm deliberately trying to be hurtful. "She wasn't alone," she says. Her voice is fierce.

I stare at her. "She wasn't?"

"No," she says, sounding angry and tired and sick of everything. "And I told the police that, too. Her friend was here. Chloe."

. . .

When people ask me how I decided to become a writer, I tell them that it happened so long ago I can't even remember. I have the perfect literary myth of origin: I was making up stories before I could even write them down. But it was a long, long time before I knew what I wanted to say.

In a way, Sara Ferdinand wasn't so far off when she said that the deaths of my husband and daughter had given me my life's material. I was thirty-four when they died, and I'd been writing my first novel for more than ten years. Circumstances got in the way—I had children, I had jobs—but I can see now that the real problem wasn't the lack of time or energy. It was the lack of perspective. Too much to write about, too many possible directions to go in. And then came cataclysm and shock and the disintegration of all that was normal. And in the clarity of the narrowing world, I wrote *Crybaby Bridge*.

It's hard for me to know how to talk about the day they died. I don't mean that it's painful, though of course it is; I mean that it's hard for me to find the right point of entry. There are too many different ways in. Think of an outdoor arena—a baseball field, perhaps. You're going to a game that will be played outdoors, but in order to get to your seat, you have to travel a network of concrete corridors and stairways. You have to go inside in order to get out again. Everything is dim and close and damp, but you find your door and go through it, and there it is: the day, the field, the game already in progress. It's stunning, the grass green like in a storybook, the drama below you being enacted by figures you can identify only by the colors of their uniforms. It's vivid, that's what I'm getting at; your eyes need a moment to adjust. Now imagine that you go back inside and walk a little way, in order to emerge from a different corridor. The view is only a few degrees off from the last one you saw, but it's enough to change things. You notice different details; there are different voices cheering or booing, and different pieces of litter, and different men selling beer. The events taking place on the grass are the same ones you'd see if you'd stayed in the previous section, but you're seeing them from a different angle. Can you really say that you're watching the same game?

What I mean to say is this: How do I begin to trace the circumference of that terrible globe of a day? Do I begin with that morning when we woke up, a family of four, in a hotel room in Fish Camp, California, and just keep going until I reach the moment when Milo and I returned to our room at midnight by ourselves? It's important to know that we were on vacation, that we'd flown to Los Angeles, rented a car, and driven up the coast. But do I go all the way back to me and Mitch sitting on our couch with maps and guidebooks? The call to the travel agent, the children fidgeting on the plane? When you're talking about an event that redrew the lines of a family, how can you possibly say that any detail is unimportant?

Okay, stop. Begin with the facts. It was July 13, 1992. Milo was nine, Rosemary was six. We'd planned a ten-day vacation, and this was day number seven. We got dressed and had breakfast, and we left to spend the day at Yosemite.

We were not a particularly outdoorsy family, and our plans were modest. See the giant sequoias, take a walk, have a picnic lunch. We hiked an easy path and spread a blanket at the edge of the Merced River, just above a ledge called Table Rock. We ate sandwiches we'd brought from our hotel, and the children took off their shoes to wade. Mitch and I lay on the blanket and enjoyed our first uninterrupted conversation of the day.

I remember that my sandwich was roast beef and that Mitch's was ham and cheese. I remember that it was warm and breezy and I felt like I could fall asleep. I remember the easy way that Mitch and I were touching: his head tilted against mine, my arm stretched across his chest. I remember leaning in, just once, to kiss him on the neck.

Perhaps you'd think that the scene was so idyllic I let my guard down. But in those places where we still allow nature to reign, I've always been more attuned to danger than anywhere else. I know how easily a foot can slip, a tree branch can crack. This wildness, this splendor, is not here for our enjoyment. We are small and so very breakable. I know the rules: Don't lean over an edge for a spectacular photo. Don't lure an animal close enough to feed it a potato chip. If you drop your sunglasses off a precipice, give them up for lost.

But the water was low and calm, or at least that's how it looked. There had been signs in other spots along our path, warnings and cautions, but there weren't any here. The children just wanted to put their feet in; they were never out of our sight. I thought the choices I was making were sensible ones. We both did. And it was several minutes before I noticed that Rosemary had taken Milo's binoculars into the water with her.

That spring and summer Milo had become interested, to a small degree, in bird-watching, and Mitch had been working to encourage that interest. The two of them had spent much of the plane ride paging through field guides, and Mitch had presented the binoculars to Milo as a surprise that morning, no more than three hours earlier. And now, in the midst of a squabble I hadn't quite been aware of, Rosemary was balancing on a rock several feet from the shore, holding the binoculars above her head, and Milo was just below her, about to grab her ankles to pull her down. I stood up and called his name, sharply, then hers, and in an instant Mitch was in the water, moving toward them. I stood and watched; for reasons I still can't fully explain, I didn't move a single muscle. I was already living on the plane of imagined loss, my life divided for a moment between the certainty that there was still time to avert disaster and the equal certainty that something terrible and irreversible was about to happen. I had been in that place many times before, seeing one of my children chase a Frisbee into the street or reach for a pot of boiling water on the stove, and I'd always emerged without incident, clutching a little too tightly at one small arm or another, squeezing and scolding at the same time. But this time there was a splash, and Rosemary disappeared from view.

Every area of study has its own vocabulary, and sometimes the language is rich, fertile, unexpectedly lovely. In the hours and months that followed, as I spoke to park rangers and police officers and, eventually, read reports of the incident, I was to learn a whole new tongue. Words and phrases that had seemed innocuous before came out of hiding, revealing terrible new meanings. Cataracts. Root balls. Swift-moving water. Waterfalls, in all their varieties: fan, horsetail, punchbowl, plunge. Tied to language as I am, when I think of that day, there's a sort of dark poetry attached to it. Words repeated, like in a sestina or a villanelle. Rushing water, jutting stones. Rock steps. Cascade.

That stretch of river *was* calm; I wasn't wrong about that. But sometimes when water is forced between large stones it becomes channelized, creating a passage that moves much faster than the surrounding currents. A park worker named Mike explained it to me, striking a balance between sympathy and not-quite-scolding. They were horrified and sad, the rangers and rescue workers, and I'll bet some of them think about it still. But they were not in the least surprised.

Rushing water, jutting stones. Rosemary was wearing a blue sundress, and within a few seconds there was no dot of color to train my eyes to. Mitch stepped up onto the rock she'd fallen from and searched wildly for a moment.

Root balls, cataracts. Swift-moving water.

I don't know if Mitch was able to spot her then or not, but I saw him make the decision to go after her. He jumped into the current and was carried away by the flow.

A drowning person does not cry out. A drowning person turns his face upward and tries to inhale. By the time I, dry and safe, could draw breath enough to scream, there was no sign of either one of them.

And then come the stark details, the words devoid of anything like beauty. The five hours it took to recover the bodies. The makeshift dam the rescue workers built out of plywood to divert the water so they could get to them. Rosemary's clothes torn off by the current. Mitch's foot tangled in the roots of a fallen tree. Both of them less than a hundred feet from where they'd begun. Milo hysterical, me a silent shell. Flying home three days later, just the two of us, knowing the bodies were in the plane underneath our seats.

Of course that day and all of the days that followed it became part of my work. It didn't feel like a choice. The profanity of death and the sacredness of grief: what more important material is there? When, in each of my subsequent books, I took time to pause and consider what we had had and what we had lost, it was something like the Muslim call to prayer. Such a powerful act. Imagine taking the time to stop your ordinary life five times a day in order to turn to something holy. A supplication, a reminder. Bearing witness. A summing-up of belief. And if, in my own life and in my own work, I didn't exactly fall to my knees and touch my forehead to the ground, I performed a sort of internal bowing. I honor you. I'm thinking of nothing else. I bear witness that Mitchell and Rosemary lived on this earth. I bear witness that they were loved. I bear witness that they are not gone from my body, from my life. Make haste to remember them. Make haste toward prayer.

\\|||/

"It is ten years since our children left."

Thirteenth-century entry in the town chronicle of
Hamelin, Germany

Chapter Fifteen

/|||\

As I stand outside the house, waiting for Roland to pick me up, I'm thinking about terror and blood-spill, the purposeful breaking of human bones. I'm thinking that I forgot to look up to see the cast-off drops on the ceiling.

Roland pulls up and rolls to a stop. "All right?" he asks pleasantly as I get in the car.

"More or less. You just missed Kathy Moffett."

"She was *here*?" He looks over at me, and I nod. "What did she want?"

"Wasn't really clear. I'm sure she thought nobody would be here. She said she just wanted to be in the house one more time. Because it reminds her of Bettina."

It's possible that it's the truth. People grieve in different ways, though I'm certain that I will never again, as long as I live, walk along the banks of the Merced River.

He shakes his head slowly. "She's an odd duck."

"You must know her pretty well?" I say.

He considers it. "Well, yes and no. Like I said earlier, I spent a fair bit of time with Bettina when she was little, though not so much with Kathy. Kathy adored Bettina, but she wasn't a real stay-at-home-mum type, and it happened pretty often that she'd go on holiday with a boy-friend and leave Bettina to stay with me for a few weeks. But later on we had a falling-out—Kathy and I, I mean—and she made it difficult for me to see Bettina. I missed most of her teenage years, I'm afraid."

"I'm sorry to hear it," I say. "Must have been quite a falling-out." He doesn't answer right away, and I backtrack. "I'm sorry. None of my business."

He shrugs. "Not like it's a secret. It's what I was talking about earlier when I said there was a bit of a saga. Kathy always said that Bettina was my daughter, and I took her word for it—the timing was right, and so on." Scattered raindrops are starting to land on the windshield; he turns on the wipers. "But eventually I got married, and my wife convinced me that we should double-check, you know. We'd talked about having kids, and she was thinking about inheritance and whatnot. She didn't want our children to have to share if Bettina wasn't really mine."

"And you found out she wasn't."

"Yeah. To make a long story short. There was a lot of drama in the middle. Kathy didn't want to consent to the test, and we ended up battling it out in court. I wish now . . . well, who knows what I wish, at this point."

He looks worn out, and it occurs to me that he's lost Bettina twice. I've sometimes thought of my own relationship with Milo in those terms: that even before this recent estrangement, I'd lost hold of him once before. Felt him pulled away by the undertow because I was busy trying to keep my own lungs from filling with water. But it's not true, not in the way it is for Roland. This isn't an ending. I haven't lost Milo yet.

"I would have liked," he says, "to go to the funeral. Would've meant a lot to me."

His face falls unguarded for a moment, and he looks tired and miserable. I feel a rush of tenderness that surprises me; I almost—but not quite—reach out to touch his shoulder. I don't know what he's thinking, but I imagine he's organizing the events of his history, arranging them in a row so he can look at them all at once. Tracing back, like running a finger along a map to follow the curling line of a river. All those years of accumulated decisions and acts of chance—is there a place where he could have made a choice that would have led him anyplace other than here?

. . .

It's late afternoon, and by the time we get back to the house, Sam Zalakis's car is gone. Roland excuses himself—he has a dinner to go to and needs to get ready—and I get myself a bottle of water from the refrigerator and go upstairs to see if I can find Milo.

He's in the library, walking around restlessly, apparently deep in thought. I knock on the doorjamb to let him know I'm here. He looks up, though it seems to take a minute before he actually sees me.

"Hi," I say. "How was your meeting?"

"Good." He stops by the table, taps his fingers on it. "Maybe."

I sit down in one of the big wing chairs. "Did Sam have anything new?"

"Yeah, a couple of things." He starts moving around again, pacing. He's not agitated, exactly, but there's an anxious energy to him, a sense of nerve endings exposed to the air. "The big one is that the blood that was on me—according to the analysis, I didn't have the kind of spatter on my clothes that you'd expect to see if I was standing right there at the moment of impact." He picks up an open can of soda from a bookshelf and takes a sip, sets it down on a different shelf. "So that's in our favor. And the prosecution won't be able to argue that I had time to change clothes and get rid of the old ones or whatever, because there are witnesses who saw me earlier, wearing the same thing I was wearing when I was arrested."

"That sounds good," I say tentatively.

"Maybe. Sam thinks that if we bring in an expert to testify about that, then he can argue that I went upstairs and found her already dead. And that the blood came from me . . . touching her. And walking through the blood that was already on the floor." He sinks onto the couch heavily, apparently wrung out by this last detail. I sit down next to him, give his shoulder a gentle squeeze.

"And you don't remember any of that?"

"No."

I think about it, try to picture it. "Do you think that's possible? No matter how out of it you were, if you'd seen that there was something wrong—if you'd seen that she was *bleeding*—you would've done something, wouldn't you?"

"That's not . . . that's not Sam's theory. Not that I went up there and saw that she was dead and then went back downstairs to sleep on the couch. He thinks that maybe I went upstairs to leave the little toy for her to find in the morning—peace offering kind of thing, which I'm sure is what I must've been thinking when I bought it—and that it was dark, and I just thought she was sleeping.

"That was the other thing. Her blood—it turns out it was on my face, too, near my mouth. Like I might have kissed her. Like I might've gone up there in the dark, drunk off my ass, and kissed her good night without realizing she was dead." He pauses, closes his eyes for a few seconds. "And the thing is, I so would've done that—I was always up later than she was, and I don't know how many times I've given her a kiss while she was asleep. But the idea that she was *dead*, and I didn't realize it because I was drunk and she was . . . she was still *warm* . . ."

His voice breaks, and I watch him struggle to get himself under control. He's slumped down so much that when I put my arm around him, I actually have to lean down to press my lips to the top of his head.

"It's horrible," I say after a moment. "Really, really horrible. But it's in your favor, don't you think, as far as the defense goes? Both this and the detail about the blood spatter being wrong?"

He takes a minute to answer. He's deep in his own head, but he pulls himself back to the conversation. "I don't know. It all depends on the jury, you know? They're going to see pictures of me with her blood on my hands—literal *blood* on my literal *hands*. That's going to make a pretty strong impression."

I nod, make a small noise of acknowledgment. I don't know why it hasn't occurred to me before now that the important task here is to plot a believable story. Not to make up something untrue, but to create a possible truth as vivid and as convincing as the one the prosecutor will be spinning.

I murmur softly, reach out to stroke his hair. When I speak, it sounds abrupt and loud in the quiet room. "Did you know that Chloe was there that night?" I ask.

He looks at me, nodding. He knows what I mean. "Yeah. Kathy mentioned it in her statement." He stands and walks to the table, begins shuffling through the papers there. "You think she killed Bettina?"

I want to be careful here. "I don't know. What do you think?"

He laughs humorlessly. "Fuck if I know. As far as we know, there were only three of us there that night—me, Kathy, and Chloe. If you'd asked me a couple weeks ago which one of us was most likely to *kill* somebody, I would've said none of us."

He finds the statement he's been looking for and skims it quickly. "Kathy says that Chloe came over to congratulate us on the engagement. I guess she would've heard about it from Joe, if she was there when I called from the restaurant."

"What else does she say?"

"Just that the three of them were there for a couple of hours, packing up Bettina's things, and that Chloe was still there when she left around eleven-forty-five."

"And did the police question Chloe?"

"Yeah." He flips through the papers, pulls out a different one. "She says the same thing, more or less. She says that she didn't stay much longer. She left ten or fifteen minutes after Kathy did, because Bettina was on her way to bed."

I think about it. "That doesn't sound right. I mean the part about Chloe coming over to say congratulations and then staying to help Bettina pack."

Milo shrugs. "How do you mean? The two of them weren't that close, but it's not like it's totally out of character. There's that whole female-bonding, 'rally around the wounded girl' thing."

"Okay, but think about what would've happened when Chloe got there. She would've found out not only that the engagement was off but that Bettina knew about Lia."

Milo jerks his head up to look at me, and I hear him breathe in sharply. "God," he says. "I didn't think of that."

"I'm just guessing here," I say. "But I don't think Bettina would have been happy to see Chloe. And Chloe would've been completely blindsided."

Milo begins pacing again. He runs a hand through his hair. "Yeah," he says. "Shit."

"They would've argued about it, don't you think?"

"Yeah, probably. Although I know Kathy wouldn't have left the two of them alone together if they were still fighting by then."

"Does Kathy's statement . . . is any of that in there?"

He shakes his head. "But by the time the police talked to her, I'd already been arrested, and everyone seemed to think it was pretty clear-cut that I did it."

I sigh. "Well, what do you think? Do you think Chloe's in love with you? Did she see Bettina as a rival?"

"God, Mom, I don't know." He sounds exasperated.

"Well, think about it. We've got to figure this out."

"Right," he says. His voice is getting louder. He's angry and scared and looking for somewhere to put it. "Because you're the detective who's going to blow this case wide open."

"Put it away, okay?" I say. That's what we used to say when the kids used a word we didn't want to hear or a tone of voice we didn't like. *Put it away, please.* I take a breath, let it out.

He pauses for a moment, closes his eyes, takes a breath. "She definitely wanted us to be together way back at the beginning, but once she and Joe got together, I thought she was over it." He shrugs. "I don't really know her that well. Honestly, except for the part where she's my best friend's girlfriend, I don't spend a lot of time with her."

"She's not just your best friend's girlfriend," I say, practically spitting out the words. "She's the mother of your child, and you have to deal with that, whether you like it or not." I hadn't realized I was so angry about this.

He stares at me with a hard expression. This is possibly the first time since I've been here that I haven't been on my best behavior with him. How long did I think it could last?

After a long moment, Milo asks, "Why are you even here?" He doesn't sound angry. Just tired.

The question feels coded, like there's a trick answer involved and I'll never be able to puzzle out the right thing to say. "Because I love you.

And you're in trouble, and I want to help." It sounds hollow, like I'm reading from a script.

Milo gathers his papers from the table and starts to walk toward the door.

"Wait," I say. "Stop." My chest tightens, and I'm afraid I might start crying. For four years I've wanted this, *four years* of knowing my son only through gossip magazines and tabloid Web sites. And now I'm here and I'm working so hard to screw it up.

He stops and turns to look at me. "What? What do you want to say?"

"I'm sorry." My voice is thick and ugly, about to crack open. I fill the words with as much emotion as I can, all my remorse and contrition and fear of losing him. "I'm so sorry. For everything."

Milo smiles a little, but not happily. "Yeah, you're sorry for everything. That's a nice way to cover your bases without thinking about whether you need to be sorry for anything specific."

I don't know what to say. Am I supposed to come up with an itemized list of everything I've done wrong in twenty-seven years? I'll do it; I'd be happy to. If he'll just give me the time. "That's not true," I say. "Not at all. I'm sorry for so many specific things. I'm sorry for the time when I—"

"If you say you're sorry for that time when I was in high school and you were on a book tour and your flight got canceled and you missed my concert, I will fucking punch a hole in the wall."

I freeze. So much fury in his voice. And yes, that was the story I was going to tell.

"You just have no clue," he says. "The things you're sorry for are not even close to the things you *should* be sorry for."

And this is where I could get myself into trouble. Because it makes me mad. I feel defensive. I want to yell at him that I did my best. I want to yell until I cry and he feels guilty for upsetting me.

But I don't. I keep my voice calm. "Fine, then. Let's talk about it. I'm not a mind reader. Tell me what I should be sorry for."

He looks at me steadily and speaks slowly and clearly, as if he's reading aloud. " 'They were exactly the wrong two to die.' "

I look down at the table, resist the urge to cover my face with my hands. It's only happened a few times that someone I'm speaking to has quoted my own writing to me, but my reaction always surprises me. There's a jolt of something very close to shame, or maybe a better word would be "exposure." It's a moment of imbalance, the private made public, but only for one of us in the conversation. It's like being caught stealing, or kissing someone you shouldn't. And always, slapped face-to-face with my own choices about phrasing and cadence, I wonder if there's a way I could have said it better.

So when Milo takes that line from *Tropospheric Scatter*, rips out the careful stitches I'd hoped would keep it in place, and lays it down before me, the sorrow I feel first is not for the pain I've caused him but for the imprecision of my own words.

Because it's—okay, it's a jarring line. It's supposed to be shocking, it's supposed to be something a parent might think privately but would never speak out loud. But it's not as horrible as it sounds. What I meant, if we strip away the pretext of fiction and acknowledge that I was talking about my own family, was that I wasn't up to the task of raising this particular child by myself. What I meant was, he deserved better, and if it had been Mitch who lived instead of me, he would have gotten it.

My career as a teacher of writing has been sporadic and not particularly enlightening for either me or my students. But it's taught me something about talent and raw potential, and I've learned that the most damning epithet I can pin to a writer (only in my head—I'm more diplomatic on paper and in discussion) is "competent." It means that the author is not completely without talent—it's not the kind of ludicrously bad writing that you can dismiss entirely—but there's no life to it, no spark. Everything's right where it should be—here's the characterization, here's the shape of the narrative, here's the climax—but it's missing something vital. There's a hopelessness to the idea of a competent writer. I've known bad writers who have gone on to become good ones, but I've never known a competent writer who was able to pull herself up above that ledge.

I was a good mother to Rosemary. To Milo—or at least so I believe most of the time—I was never more than competent.

There have never been any questions about whether I love Milo, whether I like the person he is, whether I respect and admire him and want him to succeed. And if I were to take a quiz in a magazine, ticking off boxes for all the quantitative criteria of motherhood, I'd probably earn a respectable score. Did I feed him and clothe him, soothe his nightmares, keep his body safe? Check. Take his secrets seriously, fight teachers who couldn't see his talents? Cook food that he liked, make up stories I knew would make him laugh? Yes. All of it. I would die for him; I would go hungry so he could eat; I would accept physical pain in his place.

But children are people, right from the moment they're born, and in every human relationship there's a question of compatibility. It's quite separate from the matter of love. It's about fit and friction, the carpentry of daily interaction. Some joints dovetail easily, while others scrape at every contact.

But here's what I failed to get into that sentence in *Tropospheric Scatter*, here's the casualty of my provocative phrasing and my economy of eight words: being his mother stretched me and remade me, and I wouldn't change anything about it. He was not the child I expected. But—and it took me years to understand this, maybe even until he'd almost disappeared from my life—he was the child I needed to have.

Milo's waiting for me to answer, and when I try to double back over the path I've just followed in my mind, all I manage is, "I'm so sorry." I pause for a long moment. "If I could rewrite it, I would." I'm about to go on, to tell him the rest, but his expression stops me.

He's leaning against the bookshelves, deflated but not so angry. He looks at me as if he's searching for something but has no expectation of finding it. "It wouldn't matter," he says, shaking his head. "It wouldn't change anything."

He walks out of the room, leaving me by myself.

And I know. I know that he's right.

. . .

My first novel—the one I wrote for ten years, the one that was never published, even after I'd had success with other books—was called

Hamelin, and it was inspired by the story of the Pied Piper. There's some evidence that the legend may be based on real events; it's mentioned in the town chronicle as early as the thirteenth century, and a stained glass window from the same time period, now lost, is said to have shown a man in colorful clothing playing a flute, surrounded by children dressed in white, like angels. At this distance, no one knows if there was a real man who stole away the town's children, to lead them on a crusade or slaughter them in the shadow of a mountain, but scholars think it's unlikely. It may be that the Pied Piper is a symbolic figure, representing plague or landslide or one of the many other calamities that might empty the air of small voices. It's also possible that in a time of starvation or crisis, a decision was made to send away the village's weakest inhabitants. Or it may be that "children" doesn't mean children at all but simply refers to a group of citizens—children of Hamelin—who left to find their fortune elsewhere. The one thing most historians agree on is that whatever happened, it probably had little to do with pest control; the rats didn't enter the story until three hundred years later.

What interested me at the time—I began writing the book when I was newly married, shortly before I became pregnant with Milo—was not the story's empty spaces but the vividness of the details that do remain. The street where the children were last seen, where even after seven hundred years visitors are asked not to sing or play music. The parents sitting in church, unaware that they're living the last minutes of their life *before*. The number of children lost: one hundred and thirty. The date: the twenty-sixth of June.

Such rich material. And I had no idea what to do with it. I rewrote it more times than I can remember now, trying out different voices, different styles. But I couldn't find a way in.

Thinking about Milo now, balanced as we are on the edge between regret and absolution, it occurs to me that in all that time, I barely considered a detail that belongs squarely in the center of the story. In many retellings there's one child who remains in Hamelin after the others have gone. In some versions he's deaf and can't hear the music; in others he's lame and falls behind in the procession. He's the one who tells the adults what has happened, and he's the one who complicates their grief. He's the anomaly. The one who makes it a lie for them to say, *A man dressed in colorful rags came to town and took all our children away*.

What happened to that boy after the twenty-sixth of June? Was he cherished? Was he seen as a blessing? By his parents, maybe, though it's likely they'd lost other children, and it wouldn't be surprising if they sometimes wished they'd been allowed to keep one of the stronger ones instead. A son who could help with backbreaking work, a daughter who could keep the house. And in the festival of mourning that must have followed that day, those parents might have found themselves excluded, resented. How dare they weep when they were the only ones in all of Hamelin whose house held a sleeping boy every night?

But I didn't mean to talk about the parents. I was thinking about the boy, left impossibly alone. Horrified, neglected, guilty. And maybe even jealous.

There have been times in the past eighteen years when I've thought about the parallels: the empty streets of Hamelin and the empty rooms of my house. There have been times when I've wondered—knowing it's overblown and superstitious, but not able to dismiss it—whether it's possible that by writing about one, I brought the other into being.

There's no *Hamelin* in *The Nobodies Album*, no original ending and no new one. Since the novel was never published, I didn't see the point of including it. But I wonder now if maybe this is the book I needed most to revisit. And for nobody's eyes but my own.

Excerpt from

HAMELIN

By Octavia Frost

Unpublished, 1983–1992; one possible ending, of many

/|\\\

AFTERWARD

THE MOTHERS

Frau Körtig yelled because she couldn't stand the quiet of her house. Frau Vogel was unaccustomed to washing clothes without anyone pulling at her skirt or splashing hands in the water. Frau Arbogast kept cooking too much food. Frau Millich refused to stop sewing linens for her daughter's trousseau.

Frau Braun forgot to add sugar to the plum cake. Frau Schmitt grew so thin her husband was afraid he would crush her while they slept. Frau Koch had nightmares. Frau Finzel had visions of God.

Frau Maier gave birth to a boy three weeks after the children vanished, and every time she nursed him, she wept. Frau Guss prayed every night for a new baby. Frau Schonberg wouldn't let her husband touch her. Frau Weiss was glad that the children could no longer get in her husband's way when he was in a temper.

Frau Hoster never stopped waiting for their return. Frau Jagels took to her bed.

Frau Kollmeyer would never admit it, but there was a piece of her that felt it was a relief.

THE FATHERS

Herr Finzel had a pain in his belly that none of the apothecary's herbs could soothe. Herr Arbogast was cold even in the sunshine. For the first time he could remember, Herr Bauer had no desire to eat.

Herr Hoster forbade his wife to speak any of their names. Herr Schmitt was drunk for a month, and nearly sliced open Herr Braun's throat as he shaved him.

Herr Schonberg spent his evenings carving wooden dolls that no little girl would ever play with.

Herr Weiss roared at the housewives who lingered at his stall, pinching the ducks and geese to find the ones with the plumpest breasts. Herr Jagels put sawdust in the bread dough to stretch the grain and was sent to the pillory with one of his own loaves tied around his neck. Herr Kollmeyer stopped bathing until his wife tried to sponge him down in his sleep.

Herr Maier held his new son—just born, his body freshly washed and rubbed with salt—and couldn't stop his hands from shaking.

THE ANIMALS

The horses were skittish. The dogs whined and searched. The cats slept without anyone grabbing their tails. The songbirds sang. The pigs looked for scraps in the street.

And slowly, slowly, the rats began to return.

THE PIPER

The Piper held no grudge. As far as he saw it, he had taken his payment in full.

THE CHILDREN

Johannes hopped. Ursula twirled. Alfons stopped just long enough to step away from the path and pee.

Franziska was getting tired and wondered if the grown-ups would come soon to take them home. Emmerich wondered if there would be sweets where they were going.

Gabi was giddy that she wouldn't have to do any chores today. Ingo saw a cloud that looked like a new lamb.

Heiner had never been outside the city gates before. Jutta picked up Harald, who had started to cry. Rudi thought maybe he had heard this music before, but wondered if it might have been in a dream.

Ebba smiled shyly when Thomas began to walk beside her. Leonhard hoped Mutti and Papi wouldn't be angry he had gone.

They walked through the valley and up the steep rocks, and when they got close to the peak, they stood and held one another's hands. The piper played, the mountain broke open, and the children danced inside.

Notes on

HAMELIN

From Octavia Frost's notebook,

November 2010

/|||\

Begin at the end: The long line of children, disappearing from view. The boy on his rough crutches, rags tied to the wood in the places where it rubs his body underneath his arms. How long before he stops trying to catch up?

Give him a name. We'll call him Theodor. Nine years old. He has to be nine.

Call up the pictures first. Milo, tall for his age, the top of his head already at my chin. Milo in the backseat of the rented car, reading a book while Rosemary tries to take his attention away from it. Milo laughing as Mitch steals a lick from his ice cream cone.

No, start further back: Milo barefoot, in shorts and a sun hat, smiling in his stroller. Milo barely able to stand, hugging a dog that's bigger than he is. Milo a baby in my arms.

It takes him a long time to get back to the church. Hard, even, to get the door open without losing his balance. The grown-ups, the parents, turning at the noise. He has to get the words out fast, before they look at him like he's done something wrong. Before he sees that they never expected anything else from him.

It was always Mitch whom Milo called for when he had a nightmare, when he needed help with something. For quite a long while after we were the only two left, there were always a few times a day when he would yell out "Daddy!" without thinking about it. Before he remembered there was only me.

Theodor's first memory: he's trying to walk, though he's already past the age when he should have been able to do so, and he worries that this means he's done something wrong. He uses the wooden chest in their bedroom to pull himself up, and for a minute he's seeing the world from a new place. But then he topples, and bangs his chin on the wooden corner as he goes down. He howls, as much from humiliation as from pain. His brother, Erhard, addresses the chest in a loud voice: "You stupidhead! You made Theodor fall!" And he hits it hard with the flat of his hand until Theodor has to stop crying because he's laughing so hard.

"Daddy and Rosemary died." For almost a year Milo spoke these words all the time, to everyone, a hundred times a day. He raised the subject with the woman who gave him broken cookies at the bakery and with the man standing behind us in line at the bank. A piece of paper hung on the wall in his therapist's office, with the words written all over it, urgent and overlapping: "Daddy and Rosemary died Daddy and Rosemary died Daddy and Rosemary died." It was his greeting and his good-night prayer. A riddle. An invocation. A taunt.

It created some awkward moments; there are some stories no one wants to hear. But I understood. It was a way of whittling down his grief into something he could control. Something he knew how to hold.

Don't make him a saint. He's a little boy, and he's lost as much as any of them. He's angry, and he's lonely. He yells when his mother gives him soup that burns his tongue. He laughs when his father gouges a toe on a loose nail in the floor. Sometimes it's an accident, and sometimes he does it on purpose, to see if he can get that look: the one that says they'd be happier with a house as empty as everyone else's.

We were half a family, the two of us sliding along channels that didn't quite meet. If it had been Rosemary, I would have known what she needed. Her grief would have been straightforward: sadness and guilt, spread open like pages.

But Milo was a whirlwind of anger and terror. His pain was a pressure he needed to push against. He didn't want to be held close, to have soft words murmured against the top of his head. He wanted to fight and roar and crush. He wanted to find out how much power he held. If it was enough to make other people feel as bad as he did.

He's better off, Theodor thinks, than some of the other children would have been if they'd been the one left behind. Most of the others don't even make sense on their own. Would Ursula Schmitt resort to pulling her own hair if Rudi Hoster weren't there to do it for her? Would Heiner Weiss cut off a dog's tail so he'd have someone to tease?

Children have their own logic in the same way that primitive cultures have their own cosmologies. It may seem flawed to those of us outside; we think we've advanced beyond it. We are sophisticated enough to know that the world doesn't rest on the back of a turtle. But to a child, it's airtight in its internal consistency. It's not something you can argue with.

When Theodor thinks about that day, he knows he should have seen what was coming. Knows he should have been able to prevent it. It wasn't an ordinary day, even if it had seemed so at the time. He should have noticed that the sky was an unusual shade of blue. Should have known that something was different by the way the air was so still.

So many signs: his foot had been itchy; he'd seen a dog carrying a dead goose, stolen from the poulterer's stall; when he and his brother and sisters walked toward the square, he could see that their shadows all touched, while his stood apart. It provides little comfort, but he knows that if it happens again, he'll know what to look for.

What is the right way to respond to a child tearing the pages out of a bird-watching guide, because if it hadn't been for the birds and the binoculars, he wouldn't have been fighting with his sister at the moment she lost her balance?

There weren't that many options. I knew not to scold him or tell him to stop. I did one of the following things, just one. Did I (a) walk away, leaving him to destroy the book in private? (b) stand in his doorway with my face in my hands, wondering whether or not to let him see me cry? Or (c) sit next to him on the bed and say, "Let's get rid of this thing. What do you think about burning it?"

Never mind which one is true. Tell me which one would have changed things. Tell me which one would have led us, inevitably, to an ending other than this one.

Still not getting it right. Try this:

The day they went away was like a death and a birth all at once. That doesn't sound the way he means it to; he's not breaking it down into anything as clear as sorrow or joy. He knows that birth and death are not the pure events people think them to be. He remembers when his youngest sister, Lena, was born, how angry she was to find herself in the world. And the lovely look on his grandfather's face the morning that he finally didn't wake up.

I tried, but that's not what you want to hear.
There are no pictures of Milo smiling between 1992 and 1994.

When he knocks over a basin of water, when he wakes yelling from a nightmare, he sees it in his mother's face: she is the only one in all of Hamelin who has to face such trials.

He has no doubt that they'd think of him fondly if he were gone. He's seen it happen with the others. There's never any talk of Erhard's stubbornness or Hannelore's temper fits. How Ingo was selfish and Ebba told tales. Here, they had been as much trouble as Theodor is. Gone, they're good and sweet and . . . loved.

While you're going through it, you don't know which things are going to be important. You don't know what they're going to remember.

Which matters more: that I let him stay home from school because he'd been awake with nightmares, and we made pancakes and went to the movies? Or that I yelled at him in front of two of his friends because he spilled soda on some of my notes? That I spent more on his presents that first Christmas than I had on everybody combined the year before? Or that I asked him what the hell was wrong with him when he dumped all the dirt from a potted plant onto the floor?

The adults simply mourn that the children are gone. Theodor burns to know what's become of them. His parents say things that don't make sense—they're inside the mountain, the Piper took them to a wonderful place. For a while he believes it.

He wonders what it's like there. Do they get to hear that music all the time? Perhaps they've formed their own town, a whole new city of children. He imagines them serious: Elke sweeping the dust over a threshold, Rudi and Georg learning trades. They would all need to work together; they would all need to be useful. They would have new roles, becoming far more important than the children they'd been when they were here in Hamelin, putting dolls to bed and drawing in the mud with sticks.

I pieced together a hasty religion, hoping it might bring him comfort. I spoke about heaven as if it were something I believed in. But he was always able to trip me up. He wouldn't accept a heaven with no hell, a god without a devil. No matter how carefully I thought it through, I couldn't come up with a story he'd believe.

He would have gone with them if he could. The music . . . if the adults could have heard it, they'd understand. It was like nothing else in the world.

In his dreams, the Piper comes back for him, just for him. "Come along," he says. "We'll go as slowly as you like." Whatever happened to the other children—whether the inside of the mountain is beautiful or terrible, or something in between—he wants it to happen to him, too.

The Piper leads him out of the city. The mountain cracks open. But he can never see inside.

It was all clear to Milo. Everything had changed, and if the rest of us couldn't see it, it was because of our own lack of vision. If the world could withstand a breach this great—if an organism as complex as a family could be cut in half and still asked to live—then what was the point in following any of the smaller rules?

One of the many days when I was called in to school to pick him up early, I found him on a bench just inside the door, being held on a teacher's lap. His arms were crossed in front of his chest, and she had her hands on his wrists. It looked like a hug, and I was glad to see that someone was providing comfort, consoling him, my poor desperate boy. Until I got closer and realized she was restraining him. She was holding him in place.

He's bent under the double shame: that he let them go, and that he didn't go with them.

His plate, full every day. His mother, bewildered to see him there.

Looking at a dead bird in the street, he can't find a way to see it as anything other than what it has become: an object, empty, still.

Some days he knows they're not in the mountain at all.

I will never fully know what Milo lost. There were games he and Rosemary used to play together, games no one else knew the rules to. Jokes he and Mitch shared, conversations I wasn't a part of.

And now there are songs that no one would have otherwise heard. Books that no one would have read. It doesn't make it worth it—of course not. Never. But it serves a purpose. You need a hard surface to rest your paper against. Without it, you end up writing on air.

He remembers something from when he was smaller. A neighbor of the family had become ill, and it seemed inevitable that he would die. The priest went to the man's house to speak solemn words, to smear oil on his flesh. Then the family waited. But the man didn't die; he got better. Only now that he'd been given the rites of the dead, he was no longer allowed to be a part of the living world. He couldn't sit at meals with his family; he couldn't eat or drink. He had to keep his feet bare. And Theodor heard his parents say that he and his wife could no longer share a bed.

He didn't live long, but for a time he was a curiosity in the town. The walking ghost. The not-quite-dead. Not so different from what Theodor is now.

I remember once, driving down a busy street, I saw this brief tableau: A woman pushing a stroller on the sidewalk stopped abruptly, her body tense and frustrated. As people moved around her, she lifted the baby with one hand, pulled her shirt up roughly with the other, and put the child to her breast. I could see, written in her movements, *Fine. You win. I'll expose myself on the street if that's what you want.*

It's hard to get that balance right: the child's needs and the mother's, generosity and self-preservation. "Motherhood" is not a synonym for "sacrifice," but neither is "sacrifice" a synonym for "submission." It's something that mother and child need to work out. It's something that the two of you have to learn together.

He can't be all of them. He isn't enough. Even before, when he only had to be himself—even then he wasn't enough.

But whether it has to do with strength or weakness or fate or dumb luck, he's here, and he's the only one left who can say it. He's *here.*

He's here. He would have gone with them if he could, but that isn't the way it ended. The day they went away was like a birth and a death all at once.

There are some stories no one wants to hear.

Chapter Sixteen

/|||\

After a couple of hours have passed, time enough for Milo to cool down and for me to shatter and rebuild everything I know about him, I go looking for him.

I find him downstairs, watching a movie in a cozy, denlike room I haven't been in yet. When he sees me in the doorway, he picks up a remote and pauses the action on the screen, leaving a frozen image of a kid swinging a baseball bat.

"Hi," I say.

"Hi."

I venture farther into the room, sit down on the opposite end of the couch. Neither of us says anything for a minute.

"You know," I say softly, "the other day I heard the song 'Traitor in the Backseat' for the first time. I thought I knew all your music, but I'd never heard that one." I reach out tentatively, put a hand on the back of his head. Ruffle his hair gently, like I used to do when he was little. "I loved it."

He doesn't answer, just watches me. He looks wary.

"I really liked the way you wrote about the sibling relationship. The sort of paradox that they annoy each other all the time, but they're connected in a way that no one else quite gets." I'm not sure I've ever talked to him this way about his work. Like I'm thinking about it and not just saying nice things because he's my son. "And all those gorgeous details, about seeing the ocean on the other side of the guardrail and the kids making fun of someone they'd seen, the guy who had a funny-looking tan." I smile a little bit, meeting his eyes. "Just really evocative. Made me cry, almost."

He nods. He looks down at his hands resting in his lap, but I can see he's pleased. "Thank you," he says.

"I think that might be the only song I've heard where you were really clearly writing about Rosemary. Are there others?"

He shrugs. "Not really. There's a line about home movies in 'Every Other Day' where I was thinking about her."

"Right." I nod and think for a minute before I quote the line: "'Under the sprinkler, in an endless ring / Never get older, never miss a thing.'"

Milo nods.

"And I always thought that 'Life as We Know It' was about Daddy, at least partly. Am I right about that?"

"Yeah. Not all of it, just that part about learning to drive. I remember when I was really little, like five or six, I used to think about how cool it would be when I was finally old enough to drive a car. And the way I always pictured it, I figured he'd be the one to teach me."

I smile. "He probably would have handled it better. I was not the world's calmest driving instructor."

Milo smiles, too. "I was so mad that time you grabbed the wheel in the CVS parking lot. You almost swerved us into a light pole. I was *not* going to hit that old lady."

"Probably not. I might have been overreacting. I wasn't used to judging distances from the passenger's side instead of the driver's side, you know? From where I was sitting, it looked like it was going to be close." I think for a minute, not quite trusting my own memory. "Did you actually give her the finger? After the two of us practically ran her over?"

He looks sheepish. "Yeah, that wasn't my finest moment. I was mad at you, and kind of freaked out, because she *was* a little closer than I thought she was. But, you know. Not really her fault."

I smile. "No." I look back at the TV screen, the boy's blue cap, the blur of the bat in motion. "It's really nice that you've honored them that way. Daddy and Rosemary. I think that if they could hear the songs, they'd like them."

He shrugs, deflecting the compliment. "Maybe. Aren't you going to say that they probably *can* hear them somewhere?"

I shake my head. "No. I'd like to believe that's true, but I don't really think it is."

"You've written about them, too," he says. "I mean, obviously."

He looks tentative, nothing close to angry, but I answer carefully. "Yes," I say. "All the time. Even when I don't mean to."

He nods. "Even when you think you're doing something else completely."

The upholstery of the couch is soft, something like suede but more durable. I run a finger over the cushion in a vague circular pattern.

"Clearly 'sorry' isn't the way to go here," I say. "There are a lot of things that I wish I'd done differently, but I love you more than anything else in the world, and I really, really hope that I can get back into your life, in whatever way you're comfortable with."

The words sound clumsy to me, and I regret the 'anything else in the world' part as soon as I say it, afraid he'll take it to mean that if Mitch and Rosemary were still in the world, I might love them more. But when I look at him, he's smiling faintly, looking both annoyed and amused.

"Jeez, Mom," he says. "I'm *right here*, sitting two feet away from you. In what way are you not back in my life?"

For a moment I can't say anything. I'm grateful and overwhelmed, because it's so generous and so understated and just so very *Milo*. And he can see that I'm trying not to lose it, that I'm moved almost to tears by something he said to make me *laugh*, and he rolls his eyes in a way that I know is affectionate. And then I really am laughing along with him.

"I kind of thought that was obvious," he says drily. "I mean, yeah, it's not like everything's all rainbows and puppy dogs, but if I were going to kick you out, I'd have done it before now."

"Thank you," I say, my voice still choked. I lean over and give him a kiss on the forehead.

"For not kicking you out." His tone is sardonic. "No problem. That would make a hell of a Mother's Day card: 'You raised me and nurtured me, and in return I won't send you away to sleep on a pile of garbage in the alley.'"

I laugh again and finally manage to pull myself together, wiping my eyes with a finger. I'm not sure I deserve it, and I'm not sure I won't screw it up, but for the moment I feel lucky. Blessed.

"Have you eaten?" Milo asks. "I'm starving all of a sudden."

He turns off the TV, the little boy on the screen still a moment away from hitting the ball or missing it, and together we walk to the kitchen to find some dinner.

. . .

When Milo was a little boy, we once had a discussion about the difference between DNA and the soul. I'd inadvertently, at different times, defined each of them as "the thing that makes you *you*." I don't imagine that my answer was particularly enlightening; it can be both alarming and humbling to realize the scope of your child's faith in your ability to explain the world to him. As out of touch as I was with the things I'd learned when I was young, I struggled with half-forgotten phrases about dust and breath, coils and nucleotides. I told him that it would all become clearer when he was older.

But here on the other side of "when you're older," we sometimes draw the lines *too* clearly. If I were to ask Milo now, he'd probably say what I said then: that the soul and DNA are completely separate ideas, and that they have nothing to do with each other.

Of the many gifts parents receive from their children, this is one of the best: the way they give us a new way of seeing, even after they've lost the thread of it themselves. Left to my own devices, I would never have dreamed up the idea of an album of songs that don't exist. I wouldn't have remembered that whatever we call it, there's a part of us that's essential, eternal, connecting us forward through generations and Elysium. Making us the people we are.

. . .

Milo and I talk over dinner and for a long time afterward, far-ranging conversations that move from trips Milo took with Bettina to the politics of the music industry to the temperament of the dog we used to have. We don't talk about the details of the murder case or the books I've written or anything else that might possibly unbalance us. I don't want to avoid the hard topics forever, but for tonight I'm giving us a break.

Eventually, though, when the pace of the discussion has become comfortable and soft, I do allow myself this: "So. Tell me about Lia."

We've moved from the kitchen to the living room, or whatever it might be called—the room where Roland keeps his Grammy and his coffee-table books. We're sitting on sofas that are less comfortable but more artful than the ones in the video room.

Milo gives me a look that I know well. It means that he doesn't mind my asking, but he's not going to discuss it in any great depth.

"Lia's nice," he says, deliberately noncommittal. "I like Lia."

I smile. "Okay," I say. "I won't push on this one."

He shrugs. "It's not any . . . it's just what it is."

"Right." I watch him. I'm not going to insist that he elaborate, but I'm also not going to make things easier by changing the subject.

"She's a beautiful kid," he says, after a minute or two of silence. "Sometimes I see her, and I'm just amazed to think that I had anything to do with that. So if by some chance I *don't* end up going to prison for the rest of my life, then yeah—I'd like to get to know her and maybe become something other than Uncle Milo. But I think it should be obvious that now's really not the time."

I nod and look away. I'm embarrassed that I brought it up, embarrassed that I made it seem, even for a minute, that I've forgotten how uncertain Milo's future is. What I really want to know, I suppose, is not what's going to happen next, but why Milo made the decisions he did about Lia, why he didn't step in and become her father right from the start. Or no—if I'm being honest, what I really want to know is whether or not we can reduce it to simple enough terms that I can take the blame. In some perverse way, I want him to say that it's because

Chloe got pregnant so soon after he broke away from me and he didn't want to be a part of any kind of family. Or because I gave him the idea that raising children was a burden. Or because the loss of Rosemary hurt too much for him to consider loving another little girl.

But nothing is simple, and it's *not* always about me. And Milo's right that there are more urgent matters to consider at the moment.

I get up to use the bathroom, and on my way back I stop to look at the table of photographs in the front hall. I'm drawn again to the one of Milo and Bettina sitting by the water in the midst of that strange, artistic debris. I look at Bettina, laughing and holding Milo's hand, leaning her head against his shoulder. It's a loss I'm just beginning to understand, what might have been if I'd known this woman Milo's holding on to so tenderly. This woman who loved him as much as I do.

I look over the background setting again, thinking I should ask Milo where they were that day. Water and open pipes, columns and piles of rocks stacked haphazardly. And then I notice something I didn't see before about the heavy slabs of marble and granite: some of them are carved. Carved like gravestones.

"Milo," I call. My voice is sharp. I carry the picture back to where he's sitting. "Where was this taken?"

He looks at it and sits up straighter. "The Wave Organ," he says.

"What's that?"

He doesn't answer. He's staring at the photo. "This is it. This is where I went that night."

"What is it?" I ask again.

"It's . . ." He lifts his eyes to look at me. His expression is urgent, almost wild. "It's on the bay, near the Exploratorium. It's this big sculpture that's supposed to make music when the water hits the pipes at high tide. It's, like, environmental art, or whatever they call it. It's all made out of gravestones, from when they relocated some cemetery from the Gold Rush or something."

"And you went there with Bettina. Well, obviously."

"Yeah, once."

"Was it . . . an important day? Like a first date or something?"

He doesn't quite roll his eyes. "God, Mom. I don't think I've ever been on a *date* in my life." He looks at the picture again, and his face softens. "But yeah. I just . . . it was the day I knew I loved her."

"And that's where you went on the night of the murder? The place where you fell down and hit your head, after Kathy chased you away from the house?"

He nods. "Not sure how I ended up there. I wasn't planning to go there specifically—I was just driving around aimlessly. But it's not far from the house, and I guess I just saw the turn for the yacht club, which is how you get there . . ."

"Do you remember anything else?"

"Maybe. Let me think." He studies the picture. "I was sitting right there," he says, pointing to a chunky marble platform. "And I had my phone out, and I just kept pressing redial. And I was looking at the water, which was really rough, crashing against the rocks. It must have been close to high tide, because I remember hearing these noises from the pipes sometimes, kind of a soft howling . . . or no, that's saying it too strongly. More like the inside of a seashell, but louder."

I nod, wait for him to go on.

"And, God. I just felt like my life was over. Like if I couldn't get Bettina back, then what was it all for?" He lifts a hand to scratch the back of his neck. "I wasn't thinking about jumping into the water—really, it was nothing like that—but I remember looking at the bay and wondering how it would feel to just fall into it and let it pull me away. Wondering how far away it would take me."

I tilt my head toward the floor so he can't see my face. I close my eyes and concentrate on keeping my breathing regular.

"And then finally Bettina answered the phone. And we talked."

I look back up at him, feeling a little steadier. "Do you remember any more about that?"

He's quiet, thinking. "Not much. She was upset—I already knew that. And I apologized a million times and begged her to give me another chance. Also, I remember that it was right after I hung up that

I fell down and hit my head. I think I might've been unconscious for a while. I don't know."

Behind us, in the entryway, the front door opens, and we hear Roland's voice. "Hello, everyone! Look who I ran into at this wretched dinner party and brought round for a drink."

Milo and I stand and turn to see Roland walking into the room with Joe. They're both dressed up, wearing suits: Roland's is dark and sleek, with a white shirt open at the throat, and Joe's has a faintly retro cut, accented with a bright tie. I'm not prepared for the tone of the evening to shift so abruptly, and their sudden presence, cheery and glamorous, unsettles me.

"Hi," I say, my voice a little too loud. "Chloe's not with you?"

Joe takes off his jacket and throws it over the edge of a chair. "No, we couldn't get a babysitter. She hates these kind of industry things anyway."

Joe sits down on a chair next to the couch, and Roland heads toward the bar at the other end of the room. "What can I get everyone?" he asks.

In my mind I'm plotting a murder. I don't have any idea if it's the right one, the one that actually happened, but in the early stages of conception, it's important to reserve judgment and let the story take you where it will.

Chloe hears from Joe that Milo and Bettina are getting married. She's upset by the news, because she loves Milo or she hates Milo or she doesn't want any other woman to have a claim on her daughter . . . something. She goes over to the house with the intention of disrupting things: confronting Milo, or maybe telling Bettina about Lia. But when she arrives, Milo's not there, the engagement's off, and Bettina already knows the truth. Bettina's furious at Chloe, Kathy takes Bettina's side, and . . . what? If Chloe's goal is to cause friction between Milo and Bettina, then what motive does she have for murder, after she learns they've already broken up?

No, I don't have it quite right. Not yet. But I'm not ready to toss it out entirely. I just have to find the details to make it work.

Roland carries glasses, sets down drinks. "So you two had a quiet night in?" he asks.

As I'm answering, Joe stands up suddenly. "Hey, Milo," he says. "Can I talk to you for a minute?" I watch them leave the room, feeling uneasy. I don't think Joe has looked at me once since he came in.

"I wonder what that's about," I say.

Roland shakes his head. "No clue."

"So the dinner party wasn't much fun?" I ask.

He makes a face. "Nah, they never are." He takes a sip of his drink. "I was bragging about you, though."

I look at him, confused. "What do you mean?"

He smiles. "Told everyone I had a best-selling author staying in my spare room. They were all very impressed."

I laugh awkwardly; I think I may actually blush. "As well they should be. I'm very impressive."

He laughs. "Indeed you are. The head of marketing at my record label had heard of you, and that's saying something."

I'm considering several possible answers, none of which are as witty as I'd like, when the boys come back in. They both look serious. My smile fades.

"Look, I'll just ask her, okay?" Milo says to Joe.

"What is it?" I ask.

Milo hands me a couple of sheets of paper. "Joe found this in his house. Chloe says she printed it out from a Web site called FreeMilo.com."

It's the fake interview. "I know about this," I say. "It's not real. I never said any of these things. I've already put a statement up on my Web site saying I didn't have anything to do with it."

Joe and Milo exchange a look. "That's what I figured," Joe says. "But then Chloe said that the two of you had had a lot of time to talk, and that you'd confided in her . . ." He trails off.

"Confided what? That I did an interview for this Web site?"

"No." He looks down. "She said she played 'Traitor in the Backseat' for you, and you were really affected by it. And you told her a bunch of the things that it says here: that Milo always had a dark side, that he changed a lot after his dad and Rosemary died. And also that you were really upset about Milo's keeping Lia a secret from you. And that if he could lie about something like that, then maybe he was lying about not killing Bettina."

"No." My voice is too loud; the word sounds like a small explosion. "I never said anything like that." Joe's staring straight ahead at an empty point in space. Milo's looking at me, but I can't tell what he's thinking.

"Okay," Roland says, holding up one hand in my direction and one in Joe's. "Let's not start throwing around accusations."

I try to calm down. "Joe," I say, more softly. "I don't know why she'd lie, but it's not true. She did play the song for me in the car—I was just telling Milo how much I liked it—but I never said that I thought Milo was guilty."

Joe nods, still not looking at me. "Okay," he says. "Well, maybe it was a misunderstanding." His voice is skeptical.

"I'm sure that's all it was," I say, trying to sound warm. He loves Chloe; of course he'd take her word over mine. I still can't quite read Milo's expression, but he's meeting my eyes intently, and he doesn't look angry. His eyes narrow slightly, as if he's trying to figure something out.

"When I was talking to Bettina," he says slowly, "that last phone call. She was really upset, and she said that Chloe's version of the story was kind of different from mine. Chloe told Bettina that she'd always wanted to tell her the truth but that I wouldn't let her."

I hesitate. "That's pretty much the way she described the situation to me. That's not true?"

He shakes his head. "I'm not saying I was dying to tell Bettina I'd cheated on her, but Chloe was kind of the one who convinced me. Once she and Joe were dating, she said that she wanted for all of us to be able to hang out together without Bettina thinking that she had to keep me and Chloe away from each other."

I look at Joe. His eyes are moving back and forth between the two of us. He looks wary, even a little frightened. Roland's sitting back in his chair, his expression intense but unreadable.

"Here's the thing," Milo says. "When we were talking, right after she told me Chloe had said that and I was telling her it wasn't true, Bettina said, 'Hold on, I'm going to go into the other room.' And I heard someone say something to her in the background. I'm almost positive it was Chloe."

"She was still there," I say. "At twelve-thirty. Which is definitely later than what she told the police."

"And if she overheard the conversation, she knew we were getting back together."

"Wait," Joe says, his voice sharp. "What are you talking about?"

"Chloe was at the house with Kathy and Bettina, right? What time did she come home?"

"No." Joe shakes his head. "She wasn't at your house *then*, she was there earlier, before you guys went to dinner. Remember, we both came by around six, because you and I were supposed to go over those pictures—you know, for that souvenir thing, for the tour? The program booklet or whatever. We both gave statements about how you guys seemed fine, and there was nothing unusual going on."

"Yeah," Milo says, "but Chloe was at the house later, too. She told the police that after we called from the restaurant, she wanted to come over to congratulate us. I've got a copy of her statement upstairs, if you want to see it. Remember, I called you around eleven, and you couldn't come meet me because Lia was asleep and you were the only one home?"

"I know," Joe says. "But that's not where she was. She had a meeting with a potential client. Owner of a store who was interested in selling her jewelry. It was a last-minute thing—she checked her phone around nine and saw that this woman had left a voice mail . . ." He stops to think for a moment, and I see his face fall. "It was right after you called to say you were getting married."

This is the moment where everything changes. Milo and I look at each other. I'm barely breathing. And there's the first detail.

Chapter Seventeen

IIIII

Ending a book is a nerve-racking proposition; at least, it is if you assume you'll only have one shot at it. So many moments that could come last, but only one of them is right.

The next book I finish, two and a half years from this Saturday night in Roland's living room, will not be a memoir, and it will not be an extension of anything I've written before. By then I will have packed *The Nobodies Album* away gently in a drawer, never to be seen by the world at large, and I'll have made peace with my many endings, flawed though they may be.

By that time Milo's case will be over, though it will take almost a year before the charges are dropped. It's not a simple thing to clear an accused murderer and arrest a different suspect. The next year, and the two years that follow as Chloe awaits trial, will provide an interesting lesson in narrative structure, as the two contradictory stories about what might have happened the night Bettina died become fleshed out in greater detail.

Joe and Chloe's house will be searched on Sunday morning. While Milo and I tire ourselves out by chasing Lia around Roland's courtyard, detectives will seize several items, including Chloe's laptop. A search of the computer's history will eventually lead them to a password-locked blog containing excerpts of a novel-in-progress—subject matter un-imaginative, prose merely competent—about a woman in love with a successful rock singer, who happens to be her boyfriend's best friend.

Police will also learn that three days after the murder, the computer was used to set up a new e-mail account (octavfrost366@gmail.com), through which a person claiming to be me corresponded with the webmaster of FreeMilo.com. The clothes that Joe and Kathy remember Chloe wearing that night will never be found, but her car, in spite of obvious attempts at careful cleaning, will turn up traces of Bettina's blood.

On Sunday afternoon Milo and I will make a trip to the Wave Organ, where police will later find Milo's blood on a stone, and from there we'll move outward, retracing the route to Milo's house, until we come upon a convenience store with a battered vending machine standing outside. Through the dusty, pitted glass, we'll see the prizes available for a quarter: little plastic bubbles filled with shimmering pink jewels. We'll also see that across the street from the convenience store, there's an ATM—an ATM with a security camera, containing a tape that will reveal a shadowy Milo kneeling heavily in front of the machine and digging through his pockets for change at 2:09 a.m., which places his arrival home outside the window the coroner has determined for the time of Bettina's death.

. . .

During those three years I'll travel back and forth between Boston and San Francisco often. On one of those visits, Milo and I will take an afternoon to drive down to San Jose and visit the Winchester Mystery House, which was supposed to have been our destination the day after we went to Yosemite, all those years ago. It's an exceptionally strange place, a work of evolving art—never finished, never intended to be— and it's there that I'll get the idea for my next novel. I suppose it's not unclear why this particular tale should appeal to me; sometimes I'm more transparent than I'd like.

The history of the house is this: A woman, heiress to a fortune made from the manufacture of rifles, becomes terribly distraught after she loses her husband and her daughter. She becomes convinced that she's the victim of a curse, that she's being haunted by ghosts. That she's being held responsible for the damage caused by the invention she's profited from. She believes that if the house she's building is ever completed, she'll die.

She hires workers around the clock, every hour of every day for thirty-eight years. A reclusive widow living a solitary life, building room after room, sleeping in a different bed every night in an attempt to confuse the demons. The orders she gives the workers are often nonsensical; it doesn't matter what they build, as long as they keep building. By the time she dies, the house contains nine hundred doorways. A stairway that goes nowhere. A window in the middle of a floor.

I won't say how the novel ends, but it begins like this:

People in the town had been speculating for years about what Mrs. Winchester might keep inside her safe: jewels, piles of money, dishes dipped in gold. The day she died, the day that the workers put down their tools, never to complete whatever tasks they were in the middle of, her neighbors were disappointed to learn there was nothing of value inside. Some items of clothing. Clippings from newspapers. And a velvet box holding a lock of a baby's hair.

These three years are difficult ones for Milo and Joe, who are grieving for interconnected but sometimes conflicting losses. Milo, always wondering if he'll ever remember the one moment that still eludes him—the trip upstairs in the dark to whisper good night to the woman he thought was asleep, to kiss her forehead and leave a plastic bauble by her bed—isn't sure he'll ever forgive Joe for loving Bettina's murderer. And Joe, perhaps understandably, sometimes wishes it were Milo behind bars instead.

There are times when it seems impossible that any semblance of friendship will remain between them, so it's perhaps lucky in an unhappy way that they have Lia to bind them together. Lia, heartbroken and afraid; Lia, who will have nightmares for more than a year and who will spend Christmas Eve in a prison visiting room. Lia, the ligament that stretches between them, keeping them from snapping apart completely.

. . .

But three years is a long time, and by the time the verdict is read at Chloe's trial, some good will have come from the bad. Pareidolia will record a new album, one I think is their best yet, though I may not be an impartial judge. Lia, who already has an impressive collection of loving grandmothers—in addition to Joe's mother, Chloe has both a mom and a stepmother whom we all do our best to get along with—will nevertheless come to call me Nana. And at the party celebrating Milo's exoneration, Roland and I will find ourselves alone for a moment in the kitchen. It's there that I'll look at him and wonder what, exactly, we've become to each other. It won't be anything like the way it was with Mitch; there's none of the twinning intimacy of lovers who do their growing up together. We're two people who met already knowing who we were, and that makes it completely new. There in the kitchen, I'll lean forward to kiss him, and wait to see what happens next.

. . .

Back to this night in November of 2010, not yet a week after Bettina's death, this moment I've decided to linger on: After Joe stops talking and a terrible look of understanding crosses his face, Milo will call Sam Zalakis, who will come over, even though it's late. The five of us—me, Milo, Sam, Roland, and Joe—will be up for most of the night, beginning the job of piecing together our version of the way things might have gone.

It's not a harmonious process. It's particularly difficult for Joe, who spends the first half of the night slumped in his chair, looking dazed and ill. After he's had some time to regain his balance, he joins the conversation with a frantic passion: he argues, he reverses himself, and he rages at the rest of us for believing something he doesn't yet want to believe. But he stays. And we do our best to take care of him.

Sometime around two a.m. Roland will make tea, and it will finally occur to me to go upstairs and retrieve the sugar bowl that Joe gave me, which we now conclude Chloe took from Roland's china cabinet after the murder, when she suspected I might come to town. We'll all watch as Milo takes the note from my hands and looks at it as if it's something precious. Runs his fingers over the words, as if he's reading Braille. When he speaks, his voice will be thick and hoarse. "Where did you get this?" he'll ask. "That's Bettina's handwriting."

Whatever I thought might be important about the note isn't, or, at least, not that we know of. We'll never learn when Bettina wrote those words, or what she was referring to, or who she thought was lying. But it's this clue that's not a clue, this piece of paper that turns out to have nothing to do with the murder itself, that determines how we're going to tell Bettina's story. It's the starting point for the conversation in which Milo and Roland put Bettina together out of the pieces they have.

Roland will remember a little girl, funny but lonely, who used to leave notes for him to find. Sometimes jokes, sometimes poems. Sometimes things she didn't want to say out loud. He'll remember houses she built out of sticks and grass for fairies to live in, and he'll remember the sad way she waved at him as her mother pulled her away from the courthouse after the judge ordered the paternity test. He'll remember the two of them playing charades and twenty questions and games of Bettina's own invention, and he'll remember that whenever the rules called for players to draw slips of paper, the sugar bowl was pressed into service.

Milo will remember a New Year's Eve party where he met a pretty girl and midnight seemed to hold more promise than it ever had before. He'll remember that "family" was an idea neither of them trusted, but that eventually they gave each other a home. He'll hold on to the hard-won memory that the last words they said to each other were kind ones.

Together they'll remember that Bettina never lied, and that she didn't like it when other people did. They'll remember that "Someone is lying" is a phrase Kathy used when she didn't want to hear what Bettina had to say.

It's because of the note in the sugar bowl that I'll finally start to feel like I know Bettina. It's how I'll learn that I would have liked her a great deal.

. . .

Back again to this moment in the living room, sitting with Roland and Joe. For now, we don't know how any of this will end. But Joe says something, and Milo and I turn to look at each other. For the first time, it seems possible that the story might take a different turn.

Acknowledgments

First thanks, as always, go to my extraordinary agent, Douglas Stewart, for his continuing enthusiasm, unwavering support, and flawless judgment. I am also very much indebted to William Thomas at Doubleday, for his willingness to believe that I knew what I was doing, and to my brilliant and insightful editor, Alison Callahan, whose excellent instincts, creativity, and flexibility have made this a better book than it would have been without her.

Many, many thanks to Liz Duvall, Seth Fishman, Coralie Hunter, Judy Jacoby, Marcy Posner, Nora Reichard, Alison Rich, Shari Smiley, and Adrienne Sparks, for their remarkable behind-the-scenes work.

I am grateful to several wonderful friends and colleagues, including Jennifer Allison, Susan Coll, Katharine Davis, E. J. Levy, Ann McLaughlin, Leslie Pietrzyk, Dana Scarton, Amy Stolls, Paula Whyman, and Mary Kay Zuravleff, for their early reading, suggestions, and support.

Thank you to the Virginia Center for the Creative Arts, where I spent a wonderful and extremely productive two weeks; D. P. Lyle, for his consultation about forensics; and Garrison Keillor's *Writer's Almanac*, which alerted me to some fascinating information about the Pied Piper of Hamelin at exactly the right moment.

Warm thanks to my family, including Doreen C. Parkhurst, M.D., William Parkhurst, Claire T. Carney, Molly Katz, David and Lynette Rosser, and Matthew and Margaret Rosser.

And finally, as always, endless love and gratitude to Evan, Henry, and Ellie, my three sunshines.